GW00703387

To Alan and Linda
with best wishes
John

MARSILIO

John Stewart

TWO TWENTY PUBLISHING

First published 2005 by Two Twenty Publishing
PO Box 220, Harrow HA3 5SW

A catalogue record for this book is available from the British Library.

Designed and typeset in Monotype Bembo by Discript Ltd, London WC2N 4BN

Printed in India by Thomson Press

ISBN 1 905479 00 X

To the spirit of Renaissance

Acknowledgements

My grateful thanks to Joan Crammond for typing the manuscript and suffering the seemingly endless additions and corrections to it; to Clement Salaman for his encouragement, and to Adrian Bertoluzzi for helping with research and answering my many questions. My thanks to Valery Rees for the considerable time and care she gave in reading the text, and for her helpful suggestions, and to Phyllis Thompson who, from her delightful villa near Todi, drove me round the Umbrian towns relevant to the book. The information gleaned was vital. My thanks also to David Smith and Linda Proud Smith, who responded readily both to my enquiries and those of my publisher, Jim Whiting, and to Arthur Farndell for proofreading and for his help so willingly given. I am grateful to Charles Hardaker for supplying the drawing for the title page and to Brian Hodgkinson for the cover photograph.

J.A.S.

LIST OF CHARACTERS

(H – historical; F – fictional)

H   Acciaiuoli, Agnolo – Friend of Cosimo. Had a wide knowledge of French affairs.

H   Alfonso, King of Naples.

H   Antonino (Little Anthony) – much respected Archbishop of Florence.

H   Argyropoulos, – Greek philosopher. (Aristotelian).

H   Barbo, Pietro – Cardinal – nephew of Eugenius IV. Later became Pope Paul II.

F   Bembo, Ginevra – Venetian – wife of Febo Loredan.

F   Benedetto – one time servant of the Carrucci.

F   Bernardo – bodyguard of Carlo Pucci.

H   Bessarion, Ioannos – Cardinal – a Greek who studied under Gemistos Plethon, and championed the cause of union between the Greek and Roman churches. Was made Cardinal by Eugenius IV. A leading scholar of his time.

H   Borgia, Alfonso – Cardinal, native of Xativa in Valencia. Became Pope Calixtus III, April 1455.

H   Borgia, Roderigo – made Cardinal by his uncle Calixtus – later became Pope Alexander VI.

H   Calandrini – Cardinal – present at the election of Pius II.

F   Carrucci, Coluccio – son of Orvieto nobleman.

H   Castiglione – Cardinal – present at the election of Pius II.

H   Cavalcanti, Giovanni – son of a Florentine nobleman and life long friend of Marsilio Ficino.

H   Cesarini, Giuliano – Cardinal – advocate for the Latin cause at the Council of Florence 1438. Lost his life at the battle of Varna against the Turks in 1444.

H   Colonna, Odo – first Pope after a period of schism – named Martin V – elected 1417.

H   Colonna, Prospero – Cardinal present at the election of Pius II.

F   Crito, Count Giorgio Gemistos Thulwino Dandolo – the heir of an old Byzantine family. Married into a branch of the Dandolo family.

F   Dandolo, Countess Caterina wife of Count Crito.

F   Dandolo, Portia – daughter of Crito and Caterina.

H   Estouteville, Cardinal of Rouen – wealthy, with French royal connections.

H   Eugenius IV – Pope at the time of the Council of Florence.

H   Ficino, Alessandra – wife of Diotifeci and mother of Marsilio.

H   Ficino, Diotifeci – Doctor and father of Marsilio.

H   Ficino, Marsilio – 1433–1499. Philosopher and leader of the Platonic

Academy in Florence. He was patronised by the Medici, and translated the works of Plato, Plotinus and Hermes Trismegistus. He became a priest and later a Canon of Florence Cathedral. He was also a physician and an accomplished musician. He corresponded with many of the leading political and spiritual figures of the time including Dean Colet, Dean of St Paul's Cathedral, London, prominent theologian and founder of St Paul's school. Ficino's influence on Shakespeare is analysed in detail by Jill Line in *Shakespeare and the Fire of Love,* (Pub. Shepheard-Walwyn, London 2004).

H Foscari, Francesco – Doge of Venice 1423–1457.

H Foscari, Jacopo – wayward son of Doge Francesco.

H Frederick III – German Emperor.

H Gemistos Plethon – Byzantine Platonist who was based at Mistra in the Vale of Sparta. Taught Bessarion and was present at the Council of Florence. Cosimo de' Medici attended his lectures and was inspired to found a Platonic Academy.

H Gianvaccorti – Lord of the Val di Bagno. Betrayed Florentine trust.

F Giovanni, Father – priest benefactor and teacher of the young Carlo Pucci.

F Gonzaga – violent follower of Riddo.

H Hunyadi, Janos – Hungarian Captain General, hero of the battle at Belgrade in which the Turks were defeated. Father of the future King Matthias.

F Jacopo – faithful servant of the del Monte family.

H John VIII – Byzantine Emperor – attended the Council of Florence in the hope of obtaining aid against the Turkish menace. Penultimate emperor before the fall of Constantinople.

H Ladislas V – young King of Hungary at the time of the battle of Belgrade.

H Landino, Cristoforo – Florentine scholar, an expert on Dante and a friend of Marsilio.

F Loredan, Febo – young Venetian nobleman and friend of Marsilio.

F Maddalena – Anna del Monte's kind but talkative friend.

H Manuel II – Byzantine Emperor – father of John VIII.

H Martin V – Pope. (see Colonna).

H Medici, Cosimo de' – head of the Medici house and uncrowned ruler of Florence.

H Medici, Giovanni di Cosimo de' Medici – the younger and the favourite son of Cosimo.

H Medici, Lorenzo di Piero – Cosimo's grandson, the future *il magnifico*.

H Medici, Lucrezia – much-admired wife of Piero di Cosimo de' Medici.

H Medici, Piero di Cosimo de' – elder son of Cosimo.

F Monte, del, Andrea – elder son of Carlo and Anna del Monte.

F   Monte, del, Anna – devoted wife of Carlo del Monte.

F   Monte, del, Carlo – father of his house.

F   Monte, del, Giovanni – Lord of the Alberti del Monte fortress (a fictional township). Younger son of Carlo and Anna del Monte.

H   Neroni, Diotisalvi – a Medici supporter trusted by Cosimo.

H   Niccolo, Papa – Pope Nicholas V, humanist pope and friend of the Medici.

F   Niketas – a Greek of questionable intent who tries to influence Febo Loredan.

F   Paolino – has a post at the Vatican Library. Friend of Andrea del Monte and Carlo Pucci.

H   Piccolomini – (see Pius II).

F   Pitti, Luca – wealthy Florentine – builder of the Pitti palace.

H   Pius II – Aeneas Sylvius Piccolomini [formerly Bishop of Siena].

H   Plethon – see Gemistos.

F   Pucci, Carlo – befriended by Andrea del Monte.

H   René of Anjou – help was sought by Cosimo. Had designs on the Kingdom of Naples.

F   Riario – tyrannical warlord ousted by Count Crito with Sforza's soldiers.

F   Riario, Lucrezia – 'daughter' of warlord.

F   Riddo, Ubaldo – unscrupulous churchman and enemy of Carlo Pucci.

H   Sforza, Duke Francesco – Duke of Milan and close friend of Cosimo.

F   Simone and Maria – neighbours of Gonzaga. Befriended Carlo Pucci.

H   Soderini, Tommaso – firm supporter of the Medici.

H   Soderini, Niccolo – brother of Tommaso but distrusts the Medici.

H   Tebaldo – Cardinal. Present at election of Pius II.

F   Tiepolo, Lorenzo – Venetian merchant and nobleman.

F   Tiepolo, Valeria – daughter of Lorenzo.

F   Tiepolo, Vitale – impulsive son of Lorenzo.

H   Vladislas I, Jagiellon – King of Poland and Hungary – killed at the battle of Varna 1444 while fighting against the Turks.

CHAPTER 1

Father and Son

It was growing warmer, yet the cool spring freshness of the morning lingered. The sky was cloudless and Florence, her spires and turrets etched against the flawless blue, was at her best. Vigour, colour, bubbling talk and laughter filled her narrow canyon streets. Who could fail to feel their spirits rise on such a morning?

Dr Diotifeci Ficino had reason, more than most, to join in the general mood of buoyancy. Was not this the very day he was to take his gifted and beloved son, Marsilio, to meet the uncrowned guardian of the state, the great Medici, Cosimo himself? But Dr Ficino was not buoyant. He was angry, seething at the treatment he had suffered at a merchant's palace. By the living God, he was a Doctor, not a goatherd. Striding through the crowds, he struggled to be gracious to the many who acknowledged him, grateful one-time patients now in health. His anger was receding. It was not the first time that he had been summoned and dismissed as if he were a peasant, and experience told him that it would not be the last.

Shaking off his ire, he turned his mind to present needs. He quickened pace. Above all, he must not be late for his afternoon appointment at Careggi. To be so would be disrespectful and also very stupid. Only a fool would take Cosimo de' Medici for granted. Not that the great man stood on ceremony. It was his silence and his discerning mind that Ficino feared to slight. Anxiety furrowed his brow as he hurried through the courtyard to his house adjacent to the hospital of Santa Maria Nuova.

"Is Marsilio ready, Alessandra?" he called out to his wife, his voice loaded with impatience.

"Yes, he's ready," she responded, emerging from the larder. "He's always ready. You know that, husband."

"Yes, yes; we need to leave at once . . ."

"At once! You'll be early, *very* early!"

"I know, but I've still to hire the mules at Porto al Prato. All sorts of things are . . ." He left the sentence in mid-air. "I don't mind being early but we must, at all costs, not be late!"

Alessandra inclined her head knowingly. Age, though evident, had not erased her looks.

"I sense you didn't have an easy morning."

"No! I was insulted by someone barely sixteen. These strutting family peacocks are the curse of Italy."

She smiled and Ficino remembered once again why they were man and wife.

1

"Surely most families are respectful?"

"Yes, but I wish they wouldn't smile as if they were doing us a favour."

"Oh dear, we are upset this morning."

"And every right to be! Where's Marsilio? Is he ready?"

"He's in his room with Cristoforo Landino, studying some manuscript . . ."

"Landino! He's one of the best minds in Florence. How does he spare the time?"

"Well, he's here and he brought young Giovanni with him."

"Cavalcanti – he's only nine years old!"

"I know, my love, but Giovanni is devoted to Marsilio."

"The way Marsilio's heading he'll have half of Florence in that tiny room of his. – Marsilio," Ficino called. Landino or no Landino, they needed to get moving.

"Yes, Father."

Ficino could hear the footsteps. There was no delay. It was always like that – instant obedience. At one time he had been concerned that Marsilio was not like normal boys and much too good, but he soon stopped worrying. Marsilio had a blessed nature. It was his natural state. Yet his tranquil nature was not partner to a leisured programme, for he studied long and hard and with amazing zest.

Marsilio was first down the stairs, his slightly stooped and smallish figure closely followed by Landino, who was of similar height, with young Giovanni on their heels.

"Cristoforo! Good to see you," Ficino greeted warmly. "And Giovanni. You're growing taller by the day!"

"He is," Landino nodded. "Give him another year or two and he'll be looking down on all of us!"

"I'm afraid Marsilio and I are off to Careggi," Ficino explained. "I'm sorry we have to leave you."

"That's all right, Doctor. Marsilio told us, and in any case I'm due at Fiesole early this afternoon to see my friend Andrea Alberti del Monte. I believe you know his father, Sir."

"Yes, Messer Carlo. His leg is troublesome, so I'm a frequent visitor. He's Venetian but has lived here for many years – a great friend of the Medici. Well, Marsilio, it's time to go. By the holy saints, I'd almost forgotten the Trebbian wine." He smiled at Landino. "Just a token gift for the great man!"

Landino nodded. "May we walk with you? I need to take Giovanni home. After that there's an old nag stabled for me just beyond the walls."

"Of course."

All this time Marsilio had remained silent but he could see his mother's eyes were full and close to tears.

"All will be well, mother. Be content," he whispered quietly.

As father and son approached Careggi, the ordered neatness of the vineyards stretched out in all directions. After the bustle of the city and the chaotic squalor just beyond the walls, the calm was tangible. Two sturdy field hands working near the roadway called out a greeting and Marsilio waved back, but the young man was under no illusions. The Medici servants were sturdy for a purpose. Unexpected visitors would soon be questioned, for even with Cosimo's modest unpretentious ways, envy and its child, plain hatred, were ever grumbling and no one could predict when some unbidden chance might launch their murderous spite.

The ground began to rise as the roadway twisted to the right.

"We're almost there, Marsilio."

"Yes, Father. It's difficult not to run with the excitement."

"Son, excitement is a natural human trait."

"I know, Father, but I can't imagine Socrates being excited."

"But you're not Socrates," Ficino almost countered but he held his tongue. His son was not a scholar who paraded erudition and never gave a thought to practice. If that had been the case, he would have viewed Marsilio's comments as precocious rubbish.

A girl's cry suddenly disturbed the silence and with equal suddenness the girl rushed by, her skirts held high for speed. A young man was following with equal urgency but when he saw the Doctor and his son he stopped, bowing his head instinctively.

"Ah, Pietro," the elder Ficino said evenly. "How is your worthy father?"

"Much better, Sir; thank you, Sir."

"I'm very pleased to hear it. Please give him my good wishes."

"I will, Doctor. Thank you, Sir."

Pietro was undoubtedly embarrassed. He looked away, twisted his feet awkwardly and, saying "Good bye", walked off down the path that he had come.

"Father, I think that we have spoiled a little tryst between the vines!"

Ficino looked at his son's smiling face and was amazed. He had assumed Marsilio's distaste, yet there was not the slightest hint of disapproval.

Diotifeci had also assumed that his son would eventually embrace the Church. Nature had not endowed him with those features attractive to women. Yet, Marsilio did not live within an empty, loveless world. On the contrary, he seemed, at times, to be on fire, transported by the sheer delight that was the wages of his studies. Philosophy was his mistress and here was love that very few had glimpsed, much less understood.

The Careggi Villa was looming closer. Ficino could see the guards patrolling the upper walkway. Plainly they could observe the field hands' signals and would know well in advance if trouble were approaching.

CHAPTER 2

Fiesole

The climb to Fiesole was getting steeper, the last stretch before the level of the town's Piazza. Cristoforo Landino's ageing horse was straining and digging in its hooves to get a grip. At once Landino dismounted and the horse, snorting gently, nodded twice as if in thanks.

Landino loved the old Tuscan town. The air was so much fresher here than in the city down below. The smells of Florence and the rowdy energy of her citizens were stimulating but they also prompted an escape. Bearing right, round the edge of the Piazza, Landino took a cart track which climbed towards the higher ground and there it was, the rambling Alberti del Monte villa some way from the summit of the hill but with a spacious view of Florence far below.

As in the morning, the sky was cloudless. It was warmer but a slight breeze kept the heat at bay. This was heaven while yet confined to earth, Landino thought.

At the gates his friend Andrea and the old family servant, Jacopo, welcomed him. Andrea was about thirty, the same age as himself. It was only his third visit to the villa, but right from the beginning he had felt included as a family friend.

Jacopo led the horse away and the two good friends made for the garden seat which overlooked the city.

"Father is in one of his melancholic moods," del Monte confided. "It's been plaguing him for days."

"Marsilio is subject to the same depression too."

"But he's only twenty!"

"Youth doesn't guarantee protection. Of course, in Marsilio's case it's due to too much study."

"That puts it mildly! Has his father recommended any medicine?"

"Not that I know of. Marsilio himself recommends long walks and fine music."

"Not much help here, as father can barely walk and I'm no musician!"

"There must be someone living close who plays the lyre. What brings the trouble on?"

"In this case, Constantinople!"

"But the city hasn't fallen!"

Andrea turned round deliberately on the bench and looked directly at his friend.

"The Turks are casting massive cannons in the shadow of the walls."

"To smash the triple walls," Landino murmured pensively. "God help the city and its people – but how did your father get this information?"

"From Venice. He passed it on to the Medici, yet what can they do? What can anybody do? Perhaps I didn't tell you – father knew the Emperor Manuel extremely well."

"The father of the present Emperor?"

"Yes, and father spent months at Mistra in the vale of Sparta. For him this tragedy is close."

Landino suddenly stood up.

"I think I ought to go inside and pay my respects."

"Yes, let's see what we can do to cheer things up. Did I tell you, I'm off to Rome in four days' time."

"Are they giving you a Cardinal's hat?"

"A red hat! No, I'm not dissolute enough for that!"

Landino laughed but he noticed that Andrea failed to state the nature of his mission, though Landino, discreet as ever, felt there was good reason and so did not press the matter.

They found del Monte's father not inside, but seated underneath an awning in the garden.

"Cristoforo! What a welcome surprise," he exclaimed, his dullness for the present set aside.

"And what a glorious day, Sir. Fiesole is idyllic."

"The sun's work, Cristoforo. He shines on all of us and makes no prefer-ence. Florentines, Venetians, Milanese and *even* Romans share an equal bounty."

Andrea laughed heartily, recognising his father's sideswipe at the clergy.

"My family knows I'm not too keen on high-born clergy," the old man countered to explain his son's amusement. "I must say, though, that our present Papa Niccolo has tried to help Byzantium, but all the lords of Italy are much too busy squabbling amongst themselves to send assistance. This confrontation in the north is madness and this convenient love affair linking Venice and Alfonso's Naples cannot last. Francesco Sforza of Milan, Doge Foscari of Venice and Cosimo de' Medici of Florence are all men well above the average. They should be as one. When will they wake up and send a joint force to save the city of Justinian? Alas, I fear the worst. The unthink-able is about to happen. Constantinople will fall and then we'll have the wringing of the hands and what a lamentation there will be when it's too late."

"Father wrote to all three northern leaders just after Natale," Andrea interjected.

"Yes, but keep that to yourself, Cristoforo, as most would sneer that I had grandiose dreams above my station. The truth is that I know them well and have good reason to respect them."

"Am I allowed to ask, Sir – what did the great Medici say?"

5

"You'll be discreet I'm sure – the truth is he said little. I personally took the letter to Careggi and after reading it he raised his eyebrows, as he does, and chuckled. Then we laughed. We're good friends, Cristoforo. It's friendship that allows me to remain here at Fiesole in these troubled times – friendship with the Medici and friendship with Doge Francesco Foscari. Venice and Florence cannot be at odds for long. The situation's much too crazed to last." He paused. "You know, I feel so much better than I've felt for days. Andrea, can you find that wine Dr Ficino kindly brought the other day. And, where's your mother?

"Visiting her friends just up the way."

"We'd better keep a little by for her."

"Now, Cristoforo, tell me more about your studies on our Dante."

CHAPTER 3

Careggi

Cosimo was playing with his young grandson, Lorenzo, when Dr Ficino and Marsilio were announced. At once he looked up and greeted both Ficini.

"Children are profoundly simple," he observed, "and their blissful world is something we have long forgotten. What do you think, Marsilio?"

Straight into dialogue; there were no preliminaries. In many ways it was a compliment, a mark of informality, yet even so Dr Ficino felt ill at ease, though Marsilio had no such difficulty. He looked straight at Cosimo's amused and slightly sardonic face, and smiled. For a moment he glanced down at the four-year-old playing with his wooden blocks, then looked up again.

"Children may be close to bliss, Sir," he said gently, "but they're at the mercy of prevailing company."

Cosimo's smile widened.

"Explain yourself, Marsilio."

"Their parents and their tutors, their friends and their surroundings, such is their company."

"True, Marsilio, but some seem to rise above their adverse circumstance." Cosimo's eyebrows lifted slightly.

"A predisposition that the Lord has planted, Sir."

"You are discreet, Marsilio. I feel you know much more than you are saying – Doctor, Marsilio, please take your ease."

Cosimo casually indicated the chairs about the room. It was the great man's library, where he allowed no fussing interference from his wife. Marsilio was fascinated by the numerous books that lined the walls, but Dr Ficino still felt uneasy, aware that, apart from the Pope, they were in the presence of possibly the most influential man in Italy. His unease, though, was quite irrational, for Cosimo was his patient. This time, however, the roles were different and it had unsettled him.

"Doctor, may I first impose on you? Our cook complains of pains and has been suffering for some time. If you could see her . . ."

"That would be my pleasure, Sir."

"I'll take you through. Come, Lorenzo. And Marsilio, feel free to scan the books. I'll be back presently."

Marsilio stood up. The cook's pains were no doubt real enough but he also sensed the whole thing was a ploy so that Cosimo could question him alone.

In no time Marsilio was immersed in the wealth of learning that surrounded him. All the great names, it seemed, were represented. Years of study, he thought, but this did not daunt him. Instead, it filled him with exhilaration. Cristoforo would love this, he mused, thinking of his friend Landino. What a treasure house. It made him want to shout with joy.

"You're already busy, I see." Cosimo had returned. "I'm told you gobble manuscripts like ripe fruit from a tree!" Cosimo arched his eyebrows, clearly expecting a reply.

Marsilio smiled discreetly. It was not his place to trade in humour with someone like Messer Cosimo.

"The fruit here is abundant, Sir. This is a wonderful collection."

"Well, Marsilio, it's yours to look through when you will. Often I'm not here but we can make arrangements for your ready access. Sit down, my boy."

Marsilio was amazed. He had not dreamed of ever being so fortunate. Cosimo indicated a chair and they both sat down.

"Tell me, Marsilio, how are your Platonic studies?"

"They're fairly constant, Sir."

"That's what I'm told. Now, Marsilio, how do you explain Socrates' statement that 'knowledge is simply recollection'?"

"Well, Sir, if knowledge is simply recollection it must be within, already part of one's inner being."

"But, Marsilio, that doesn't make sense. What about my bank transactions and book keeping methods?"

"With respect, Sir, that is information."

"Some might describe your answer as 'convenient'!"

"It's not 'convenient', Sir. It is how it is."

Cosimo chuckled.

"Go on, Marsilio."

"The knowledge that Socrates refers to is of God – in Platonic terms, the One. Information is knowledge of diversity and is a tool for living in the daily round."

"Well answered, Marsilio!"

The conversation continued, with Marsilio answering all the questions he was asked. In fact, it was clear to Cosimo that the questions stimulated the young man; so much so, that he glowed with energy.

"The soul's relationship with God has always fired my interest," Cosimo said evenly. He had introduced a question dear to his heart. "Have you studied this?"

"I have studied various scholars on the subject, but my understanding is partial. Yet I strongly feel that by trying to cognise God we reduce His size to our human scale, but by loving Him we enlarge our mind and raise ourselves towards His immeasurable breadth."

Cosimo nodded.

"Most interesting, Marsilio," he said pensively. Cosimo was impressed.

"Well, my boy, I really have enjoyed our meeting and I can promise you it will not be the last, and remember, I will expect you to use this library. Ah! I hear your father coming. Well, Doctor, did you diagnose the trouble?"

"Yes, Sir, the girl is pregnant!"

Cosimo burst out laughing.

"Did she volunteer the father's name?"

'No, Sir, but she protested her amazement. She did not understand how it could have happened!"

"I see." Cosimo looked at Ficino with undisguised amusement. "Another case of divine intervention, perhaps! So there it is; Careggi is to have another pair of little dancing feet."

For a moment Cosimo was still, as if he had retired within himself.

"Dr Ficino, Marsilio, there's a group of scarlet-robed officials waiting for my presence. I must not linger, as is my inclination, but my good wife will have refreshments to help you on your way. I'll take you through. Marsilio, you go first."

Cosimo caught the Doctor's arm as they left the room. "Diotifeci, your son is most remarkable."

CHAPTER 4

Rome

Rome was hot but not oppressive and on the Palatine there was a gentle breeze. Andrea looked down on the old Circus Maximus, long since plundered of its stonework. Turning round, he picked his way through the ruined grandeur to the other side that overlooked the Forum. One temple, consecrated to the Church, was still intact, but most were badly pillaged, though the two triumphal arches of Titus and Septimius Severus were still in place and, of course, there was the colossus of the Flavian Amphitheatre.

"Messer Andrea del Monte."

Andrea spun round, immediately on guard. Caution was obligatory. Rome was not Florence and certainly not Venice.

"Ah, Messer Paolino. Having a break from your duties?"

"Yes, this is my renewal time. These ancient ruins bring their calm."

"They do indeed. Thank you very much for showing me round the Pope's new library yesterday. It was most generous of you. I have a friend in Florence who would be fascinated by the collection. Ficino is his name. He's young, so I doubt if you'll have heard of him."

"On the contrary, I have. He's a kind of prodigy, I'm told, and famous for his memory."

"Yes, his memory is amazing."

Paolino's slight frame, and moderate height gave an air of refinement. His eyelids were distinctive, though. They drooped markedly each side, rather like a portrait he had seen of Cardinal Bessarion. He had yet to meet the famous Greek and it was likely that he would, for as a Medici bank official he was viewed by many as a diplomat of Florence. Indeed, he had already attended one high-level reception, even though he had been only a week in Rome. His father had been pleased, though much amused, by his appointment. "Cosimo's up to his old tricks," he said. "He's hired your ears and eyes to find out what's going on in Rome."

From their vantage point Andrea and Paolino watched the scene below. A few distant figures were casually walking amongst the ruins of the Forum. Some were carrying swords – young aristocrats, Andrea guessed, with nothing much to do. For a time they passed out of view and then there they were again.

"Colonna!" Paolino observed with an obvious note of caution.

"And there?" Andrea pointed in the direction of the Capitol to another group of swaggering youth.

"Oh no!" Paolino exclaimed. "It's the Orsini. They're all young bloods.

There's bound to be a fracas if they meet. Dear God, I think they've seen each other."

"They have," Andrea confirmed. "I can hear the shouting."

"Taunts and insults!"

The rivalry of the two great families had festered for generations. Andrea understood the danger of the situation well. It only needed one mad fool to draw his rapier for tragedy to strike, and after that the inevitable vendetta which could keep on claiming lives for years.

From their vantage point the shouting and the gestures were like actors over acting – puppet figures jerking on a string.

"Look!" Paolino pointed vigorously.

"Two Red Hats!"

"They've seen the trouble and they're moving quickly."

"Yes, for Churchmen! But, Paolino, will the young bloods heed them?"

"They will. They're already shuffling off."

"Let's climb down and have a closer look."

"Do you think that's wise?"

Andrea made no answer but rushed quickly down the hill with Paolino close behind him, breathing heavily from the effort.

"Do you recognise the clerics, Paolino?"

"Yes. Just a little closer – yes, by the sacred Mother, it's Bessarion and the other man, – I think that's Alfonso Borgia."

"The great Bessarion I know about, but who's Alfonso Borgia?"

"A Spaniard from Xativa in Valencia – a skilled diplomat in his time, who served Martin V and Eugenius IV with distinction. Now he's old and smiles at everyone."

"How old?"

"Seventy-five, I believe."

"Too old to be elected Pope!"

"A compromise candidate – you never can be sure."

The crowds following the Colonna and Orsini had dispersed and the Churchmen, deep in conversation, were receding too.

"Paolino, what's your view of Bessarion?" Andrea asked on impulse.

"Ah, now, there's a man! Substantial, deep – a man born for the Papal throne."

"Would they elect him, though?"

"Never! He's a Greek!"

Andrea laughed. Paolino hesitated briefly, then joined in.

"I need to get back to the library, Sir . . ."

"Andrea is the name!"

"Well, as I said, Andrea, I need to go, otherwise they'll lock me up inside St Angelo's walls!"

"Do you come here most days?"

"Yes, at about this time."

"Perhaps we may meet again."

"I hope so, Andrea. God's blessing on you."

"And on you, Paolino."

Andrea watched his new friend go. The ankle length gown of the clerical secretary, though light, would be hot, but then he must be used to it. Paolino was the perfect contact, the kind his father always recommended. Men striving for the top were mostly useless, he had told him, for they were always careful what they said and were always on the lookout for someone more important. In other words, they rarely gave you full attention. Of course, the real men at the helm were different. You were fortunate when you had their trust.

Andrea walked slowly towards the road that ran between the Palatine and Capitoline which in times past had been crowned by the Temple of Jupiter. Subject to the rivalry of the powerful Roman families, Rome was volatile and the Pope was not immune. More than once rioting crowds had driven the reigning Pontiff from his seat. Indeed, not long past, Eugenius IV had escaped down the Tiber underneath a shield.

A week was but a moment. It would take at least three months before he grew to be familiar with the city. One thing was very plain to see – the numerous black-robed clerics, especially in the area round St Peter's.

Without a doubt, Rome and the Papal lands were difficult to control. The reigns of Popes were mostly short and new Popes often brought new policy. Then the beneficiaries of the previous Pope would naturally grow hostile to the new man's moves. In fact, stability was not easy to achieve. Add to this the changing pattern of alliances between Florence, Naples, Milan, Venice, France and Spain and, of course, the Holy Roman Emperor. These were the ever-shifting pieces on the games board.

Del Monte had now reached the river bank, the mighty Tiber, eternal like the city, though a city greatly savaged since its fall one thousand years ago. What a place this must have been in Trajan's day – mistress of a mighty empire from Britain to Arabia – an amazing feat. Yet time grinds all to dust.

Absorbed in his thoughts, Andrea was at first oblivious of the rag-clad figure noiselessly drawing close. He turned instinctively and saw two large sad eyes observing him. There was no aggression in them, but there was intelligence.

Del Monte nodded briefly.

"I was hoping, Sir, that you might help me." The man spoke in a measured way, without any animation.

This is different from the usual wheedling patter, Andrea thought. Then it struck him suddenly – there was no smell! He looked anew at the man standing quietly before him. His face and hands were clean, which for a

12

vagrant was most unusual. This was no normal beggar and he was so amazingly passive. Indeed, not unlike Marsilio when he was reflective.

"What is your name?" del Monte asked evenly.

"Carlo."

Instantly Andrea was alerted. Carlo was his father's name and, at one time, his state had not been greatly different from that of the man before him, a man much younger than he looked, Andrea guessed. Who was this man? And was it wise to get involved?

For what seemed an eternity, Andrea pondered. Part of him resented the intrusion, if not presumption, of the man before him. Indeed such beggars were the very name of trouble, their sweet words honeyed by pretended innocence. Yet his other part, the part that knew about his father's early sufferings, counselled hard against rejection. Give him a chance! At least listen to his story. Obey your instinct!

"Let's eat," he heard himself pronounce with some surprise. The words had spoken of themselves. At once his mind swung back to doubt. He was a fool, an idiot. This bedraggled figure at his side was well rehearsed, his game played many times before. Yet Andrea knew his invitation was exactly what his father would have done. "Use your inner sense and seize the moment"– those were his very words. The die was cast.

"There's a place quite close."

"Thank you, Sir," was all the rag-clad figure said.

They took their seats beneath a canopy, well away from all the others present, who did not hide their plain disgust. Certain that they would be told to move, Andrea slipped the waiter a fat tip. It worked wonders and wine was swiftly brought.

"Well, Carlo, what's your story?"

"May I first ask, Sir, who are you?"

Not a fool this Carlo, del Monte thought.

"You may ask, of course. My name is Andrea Alberti del Monte and I'm a Florentine."

"So, you breathe the full free air of Florence. You have the saintly Antonino as Archbishop, as well as the Medici."

"Yes, but there are limits." This rag-clad man was well informed.

"But not as narrow as they are here."

"You speak with some authority."

"I was dismissed for being over-fond of Plato's pagan teaching."

"But surely Papa Niccolo is sympathetic to Platonic thought?"

"How could I approach the Papal chair? I was labelled heretic and it was believed."

"And you fell foul of this?"

Carlo nodded.

"That's when my troubles started. I lost my room, so thought I'd make

13

a new beginning in Siena, but on the way was robbed of everything and also badly beaten. The care of a local monastery restored me, but someone called from Rome who knew me and once again I was the 'heretic'. Need I go on? I'm here. I saw you walking from the Forum and I was drawn to you. That's my story."

Bread and cheese were put before them together with a bowl of olive oil and they began to eat, but del Monte noticed that Carlo did not rush to eat.

"Carlo, I sense you haven't told me all."

"Sir, do you really want to hear about the open drains of Rome?"

"You were a scribe or secretary to a promotion-hungry cleric. Is that right?"

Carlo made no answer.

"Your silence is articulate, my friend."

"I'm sorry, Sir. I made a vow to let the Lord be judge, otherwise I fear the lust for vengeance might destroy me."

This, Andrea felt, explained at least in some way the strange tranquillity about the man.

"How do you survive; I mean, eat and sleep?"

"There is compassion in the monasteries, Sir."

For a time they ate in silence but Andrea's mind was busy. This was no ordinary meeting with chance its explanation. The man before him had been sorely tested but had not succumbed. He clearly had an inner strength above the average and Andrea felt it was his duty to befriend him. Even so, he would move slowly. He would watch him for a while, test him with some unimportant letters and, if he acted as he thought he would, things could then be permanent.

"I think you ought to leave this city for a while, my friend," del Monte suggested knowingly. "The full free air of Florence, I suspect, would suit you well!"

"I would be very grateful, Sir," Carlo answered quietly. He smiled and del Monte knew that it was from the heart.

★

Andrea Alberti del Monte, like his father, was a handsome man. He had an easy manner, but also like his father he distrusted high-placed clergy so vehemently that his friends made fun of him. Women found him attractive, but he rarely gave them hope and so he gained a reputation of being aloof and arrogant. In truth, he could not stand the empty headed talk of clothes and neighbours, yet when he did find someone he could love, the world was his to give. That had happened twice but both had died – one three months after they were married.

Though affable and easy in his manner, Andrea was a lonely man. Of course, his family wished him to re-marry, yet there was no hint of pressure.

His dear sweet mother, with the backing of his father, would not allow it, though his mother often said he ought to visit Venice. With Venice and Florence locked in confrontation, that had not been an option, but things were changing now. All three northern City-states were tired of war. Again the menace of the Turks was concentrating minds. Florence, Venice and Milan dearly wanted peace. Milan was always fearing trouble from the French, and Venice, dangerously overstretched, was disquieted by the Turks. What was needed was a firm alliance. Without it Florence would be subject to the power of Naples and the Papal States. With it, all hopefully could be held in balance.

At last Andrea's mother's wish was coming to fruition, for, with Cosimo's blessing, the orders had arrived that he should go direct from Rome to Venice. There was no one better suited for the mission, since his noble father and the Doge Foscari still held each other in considerable affection.

Arrangements had been made that he should travel from Ancona, and his newly appointed secretary, Carlo Pucci, was to journey with him. The one-time vagrant's fortune had amazingly transformed itself and, what was more, he now had access to Andrea's manuscripts copied for him by his young friend called Marsilio.

The day before they set out for Ancona, the awful news arrived that Constantinople had been sacked. Rome was stunned. The Emperor Constantine was dead, killed fighting in the breach, and a Turkish flag now fluttered on the church of Holy Wisdom.

CHAPTER 5

Venice

Almost ten years had passed since Andrea's last visit, but as the ship glided towards the Molo the familiar sights of Venice greeted him like old friends: the Ducal Palace, the Campanile, the lion of St. Mark perched on its column and the buzz of boats darting past each other with such apparent recklessness. Born in this watery city, he had spent much of his life here and was strongly drawn to it, yet in his heart he was a Florentine.

In 1438, when the Byzantine Emperor John VIII called while en route to Italy, the splendour of his welcome had amazed the citizens and the Doge Foscari had revelled in the grandeur, for Venice was in love with ceremonial pomp. Now Constantinople was a Turkish stronghold. The Doge was over seventy, broken-hearted at the banishment of Jacopo, his wayward son, and the coffers of the city were depleted, bled dry by endless warring on the plains of Lombardy. Venice wanted peace, but the Serene Republic, as she called herself, was conscious of her dignity, and an abject peace she would not tolerate.

It was the Turks who fired the growing worry of the city fathers. The Eastern fortress trading ports, which had for generations stood inviolate, were vulnerable, for nothing seemed to satisfy the conquering Sultan. Though unthinkable to the powerful trading state, the fear, a deep Venetian fear that their mastery of the sea could now be challenged, was no longer just the academic topic of eccentrics.

Even before he stepped onto the Molo, Andrea sensed the sombre atmosphere. The great city, historically their mother city in the east, had fallen. Uncertainty was in the air and taxes had been heavy for too long. However, a swarm of porters quickly descended, jostling for his trade, though his belongings and Carlo's modest chest were disappointing business.

Carlo, Andrea's secretary, had never been to Venice and was utterly amazed. No trees, no hills, just buildings standing as if by magic on the water.

Carlo still awoke each morning surprised to find the unfamiliar comfort of his bed. Gratitude was his natural response, especially to the generous-hearted man that he now served, but what amazed him most was that he, long hounded for his love of Greek philosophy, had found a master dedicated to the same tradition. The vivid memory of the strange compulsion which first drew him to Andrea still remained, and what was even more intriguing was his newfound friend's response. "When you're ready for a teacher," he had said, "one surely will appear," though he made it very clear that he was not the teacher.

The walk to the Dandolo Palace was short. For Andrea the familiar building held so many memories. This was his birthplace, where he had played in childhood, but he felt a wave of sadness too, for Grandpa and Grandma Dandolo, as he had called them, had passed on and the big-hearted family servant, Pietro, was dead as well. Andrea had been named after this 'Grandpa', not his real grandfather but his father's friend and benefactor.

He was just about to pull the bell cord when the heavy door abruptly opened and there before him was the Count, tall and impressive as ever.

"Andrea, I know we've been expecting you, but what a welcome surprise!"

They embraced.

"Count, may I introduce Carlo Pucci, my secretary."

Carlo bowed, and after general pleasantries they went inside.

When Carlo was taken to his rooms, the Count turned directly to Andrea.

"I'm known as Count Giorgio Gemestos Tulwino Dandolo – more names than most royalty could boast, but to you Andrea and to your family I'm Crito, plain simple Crito. It *is* so good to see you. How are your noble father and your dear mother?"

"Thank the Lord, they're well, but Father's leg . . ."

"Yes, I have heard – and your brother Giovanni?"

"He's mostly at the del Monte fortress."

"I know it well," Crito smiled.

"And *we* know well that it was you who won back my mother's family home!"

"Yes, thanks to Francesco Sforza's help."

"Sir, does your known friendship with Sforza and the Medici compromise you here?"

Crito shook his head.

"Alliances are always changing and it's useful to have ready contacts. Anyway, I'm the eastern expert, not that they ever listen! Tell me, Andrea, this secretary of yours, who is he? There's something about him, something I can't quite . . ."

"I know, I feel the same! I've questioned him at length and he answered openly, yet like you I feel there's something else. He's an orphan and can't remember his family – says an old priest befriended him, and that is it. But you're right. I share your puzzlement."

"Ah! I hear familiar footsteps – it's Caterina."

"Beloved Andrea!"

They embraced.

Caterina was just as beautiful as he remembered. To her the role of countess was simply natural and Andrea told her so.

"You've brought a needed shaft of sunlight, my Andrea. We're all so

17

tired of war. Crito's mourning for the city of his ancestors and most are mourning for their ducats. Taxes have been heavy!"

"It's all turned out exactly as Grandpa repeatedly predicted," Andrea observed.

"Well, yes," Crito agreed. "We've been much too busy capturing cabbage patches in the valley of the Po. So you're here to see Francesco?"

Andrea nodded.

"He's greatly failed, Andrea," Caterina interjected.

"The way they've hounded Jacopo, his only son, has tortured his declining years," Crito added forcefully.

"Do you think my embassy will be useful?"

"Have no doubt, the Doge will welcome you with open arms. He and your father were very close. They used to talk and joke for what seemed hours!"

"Andrea," Caterina interrupted brightly, "We'll have a jolly time this evening, and how we need it in this gloomy city."

★

Andrea looked up at the ornate stairway which led to the ducal chambers. His Grandpa Dandolo had climbed these very stairs countless times and his father, too, had climbed them, though infrequently. Guards were watching every move he made. Indeed, the Doge lived like a queen bee in a hive surrounded by a swarm of warriors. No one could get through. Venetian planning and efficiency had seen to that.

Andrea was escorted with due dignity and announced. Then, proceeding to the ducal dais, he bowed low.

The Doge, no longer steady on his feet, was helped down from his ceremonial chair and then he stood, his arms outstretched, a smile brightening his tired, emaciated face.

"Andrea!" Impatiently he dismissed his close attendants. "My boy – how good to see you! And how is that old rogue, your father? Well, I hope."

"His leg, your Serenity, is always troublesome."

"I know, I know. And are you married, my boy?"

"My wife died, Sir."

"My sympathy, my sympathy." The old Doge had acquired a habit of repeating words. "Human existence is precarious, and the schemes and plans of men are ripples on the ocean. How I wish that I could see your father."

"His leg, Sir, would make it difficult. As it is, he has to measure out his walking."

"Ah, yes, but it's a pity. So you've come from the Medici. We have been angry with them. 'Perfidious Florence' has been echoing on the walkways. We see it as betrayal, for we took their side, and at some cost, against Visconti of Milan."

Andrea swallowed, not quite knowing how to answer.

"My feeling is that Cosimo and the Signoria saw the balance shifting . . ."

"In our favour! He's much too fond of Sforza!" The old man grunted. "Listen, all we're doing on the plains of Lombardy is stuffing ducats in the pockets of the useless mercenaries! It's time for peace, Andrea. Venice and Florence are free republics. We should never be opposed. Cosimo is long-headed, yet even so this one he's got wrong!"

The old Doge was venting his annoyance, and del Monte felt it better to be quiet, for the truth was that Venice had been over-active on the plains of Lombardy, and Florence feared her northern trade routes could be cut.

"Let there be no doubt, Andrea, peace is what we crave; peace with honour!" Foscari growled. "The Serene Republic will not suffer gross humiliation and, Andrea," his tone turned confidential, "we need a sweet-meat, though this I never said."

"I really am quite deaf, Sir!"

The Doge smiled briefly.

"The Pope plans to gather all his wayward chickens, but there'll be far too many round the table to agree. It'll happen with smaller groups behind closed doors, three or four together to hammer out the detail. We all want peace, and not to sign a treaty would be madness, for the Turks are like a storm-cloud darkening the sky. But I do not trust the Naples of Alfonso. He's a foolish man playing games without the gold to lay a wager. Does he not know the Turks could strike his kingdom first? Florence, Milan and Venice must stand firm together. I admire Cosimo de' Medici. I admire Francesco Sforza. Let's treat with honour and let's keep the French out of Italy! My God, Andrea, why did Sforza and Cosimo bring these barbarians into Italy?"

"The situation was desperate, Sir," del Monte answered respectfully. "Florence was in peril . . ."

"Cosimo brought it on himself by siding with Francesco Sforza. Anyway, we would have stopped well short of seeing Florence fall."

Hot air, del Monte thought, but he kept his peace.

"Andrea, we want peace, and Cosimo, I know, is longing for the day – and so is Sforza. Let honour be our bond."

Fine words, Andrea thought; the diplomats would have to struggle with the detail, and tetchy detail it would be, for the pride of city states soared like the Campanile. And the French, dear God, let's not even think of them. How could a divided Italy stand against their will?

"Now, Andrea, I want to hear about your family." The Doge had firmly put affairs of state aside and listened closely to all Andrea's news. Then the old man turned to reminiscence, escaping from the painful present to the fun and humour of a happier time. He laughed and chuckled and Andrea listened with fascination. He was hearing first-hand history, for whatever the power-ful Doge of Venice said *was* history.

Andrea did not mention the ill-fated Jacopo, the Doge's wayward son. The subject was too personal, too close. All Venice knew, of course, how deeply the old man had been wounded by it all. He loved his son despite the young man's failings. Jacopo had been banished then pardoned, and then banished once again due to a fatal stabbing for which his guilt, though not completely proven, was still assumed. Venice was divided by the issue, and guilt seemed more to be a question of belief than fact.

The Doge's counsellors were growing restless. There was business to attend to and the old man did not hide his irritation, yet he was the Doge of Venice. He knew the rules, however reluctant he might feel. Wearily Foscari struggled to his feet for, bound as ever to his duty, the Doge had no alternative.

"My warmest wishes to your father and to your lovely mother, and my compliments to Cosimo for his choice of messenger. Another might have ended crumpled at the bottom of the staircase! Your visit's been a tonic."

"Your Serenity." Del Monte bowed, slowly moving backwards. The Doge smiled, and then the light about his face went out as if a candle had been snuffed. Ducal duty and a painful loneliness had returned.

★

Having seen the Doge, del Monte's duty was to make his way to Florence by the quickest route. This time it would be overland and through Venetian territory. There was no danger, for he had a letter of safe passage with the ducal seal and a six-man bodyguard to escort him to the border, but first there was the evening's dinner party, the 'jolly time' the Countess had suggested.

Andrea was amazed to notice that his newfound secretary was included. Crito never had been one to stand on ceremony. As he often said, an arrow on the battlefield does not choose between a pike-man and a Count.

The table was laid for five – the Count and Countess, Carlo and himself, with the final placing no doubt for Caterina's sister, whose husband was presently at Modon.

Wine was served before the meal and Carlo, finding his new circumstances more like a fairy tale than fact, was talking to the Countess. Crito and Andrea were discussing Rome and its administration.

"Rome has always been a mystery to me," Crito remarked. "*Is* the Pope's word sovereign?"

"Rome is ruled by families, with the Pope as referee!"

"Spoken like your father," Crito chuckled. "Ah, here's our daughter. Portia, my dear, do you remember Andrea?"

"I do, father, but does your friend remember me?"

"Well, I remember..." Andrea hesitated, "I remember a gangling ten-year-old!"

"Yes, and that was ten years ago!"

"Madam, you have revealed your age!"

"Sir, is it supposed to be a secret?"

"It is the custom."

They all laughed heartily.

Although pretending casualness, Andrea in reality was shocked. Superlatives seemed to crash before her beauty. She was very like her mother, regal, calm, though with a youthful lissomness. Why was she not married, or at least betrothed, for half of Venice must be knocking at her door. Was this the reason his mother had been urging him to come to Venice? It could well be so, for she and the Countess were great friends and letters passed between them frequently. Somehow he felt uneasy. It was almost too good – too perfect.

"When you return to Florence, Sir, will there be further embassies?" Portia asked.

"Nothing has been said."

"Surely if they want to smooth the road to peace they'll send you to Milan, for both our fathers know Francesco Sforza."

"I doubt it, Portia. Cosimo and Sforza already get on well."

"Yes, but the Medici haven't been to Venice, Sir, to have a friendly audience with the Doge. You could tell Francesco Sforza face to face that we *do* want peace and you could tell him that you heard it from the old man's lips. I think you'd find the Doge would like it if you did."

Was this Portia or her father speaking? Even if it was her father's thought, she'd understood the situation well. Beauty and intelligence together in such measure were impressive.

"What you say I cannot fault but, Portia, I must wait until they ask."

"They will, Sir."

What did she know? Was this her father's thinking also?

"I see you've added prophecy to your table of accomplishments," he smiled. "Portia, my name is Andrea."

"I've heard." A mischievous glint flashed in her smile and when it passed the glory of the smile remained.

"Andrea!" Crito intervened. "Carlo tells me there's a second Plato now in Florence."

"You mean Marsilio. Yes, his reputation's spreading fast. He's young, just twenty years of age. His powers of concentration are phenomenal and he's captured the interest of Cosimo."

"Does he know Greek?"

"Not as well as he would like."

"For Plato you need Greek," Crito countered bluntly. "Ah, here's our meal. Let's take our seats."

★

Andrea del Monte found ample time to reflect as he set out next morning.

For one thing the audience with the Doge had been ludicrously one-sided. The old man had commandeered the conversation and he had hardly said a word. In a sense there was no need, for Foscari said it all. He wanted peace and he wanted an alliance between Venice, Florence and Milan. His most significant remark though was his secretive aside, his 'sweetmeat' as he put it. Of course, Foscari wanted Cosimo to hear it. Venice needed something, an extra border town to satisfy her honour and the Senate needed a 'success', otherwise the peace would be stillborn. And, of course, his disdainful aside about Alfonso was also tailored for the Medici ear. In other words, the Venetian alliance with Alfonso, King of Naples, was not something to be seen as hewn in stone.

Doge for thirty years, Francesco Foscari was a legend, but his time was running out. Who would succeed him? This was a question he would certainly be asked, yet Crito had offered no clear answer when he brought the subject up. There were a number of older men, he said, but no young man to match Francesco in his heyday.

Then there was the East, of course. The shocking fall of Constantinople had produced a tidal wave that penetrated to the meanest walkway and canal. Now the eastern trading fortress ports were under threat, and the Turkish navy, growing all the while, was challenging Venetian mastery. The Count's words had been forceful: "Tell the heedless west that the Venetian navy is the wall that keeps the Turks at bay. It is this city's navy that allows the squabbling on the mainland to continue. Tell them to wake up!"

Portia had disturbed Andrea's easy ways. Her patrician beauty, married to a keen intelligence, made her special. True, she was delightful company, but behind the scenes he sensed the expectations of the Countess and the hopes his mother had been nurturing. Perversely, so it seemed, he felt resentment, for it appeared to him that he was being subtly pressed to act. In fact, the lack of overt pressure made him imagine the supposed coercion to be stronger.

Marriage was a lottery, and many marriages ended up as loveless shells. With Portia, though, he stood more chance than most. Then why this hesitation? Somehow the spark had not ignited, and he wondered why.

The galley which transported them from Venice was now gliding to the mainland jetty. Horses and a Venetian bodyguard were waiting for the ongoing journey. He shrugged. They would be on the road for many days – time in plenty to review his thinking.

CHAPTER 6

Family Matters

With five sons, two daughters, and servants appropriate to his station, Dr Diotifeci Ficino's house was full. During the day, of course, there were tutors calling to instruct the girls. Fortunately, the house, adjacent to the hospital, reflected the dignity of his profession, and as a doctor well acquainted with the dwellings of the poor he knew how fortunate he was.

In the morning and the afternoon the younger boys were out at school. Marsilio, his eldest son, was often at the University, though he also spent time studying at home when the candles burnt both late and early. In fact, study was as near to constant as sanity would allow.

Not surprisingly, Dr Diotifeci's expenses were heavy. Indeed, his fees just balanced his commitments. All was well as long as he was sound in health yet now that he was over fifty life's uncertainties could not be long ignored. So far he had been tolerant of Marsilio's philosophic studies, but if patronage were not forthcoming soon sheer necessity would force him to insist that Marsilio devote more time to medicine and helping in the family practice.

To curtail Marsilio's work would be unfortunate. He knew it would distress his son, yet prudence and sound common sense dictated it. Still, he hesitated. He would have a quiet word with his good friend Antonino. The saintly Archbishop was often at the hospital, visiting the sick. He would understand Marsilio's hunger for his studies and know how to strike a balance with necessity.

★

Marsilio, of course, was reading widely and with an application and enthusiasm that made his friend Landino marvel. The wisdom of the Greeks, with the impenetrable commentaries of the Latin translators, Marsilio absorbed with little difficulty. But for him the theories, the conflicting opinions and the colouring of belief all paled before the eternal simplicity of Plato.

What were the young Ficino's plans? He had no plans as such, other than to penetrate and understand the human quest which all these ancient teachers had pursued. Sometimes he was on fire with what he had discovered. At other times a dark depression would engulf him. The untroubled blissful state that he had read about and fleetingly experienced, he longed to know in full, yet this seemed very distant.

Young Ficino knew his father wanted him to focus more on medicine and thus secure a steady income. He also knew that Bologna, much favoured for its schools of medicine, would be his destination. There his philosophic studies would be drastically curtailed. This bleak prospect chilled his very being and was opposed to all his inner promptings but he understood his father's point of view and when it came to it he would obey. Meanwhile there was a pause, a respite as it were, and hopefully some time as yet to further penetrate the wisdom of the Greeks. His father had seen Antonino, and he sensed the good Archbishop stood against a premature decision. There was still hope, and Marsilio knew he had to formulate a presentation of his work that would attract the hand of patronage, for without such backing necessity would demand a medical career.

The favour of the mighty Cosimo was, of course, his constant dream, but the great man, burdened hourly by the current diplomatic ferment, had little time for struggling scholars. Still, hope remained, for with Cosimo's backing he would be free to work. How he longed for space, and even though he revelled in the sparkling wit and humour of his fellows in the city, he loved the tranquil hills, the sweeping vistas and the neat well-tended rows of vines. The narrow bustling, often-smelly streets of Florence might be stimulating, but peace was in the silence of the country.

There was so much to investigate, as the Latin writers had uncovered many scholars that he longed to study. Cicero and Boethius he had absorbed, of course, but his reading had revealed so many treasures yet to be explored. Tantalising names like the legendary Plotinus, Porphyry and his disciple Iamblichus, and the patriarch Proclus all awaited his investigation, but he needed Greek. There was so little time, and even with his capacity and energy Marsilio's enthusiasm and the hours available simply did not harmonise. So by sheer necessity he had to bring some measure to his study. However, walking greatly refreshed him, and this was why he loved the countryside. The open space was liberating.

CHAPTER 7

A Brief Homecoming

It was late evening when at last Andrea climbed the hill to Fiesole and, after washing and putting on fresh clothes, he joined his parents for a night time glass of wine. Del Monte's parents were hungry for every scrap of news from Venice. It had been their home for years, the place where he, their eldest son, was born. The tall Count Crito and the Countess Caterina were to them like family, and the memory of shared danger held them close.

Andrea recounted every detail, including Portia's presence at the dinner and also in the morning when he left for Florence, but his mother wanted to know more.

"You haven't said a thing about the lovely Portia! How did you find her? Did you talk?"

"Mother dear, she's very beautiful and regal like the Countess. It's a mystery why she's still unmarried. Carlo, my newfound secretary, heard some gossip that she spurned an offer from the Loredan family. They were *not* amused, it seems."

"But how did *you* find her?"

"I know what you're trying to say, Mother. She's wonderful. Her patrician beauty is striking and she's intelligent. I'd be mad to let her slip. Yet I feel unmoved. There . . . there is no spark."

His father gave a chuckle. "I was blind as well, Andrea. I did not really see your mother until Francesco Foscari woke me up. Don't worry, son, the spark will come!"

"Well, everybody seems to want it," Andrea responded casually. He shrugged. "I'd better swim with expectation."

"Andrea!" his mother exclaimed. "How can you be so indifferent? You'd be marrying a virtual princess!"

Her husband burst out laughing. "Don't worry, dear, Andrea will come round. Men take a little time to see the obvious!"

Andrea's mother would not let the matter rest but continued listing Portia's many accomplishments, especially her aptitude for Greek and Latin. Andrea smiled. He knew his mother had his happiness at heart, but it was impossible to resist a touch of ridicule.

"Mother, if you go on much longer you may convince me I'd be marrying a manuscript!"

This time they all laughed heartily, the subject of betrothal for the moment put aside.

"Tell me about this Carlo, this 'stray' you found in Rome," his father asked.

"He's an unusual man," Andrea began – then detailed all the sequence of their meeting.

"You're just like your father," his mother murmured wistfully.

"Is he competent?" the elder del Monte asked.

"Yes, he gets things done."

"Test him with responsibility, my son – a little to begin with, but test him. By what you say he has an inner strength."

Andrea nodded.

"I haven't asked you about Francesco yet."

"The Doge, you mean."

"Yes, but let's keep that subject for the morning."

"He sent his warmest greetings to you both."

"He was good to us. God knows he made mistakes, but at least he made them grandly. Timidity is a word he never knew. – And tomorrow, where are you going?"

"To see Cosimo."

"Where – Florence or Careggi?"

"Careggi."

"Good. I always found his mood much lighter there. Well, it's late, Andrea. If you feel the way I used to feel, you'll sleep."

"That I guarantee!"

★

The fortress villa at Careggi always made del Monte pause before he rode the last remaining distance to the entrance. The will of Cosimo was sovereign here, but in Florence, where his wealth and power were based, he needed broad support. The Medici party was widely founded and his stubborn stand against Venetian ambition was applauded, but his backing of their old persistent enemy, Milan, they did not, or simply would not, understand. They did not fear, as he projected, that the city's trade would greatly suffer if Venice were allowed to swallow up the plains of Lombardy and thus control the trade routes to the north. Venice was a merchant city ruled by merchants. They would support their own.

Now the winds of circumstance were changing. Venice, Florence and Milan, all for their separate reasons, wanted peace. Cosimo's stand had been vindicated and the balance of power restored. What was more, unpopular taxes could be eased. Del Monte was well aware of the resentment fathered by the war taxation. Some families who had suffered penal rates saw the hand of Cosimo. Indeed many, including del Monte, assumed Medici used taxation as a weapon to weaken opposition and to bring the troublesome to heel.

The weather had grown hot, and Andrea was shown into the cool inner hall, where he found the great Medici drooped and weary. Indeed, as often was the case, when tensions were released the underlying strains began to surface and del Monte surmised that this explained the haggard look. Nonetheless, Cosimo listened intently, but with little comment to all Andrea had to say. Doge Foscari's 'sweetmeat' caused some brief amusement. Amusement, though, was not his mood when he raged about the shameless treachery of Gianvaccorti, Lord of Val di Bagno.

Gianvaccorti, after protesting his loyalty to Florence, had in the meantime secretly exchanged his lordship for lands in the Kingdom of Naples. No doubt Alfonso's offer had been tempting. Fortunately, the town, staunchly Florentine, had rebelled and closed the gates, sending Gianvaccorti packing. Cosimo sighed. "It all cost florins, florins we could ill afford – a tedious but dangerous distraction stirred up by idle minds and all too typical. If half the energy we spent in squabbling amongst ourselves had been active in the East, Constantinople would not have fallen!" As the conversation flowed, Cosimo spelt out his hopes for an alliance.

Time was slipping by; in fact, half an hour had passed and Cosimo showed no sign of stopping. Del Monte knew that such a lengthy private meeting was a mark of favour. He was fortunate.

"I like talking to you, Andrea, for I'm certain I'll not hear my indiscretions in the street next day!"

"When it suits me, Sir, my memory is quite dull!"

Cosimo chuckled.

"Now, the future." For a moment Medici was silent, then he looked directly at del Monte. "The Signoria would like you to visit Hungary."

Del Monte swallowed.

"I know absolutely nothing about Hungary, Sir!"

"That's probably an advantage. We want fresh eyes. All the papers will be ready for you at the Palazzo della Signoria, and all and sundry will doubtless try to shower you with their expertise. Just keep your counsel."

"Yes, Sir."

"And, I almost forgot – I've first arranged for you to visit Duke Francesco Sforza in Milan. He knows Hungary's leading general and will give you a letter of introduction. The personal touch is always useful, for we're all human beings – even dukes and generals and even the Medici."

Cosimo rose slowly to his feet. He looked brighter, del Monte noticed; the haggard covering had gone.

"You've found yourself a secretary, I understand."

"Yes Sir, Carlo Pucci is his name. A fine man and most reliable."

"A Platonist, I believe."

"Yes, every piece of text I give him he soaks up like a sponge. I hope to introduce him to young Marsilio tomorrow."

"Ah, Marsilio!" Cosimo stood silently for a moment. "Yes – yes, that is good."

CHAPTER 8

Carlo

Initially what struck most people about Carlo Pucci was his jutting chin. His nose came second. It was long and straight, though not too long; but when people got to know him it was his eyes and the tranquillity they conveyed that held attention.

His last two years in Rome had been a nightmare, but adversity had taught him much. He had learnt the art of patience and knew of its rewards. Again, a strong belief in grace had grown, for in those years of deprivation it seemed that grace had saved him every day. Of course, his meeting with del Monte was grace abundant. His life had changed dramatically and the income that he once received as scribe and secretary to the narrow-minded Roman cleric now appeared derisory.

"Carlo!" a voice called cheerily above the echoing din of the narrow street. Carlo scanned the bustling crowd to see Cristoforo Landino's waving hand. Those dark arched eyebrows were unmistakable.

"Messer Landino!"

"Cristoforo! Cristoforo to you, Carlo. Tell me, where can I find my friend Andrea?"

"He's with his parents at Fiesole."

"My poor old nag will not be happy. That hill's a killer! Well, Carlo, you were striding out quite purposefully before I hailed you."

"I'm bound for the Ficino house to see the young Marsilio. Messer del Monte insisted that I visit him," he replied loudly above the noise.

"Is it your first visit?"

Carlo nodded.

"Do you know the way?"

"Only vaguely."

"I'll walk you there. Mark my words, one day Marsilio will be master of us all. – Eugh, what a smell! Why don't people flush their drains?"

"Who's that, Cristoforo?" Carlo asked, pointing to a diminutive cleric with young priests fussing round him.

"That's our good Archbishop, Antonino. The priests are there for his protection, but he doesn't need them. The people love him. No one would harm a hair on his head!"

"Messer del Monte has great respect for him. He lives the life of a simple priest, he told me."

"Yes, when it comes to bishops he's the great exception!"

There was no quick passage through the jostling crowds. Eventually, as they neared their destination, Landino pointed.

"Through that courtyard entrance – you can't mistake it. I'm tempted to come with you, but I must not miss Andrea before he disappears again, for there's a manuscript on Dante that I want him to enquire about."

★

Carlo was shown upstairs to Marsilio's room by one of the housemaids. She knocked, and after a brief delay the door opened. Before him Carlo saw a smallish man, with a young, yet ageless face. It was the smile of greeting that captured him. It seemed so totally at rest and made connection in a way that was both unfamiliar yet wholly natural, like the meeting of old friends, deep and unreserved.

"Messer Ficino," Carlo began.

"Marsilio, please," Ficino countered gently.

"Then let it be Marsilio and Carlo."

"And one in friendship," Ficino added. He cleared a chair piled high with books and manuscripts and pulled it forward for his guest. They both sat down.

"Andrea said you had a difficult time in Rome. Did you try Cardinal Bessarion?"

"I did, but couldn't breach his wall of secretaries. When you're down and out and look it, humanity turns away."

"Boethius said something very similar in his 'Consolation', but God Himself never leaves a man."

"Yes, I do believe it was His grace which drew me to Messer del Monte."

"I'm sure it was, for God is the ever present witness, and His grace is love in action. That's what the great ones teach."

"The old question still prevails, though – who is God? What is 'the One'?"

Marsilio smiled, almost mischievously.

"God is a single stillness, an unchanging unity," Marsilio said quietly.

"So profoundly simple," Carlo mused.

For at least an hour Marsilio opened up what Carlo felt to be a treasure house of thinkers and their wisdom.

"I hope to collate my researches into, say, four books, as I need something tangible to show and to be recognised, for without patronage I must needs become a doctor!"

"Grace will be your friend, I'm sure, Marsilio."

Then the topic turned to the Alberti del Monte family and their idyllic villa at Fiesole.

"It would be a perfect place to study, Marsilio."

"Yes, Carlo." His wistful note was eloquent.

"Tell me, how do you survive university life?" Carlo probed. "Those dreary rooms and your fellow students intent on everything except study must be . . ."

29

Marsilio laughed. "It's not as bad as that!"

"In Rome it is, with anti-papal republicanism and rioting a way of life!"

Marsilio laughed again. "Some must study, Carlo," he added quietly.

"You're right, of course, but the endless practical jokes are tedious."

"It's high spirits, Carlo."

"Do you have trouble?"

"Very little. Some try to provoke me but soon give up. It's a game and it's best not to take it too seriously."

"There are some nasty characters about, though!"

"Yes. One gave me trouble not long ago but the others ganged up against him and I was left in peace. In the main I'm accepted as I am. There are some natural wits, of course, and they can be very funny."

Marsilio then regaled Carlo with some humorous incidents he'd encountered and these were matched by Carlo.

Suddenly, yet without abruptness, the meeting came to an end.

★

"How did you fare with Marsilio?" del Monte asked when he and Carlo eventually met that evening in Fiesole.

"It was like meeting someone I had known all my life. He's completely down to earth, yet he seems to leave the earthly sphere when he talks about the nature of the soul and God. Indeed, he shone with sheer delight. He's such good company and I feel that I can go and see him any time I like – and those manuscripts he was reading! Some writers seem to make obscurity a god, but they didn't daunt Marsilio! He cut through their convoluted thinking like a knife, and quickly too! What a mind!"

"So the meeting was successful, it seems," del Monte said, his voice accompanied by an understanding smile. "I'm not surprised. If I were prone to gambling I would have wagered on it. What's he working on at present?"

"He says he hopes to collate his researches. He's doing what the world expects, otherwise there'll be no patronage."

"You sound as if you have some reservations?"

"It feels like a diversion, but who am I to judge. Landino has encouraged him."

"A necessary road perhaps, but not the main highway. Now, talking of Landino – he's asked me to look out for Dante manuscripts when we're on our travels. I told him I would give the task to you."

CHAPTER 9

Setting Out

Del Monte, born in a city where law was sacrosanct and where the Doge was elected, had a deep mistrust of unrestricted ducal power. This view was strengthened by the freedom or, as his father put it, the 'ordered free-for-all' that he enjoyed in Florence.

Milan, in del Monte's mind, was linked with the Visconti and the bestial behaviour of their later dukes, though Sforza, married to the daughter of the last Visconti duke, was made of more substantial stuff. Having steered his way successfully within the ever-treacherous labyrinth of Italian politics, no one could describe him as naïve. Yet he was a Duke, with ducal power; the law was in his breast. Such were del Monte's musings as he neared Francesco Sforza's city. It was hot, and his companions, Carlo and the two-man body-guard, rode in silence. Looking about him, del Monte noticed that almost every corner of the rich flat countryside was cultivated. This was the favoured farmland with a ready market, land unspoiled by marching armies. Such damage, no doubt, was all too evident closer to the border with Venetian territory. There the resulting misery of the peasantry had to be appalling.

The walls of the city were looming large in the haze, and as the party drew closer the shacks and buildings outside the perimeter became more numerous. As always, property within the walls was at a premium.

Once inside the city, it was the sense of purpose that he noticed first. With the new Duke, his fame unquestioned as a soldier, perhaps there was new pride and hope. Stonemasons were busy at the cathedral, and work at the Sforza castle was proceeding at a pace. The towering walls were massive, and clearly costs were soaring, but that meant taxes; not the way to court popularity, del Monte thought. Again, the city entertained a strong republican sentiment. While Francesco Sforza lived, all might be well; what happened after that would be quite another matter.

Duke Sforza's chin receded and when he stood upright, like the soldier that he was, it almost disappeared. He had a square, honest, almost kindly face, though del Monte sensed a keen incisive mind – very much a man of action, was his conclusion. Instinctively he liked him.

Their brief and formal greetings over, the Duke began at once to praise the merits of Hunyadi, the Hungarian general del Monte planned to meet. Hunyadi, the Duke recounted, was a man of considerable courage, battling against both intrigue at home and the insatiable Muslim Turks, their sights, no doubt, fixed firmly on the fertile lands of central Europe. "Opinion has it that Buda is impregnable," Sforza grunted, "but being an old soldier, I treat such claims with circumspection. Cosimo and I, and indeed Foscari, know

31

just how dire the situation has become. Hungary is the bulwark, the wall that keeps the Turks from sweeping on. Hungary needs support."

Del Monte nodded. Fine words, he thought, and spoken with sincerity, but what would happen on the ground?

Without a pause Sforza switched to the details of his journey. "An experienced guide will accompany you to Basle and Constance. There you'll need to contact the Medici agent who will arrange your onward journey."

Del Monte had learned all this before leaving Florence but made no comment. The important thing was Sforza's letter of introduction to Hunyadi.

"How's your father?" Sforza asked abruptly, again without a break.

"He's well, Sir, but for his leg. He wished me to pass on his greeting and remembrances."

"And remembrances they are!" the Duke retorted, his face alight with pleasure as he recounted what he called the good times past – "though maybe not so good in fact," he added wryly.

It was all so like his meeting with the Doge, del Monte mused. Men, in the end, were human beings and in their shared humanity they received reward.

As with the Doge, the meeting with Francesco Sforza had gone well. From now on, though, it would be different. In Basle and Constance and in Munich and Vienna he could not trade upon the goodwill of his father. Buda, though, would be the test. There pleasantries would be wasteful luxury, for the Turks were close and full of conquering zeal.

★

It had never happened before, not to her or to any of her friends. Portia had always walked freely on the walkways, though with a burly servant in attendance. The more obscure walkways she avoided; that was prudent. In any case there was little chance of trouble. Yet, for all that, Portia was attacked in broad daylight, her attendant caught off guard and thrown head first into the canal. Being her father's daughter, rage arose instead of fear. Portia fought back and, taken by surprise, her two assailants failed to press home their advantage in the brief time that the walkway was deserted. So, with Portia screaming desperately for help and her servant shouting as he scrambled out of the canal, the two men took flight.

For a short time Portia felt elated, then she started shaking, and with her servant close beside her she hurried home, going straight to the refuge of her bedroom. The shaking soon subsided, but the turmoil in her mind continued, and her confidence, her usual strength, simply disappeared. She was like a galley that had sheered its moorings and was drifting helplessly. It all seemed so unreal. She braced herself.

"I must see father," she muttered, getting up abruptly from her bed.

The Count rose angrily from his seat when Portia told him what had happened.

"Did you tell your mother?"

"No. I thought she'd worry."

"Good girl. What about your guard, Matteo?"

"He promised to keep it to himself."

"And the people who heard your screams and Matteo's shouts?"

"I told them that there'd been an accident and as Matteo was dripping wet and with the smell from the canal it was convincing."

"Very good. Gossip's the last thing we want! But, Portia, is there nothing you can remember about the men?"

"Well, I thought I recognised the voice of the smaller man but I can't be sure. They were dressed like servants. Oh, I'm not sure of anything, father!" she burst out, visibly distressed. "I've always felt so confident, but now I don't even know what I was confident in."

"Come, my dear," the Count said gently, drawing her close. "It's still much too immediate. You'll feel better after a good night's sleep."

"It's not like that. It's deeper. I feel lost. I've never felt like this before!"

"You've been badly shocked, my dear. It does strange things, and in a day or two you will be fine." He held his daughter reassuringly but he felt concerned. Clearly, she needed some direction. "You've told me more than once that when you're still you sense a presence, indeed a mighty presence, if I recall aright."

"You do, father."

"Well, Portia, that is the presence of the Lord. It's always present. It always is and it never becomes. Trust in that, my love."

"And not in that which is always becoming but never is – the *Timaeus*, father."

"Well remembered!"

"How could I forget! I used to sing it out in verse when I was ten!"

"What a tedious father I must have been!"

Portia laughed softly and kissed him on the cheek.

When she had left, the Count sat pensively behind his desk. What a daughter! And who in heaven's name could match her. Del Monte could, but he was so damned casual. Despite the mothers' scheming, it would depend on Portia and Andrea, of course. There could be no coercion. But who had attacked her and for what purpose? Someone seeking ducats? He hoped that it was simple robbery, since undiscovered motives were disturbing. In future he would provide two guards for her protection.

CHAPTER 10

On the Way to Buda

Carlo had found the small inn by chance and had enthused about it to del Monte. It was clean, of course, like most places in Constance, and with a friendly landlord, tolerant of his stumbling attempts at German. It was the perfect place to wait for Messer del Monte, as it was quiet and clearly not a noisy fashionable haunt. Carlo ordered white wine and chose a weatherworn garden bench outside from where the lake was visible, its freshness carried on the air.

For Carlo the miracle was continuing. Indeed, after almost three months he still found his situation quite unreal. Only this morning he had been Messer Pucci, enquiring after Dante manuscripts at the Cathedral, where he had been treated like a visiting prince.

One huge blessing in his poverty and misfortune-ridden past had been his education. As a young boy, the old priest who had befriended him was uncommonly patient with one who thought more often of his stomach than his Latin conjugations. Now, this thorough grounding was bearing fruit, as it was plain that Messer del Monte trusted him with his more important work.

Carlo yawned, while absently taking a dog-eared piece of paper from his pouch, one of Marsilio's copies. He began to read, but his eyes were heavy. The afternoon was warm and for him not a good time for mental concentration.

He came to with a start, the paper lying on the ground. Automatically, he bent down to pick it up, at the same time noticing two men sitting a dozen paces away at the other side of the garden. Dressed in vivid tunics, they had arrived while he had drifted off. They were Italian, Florentine by the sound, and talking freely, confident, he presumed, that they would not be understood. Feigning sleep, Carlo closed his eyes and listened.

"Niccolò, I thought you were for the Medici; your brother is!"

"Tommaso's playing safe, but I'm tired of our republican pretence. Nothing happens unless Cosimo nods – nothing!"

"Well, it was just the same with the Albizzi."

"But that doesn't excuse the Medici. Listen. You're connected to the Menetti. You know how Cosimo's fleeced Giannozzo, and no one can call Giannozzo a traitor. No, he's a straight and honest man!"

My God, Carlo thought apprehensively, if Messer del Monte arrives in the middle of this it could be awkward. Should he slip out and warn him and at the same time risk being noticed or should he trust that Messer Andrea would be some time, as he had said. Carlo sat on undecided and continued listening. It was fascinating.

"Of course Giannozzo is honest. No one would dispute that, Niccolò, but my kinsman might just bend a little. All he needs to do is play the game and be discreet. That's all the Medici ask. But no, Giannozzo stands aloof. He loves his lofty independence."

"What's wrong with that ? Are we Florentines or are we not? The way things are we might as well have a dukedom like Milan!"

"Well, if we didn't have the Medici we probably would! Our constitution is unworkable!"

"That's the excuse used by Medici apologists!"

"Niccolò, I've a lot of sympathy with your views, but I still think we could do a lot worse than Cosimo. Sforza tried to pressure him to grab the ducal power, but Cosimo was adamant he would remain a citizen."

"Surely, Giovanni, you don't believe that tale!"

Carlo was becoming more and more concerned. If they did not leave, and soon, he would have to make a move. Yet he still sat immobile, as though rooted to his bench.

"You may be right, Niccolò; even so, I feel we should be careful. We could end up in a much worse state. Cosimo showers his wealth on city projects..."

"And the wealth of others, too. You ask Strozzi! He's been shorn. Anyway, this conversation hasn't happened."

"Niccolò, have no fear. It's safe with me. Would you like another, before we go?"

"No, thanks. I'm due at the Cathedral in not too many minutes."

"Right. I'll walk with you."

Carlo, still feigning sleep, listened as they left. "Thank God," he muttered to himself. He had desperately wanted to see their faces, but he knew he dared not look. Standing up, he took his mug inside and asked for a refill. He needed it. He was disturbed, for the man named Niccolò had made sense and had questioned Carlo's view of Cosimo as a wise ruler, a reflection of Plato's philosopher king. Had he been naïve? Who was this Cosimo that del Monte kept lauding to the skies? Was Niccolò correct? Were the Medici busy with the usual political power game which he observed in Rome? "Calm down, Pucci," he chided himself, as he returned outside. "Your present fortune is based on the magnanimity of Andrea del Monte. He trusts the Medici, so maybe you should have a little trust as well."

He walked over to the garden fence that overlooked the lake and breathed deeply. The air was like a tonic.

"Carlo." His name reverberated loudly. "I'm sorry to have kept you waiting, but these bankers do pontificate!"

"I'm glad you did, Sir," Carlo returned, immediately describing what he had heard.

"Niccolò Soderini. I met him just now on his way to the Cathedral," del

Monte remarked casually. "He's been talking rather much of late. Cosimo knows all about it, and his brother Tommaso's trying to make him see some sense."

"But what he said did have the ring of truth."

"Carlo, Florence is proud of its constitution. It has many excellent features but it's not perfect. How can it be, when a new Signoria is elected every two months and is free to cancel the work of the previous one. Nothing can proceed with confidence. In this situation ruling factions like the Medici endeavour to control elections, but that's by no means easy. So men like Cosimo work hard behind the scenes to establish continuity."

"Niccolò was damning when it came to penal taxes."

"Taxation is a tool to curb ambition and to discipline the proud who love to be obstructive. Carlo, better the tax of the Medici than the axe of ducal power!"

"I know, but penal tax will cause resentment, and that resentment could explode!"

"Yes, thank God it's Cosimo at the helm, for the whole sad business needs a father's care. He often says that he would like a senate as in Cicero's time, but that would be difficult."

"Why?"

"They'd fight it tooth and nail."

"For what reason?"

"No doubt to protect their constitution and mostly, I would guess, because it's there to fight! Carlo, take my advice, keep clear of factions, for, as you rightly fear, there could be trouble ahead."

Carlo nodded. He had already resolved to keep his distance.

Del Monte extended his arms full stretch above his head and yawned.

"No more bankers today, thank heavens," he said with vigour. "Let's explore the lake edge, Carlo, and, by the way, we don't have to visit Munich. It's Vienna next."

★

The Danube's flow was full and steady. The wind had a welcome freshness, for the sun was hot. The boatman and his two assistants had, with a modest sail, managed to achieve a down-stream speed that was quite impressive.

"At this rate," del Monte called across to Carlo, "we'll be in Buda in no time."

"And with these back rests this surely is luxurious travel," Carlo responded, trailing his hand into the water and letting his fingers skim its surface.

Del Monte turned to check the second boat's position.

"Our guards are just behind. They seem to be enjoying the luxury, too."

"After Vienna, luxury's heaped on luxury! Vienna is a rich and growing city, Sir."

"Yes, and a glittering prize for the ambitious Turks," del Monte almost added, but he checked himself. It seemed a grossness to disturb the quiet idyll of the river. There was just the swishing of the water as the boat sailed on, and now and then the sound of straining wood. The scenery was undulating, but when the Danube turned to flow due south to Buda it would be more dramatic.

Being closeted with the bankers, del Monte had seen little of Vienna, but what he had seen was impressive. Bankers, he grumbled to himself, all they did was justify their idleness and magnify their occasional success. In short, they talked about themselves. Only one man had told him simple facts. He was the man for Cosimo.

"Would you like to live in Vienna, Carlo?" he asked suddenly.

"They don't speak Italian, Sir!"

"How inconsiderate of them! – Look, Carlo!" he added, pointing to an oarsman struggling up-stream. "That's the other side of our good fortune."

"And one that we'll avoid."

"Except that our homeward journey overland to Venice may make a struggling oarsman's lot quite tame."

Coming up on the right was the fortress of Esztergom, perched high upon its cliff. Now the dark wide river would turn south, then north, before sweeping once more in a long bend to the south and Buda. They might arrive by late afternoon if his calculations were correct. Of course, the boat-man would know precisely.

Buda! He had no idea what to do or what he should expect, for the restless aristocracy had a violent history. All he had was the name of Janos Hunyadi and the letter of introduction from Francesco Sforza. There was nothing for it but to await events. The wooded hills, now on both sides, seemed to have no end, and the varied richness of their colours was arresting. How different from the watery city where he had spent his early days.

CHAPTER 11

Husband and wife

Messer Carlo Alberti del Monte and his wife, Anna, were in their favourite seats underneath the awning in their villa garden at Fiesole. Anna was sewing, and her husband was sitting with his eyes closed. A bee buzzed close, but neither reacted, and their old black cat, which had commandeered a vacant chair, looked up, blinked and then went back to sleep.

"I met my old friend Maddalena in the Piazza this morning. Are you awake, Carlo?"

"Yes, dear, I'm listening. What was Maddalena's grand crusade this morning?"

"Carlo!"

"She loves talking, Anna."

"I know, but she's always very kind."

"She is. Anyway, you were about to tell me . . ."

"Maddalena was saying that the Medici have grown very unpopular. Everybody's grumbling."

"And what did you say, dear?"

"That we heard very little criticism."

"Good; you're right. People know we're friendly with Cosimo, so they hold their tongue. But Anna, the situation has been dire for quite some time and taxes have been very high. Last year it was critical and here we owe a lot to Cosimo's old friend Agnolo Acciaiuoli, who persuaded René of Anjou to send French troops."

"Yes, you told me at the time, but they were brutal!"

"That's a mild word for it. They alarmed us more than they hurt our enemies, but they had the desired effect, for neither Venice nor Alfonso of Naples could see an end. So, thank God, it's peace."

"You never told me it was quite so serious."

"Did I not, dear?"

"You know you didn't!" She smiled, leaned across and touched his arm.

"What else did Maddalena say?"

"That Cosimo had taken the opportunity to tax his opponents to near ruin!"

"A lot of this is exaggerated. Anyway, most of the families have well-secreted reserves. They'll not starve. Anything more?"

"When Cosimo goes, it's held that the citizens will reject his sons, for they will reap the harvest of resentment."

"Yes, it will be an anxious time; though, when it comes to it, I feel they'll back stability, and when the war is past a lot of this will be forgotten."

"What do you think of Piero and Giovanni?"

"Cosimo's eldest son, Piero, is honourable, courteous and reliable, but he doesn't have his father's flair. The poor man's crippled with arthritis. Even so he has one major asset and you know her well!"

"His wife, Lucrezia. She *is* a major asset, for everyone adores her, and she's a poetess as well. I think she's wonderful."

Carlo nodded.

"She is."

"And what do you think about their younger son, Giovanni!"

"He may be our neighbour soon. I hear he's shown interest in the villa Belcanto owned by the Bardi family, but keep that to yourself, dear."

"I'll tell Maddalena!"

"You rogue!"

They both chuckled.

"Where were we? Ah, yes, Giovanni. He's good company, full of fun, loves music and has an eye for excellence in painting. He's also a good businessman and a responsible citizen. In fact, he's Cosimo's favourite."

"But he's so very fat, Carlo."

"He eats too much, I grant you. Indeed, he needs to diet, but I doubt he will."

"His poor heart!"

"And my poor leg. Did I tell you that Dr Ficino and Marsilio are due later this afternoon?"

"No, dear. They're always welcome, of course. Young Marsilio is a wonder. He's so very tranquil."

"I know. I've never known anyone quite like him."

"Carlo Pucci, Andrea's 'stray' as you call him, has a similar quality."

"Yes, but not as established as Marsilio. An interesting man, though."

"He's fine featured, almost aristocratic in appearance."

"That doesn't say much, dear, for most aristocrats look anything but aristocratic!"

Anna laughed lightly.

"My darling husband, you haven't lost your touch."

For a time they sat in silence. The only sound it seemed was Anna's thread as she drew it through her tapestry. Carlo closed his eyes.

"I wonder where Andrea is now, Carlo."

Carlo shook himself. "Sorry, I almost nodded off. He's probably in Buda."

"Is he safe?"

"Oh yes, he's precious property. An envoy with the ear of Cosimo and Sforza will be listened to. He'll be guarded well, have no fear."

"Do you think he'll marry Portia?"

"I hope so."

"If he does, he'll be very wealthy, but Andrea never seems to think of money – just like you, my husband!"

"Father and son may not be as indifferent as they seem. Remember, when I married you I married a fortune!"

"When we married, dear, I had no fortune. It was Count Crito and Francesco Sforza's soldiers who regained our family's lordship and it's our second son, Giovanni, who's making it successful."

"Yes, he's doing very well."

"And so is Andrea, dear. We are fortunate to have such sons."

"Yes, Anna, we are."

Once more they lapsed into companionable silence, and this time Carlo fell asleep. Anna smiled and then she closed her eyes as well, though not in sleep. It was a prayer, a simple child-like prayer: 'Dear Lord, our happiness is so unique. Please let your grace permit it for a little longer. Even so, Thy Will be done'.

★

Carlo del Monte woke up not long before Dr Ficino and Marsilio were announced. He stood up as they approached. As usual, his leg hurt, but he was used to that.

"Ah, Doctor, welcome again. Your care is much appreciated. And Marsilio, welcome too."

After reciprocal greetings, Dr Ficino went straight to work and, knowing what was required from previous visits, Jacopo the family servant had provided a bowl of water. Carefully Dr Ficino unwound the bandage.

"Good," he said quietly. "There's no discharge and the swelling's down. I think we'll dispense with the bandage and let your leg enjoy some air, but I'll need to check it again soon."

"Doctor, I feel a total fraud dragging you here, all the way from Florence. I'm sure Marsilio could check things first and save your precious time."

"If you're happy with that, Sir – yes, of course," the Doctor smiled. "There's one proviso though, that he examines your leg first, before you start on Plato. Otherwise I fear your body's needs might be forgotten!"

Del Monte laughed. "I always knew I had a wise doctor! Ah, here comes my good wife. She wants to show you her herb garden. I'm afraid I must admit to a little devious planning, for I want to have a brief word with Marsilio."

"Brief, Sir!?" The Doctor's amusement was evident.

"Of course," del Monte returned, an obvious twinkle in his eye.

When Dr Ficino and Anna left, Carlo del Monte began to talk at once, and Marsilio, who was fond of the old man, listened intently.

"When I was in Mistra about fifteen years ago I copied out part of Plato's *Parmenides*, on the nature of the One, that Absolute One, but I've mislaid it and it haunts me. I've looked everywhere! I can remember the sense of wonder I experienced, but not the passage. Could you find it for me, Marsilio?"

"'If one is,' Parmenides said, 'the one cannot be the many.' Is that the part you mean?"

"It is!" del Monte exclaimed. "Could I impose upon you to bring me a copy on your next visit?"

"I can write it out for you now . . ."

"Now! You remember it!?"

"Yes, Sir."

"My heavens, what a memory! Marsilio, could you recall it before you write a copy out for me?"

"Of course, Sir." Marsilio smiled. How tranquil the young man was, del Monte thought. Yet, he also sensed the fire of sheer delight.

"Thank you, Marsilio."

"I'll start from the beginning:

If one is, Parmenides said, the one cannot be many.
> *Impossible.*
Then the one cannot have parts, and cannot be a whole?
> *Why not?*

"Just a little slower, Marsilio," del Monte interjected.

Marsilio nodded.

Because every part is part of a whole, is it not?
> *Yes.*
And what is a whole? Would not that of which no part is wanting be a whole?
> *Certainly.*
Then in either case, the one would be made up of parts; both as being a whole and also as having parts.
> *To be sure.*
And in either case, the one would become many and not one.
> *True.*
But surely it ought to be one and not many?
> *It ought.*
Then if the one is to remain one it will not be a whole and will not have parts.
> *No.*
But if it has not parts, it will have neither beginning, middle, nor end, for these of course would be parts of it.
> *Right.*
But then, again, a beginning and an end are the limits of everything?
> *Certainly.*
Then the one having neither beginning nor end is unlimited?
> *Yes, unlimited.*

"Marsilio, that's enough for the moment. My old mind's been over-stretched! One, one without a second, absolutely one, and so profoundly simple. And Marsilio, what a phenomenal memory you have!"

"When you love your subject, Sir . . ."

"I think there's a little more to it than that. Ah, here comes your father and my darling wife."

"Well, I know where to come when I need advice on herbs!" Dr Ficino said loudly as he approached. "Your good lady is a mine of information, Sir!"

"She is," del Monte agreed emphatically. "I keep telling her to let the knowledge that she has be known."

"My dear, there are many who know much more than I. I'm just a part-time gardener and before my head is swollen any further, I think we ought to have refreshments. They should be ready now."

CHAPTER 12

Buda

Buda was on the hilly western bank of the Danube as it flowed southward from Esztergom. It was not at all what Andrea del Monte had expected. He had imagined a massive all-embracing wall inside which the city would be guarded, when in fact only the citadel was fortified, leaving two major churches outside the wall.

The sky had clouded over as they approached Buda, and when they disembarked it began to rain, a heavy downpour, without a breath of wind. All seemed grey and dreary and after the warmth of the day it was now quite cold. These first impressions were distinctly gloomy, del Monte thought, as he stood with Carlo on the wooden landing stage. Other boats moored nearby moved gently on the eddies by the river bank. Some thirty men were loading and unloading boats. Del Monte felt completely isolated.

Then, as if from nowhere, he saw a troop of soldiers heading straight towards him. Were they friendly, he thought defensively, for God knows what political developments there could have been. He waited till a few paces short of him the soldiers halted by command. Their officer stepped forward and saluted.

"Welcome to Buda, Excellency," he said in perfect Italian.

Del Monte acknowledged the greeting with due formality. Clearly he was seen as an ambassador.

"We have been asked to conduct you to your quarters, Sir, after which, when you are refreshed, the Captain General will receive you."

The rain was still pouring down. Del Monte felt a coldness on his shoulders; the damp was seeping through. Walking casually with him and Carlo Pucci and apparently oblivious of the rain, the officer made pleasant conversation. The road was strengthened with stones but still muddy and del Monte's shoes were quickly saturated. An inauspicious arrival, he reflected, his eye catching the knee-high boots of the Hungarian striding out beside him.

The stone-walled rooms that were his quarters were draped with tapestries, and, most importantly, there was a fire. The furniture was austere, reflecting in del Monte's mind the harsh realities of the city's situation, for the proximity of the Turks was like a threatening storm darkening the southern sky. How easy for their galleys to navigate the river. Dread of the Turks was in the air, fed by memories of Kosevo, where the flower of Serbian nobility had been slaughtered in 1389 and also by the disaster at Varna in Bulgaria in 1444 when King Vladislas Jagiellon of Hungary and Poland had died and the famous Cardinal Cesarini had simply disappeared. This was not the farcical

43

game the mercenary generals played in Italy and mislabelled war. This was a clash of cultures in which mercy was a word that few acknowledged.

After an hour to rest and change, Andrea and his secretary were conducted through the narrow streets of the citadel to meet the Captain General, Hunyadi. The anteroom into which they were shown was decorated with a fresco, Gothic in style, of some Hungarian saint, but del Monte had no idea who it was. The door opened and the Italian-speaking officer who had met them at the jetty stood before them, doubtless to act as the interpreter.

Hunyadi was broad and strong, a man used to hardship, a man of action, moulded by necessity and practised in the art of snap decisions. He spun out his greetings in hesitant Italian, at once returning to the comfort of his own familiar tongue which the officer deftly interpreted. Del Monte was surprised how quickly the process became routine.

"We are honoured by your visit, Messer del Monte," Hunyadi continued. "You come well recommended as the emissary of the great Medici, renowned throughout the breadth of Europe as the head of a commercial house that can be trusted. Wisely, Cosimo de' Medici wants to know the situation here first-hand. Nothing beats the intimacy of being present, and you are present, my friend. Have you any questions?"

"What drives the Turks to wage perpetual aggression?" del Monte asked.

"It's not perpetual, even though it seems so, for it depends upon the nature of their Sultan. I know one thing, though, they are belligerent at present, and we must stand up to them or else be over-run. Tell them in Italy that Hungary is fighting not just for Hungary but for all of Europe too. This is a struggle for survival and not a petty skirmish between two boastful princes!"

"But, Sir, what drives the Turks?"

"A fanatical certainty. The white-robed janissaries are the worst. They seem to be possessed."

"I'm told they're trained from youth . . ."

"They are, but they're not invincible. They're flesh and blood like any man. They will be stopped, for we too have a holy faith, we too are certain!"

Del Monte was impressed, for he knew Hunyadi meant exactly what he said. The Captain General then turned to commerce and the need to foster trade and promised that his visitor would be introduced to the city's leading merchants. Del Monte expressed his thanks and enthusiasm, knowing Florence's commercial houses, not least the Medici, would be pleased.

It was growing dark, and servants were busy lighting numerous candles. Suddenly the large hall was magical, the sombre atmosphere transformed as the colours of the full-length portraits and the tapestries came to life.

With a sharp command Hunyadi ordered wine, and del Monte let it be the signal to stop Carlo taking notes. For some time they discussed the ever-shifting pattern of Italian politics and the current hope for peace and, much to Carlo Pucci's surprise, he was included in the conversation – del Monte's doing, of course. In fact, Carlo had the distinct feeling of being groomed for something.

It was clear that Hunyadi's main interest was in Venice, for Hungary and Venice shared a border which was by no means always friendly. Now a common enemy had united them – both shared the task of holding back the Turkish tide.

After a second cup of wine Hunyadi questioned del Monte on the New Learning.

"What is this New Learning that is transforming Italy?" The interpreter translated with a seamless ease that made del Monte marvel.

"Well, Sir, if you asked a group of thirty their opinion you might get thirty answers. For my part, though, its essence is the rediscovery of Plato. What do you think, Carlo?" he added, turning to his secretary.

Carlo Pucci gulped and shifted uneasily on his ornate wooden chair. Panic was close, but his better part spoke out.

"I see the New Learning as a child of the ancient wisdom of the Greeks and Latins, with Plato, as Messer del Monte says, a pivotal centre." His eyes scanned the hall, focusing on the two guardsmen flanking the door, – powerful individuals. That's it, he thought; this was his lead. "Somehow, Sir, we have escaped the old monastic anonymity, for the individual is now prominent in every walk of life. That's how it seems to me, but what the link with Plato is, is something I would have to study." He smiled tentatively, hoping he had expressed himself with dignity.

"You're right about the individual factor, Messer Pucci. That very point struck me forcefully when I was with Sforza in Milan. Yes, you're right."

At a brief gesture from Hunyadi their cups were filled again. Del Monte guessed the battle-hardened soldier was no stranger to such evening solace. The conversation continued, with Hunyadi spelling out the following day's appointments, including the church leaders, the bankers and the merchants. The young King Ladislas V and his regent were at Esztergom, Hunyadi explained, but del Monte was not unhappy to miss the royal audience. The real ruler was the man before him, Janos Hunyadi.

CHAPTER 13

Back to Venice

What had he achieved in Buda, del Monte asked himself. Very little, was the honest answer, yet he had made contacts and contacts were the life-blood of diplomacy and trade. He fully understood the perils that Hunyadi faced. These he would communicate in no uncertain terms, though he did not think that help would be forthcoming from the North Italian cities. Venice had its own Turkish threat to face, while Florence and Milan were over-taxed, their gold reserves impoverished by the costs of war.

Hosted by the officer who had acted as interpreter, he had met many of the city's dignitaries in the three days of his visit. Carlo kept careful notes, yet even so remembering names was by no means easy. The Buda merchants made some strange requests, though not so odd as to surprise the merchant house in Florence. The Medici, of course, prided themselves in supplying what was wanted, regardless of its rarity. Banking, though by far the most important, was not their only interest.

Del Monte had been obliged to visit Pest, which lay across the river. Unlike Buda's hilly terrain, Pest was built on level, sandy soil and was diffi-cult to fortify. It was politic, of course, to pay respect to this proud town and listen to its elders.

Although the hospitality had been generous, too generous in many cases, del Monte was pleased to set out for the south and Venice. He was tired of travelling and looked forward to some ease and comfort in the familiar city of his birth.

The Hungarians had been helpful, almost to a fault, providing him with an escort and a well-experienced guide. Del Monte felt embarrassed, for he had done so little and received so much. The truth was that they liked the unpretentious ways of one so clearly cultured and so well connected. He was completely unaware of this, but Carlo Pucci noted it; he had read the situa-tion perfectly.

Pucci was also aware that del Monte had been slowly easing more impor-tant work in his direction. Nothing had been said in any formal sense, but del Monte in his languid way had introduced him more than once as his 'assistant'.

★

The guide's Italian was basic, and with his air of angry isolation he was not up-lifting company. Even so, he was experienced and knew exactly where to go and when to stop. Clearly, he had made the journey many times. Del Monte saw their Hungarian escort to be more a token than substantial, for they were little more than boys in uniforms. The hardened troops had sterner duties.

It happened near to midday, not too far from Zagreb. The heat and lazy rhythm of the horses was soporific, so when they saw the troop of Turkish Janissaries they first were unbelieving. Would they perhaps wake up to find it was a mirage? Two of the young soldiers did wake up, however, and promptly bolted, but the others were too mesmerised by fear to move.

The two burly Florentine bodyguards gripped their swords instinctively; for them the reputation of the Janissaries was not so harshly real. The taciturn guide opened his mouth to speak but failed to say a word for, as he judged it, there was little point. In his mind, death had made its appointment.

Carlo Pucci remained calm, an eerie calm. It had happened before in times of extremity, and this certainly was extremity, for the dreaded reputation of the Janissaries left little room for hope – yet there was no surge of panic. He looked across at del Monte sitting impassively on his horse. If frantic thoughts were racing through his mind he did not show it, but fear did grip del Monte's stomach. The curved scimitars of the Janissaries inflicted frightful wounds. With helpless fascination he watched the Turks approach. In the windless heat their loose white garments hung limp. Strangely, there was no hint of aggression, none at all. Then it struck him – this was a deputation, a mission, not unlike his own party, with papers of safe passage.

"Keep calm," he called out quietly. "Do nothing provocative." He kept watching. They were close to hailing distance. Del Monte sensed their confidence and discipline. He also noticed two turbaned figures in sandy-coloured robes, diplomats perhaps or even merchants. The Turks, he knew, traded with Venice.

He had learnt a little Turkish, words of greeting and thanks, but little else.

"May the merciful and compassionate Lord bless your journey," he called out, hoping his Turkish would not be taken as an insult.

The Turks halted and one of the Janissaries, no doubt their leader, called in reply, bowing elaborately. Del Monte recognised sufficient words to know his answer to be friendly. He also bowed and then both parties quietly continued on their way. When the Turks were well distant, relief burst out spontaneously. Meanwhile the two young Hungarian soldiers who had panicked quietly drifted back. Del Monte pretended not to notice.

"The Turks are human beings, too, it seems!" he quipped to Carlo.

"Yes, Sir, but I'm glad you knew some Turkish!"

"I only hope that what I said and what I meant to say were similar."

"Well, Sir, at least they did not use their scimitars!"

"Thank God – and Carlo, I'm tired of all this 'Sir' and 'Messer'."

"Then how shall I address you?"

"I have a taste for 'Excellency'", del Monte said flippantly.

"Excellency or Your Excellency?" Carlo returned, matching his mood.

"Your Excellency, I think, and could you grovel a bit, – for God's sake, Carlo, my name is Andrea!"

"Yes, Sir."

At that they both exploded into laugher until the tears ran down their cheeks, as shock and tension were released. The sour-faced guide looked on with patent disapproval, but he had a new respect for these soft Italians. His tensions were releasing, too, and he knew his favourite inn was close.

For Carlo the new familiarity had a disproportionate effect. It was as though he now remembered something, something long forgotten. The cloying subservience, born of his years in Rome, had been eroding ever since the marvel of his meeting with del Monte, and now its shadow had disappeared completely. He was puzzled, though. What was this elusive memory, just out of reach?

In three days' time they would be in Venetian territory. Carlo knew the plans, but he was puzzled as to why the eastern Adriatic strip belonged to Venice, for, with the vast bulk of Hungary behind, it seemed unreasonable. Why did Hungary tolerate it? He put the question to del Monte.

"They fought about it some thirty years ago, but Venice would not budge. On the face of it, the Hungarian case is strong but the problem coast-line with its numerous islands is a breeding ground for piracy. Only Venice can police it, and policing it is vital to Venetian trade. So reason, and a few judicial ducats I would guess, secured the day."

"Venice is wealthy!"

"Very. Her coffers may be depleted at the moment, but in a year or so they'll be just as full as ever. The Great Sea is a Venetian lake. Trade is their life-blood and their word their bond. Even their enemies trust them when it comes to commerce!"

"But their lake is shrinking, Andrea."

"Yes, like Hunyadi's Hungary, the Turkish threat is real and present."

"The Turks have one huge advantage."

"What, Carlo?"

"Fear. We anticipate defeat!"

"You're right. We need a victory but, Carlo, let's leave such gloomy thinking for another day and thank the Lord we've met the Janissaries face to face and lived."

"Amen to that. I thought my hour had come."

"You looked quite calm."

"Yes, at the time, but afterwards I shook a bit. Andrea, isn't it strange how the horses walk in tandem. They seem to know we want to talk."

"They probably do." Rounding a bend, he exclaimed, "Oh, look – a village at long last. Our guide is beckoning. He clearly knows the inn!"

"I don't care how rough the vintage is; I'll drink it."

"So will I, Carlo, and just think of it, within the week, if God allows, we'll have the best, within the warmth and friendship of Count Crito's palace."

CHAPTER 14

Needed

"Back in 1438, when my old master, Gemistos Plethon spoke in Florence, Cosimo was inspired to found a Platonic academy, but as far as I have heard *nothing* has happened. So what's going on?!" Count Crito paused, peering with pretended fierceness at del Monte.

"Please, Sir, it's not my fault," del Monte protested with mock schoolboy deference. "Ask Cosimo."

"Seriously, though, has anything been initiated?"

"There are loose groupings – meetings of like minds, but that's always happening. No, as far as I know, nothing else has happened. I think he's waiting."

"What for?"

Del Monte did not answer immediately. They were both standing looking out from the first-floor window over the busy entrance to the Grand Canal, towards the monastery of San Giorgio Maggiore and its campanile.

"I don't know why I said he's waiting. It just came out, but clearly if there's to be an academy it will need a leader."

"And one with great authority, to keep the volatile scholars together." Count Crito shook his head. "No wonder there's delay! – Ah, Carlo! We thought we'd lost you."

"I was out exploring, Count," Carlo answered, as he joined the two men at the window. "What a wonderful city!"

"Say that in November when the north wind's blowing!"

"I can imagine, Sir!"

For a moment they were silent as they watched the ever-changing pattern of the gondolas and boats as they plied the waterway.

"Carlo," Crito said abruptly, as if giving a command, "who would you choose to lead a Platonic academy in Florence?"

"Well, Sir, only one name comes to mind."

"He's too young, Carlo," del Monte interjected, anticipating the answer. "And also, Florence is awash with proven scholars."

"Is this a private conversation?" Crito asked mildly.

"I'm sorry, Count. Carlo is recommending young Marsilio Ficino."

"Oh yes, you mentioned him before."

"He's quite remarkable," Carlo pressed, "and Plato is for him a way of life."

"Carlo's right," del Monte said emphatically, "but I still believe he's much too young."

"Maybe that's why Cosimo is waiting," Crito concluded pensively, "for, knowing him, he'll take his time before he speaks. – Ah, I think I hear the ladies. By the way, my daughter's friend and second cousin, Valeria Tiepolo, is joining us. If she's a little quiet this evening, pretend you haven't noticed – family trouble!" The tall Count nodded knowingly.

As they entered, Portia felt in turmoil. Gone were her supreme self-confidence and her flashing wit, yet her natural poise disguised all this. She did not know if she were in love or even what love was, but she knew she wanted Andrea. The incident on the walkway had unexpectedly smashed the glittering shell of her protected life and left her vulnerable. She wanted him to care, but did he care? He was so casual and languid that she sometimes wondered if anything would excite him. But there it was, she *was* attracted.

As Andrea approached, she immediately felt a rise of panic, but her poise just held. Pretence, though, was impossible. She could not hide her feelings, yet even in the midst of this confusion her mind kept circling its unending commentary. Why the violent swing from total confidence to tumult? 'Neither are real, you silly girl,' she rebuked herself. 'Your confidence was a brittle edifice waiting for destruction and your present chaos is wild emotion. You are neither of these two extremes. Hold firm.'

"Portia, you look lovely," del Monte greeted her, smiling in his usual friendly way.

"Thank you, Sir," she stammered, immediately critical of her lame reply.

For a moment he stood gazing at her quizzically. "The same beautiful 'princess' and yet . . . ," he paused reflectively. "You've changed."

"Changed? What do you mean, Andrea?"

"You're more open somehow."

"Am I?"

Suddenly she found herself speaking about the incident on the walkway.

"Good God," del Monte exclaimed.

"Quiet, Andrea; only father knows."

"Are there any clues?"

"None!"

"I would like to visit this walkway. Could we go there in the morning?"

"Yes, of course." A sudden sense of joy shone in her face. He did care. She was certain of it and she felt her tensions ease. Casually she scanned the company.

"Oh, Andrea, look!"

"What, Portia?"

"Carlo and Valeria."

"Oh heavens," he whispered. "They're both alight!"

"You're right, Andrea. They can only see each other."

"I see a tragedy in the making."

"Maybe it's just a passing wonder," she murmured.

"Not with Carlo. He doesn't dance upon the surface."

"And neither does Valeria! The trouble is immediate, Andrea, for the Tiepolo family is talking to a prominent branch of the Loredan family. The proposed suitor is such a pompous fool. He hasn't grown up!" Portia spat out the word. "The pressure's on and poor Valeria is beside herself. This will make it ten times worse!"

"Maybe," del Monte said quietly, but there was a steely look about his face that Portia had not seen before. Even so, what could he do? Carlo had neither wealth nor property and Valeria was a Tiepolo. It was a hopeless situation. Perhaps by morning the brilliance of a sparkling evening would become a passing fancy. Portia shook her head. She had not seen her gentle friend Valeria look like this before. And who was Carlo Pucci? Who was this man who only months ago had been a vagrant on the streets of Rome?

★

The morning air was cool, but the dank smell from the canal dispelled its freshness. The sun was catching the tops of the buildings but was not high enough to light the gorge-like walls rising from the water. Del Monte and Portia stood, her arm in his, scanning the walkway.

"So this is where it happened, Portia."

"Yes, Andrea, just here," she answered, pointing out the place but more intent on the new unspoken intimacy between them than on the walkway incident now two months old.

There was little to see; just the smooth curved wall that the walkway followed and a plain door flush with the wall, without a handle but out of view from where Portia was assaulted.

"I wonder what's behind that door?" del Monte mused.

"Probably a warehouse fronting onto a canal on the other side." Portia suggested.

"Do you know who owns the property?"

She shook her head. "I'm sure that father could find out."

"Another question. Do you use this walkway often?"

"I did — but not now. Father's orders. It's the quick way to Valeria's — I mean, the Tiepolo villa."

"Well, I think we've finished," he said briskly. "Let's go back."

She put her arm in his again and off they went. He seemed quite happy that they were walking arm in arm in public. Portia knew, of course, there would be gossip, but she didn't care!

"Have you spoken to Valeria since the dinner party?" he asked her, as they walked.

"Yes, she stayed the night, as she often does, and we talked late. Her father is ruthlessly using her to secure a family alliance and she's determined to resist, especially after meeting Carlo. She says she's never known such fine affection."

"How did she describe him?"

"As strong, yet very gentle. Apparently he talked a lot about your friend Marsilio."

"Yes, he's very struck by him! What did he say?"

"That Marsilio has a brilliant, penetrating mind and it was his air of sweetness that made his presence so attractive. There were other points, for Valeria remembered everything that Carlo said, it seemed. Oh yes – he was emphatic that Florence had yet to realise Marsilio's special qualities."

"That could well apply to Carlo, too! But who is Carlo Pucci? I still find myself asking this question. I presume Valeria knows he has no wealth or property."

"Yes, he told her, but she says she doesn't care."

"Poverty has a habit of making sure you care!"

"I fear that, if her father tries to force his will, she'll run away."

"Where to!? The open road's no place for her."

"My grandmother ran away!"

"That was different. She was up against a scheming guardian, but Valeria would be defying her father."

"A father in name but not in deed!"

"That may be, but the law is on his side and, Portia, God help the servant who tries to help her."

"Why is this allowed to happen!?"

"Families rule. Their pride is sovereign!"

"Andrea, I've just remembered – the servants! What we saw last night, they saw. You know how much they gossip and gossip funnels round the walkways like the wind. Her father could lock Valeria in her rooms."

"I doubt it. They wouldn't want the Loredan family to hear the rumour."

"They certainly wouldn't. Speaking of rumours, Andrea, we're approaching the Grand Piazza. Shouldn't *we* be formal?"

"I'm happy to have your arm in mine; aren't you?"

"Oh, yes, Andrea," she answered softly.

"Then damn rumour!"

She gripped his arm tightly, her heart content, certain that the future was secured.

★

When they returned to Portia's home, del Monte went directly to see Count Crito, who was busy in his library.

"Did you discover anything?" Crito asked at once.

"One possible lead, that's all. Who owns the building behind the door without a handle?"

"Some merchants use it jointly."

"It might be fruitful to check exactly who they are."

"Are you suggesting that Portia's assailants could have used the door!?"

"Yes, and planned to use it for their real objective of abducting her."

"You have your father's flair. Yes, I'll make enquiries. Now, Andrea, I've contacted the Doge's secretariat, but Foscari's seeing no one. Apparently he's ill. My feeling is that the old man's pining for his son."

"I suppose there's no chance of Jacopo's exile being lifted."

"No, the law's the law, and the Doge's enemies are vindictive. He in turn reacts by being stubborn. The Ducal Palace is not a happy place at present."

"I'm sorry; I rather like the old man."

Both men were standing. Crito had his arms folded, and his eyes were closed in concentration. For some time they were silent, and del Monte sensed the Count was ill at ease. Captured by a single thought, they both sat down, and for a moment the Count remained pensive, then looking up, he smiled and said: "My wife has been whispering in my ear for months, and I believe your mother has also been whispering to you."

"Yes, Count, I've been subject to a little gentle pressure. Sir, the answer's 'yes'! May I formally ask for your daughter's hand in marriage?"

"Thank God – oh yes! We'd hoped for this, Andrea. Our daughter's special, and after the death of our beloved Giorgio, you will be our son now. Dear Caterina will be much relieved, for in the spring you seemed so . . .", he paused, "well, so indifferent. But this time I noticed things had altered. Why the change of heart, if I may ask?"

"This time I felt that I was needed. Before I didn't. I don't know, Sir. It's simply how it is. Your daughter's wonderful."

They shook hands firmly and affectionately.

"It's a pity father will have to miss the marriage. It would be impossible, with his leg . . ."

"We could come to you."

"Would you, Sir? That would be perfect."

"Now, Andrea, we've had the good news. I know that you intended to rest here for a while, but, alas, the Signoria are calling. The message came by way of the secretariat this morning. They want you back in Florence."

CHAPTER 15

Back to Florence

Carlo was untroubled by hope. Reason dictated that any relationship with Valeria Tiepolo was out of the question. He was penniless, and she was a Tiepolo, and that was that. Yet her loveliness lingered, as did the sweetness of her nature. Andrea, his friend and benefactor, remained completely silent on the matter and, if sympathetic, he kept that to himself. Certainly on the long journey back to Florence there was ample time to talk, but Andrea pointedly confined the conversation to things political and the stupidity of Christian princes who kept squabbling over trifles while the Turks were growing stronger by the day.

"Even in Buda," he maintained, "with the Turkish menace darkening the horizon, Hunyadi's strength is looked upon with murderous suspicion."

"By whom, Andrea?"

"The jealous regent of young King Ladislas."

Carlo nodded. "Yes, that's predictable."

They were on the road north-east of Florence where the vistas and the hill-top towns of the Romagna entranced the eye. It was difficult to believe, del Monte thought, that such compelling beauty could be the home of family greed and merciless vendetta, but it was so, alas.

Del Monte reined his horse to a halt. "Carlo, what is that passage from the *Laws* that Marsilio sometimes quotes? The Athenian . . . something . . ."

"You mean the Athenian Stranger, who wonders if human affairs are worth serious effort?"

"That's the one! Yes, and he says that it's our unhappy lot to take them seriously."

"That sums it up," Carlo agreed knowingly.

"It certainly does."

"Are we far from Florence?"

"Just one more noisy inn, and then tomorrow morning we'll have some peace!"

★

The first day back del Monte rode to Fiesole to see his parents, while Carlo remained in Florence, mostly in the company of Marsilio, with whom it seemed quite natural to talk about Valeria. He described her finely etched beauty, her gentle nature, and how they thought as one. Then he explained who she was, how they met, and how the tenderness he felt for her was almost painful. But why? The experience was completely new to him.

"Oh, why am I telling you all this, Marsilio? For it's a hopeless situation. In any case, I'll probably never see her again."

"I think you will," Marsilio responded quietly.

"How so?"

"You've told me that Andrea is to be married here in Florence." Carlo nodded. "Well, I would guess the bride's best friend will be in attendance."

"The Tiepolo family would never let her out of Venice!"

"Maybe," Marsilio responded mildly.

Carlo stood up impulsively, but he could not pace about for the room was much too small.

"Seeing her again would simply be a torture!" he said frustratedly.

"Carlo, the Lord has put an angel in your way; be careful of her wings!" Marsilio's smile bordered on the mischievous. Then, as if by some unspoken will, the subject was suspended. Sitting back, he pushed his manuscript aside and stretched his arms above his head. "I've been seated at this table since early morning, and now it's early afternoon." He sighed. "I need to get some air and walk. Will you join me, Carlo?"

"Of course."

Heading for the Duomo, they moved slowly. It was much too warm to hurry, but mercifully there was a breeze. Judging by the waves and greetings, it was clear the young Ficino was well known and that his slight bent figure was familiar to many on the bustling streets. Suddenly Carlo froze.

"What is it, Carlo?"

"It's him!"

"But who?"

"That well-fed priestly figure striding forth. He's the man who threw me on the street."

"You were his secretary, but you never told me who he was."

"You know him?"

"Not personally."

"Keep it like that!" Carlo snapped.

"He's recently been made a Canon and is working closely with Aeneas . . ."

"Piccolomini!"

"Yes, the Bishop of Siena – probably the most gifted politician in the whole of Italy, and many say a future Pope. Your friend the Canon is doing well."

"He's no friend of mine," Carlo spat.

"He's not worth it, Carlo," Marsilio admonished mildly. "Don't waste your energy."

"I know, but it's difficult, for seeing him again brings the hateful past to life. He's clever, there is no doubt of that, and hooking onto Aeneas Piccolomini is the proof. Aeneas was in Vienna when Andrea and I were there, but we didn't meet him."

"He's worked closely with the German Emperor, Frederick, for years and was his envoy to Pope Eugenius at a rather crucial time. Did you have an audience with Frederick III while you were there?"

"No, he was at his summer palace. The local gossip wasn't flattering. Most labelled him as idle."

"The very ruler that the Sultan likes!"

Once at the Duomo, they headed up the Via Larga towards Cosimo's new palace and San Marco.

"I'll be seeing the inside of this place tomorrow morning," Carlo remarked casually as they approached the palace. "Andrea and I are to present ourselves at ten. Who is that entering?" he asked, seeing an important-looking official hurrying through to the courtyard.

"Diotisalvi Neroni."

"He looks very authoritative."

"Officials often do," Marsilio said with his usual mildness, but there was a twinkle of amusement in his eyes.

★

Frequent callers and the pressures of immediate business gave the palace on Via Larga a much more busy feel than that at the Careggi villa. Conscious of appointments, Cosimo had no leisure for a lengthy meeting yet, even so, his measured way of working remained the same.

Andrea del Monte did most of the talking, but Carlo was also asked for his impressions, especially about Francesco Sforza and Milan. Carlo wondered why until, at the meeting's end, Cosimo made his reasons plain. Messer Pucci was to be entrusted with a letter to be handed personally to Francesco Sforza. For his part, del Monte was to make a study of the City States that were party to the pressing need for peace. Although these orders had the seal of the Signoria, it was clear that Cosimo was their author. He liked to hear the independent, unofficial view of men who told him what they saw and not some pro-Medici fiction which officials thought might please him.

"We need more time to discuss your findings on the way to Buda," Cosimo concluded, getting to his feet, "hopefully at Careggi in the not too distant future." He laid his hand on del Monte's shoulder. "Now, Andrea, I've heard a rumour which links you to Count Crito's daughter. That does warm my ageing heart."

How did he learn so quickly, del Monte thought, but he held his peace.

"I'm sorry I must let you go," Cosimo continued, "but the Lord Priors are due and if I keep them waiting I could end up chained in the Bargello!" Humour flickered briefly and his eyebrows lifted in their characteristic way.

CHAPTER 16

At the Sforza Fortress

Carlo Pucci was given an experienced guide for his journey to Milan and, judging by his size the man was meant to be a guard as well. Three more guards accompanied them but were asked to follow at a distance. Anonymity, it was thought, would not excite the greedy.

The letter, clearly of the first importance, was strapped safely to his person. So why had he been chosen, he asked del Monte. "Who do you know in Florence? – your landlady, Cristoforo, Marsilio, myself – you're an unknown, Carlo, and you're discreet. You'll not be talking in the tavern."

"But, Andrea, the letter's sealed!" Del Monte smiled, and Carlo's puzzlement remained.

The four-day journey to Milan was relentless for both men and horses, with the minimum of rests. His relief was tangible when Carlo eventually handed the letter to the Duke. Sforza received him with blunt courtesy and read the letter carefully, while Carlo scanned the modest antechamber with its plain substantial furniture. Then Sforza spoke in low tones to his attendant, who hurried from the room, leaving Carlo and the Duke alone. The guards were on the other side of the tall twin doors.

"Messer Pucci, there'll be no written reply, but tell my friend, the great Medici, that I much appreciate the warning. That's all. Oh yes, and tell him I'll keep him well informed. Now, Messer Pucci, you'll have an escort in the morning. This city's full of the most observant people – from other cities," he added strongly. "Venice has her agents, Rome has the Church, of course, and Naples has its spies. Then there are the French, even the Sultan . . ." But there Duke Sforza stopped abruptly. Carlo, however, pretended that he had not noticed.

Sforza stood up, bringing the audience to an end, as an official entered and announced, "The Bishop of Siena has arrived, Your Grace."

For a brief moment Sforza betrayed annoyance, but he soon recovered.

"Ah, Aeneas Sylvius Piccolomini. Have you met him, Messer Pucci?"

"No Sir, but I'm told that he's a skilled diplomat."

"Yes, this old soldier Sforza will be easy prey!"

"I'm sure you'll command the high ground, Your Grace."

Sforza laughed. "Well said; – Tommaso!" he added, beckoning his attendant who had just returned. "See that Messer Pucci receives our hospitality."

"Your Grace," Carlo Pucci acknowledged, bowing low. The brief audience was over.

Since the mention of Aeneas Sylvius, Carlo had found it difficult to concentrate, knowing that the Bishop's secretary, his old enemy Ubaldo Riddo, was probably in the building, too. If there were some reception in the evening they could well meet. The thought made Carlo Pucci shudder.

★

There *was* a reception and Carlo was invited. He found himself mixing with ducal officials, magistrates and bishops, even a cardinal and, when one friendly bishop questioned his profession, he answered, "Just a messenger." But Sforza, who overheard the comment, intervened. "A messenger from the great Medici is more than 'just a messenger'!" The bishop rumbled with a laugh, and Carlo moved discreetly on.

Piccolomini was still not present and Carlo began to feel that his anxiety was misplaced, assuming that the busy man was on the road again. He relaxed, that is, if relaxation was the term to use, since he felt completely out of place. Suddenly he heard a voice behind him.

"Always watch your back, Messer Pucci." He froze. He knew the sneering voice so well, but made no comment, quickly merging with a group of wealthy-looking dignitaries, yet still aware of Riddo's cloying and unsettling presence.

Ten minutes later the same voice spoke again with a gloating hiss. "I've already warned you, Messer Pucci, always watch your back." Carlo's heart was pounding. Unreasoning fear, born of his sufferings in Rome, began to fuel panic. Then suddenly Marsilio's gentle presence and the memory of his enigmatic smile flooded through his mind. Instantly he was calm and fearless too.

"Why should I watch my back, Sir?" he said loudly enough for those close by to hear, including Sforza.

"You snake!" Riddo hissed, but instantly in soothing tones he spun a honeyed web. "Habitual posture, Sir, is our enemy and don't I know it well." His smile was keen, inviting, understanding.

"Indeed," Carlo responded coldly.

The deception succeeded with all but one, the evening's host, Duke Francesco Sforza, who, after a judicious interval, contrived to have a private word with Carlo.

"Messer Pucci, what was the smooth cleric up to? Do you know him?" Consistent with his nature, Sforza was direct. Carlo swallowed.

"I was his secretary in Rome, your Grace,"

"Yes . . . ?" Sforza clearly expected more, and Carlo, giving up all hope of circumspection, told his story straight.

"So he resents your new prominence, Messer Pucci."

"He fears it, Sir. I know too much!"

"About what?"

"Fraud and perversion."

"Have you evidence?"

"No, Sir – it's his word against mine."

"Well, Messer Pucci, Piccolomini has offered this viper as an expert aide in the coming peace negotiations."

"Riddo is very clever, Sir, and a master of detail. I'm sure Piccolomini's offer is genuine and I doubt if he would know about the darker side."

"May I call you Carlo?"

"Of course, Sir."

"Well, Carlo, I think I'll take this viper on. I'll have him watched and also learn about his friends and, Carlo, tell my good friend Cosimo all about this conversation."

"Yes, Sir."

Sforza smiled briefly. "You see, you're more than just a messenger! Now, while we've been talking, Riddo has been kept in conversation by two of my advisers, his back to the door to ensure he cannot see you leave. I'm remaining here, but you, my friend, will slip through there." Sforza pointed to a door fashioned as part of the wall. "On the other side you'll find a guard and he will take you to your quarters. Sleep well."

"Your Grace."

Even though his mind buzzed with questions, Carlo did sleep well. Next morning those questions were still there and the central one, the content of Cosimo's letter, seemed to hold the key. But the questions and surprises were not over, for when he saw the guard drawn up to be his escort he was amazed. There were six of them, and from the Ducal Guard! Carlo could only conclude that it was a mark of honour to Cosimo, Sforza's long-time ally and his friend.

No day passed without the conjuring of Valeria's presence, and now, as the city walls receded, his mind grew busy yet again. This time, though, there was a difference. The image of the hopeless supplicant had changed. A new dignity had been given to the dream, for it was a dream. Still, there was a difference in perspective, a difference in belief which seemed to resonate with something in his nature. He shook himself. Facts, Carlo, facts! However much you dream, she'll not be waiting at del Monte's villa.

CHAPTER 17

Febo

Febo was not from the premier branch of his family but even so he was a Loredan and as such commanded due prestige. Largely blind to his defects, his father indulged the young man's youthful pranks when others would have been disgusted. Most saw the twenty-three-year-old as vain, an arrogance covering his lack of real achievement.

Loredan's frustration was mounting, however. Two prominent families had rejected his son's suit, and even the Tiepolo family, after initial enthusiasm, were slow to make a firm commitment. Febo blamed the Count's haughty daughter for poisoning his reputation, an accusation his father classed as simply wounded pride, for Portia Dandolo was a prize for any man.

On reflection, even Febo felt the planned abduction of the proud and scornful Portia had been stupid. True, her rejection had maddened him, but what could he have done except humiliate and frighten her and if he had been recognised and charged, the lower dungeons could have been his lot. Thankfully, the plot had failed but there was one problem – the thick-necked servant who had helped him was asking favours which would doubtless grow to be a habit.

Now the Tiepolo girl was being tedious. Imagine being rejected by a Tiepolo! It was too much. Damn the lot of them. All he wanted was to be someone, to do something, something worthy of a Loredan. That was his right, but earning his position had not occurred to Febo. Yet he had a gift, an artist's gift with colour and design, though grossly overlaid by his ambition to be a great commander like his famous kinsmen.

For all his posturing he was sensitive to detail and prone to worry, a tendency that sometimes grew obsessive. Indeed, the fear mounted that his thick-necked accomplice might betray him. It was so easy to drop an unsigned note into the denunciation box. In desperation he joined a convoy escort bound for Crete, as a humble naval trainee, a move that greatly cheered his father. But much to his dismay, his servant, too, had joined the same ship as a sailor.

All went well until they left the fortress port of Modon on the southwest Peloponnese when a sudden storm scattered the convoy, and separated Febo's galley from the squadron. They had been driven close to some islands on the southern coast. All had survived the buffeting, and spirits were high until the look-out yelled the dreaded words, "The Turks!" Even then Febo's mind was spinning tales of glory he would tell the open-mouthed in Venice, but when it came, reality was anything but glorious.

Shouting, screaming, slashing, cursing, and the pungent smell of sweat blended in the frantic chaos of the battle. Wounded men, dead men, men tossed overboard like discarded waste, and blood, blood everywhere, covered the decks of both ships as they heaved together.

Febo, with both helmet and breastplate, battled with the rest. One wild-eyed Turk came straight at him. Febo swung and caught him on the arm but the Turk kept coming on until someone else dispatched him.

"Why are we killing each other?" Febo yelled at the unheeding mass. Then someone clubbed him from behind.

He came round to the sickening, silent aftermath. They had won but at a heavy cost. There were no prisoners. He was not surprised, having seen the reckless way the Turks attacked. Febo felt no great elation at the victory, and tales of glory were no longer in his thinking. Why had he survived, he puzzled, for half the crew were dead.

They were drifting close to an island. The sea was remarkably calm considering the recent storm. The captain sat immobile, completely drained. There were no seriously wounded survivors. Then Febo noticed that his thick-necked servant was not amongst the living, though in his mind the incident of the walkway was now completely insignificant.

Eventually the captain stirred himself. "We're returning to Modon, men. We'll take the Turkish boat in tow."

At last Febo had his hour of glory. He, being a Loredan, and his captain – the only officer to have survived – were feted by Modon's fortress commander, though perversely Febo did not want the plaudits. He was grateful to be sound in limb and to have escaped, but that was just the chance of battle, for better men than he had died.

Crete was no longer of interest and, as no immediate convoys were scheduled for the homeward journey, Febo found himself with ample leisure to explore the fortress town.

On the fourth morning he fell into conversation with a friendly Greek, while strolling on the sandy beach beneath the massive walls on which the Lion of St Mark was fashioned in relief. The Greek, Niketas by name, had a stocky, ageless look – thirty maybe, even forty, it was difficult to tell. Before the sea-fight Febo would never have spoken to such a stranger. It was different now, and for a reason he did not understand. It just seemed that he had woken up.

The Greek was personable and the conversation easy. He was a great admirer of Venice, so he said, and knew her recent history well. The enemies of Venice were his enemies, he roundly claimed. Febo felt the Greek was overdoing it, but no matter. They met the next morning and the next day too, when Niketas suggested that they eat together in the evening. Febo willingly agreed. It passed the time and the Greek was entertaining.

That evening the conversation took a different turn. Niketas was set against the Duchy of Milan – music to most Venetian ears, but Febo was completely puzzled. Why would a Greek be so engaged about Milan, far distant from his borders, especially when the Muslim Turk was hammering at his door? It made no sense. Yet Febo laughed and joked and drank his wine. Niketas might hate the Milanese, but he was much too far away to cut their throats. It mattered not.

Next night they met again, when the theories of the Greek were even more bizarre. Milan had made a deal with Genoa to share the spoils, if the Genoese would send their galleys with the cannon into the Lagoon. Febo doubled up with laughter. No one could have dreamt a fiction quite so mad, yet Niketas meant it, which made it even more hilarious.

Niketas was off to Kalamata in the morning. It was the last night he would see his good friend Febo, and so began the toasts – "to Pericles!" Febo declaimed grandly – "to Doge Foscari," Niketas returned, and thus they carried on until the landlord threw them out.

"Now, my good friend Febo," Niketas said roundly, slapping Febo on the back, "don't forget to warn your friends in Venice that Milan's a serpent." His voice hardened. "They take advantage when you drop your guard! You're a Loredan; they'll listen to you."

"I'll tell them everything, my friend," Febo said, pretending seriousness. This Greek was quite good fun, but such an idiot when it came to politics.

Suddenly the Greek strode off into the darkness of the night as if he'd never had a drink. "That man is bronze. He isn't human," Febo muttered. Then he headed for the ramparts where the wind, he hoped, might sober him. "Febo, my son, you're drunk," his muttering continued, "and you've changed, by God you have. Ten days ago you'd have taken what that crazy Greek said seriously, boring all and sundry in the process."

He swayed, steadied himself with elaborate care, and then continued on his way. "Come to think of it," the mutter now a whisper, "you never would have spoken to the Greek at all! A Loredan," he said with deep-voiced dignity, "doesn't do such things!" and he roared with laughter.

On the parapet the fresh air almost knocked him out. Not such a good idea, he thought, yet he enjoyed the wind. It was free and just the way he felt.

It took two days for Febo to recover fully. Meantime the convoy had been gathered, and on the following morning he joined it for the homeward journey.

★

The comments started when he reached the Molo. "Febo, you look well." – "By heaven, Febo, you've changed" – "You're a new man, Febo!" His father was amazed, even to the point of tears, something that he masked by pulling on his greying beard. What had happened to his haughty, brittle-tempered son, who had so recently driven him to despair?

"My son, your exploits are the talk of Venice. You've made an old man happy."

"I'm no hero, father. The so-called glorious battle was chaotic slaughter, ruled by little more than chance."

"It needed courage to hold your ground, my son."

"On a galley, father, there's nowhere you can run!"

"You could have jumped!"

"I would have if I'd thought of it!"

His father laughed. He liked his son's new realism.

"How did you find Modon?"

"Boring, father, but I met a crazy Greek called Niketas who helped to pass the time," and Febo then described the Greek's obsession with Milan. "He was amusing, but completely mad."

His father pondered for a moment. "Did you tell the Governor about this man?"

"I didn't think the subject worthy of his time."

"I wonder." His father paused. "What if your Greek acquaintance was a convert to Islam?"

"My God! That would explain it all. They want Venice to be occupied by war in Lombardy so that they can have a freer hand. But, father, it was schoolboy stuff in Modon. My Greek friend was such a joke!"

"There'll be others, though, and they'll be more sophisticated. You ought to tell Count Crito. He's the Eastern expert."

"Count Crito!" Old attitudes and fears came crowding in and his new-found freedom vanished. 'No, damn you', he grated to himself, 'I'm not going back.' His protruding jaw shot out defiantly.

"Father, I'll go straight away."

Loredan nodded, clearly pleased by his son's resolute behaviour.

On the way to the Dandolo Palace Febo's doubts were rampant, but even so his resolve did not waver. Once there, he was quickly shown to a waiting room and there he remained, his heart pounding, though determined to be free of fear. He could hear approaching footsteps and assumed it was a servant. To his surprise it was the Count himself, tall, commanding, yet with an open smile of welcome. Miraculously, Febo's tensions faded – freedom had returned.

"We've heard you've had a little trouble with the Turks," the Count said easily.

"Yes, Count, our galley was attacked."

"A messy business, war at sea. Thank heavens I've always had the earth beneath my feet."

"You fought the Turks, Sir?"

"Yes," the Count said briefly. "Not a pleasant memory."

Febo was amazed and humbled too. The famous Count was talking man to man.

"Was it very rough?" the Count asked mildly.

"Most of it I didn't see as someone clubbed me from behind."

"A happy respite. Some are taken, some are not; it's all quite inexplicable. Thank the Lord I'm much too old for all that now. Well, Febo, no doubt you have a reason for your visit. Let's sit and you can tell me all about it."

Febo was won over. Count Crito was a Count indeed.

"Well Sir, father suggested that I should tell you of some meetings I had at Modon with a Greek." And Febo then recounted what had taken place. "Though I can't imagine this man to be a top-grade spy; he seemed far too naive."

"Yes, but it confirms for me the widespread thrust of Turkish policy. They are insatiable, and only our much-stretched navy stands between them and the shores of Italy. We're not at war, at least not officially, and we'll complain about this unprovoked attack, though they'll doubtless make a counter claim. It's hardly worth the effort. Christendom must wake up. I write to my old friend Francesco Sforza; I write to Cosimo and my friends in Florence, but letters end up on a pile. Indeed, I've sent so many that I risk being classed a bore."

"The Pope has been active, Sir," Febo ventured respectfully.

"Yes, but he's had scant support. He talks of a crusade, and one should be grateful that he talks at all." The Count shook his head vigorously. "I detest the very word crusade but, as my ancestors were robbed and driven from Constantinople by the so-called Fourth Crusade, it's understandable. A war defending our way of life and land I understand, but a holy war I don't. Greed and lust for power seem much more honest motives!"

The Count smiled, and Febo felt drawn to his strong straightforward nature. All at once the secret of the walkway incident loomed darkly in his thoughts, but he turned his back on it. This was not the time to trouble the Count or to indulge the freedom of confession. A triviality was a triviality; just let it be, he told himself.

The Count was still smiling and Febo wondered why. Then suddenly he knew. "Febo, would you like to go to Florence?"

"Me, Sir – why – yes if . . ." Febo was completely taken aback.

"Your father will have to agree, of course."

"He won't mind, I'm sure, but Sir, we're still at war!"

"That's history, or it will be soon. The whole campaign was stupid, little more than pride and posturing."

Febo's wide-eyed look betrayed his shock.

"Don't worry, Febo, Francesco knows my views. In fact, they all know at the Ducal Palace, for I've consistently argued for a truce and a transfer of resources to defend the East."

"Yes, Sir, father told me, but Sir, why Florence?"

"Febo, this is not a plan that I've been nurturing, for it's only just occurred to me. You've seen the Turks in action and you've met a Turkish spy – for no doubt that's what your Greek friend was. Tell this to the Medici. Describe the suicidal frenzy of the Turks' attack. They know about all this, of course, but do they *really* know it? You're a Loredan. Perhaps they'll listen, for I don't think that they hear me any more. I've probably warned too often. Why, oh why do we wait until the enemy's knocking at the door?" Count Crito laughed lightly. "Boethius said that human affairs are fraught with anxiety; they never prosper perfectly and they never remain constant. We can but do our best. Well, Febo, tell me, how is your father?"

Febo felt himself at ease, even happy, as the conversation carried on informally. A month ago he never would have dreamt of such a meeting. The powerful memory of the freedom he'd experienced had returned, yet there was something missing, but he knew not what.

When he took his leave, the Count's warm handshake and his invitation to call at any time was genuine. Nothing had been said about the awkward subject of his rejected marriage suit. For Febo, though, all that was in the past. He would also ask his father to withdraw the stalled attempt of marriage to the Tiepolo girl. 'What's the point of marrying a girl who doesn't want you,' he murmured as he walked towards the Grand Piazza. The logic was so simple and, what was wounded pride he asked himself, thinking of the yells of pain and the mindless slaughter he had witnessed.

He walked on, nodding here and there to people that he knew. Then the dark memory of the incident on the walkway rose again. It was past and unnecessary, but there it was. Florence, he thought – all would be resolved in Florence. He stopped and looked at the horses above the entrance to San Marco. Yes, all would be resolved in Florence. What a strange prediction.

CHAPTER 18

Messer Pucci

Cosimo looked exhausted. His eyes were closed, and Carlo seriously wondered if he were asleep. Then one eye opened and Carlo knew the great man had been very much awake and had heard his every word.

"You're in some danger, Messer Pucci," he said bluntly.

"I don't quite understand, Sir." Carlo's voice was tentative. "I knew the Duke was being careful, but I felt that it was more a mark of honour to yourself."

"Duke Sforza doesn't waste his time on gestures," Cosimo barked, and Carlo felt that he had spoken out of turn. "The ducal escort was a message, Messer Pucci, a measure of the Duke's concern." Cosimo paused, letting his words have maximum effect. "There are powerful forces outside Italy who want to see us warring and divided. It suits their own expansion. If well-placed, their agents can be paid extremely well and a Churchman short of funds and maddened by his lust for power..." Cosimo paused and lightly shrugged his shoulders. "This friend of yours from Rome, the one who showed so much concern for your back, tell me more about him."

Carlo pressed his lips together tightly as he felt the rise of bitterness and anger. 'Pucci, keep calm,' he told himself. 'Just stick to facts.'

"Well, Sir, his public face is charming and very gracious. He entertains in lavish style and his guests are loud in their appreciation, but when they've gone and the door is closed his other self takes hold. I've witnessed it so many times. My fault was my complacency, for I stayed too long."

"Yes, but what happened behind closed doors?"

"He almost always criticised his guests and 'peasant' was his favourite jibe for even his exalted visitors."

"I often think like that myself," Cosimo said dryly. "Go on."

"The women, when they came, came late, and one night I heard a scream and hurried to investigate. His door had not been fixed and eased ajar. There were two girls with him, not Italians; it was pretty compromising, Sir. He saw me and I knew at once *he knew* that I had seen too much."

"So the fool panicked!" Cosimo snorted.

"Yes, Sir, but he took time to blacken my name before he threw me out."

"You lived in his residence?"

"Yes, and ate there too."

"So you were on the street with nowhere to live, next to no money – for he paid you little I imagine – and, as he had defamed you, you couldn't find employment – right?"

Carlo nodded.

"So, as I've heard, in desperation you set out for Siena or any place away from Rome, but you'd hardly left the city before you were beaten up and robbed. That was probably his doing as well."

"I never thought of that."

"But why didn't he complete the job? Perhaps his henchmen thought they had and when he saw you back in Rome and on the street he knew the hazard of the gutter would oblige. How did he finance his parties?"

"He oversaw a Vatican building project."

"Say no more!" Cosimo interjected. "What else?"

"Well, there was the Foundling Hospital, and fund-raising events. I know he'd never let me handle the accounts."

"You say he's clever."

"Very."

"The man's a fool! He panicked when he threw you on the street, and I fear that he may do the same again. It's your word against his. Petty fraud is commonplace, and the Church would close its ranks behind him. He has nothing to worry about, but he'll doubtless panic and that's the trouble. That friendly giant, Bernardo, whom we gave you as a guide, can be your shadow for a while."

Carlo was completely stunned and looked it. Cosimo was amused, but only those who knew him would have noticed.

"Andrea tells me that your Latin's good and you even know a little Greek. Who taught you?"

"Father Giovanni, a village priest just outside Assisi. I was brought to him at the age of four."

"By whom?"

"A peasant woman, I was told, who said my name was Pucci."

"Did she tell the good priest who your parents were?"

"Father Giovanni didn't see her, but he was told she grew emotional and ran off. She was an innocent soul, it was said, a kind of village simpleton."

"And how did you get to Rome?"

"I looked after Father Giovanni until he died, and when the new priest came he suggested, quite rightly, that I should earn my living in the world. He knew an impressive Churchman, he said, and wrote me a letter of introduction. So that was how I came to know Ubaldo Riddo. I was accepted as a junior secretary – a very timid and bewildered Pucci!"

"And he exploited that."

"I'm afraid so, Sir."

Once more Cosimo closed his eyes. Carlo sat watching quietly. What was occupying that sagacious mind? And what a mind, he thought – measured, unhurried, yet needle-sharp and guided by an ever-present common sense.

Cosimo looked up. "You will remain in the employ of the Signoria. There are no specific tasks at present, but in the meantime you can assist Andrea. And get to know the treasures of the city. Marsilio will help you there, and remember, be ever vigilant." Slowly he stood up and to Carlo's amazement he stretched out his hand. Carlo grasped it.

"Thank you, Messer Pucci. Your calm demeanour is impressive."

Why did he call me Messer Pucci, when the custom was Messer Carlo, or simply Carlo? And he was not the only one; even Bernardo did it. Well, that was how it was.

★

Carlo knew that his interview had gone well and that the great man had shown him considerable respect. It was strange, though, that he called him Messer Pucci, when Andrea was Andrea, and Marsilio, Marsilio. He skipped down the stone steps to the courtyard, past Donatello's David and then outside. It had grown colder and a chill wind was blowing down the Via Larga. He buttoned up his tunic and hurried on towards Marsilio's house. Only then did he realise that the familiar bulky form of Bernardo was just behind him. It was the new reality.

"Winter's on the way, Carlo," Marsilio said in greeting. "Ah, Bernardo . . ."

"I'm looking after this one, Marsilio," Bernardo nodded towards Carlo. "It's the master's orders."

"You can look after both of us, Bernardo, for it's time for our usual walk."

"Messer Cosimo told me to become acquainted with the treasures of the city," Carlo remarked. "Could we visit one today? – Maybe a Masaccio fresco that Andrea keeps praising? Is that possible, Marsilio?"

"Of course. Let's cross the river to the Brancacci Chapel. *The Tribute Money* is wonderful."

They walked briskly, the chill wind an incentive.

"Andrea called yesterday with a young Venetian named Febo Loredan. You would have enjoyed the gathering, Carlo. He was full of questions. Alas, to his disappointment, he's been recalled."

Carlo was puzzled, remembering that a Loredan had been rejected by both Portia and Valeria and had been less than gracious, but he kept that to himself.

"Andrea told me that Loredan survived a sea-fight with the Turks and that he'd had a kind of Damascene experience."

So that explains it, Carlo thought. "By the sound of it, Marsilio, we'll be seeing him again. We ought to form a group – you know, of strays like me!"

"That's impossible, for I never know when father wants me with him on his rounds."

"Marsilio, I have a silly question: why does the great man always call me Messer Pucci? He calls you Marsilio and he calls Andrea, Andrea."

"He's known us longer, Carlo."

"There seems more to it than that."

Marsilio turned and looked at his friend in profile and a familiar smile played on his face. "It's that aristocratic look you have!"

Carlo laughed. "Now you're mocking me, Marsilio! Heavens, this wind is really biting!"

"The depth of winter's herald."

"When it comes, will 1454 bring peace?"

"God's will is not predictable, but grace arises when efforts are sincere, we're told."

CHAPTER 19

Illness

At the end of February 1454 a letter arrived from Venice at the Alberti del Monte villa in Fiesole, and when Andrea's mother read the content she was devastated. Portia had been gravely ill for weeks, with little sign of change, and now a cloying depression was weakening her will to fight. The Countess Caterina and Count Crito were beside themselves. They had already lost their beloved son Giorgio, and now Portia's life was in the balance. Could Andrea come, they pleaded. Perhaps his presence would uplift her spirits.

Caterina described her daughter's symptoms, and although she emphasised the expert care Portia was receiving, Andrea still sought out Marsilio and his father. They could speak only in general terms, of course, but they gave advice on diet, while Marsilio strongly recommended the healing power of music. Andrea also drew upon his mother's knowledge in the use of herbs and, having obtained Cosimo's permission, he set out for Venice with two sturdy servants as security.

Caterina's letter also contained depressing news about Portia's friend, Valeria. She had been much relieved at first when Febo Loredan withdrew his suit, but to her dismay her ambitious father quickly found another suitor from a well-established family. If anything, Valeria's opposition hardened, and her continued disobedience so infuriated her father that he locked her in her rooms and refused to let her visit Portia, whom Messer Tiepolo blamed for all the trouble. "It took all my powers of persuasion," Caterina wrote, "to stop Crito from wringing Tiepolo's neck!"

Everything, it seemed, was going wrong and the del Monte household was plunged in gloom. Low cloud had enveloped Fiesole for days and, as Andrea left in the swirling mist, the gloom seemed universal.

★

Early each morning Carlo Pucci went to the Medici Palace to join the secretariat which dealt with correspondence personally addressed to Cosimo. Carlo translated from the Latin – the diplomatic language of Church and State – and helped in drafting letters. Though he saw little of Cosimo, he got to know his jovial son, Giovanni. Judging from his princely pay, Carlo felt his work was viewed as satisfactory. He had never had such funds before; indeed, enough to contemplate marriage and a family, but alas, that was not possible. Valeria was his vision and it was not in his nature to compromise.

He had written to the Dandolo Palace expressing his concern and hope for Portia's swift recovery and had enclosed a letter to Valeria, hoping it could be delivered without compromising either Portia, Valeria or the

Count and Countess. What else could he do? There was always hope, but the flame burned low.

★

Febo Loredan was recalled from Florence to command a galley squadron to confront an outbreak of piracy in the Adriatic. This was a task to prove young men, but it was a signal honour, too, and six months previously Febo's ego would have soared beyond the Campanile. Now, he did not even want the job, yet he dared not say so, for it would greatly hurt his noble father and it would offend the elders of the state – not a wise thing to do. The truth was that he wanted to return to Florence. There was so much there to be explored. And then there was the young Ficino, whom he visited with del Monte. He had always run a mile from Plato and the Greeks, but Ficino made it all so simple and it explained so much about the taste of freedom he had had.

The incident on the walkway still haunted him and surfaced in the most disturbing way. Perhaps he wanted to be rid of it too much. When he heard of Portia's illness he briefly called to offer his best wishes. The Count received him graciously, though it was not the time to linger or for such a thing as a confession.

The gathering of men and stores for the sweep against piracy was almost complete. Soon all would be ready for the hide-and-seek around the islands along the Croatian coast, but success was rare, for pirates, knowing every hidden cove, were a most elusive quarry.

A week before the squadron was due to leave Febo was surprised to see del Monte in the Grand Piazza. He looked strained and weary, quite unlike his usual urbane self. No one had said he was in Venice, but it was clearly him. Doubtless he was here because of Portia.

Del Monte had seen him and came hurriedly across the wide expanse of the Piazza. With no preliminaries, no greetings, del Monte burst out "Febo, do you know of any good musicians? Perhaps you've heard that Portia's ill, but she's beginning to respond to music and we need to keep the diet fresh."

Startled, Febo thought a moment. "My sister knows a flautist whom she's always praising, but I've never met her."

"Excellent. Can you direct her to the Dandolo palace as soon as possible? It's urgent."

"I'll act at once."

"Thanks. I must rush. I'm on an urgent errand for the Countess. She hasn't been too well – the strain has been awful, but she's getting better, as is her daughter, thank the Lord. Oh, Febo, congratulations on your commission. We must meet soon, before you leave."

Turning abruptly, del Monte strode off back across the Piazza and, standing quietly, Febo watched him go, while thinking just how strange the play

71

of life could be. Now for his sister and her friend the flautist. He was pleased to be of help, for it also eased the sense of guilt he felt each time he thought of Portia. Abandoning his own plans, he set out for his sister's villa. The 'great Commander Loredan', he mocked himself, 'off to find a flautist.' Then his prominent jaw shot forward in defiance.

★

Sforza's inner council had debated Milan's negotiating position exhaustively. How far should they go when the three main parties met at Lodi? What should they retain and what concession could they offer? The strengths and weaknesses of Venice were analysed in detail. No facet was passed over. Throughout these talks Ubaldo Riddo had distinguished himself. He was both brilliant and careful of the feelings of his fellow delegates, but the words of Carlo Pucci had, by no means, been forgotten, and he had his own instinctive feeling, too; somehow Riddo was too perfect. Yet Piccolomini's secretary was impressive; so much so that he began to question his misgivings. Still, he hesitated. Such an able man at Lodi would be useful. Ability, though, was not his first requirement, for he needed men that he could trust completely. Should Riddo be included in his delegation? That was the question, and one that he decided to defer until the final council meeting. Of course, he had no wish to slight the influential Piccolomini. However, his priority was the integrity of his delegation. That was paramount. Sometimes Sforza wondered why he had fought so long and hard to be a Duke. Such pensive moments, though, were brief. The Dukedom was a role that seemed to fit.

He had already requested Carlo Pucci's presence at the final council meeting and Cosimo had willingly obliged. But Pucci would be a secret witness. He knew Riddo and could have useful observations.

★

Sforza had already been in negotiations with Venice. The waters had been tested, as it were, but secretly. No one except his closest advisors and Cosimo de' Medici knew. Even so, the council he was chairing was a vital instrument and the backcloth to his final orders and decisions.

In ones and twos they gathered, until at ten precisely the Duke appeared and took his seat while glancing briefly at the minstrels' gallery. He asked for final comments and, without bidding, the council members spoke sequentially round the table. As it happened, Ubaldo Riddo was the last to speak.

"When I was a young man," he began, "my father told me how the blind Doge Enrico Dandolo turned the fury of the fourth crusade on Constantinople." Riddo paused, making contact with each council member in turn. 'Get on with it, man,' Sforza thought impatiently.

"It was a crime that weakened the great City. I can still hear the passion in his voice and, of course, the horses stolen from the Hippodrome now stand as evidence above the entrance to San Marco."

"Well, at least the Turks don't have them," one elderly counsellor

72

mumbled, and laughter rippled round the chamber. Sforza's mounting impatience was now tangible and Riddo sensed it immediately.

"Noble Sirs, I acknowledge unreservedly that I'm prejudiced, for the stories that one learns when young are prone to stick and, because of that, I've always tried to keep to facts; one being that during Doge Foscari's reign Venice has been at war and, in my opinion, mostly the aggressor. She's rather like a cat that preys upon its victims when they're unsuspecting, but that may be, of course, my predilection. What I'm trying to say in my long-winded way is, gentlemen, beware! Make no concessions. Give nothing away, for they'll swallow everything you've got. Be wary of their promises and their so-called reputation that their word's their bond. Now, as I've already pointed out, this may be deep-seated prejudice, but I must be honest; I must tell you what I feel."

Riddo sat down grandly and Sforza nodded his acknowledgement. 'Damned fool', he grated to himself; 'far better to have simply said he didn't trust Venetians in the first place. Instead he had to bore us all with platitudes that none of us believed. The man's a fool'. But there was now one certainty: Riddo would not be in the party bound for Lodi.

"My friends, those in the delegation will be notified." The Duke stood up abruptly and walked briskly to his private quarters.

Riddo was picking up his papers when a grey-haired counsellor approached. "I didn't know the horses were from Byzantium; most interesting, Sir; thank you."

"They were not the only treasures which were stolen."

"Well, as our colleague said, the Turks don't have them." The old man patted Riddo's arm and Riddo forced a chuckle. Just then a movement in the minstrels' gallery caught his eye. He looked again and saw a figure leaving. He only saw the man's back, but it looked so like that weasel Pucci.

★

It happened by chance, as Carlo did not know that Riddo had been given quarters at the Sforza fortress. Indeed, if Sforza had not summoned him he never would have heard the muffled sound of swearing when he hurried round the first tier courtyard walkway. It was Riddo, ranting. He knew the voice too well and he stopped before the studded door where the sound was most intense.

"Damn to hell that cunning wall-eyed Duke." The words were plain, aided by the simple fact that the door was just ajar. It was so like Rome, when Carlo had seen his pompous master with his women. Perhaps Riddo's self-important nature would not take the time to see the door was shut. Cautiously Carlo peered through the slit, adjusting his position until Riddo became visible. He was amazed, for the black-clad Churchman was punching his pillow with unrelenting savagery, while swearing like a stream in flood. Carlo shuddered as if witnessing something reptilian.

He straightened himself and left swiftly, his guard Bernardo close behind. Now he understood why Sforza had been adamant that Bernardo should be with him, even in the fortress. Riddo was vicious and his vindictive streak worked far beyond restraint of reason. Cosimo had been right. He, Carlo, was in danger.

Access to Duke Sforza was immediate and at once he felt assured by the great man's air of confidence. Carlo related all that had just occurred, but Sforza did little other than speculate on who Ubaldo Riddo's friends might be.

"What did you witness from the minstrels' gallery?" he asked, and Carlo guessed that that was why he had been summoned.

"According to Your Grace, Riddo has been brilliant in all the previous sessions. Then he throws it all away. But why? Why so suddenly anti-Venetian? What's his motive? In fact, Your Grace, it felt as if he was obeying orders!"

"Well, he's not going to Lodi. I want men that I can trust!"

"Have you told him, Sir?"

"I sent a 'respectful' note. He's Piccolomini's secretary. That I mustn't forget. Who knows how that busy prelate might react if I question Riddo's integrity."

"What if Riddo poisons the situation?"

"I doubt if he will. He'll pretend that all was smooth and easy with his friend the Duke." Humour played on Sforza's honest features. "Don't be fooled by the childish tantrum that you witnessed. Riddo's not a child. He'll play the smooth-tongued cleric as before, for that's his mark. Yes, he's dangerous and very clever, and his Latin's brilliant, too."

"His French is also fluent, Sir."

"My God! My friend, you've given me the key!"

CHAPTER 20

The Peace of Lodi

The Peace of Lodi was signed on the 9th April, 1454, to the great relief of Florence, Venice, and Milan. Naples, though, was still dissatisfied and René of Anjou was in a sulk, feeling that he had been used; yet this did not cloud the air of hope in the three great northern cities.

At the Dandolo palace there was a mood of expectation. Portia had recovered from her fever, but her depression still remained. The very best physicians had advised and treated her, yet to no avail. Only music seemed to lift her spirits.

It was her father who suggested that she visit Florence. He hoped the drama of the journey and the change would be a tonic. Overcoming her dull reluctance, Portia eventually agreed. To wrestle with the darkness needed courage and the Count was greatly heartened by her stand. It strengthened his decision, not lightly taken, to send his daughter far beyond the safety of her native city, the most secure in Christendom.

Crito was all the more concerned as his wife insisted on accompanying Portia: a move he did not like yet knew to be necessary. However, he had sufficient influence at the Ducal palace to assemble a substantial guard. Of course, it all depended upon Andrea. Nothing would happen until he returned from Lodi, where he had been present at the signing. Crito would not entrust his wife and daughter to anybody else.

★

Weather permitting, Valeria Tiepolo walked for half an hour each day, but on a route dictated by her father's servants. The Dandolo palace was forbidden, as was the Grand Piazza and the Molo. In fact, her walks were for her health alone – a brief escape from the confinement of her rooms.

She understood her father's anger and frustration, for by proposing marriage below her class she was flouting all the rules, and that was something no Venetian did. The talk of Carlo's rising fortune in the pay of the Medici meant nothing to Messer Tiepolo. "Scribes and secretaries are the small change of a ducat," he responded angrily. She was trapped, her gilded rooms her prison. Her brother sided with their father, the servants knew their place, and her beloved mother was no more. She had no friends except her nurse, but she, of necessity, was circumspect. So the weeks went by, with intermittent calls from priests, even a bishop stern in his admonition.

At last her strength of will began to ebb. She was being silly. Her love for Carlo was a dream, a childish foolishness, and her father was only being realistic. And Carlo, he was far away in Florence and she was not the only woman in the world. Nature would win, it always did, and then she would receive a letter telling of his marriage. Her doubts were growing.

Just when resolution was about to crumble, her nurse, at no small risk, delivered Carlo's letter, sent via her long-time friends at the Dandolo palace. Her hopes were born anew. She read the letter quickly, then slowly, savouring his every word. After the turmoil of her recent indecision she felt at peace, and for a moment she drifted into sleep. Suddenly she awoke as if disturbed. Something strange was going to happen. It made no sense, but the feeling overwhelmed her.

★

Chasing pirates needed patience and a sense of humour and, after Modon, Febo Loredan felt that he had exercised them both. Not that pirates were in any way amusing, for their mindless cruelty could often be appalling. No, it was the villagers with their colourful excuses that he found comical. His father had warned him that peasants could be cunning and, by heavens, he was right, but it was all so very farcical as well. One toothless mother, protesting her innocence, claimed the priceless carpet hanging on her wall had been the final luxury of a holy hermit, the shedding of his last possessions. "I hope so, mother," Loredan murmured, looking into her doleful eyes, "for if a throat's been slit for this the good Lord has a flawless memory!"

Towards the end of their operations they picked up three priests in a small boat who maintained that they had rowed across the Adriatic. The crew treated them with great respect, but Loredan was certain they were frauds and put them under guard. Such treatment of priests was resented, and the grumbles of the crew were barely held in check, but Loredan barked and looked imperious, an act his old self had long practised, and all contention withered. His decision was vindicated that very evening when the priests, taking advantage of their guards' respect and leniency, slipped overboard as the squadron was heading for their anchorage. Loredan ordered a sweep, but they picked up only one, who, while protesting his clerical immunity, was put in chains.

"We'll question him at Corfu," Loredan said dismissively, yet he was intrigued. Who were these so-called Churchmen? Were they robbers, using their disguise in order to gain access to unsuspecting coastal craft, or were they up to something else?

He would hand his prisoner over to the governor at Corfu, where the man's identity could be checked, but that, of course, could take some time. Loredan planned a three-day rest call at the island before a second scouring of the Croatian coastline. Then back to Venice and the vivacious flautist, Ginevra Bembo, for in finding a musician for del Monte Febo knew that he had also found his future wife. She would be a handful, but then most women were, in Febo's judgement.

His father, long since despairing of his son's inability to wed, was greatly heartened at the prospect of such a union. "And she's a Bembo!" he kept repeating to his friends.

All was well in Febo Loredan's world, except the incident on the walkway. It was always there, waiting to engender guilt and cloud his new-found freedom. His thick-necked servant had been killed, so only he knew of the incident. Should he dismiss it as a triviality or should he speak and risk unwelcome consequences? All at once the young Florentine Marsilio came to mind. He would ask *him* what to do. He would know. The fact that Ficino was only twenty did not occur to him.

CHAPTER 21

The Two Carlos

From their first meeting amidst the ruins of the Palatine, Paolino and Andrea del Monte had kept in touch by letter. The correspondence was infrequent, indeed banal at times, for when Paolino used the Church as messenger he was circumspect. However, when he sent his letters via the Medici Bank he was direct and frank. Such was his latest letter, which described a lavish reception given by the up-and-coming Ubaldo Riddo.

The guests, Paolino wrote, included five Cardinals, two of whom were French, and four Bishops, with scholarship very much in evidence. Paolino's comments were wry. In one corner, the letter ran, two experts in the canon law exchanged insults, though veiled and softly spoken in the interest of decorum.

The seventy-six-year-old Cardinal Alfonso Borgia, Paolino continued, smiled benignly at everyone. He was a general favourite, being much too old to be a rival. Also present was the great Bessarion, his long beard, the mark of the Byzantine clergy, defying Latin tradition. Piccolomini, Bishop of Siena, was there of course, the consummate diplomat, charming all he met. And then there was the host himself, wreathed in smiles and showering all with compliments, while no doubt scheming to procure a bishopric.

'Where did Riddo find the funds?' Paolino questioned, 'for a table of such bounty and so artistically displayed must have cost a fortune.' The boar's head surrounded by other sumptuous dishes and abundant piles of fruit were clear evidence that no expense was spared. So how did Riddo, still a mere canon, pay for it? No one knew, though most assumed his family to be rich.

Paolino wondered why he had been invited. Perhaps his employment at the new Vatican Library, with its air of scholarship, had caught Riddo's imagination.

Del Monte chuckled frequently as he read the letter, for Paolino's playful wit was entertaining. As he had anticipated all those months ago, the librarian was a useful contact.

Having been re-delivered from Florence, Paolino's letter had taken some time to arrive at the Dandolo Palace. It was now June, much later than del Monte had expected to be still in Venice. There had been considerable delay in obtaining papers of recommendation and safe passage and, of course, neither he nor his future father-in-law would take any chances. The Countess and her daughter were a precious charge. However, departure was now imminent.

★

As he had never pushed himself forward, Carlo's fluency in Latin was not fully appreciated until practical requirements revealed it. Because of this and the fresh intuitive quality of his reports and because Cosimo liked him, Carlo found himself included in missions of increasing importance, the most demanding being the one to London. Italians were not liked in England, and to Carlo the reason was soon apparent. The king, desperate for funds, repaid his loans by farming out tax-gathering to his creditors, some of whom, especially the Venetians, were ruthless. It was little wonder there was trouble. The Medici interests, though, seemed free of this and Cosimo's rule that loans to king and baron had to be secured, held firm. In any case, the export of goods was the main object of the Medici London branch. The factional strife of Yorkist and Lancastrian was the curse of England, Carlo wrote, but when this ended London would enjoy a huge potential.

Carlo had always known that the Medici banking and merchant interests were large, but he had not appreciated their sheer scale until his visit north. London, Bruges, Antwerp, Avignon, Geneva, Barcelona, Valencia, all had branch offices and, of course, there was a presence in the Italian cities. Cosimo had competent managers and he also had his sons, but he held the reins himself. All this, together with the cares of state and the endless political manoeuvring necessary to keep stability, was a constant labour, for Cosimo did not wield the ducal power with its tyrannical decrees. Then, of course, there were his charitable works and, by no means least, his patronage of art. What was more, he made time for philosophy and its promotion. Marsilio had access to the Medici library and could, if he so wished, always see the great man privately – and he *was* a great man, of that Carlo was completely certain.

Carlo Pucci returned to Florence in late July. With the Peace of Lodi signed and holding, he quickly sensed the optimistic mood as merchants felt the urge to trade. Cosimo looked less weary but was just as reticent as ever. Apart from questions, "Well done, Messer Pucci" was about the sum of his remarks, although he did say something unexpected just as Carlo was about to leave.

"Visit Andrea's father at Fiesole and ask him to teach you the art of disguise. Tell him I sent you!" The usual Medici smile added a note of mystery.

*

It was with considerable relief that Carlo left the stifling heat of Florence. The mule he hired was stubborn and reluctant. It clearly did not see a reason to exert itself in such a temperature, so the journey proved slow and even slower as they climbed the last slope to Fiesole, but at the top a gentle breeze rewarded them.

Messer del Monte was in his favourite seat beneath the awning in his garden and when Carlo told him what Cosimo had said he burst out laughing.

"Cosimo's an old rogue," he chuckled, then, growing serious, he explained: "I used disguise a lot in order to observe unnoticed and also when I was under threat. Is Bernardo with you?"

"Yes, he had to walk much of he way. His mule simply could not cope!"

"Bernardo's a problem. He's big and all too easy to recognise, so he'll have to be disguised as well and kept in the background if possible. Of course, you'll need more than one persona." Andrea's father continued to describe the various guises that he used. "Where's he sending you?" he asked eventually.

"He didn't say, Sir. There was no mention of a journey."

"It's probably to Rome."

"Why Rome, Sir?"

"Let's put it this way. Papa Niccolo isn't getting any younger."

"Well, if it's Rome, why the disguise? Few will remember me. I was on the streets for a year!"

"The 'saintly' Canon Riddo will remember!"

"Oh yes, he'll remember." Carlo's words carried an unfamiliar edge of bitterness. "You're right, Sir. It must be Rome, for his grace Duke Sforza hinted at it, and he and Messer Cosimo are as one. Yes, it's Rome all right, and I will surely need disguise. Messer Cosimo clearly thinks ahead!"

"He always has. Now Carlo, I've good news. Your friend Andrea is due from Venice any time. In fact, he's somewhat overdue, but then he has a precious charge, the Countess and her daughter. I hope you'll still be in Florence when they arrive."

"I hope so, Sir," Carlo responded, distracted by a sudden surge of feeling, for to him mention of the Countess and her daughter brought Valeria to mind. Part of him wanted desperately to ask if there was news of her, but the other part held firm and silent.

The two men sat quietly for some time. The old Carlo and the young Carlo, del Monte mused, they were similar in many ways, but the young man beside him was blessed with a natural tranquillity. Indeed, sitting as they were together, the peace felt tangible.

"I was half expecting Marsilio today. He looks me over every fortnight. Have you seen him since you returned?"

"No, Sir. I went to see Messer Cosimo and then straight here. I hope to visit him tomorrow."

"The energy and enthusiasm of his scholarship is phenomenal. He can read a manuscript once – once mind you, and memorise large passages. This is unusual, to say the least, and when he's fired by the right question, he is transported by sheer delight. In fact, the inner truth of Plato's teaching seems to live within him. Yet, I sense there's something missing. A presumption on my part, you may say, but that's an old man's privilege! Somehow he has still to set his course. In fact, I strongly feel he needs to master Greek."

Carlo Pucci nodded.

"He's aware of this, I'm certain, but the demands upon his time are mounting, not least from his family; yet despite these distractions, he remains very still within himself."

"And so can you, my friend," del Monte prompted.

"Maybe, but nothing like Marsilio. I think we're very fortunate to enjoy his friendship."

"Amen to that."

CHAPTER 22

Still the Doge

The sun was low and the heat had lost its intensity. The air, though, was still warm, and even as Carlo and Marsilio crossed the river there was little freshness.

"San Miniato might be a little cooler," Marsilio suggested briefly. Carlo nodded, and at once they headed for the steps that led to the higher ground.

As always, Carlo was intrigued by Marsilio's way of moving. No one could describe him as athletic, yet somehow every step appeared complete.

Once they began to climb towards San Miniato, Carlo wondered if their choice was wise. It was much too warm, but Marsilio climbed on, step by step, apparently unperturbed. The sheer simplicity of his movements was arresting, so much so that Carlo also fell to being simple in the way he moved. He smiled. Example was the surest teacher.

When they reached the open ground beneath the monastery, Carlo felt refreshed, not tired and panting as he had expected, for the climb had been steep. He glanced across at Marsilio, whose rhythmic breathing showed no sense of strain. He looked totally at peace and divorced from all distracting thoughts; so, in a similar way, Carlo followed his example. This he felt to be completely natural. The presence deepened. It had no end and no one lived apart from it.

"Carlo." Marsilio's voice seemed to sound within him.

"Yes, Marsilio."

"This morning at the Duomo I overheard two bishops talking. One said loudly that Canon Riddo was about to join their number – number meaning bishops, I assumed. We can't be sure, of course."

"I'm sure. He's crawling up the rickety ladder." Carlo had forgotten all about the present moment. Past wrongs, recent threats and future uncertainties filled his mind. "Marsilio, a bishopric could take him out of Rome," he added hopefully.

"I rather gathered from the asides and innuendo that Riddo would remain in Rome and would, to use their words, 'continue to be very useful.'"

"Yes," Carlo ventured flatly, "he'll be where the power is. Power and wealth – he wants it all."

"A common malady."

"With him it's all-absorbing."

"Yes, Carlo, but however selfish they may be, most men have a spark of good. In Riddo's case it could be his Achilles' heel!"

Marsilio was smiling, that familiar smile that Carlo knew so well. Fully present, Marsilio had not strayed outside the stillness. For Carlo this example was another powerful lesson.

"Marsilio, please say something more about the all-embracing One – Plato's unity," Carlo asked, turning to his friend, and in that moment Marsilio seemed to shine.

★

Andrea's father could pretend no longer that all was well. Andrea and his precious charge, the Countess and his future wife, were three weeks overdue. Del Monte had sent a letter to Cosimo, who in turn had sent a troop of horse. They could patrol some miles the other side of Rocca, but beyond that permission would be needed.

His dear wife Anna was sleeping only fitfully and he slept little better. He consoled himself that Andrea and his party were well guarded by eight of the Serene Republic's best men. Crito would have seen to that. Then there were Andrea's own two bodyguards. Eleven men, including Andrea, were a powerful deterrent to simple brigands, but if sponsored by some wild-eyed lord in search of ransom . . . He stopped. It was too painful to pursue this line of thought!

The road from Ravenna had been free of incidents for some time, so why now? Del Monte was maddened by frustration knowing that in younger years he would have long since left to scour the area. Now all that he could do was wait and pray. Hopefully the delay had some simple explanation, for that was often the case in such situations. But the Romagna was the Romagna. He knew its lawless reputation well.

★

It was the death of his son Giorgio which drew Count Crito close to Doge Foscari, and when the old man heard of Portia's illness he was most solicitous. It had never been in Count Crito's nature to be sycophantic, and in the heady days of the great Doge's reign he had rarely been included with the favoured. Now he was amongst the few the Doge could bear to have about him. As Doge, Foscari was obliged to see a stream of visitors, and as some were prone to gossip he soon learned of Tiepolo's treatment of his daughter. Such news was commonplace, but when Foscari heard how Valeria had been barred from visiting her sick friend Portia, the old man raged, demanding all the facts.

"I'm still the Doge," he thundered at his counsellors, "even though you want me in the grave! What has Tiepolo been up to? Find out!"

Foscari was right. He was still the Doge, and even if they wanted to, no one dared ignore him – at least, not yet!

As ever, the Venetian secretariat was efficient, and the Doge was soon informed of all the details, including those of Carlo Pucci, who had gained the trust of Sforza and Medici. The story reminded him of another Carlo, his old friend Andrea del Monte's father. This made Foscari even more

83

determined to create a fuss, for all knew Tiepolo had not transgressed the law. Foscari knew it too, of course, but he was stubborn and demanded that Tiepolo be brought before him.

Tiepolo was unrepentant, even disdainful, knowing that the aged Doge would soon be off the stage. This fuelled Foscari's fury, and he called Tiepolo a hard unfeeling monster. Tiepolo had miscalculated, for the story of the clash raced round the walkways like a northern wind. If it had been other than the old declining Doge, Tiepolo would have filed a suit. But that was not all, as Foscari, the stubborn fool, had demanded that his daughter and her nurse be bought before him. Tiepolo was enraged yet powerless. Though the law was on his side, public sentiment had sided with the Doge, and he felt obliged to acquiesce. In any case, his hopes for an advantageous marriage had evaporated. After all the gossip no family would be interested.

Doge Foscari was captivated by the sweet girl when she arrived. "You're very beautiful, my dear," he murmured gently. "And you have spirit – eh!" He smiled as though they shared a secret. "I knew your mother," the old man nodded. "She was a very lovely lady, yes, a lovely lady, and you're so like her." He patted Valeria's arm affectionately. Tears came to her eyes. She could not help herself.

"I'm sorry, your Serenity, but you are so kind."

"Don't worry, don't worry. I'm just an old man who is uplifted by your sweetness. Have no fear. I'm sure that all will happen as it should."

Valeria was completely overwhelmed by the situation but, being trained from youth as to how she should behave, she held her poise. The Doge went on at length in praise of 'Messer Carlo', recounting how he had impressed both Sforza and Medici. The Venetian secret arm was like a universal presence, and the Doge was always well informed.

Foscari's praise continued as he listed Valeria's accomplishments – her expertise in Greek and, of course, Latin. "And you play the lyre, I'm told."

"Yes, Sir, but only in my chamber."

"Perhaps you'll bring it here one day to soothe an old man's spirits."

"I fear my playing might have a less than positive effect," she blushed.

The Doge's chuckle rumbled deeply. "We'll see, we'll see," he laughed.

The ever-present counsellors were growing restless. Nothing much had been said. There had been no criticism of Messer Tiepolo, but the old man had made it very plain where his sympathies lay.

"The Doge," Foscari concluded grandly, "will be an old and loving uncle. Have you noted that?" he barked, turning to his secretaries.

"Yes, Serenity."

"Good!"

He leaned forward, whispering confidentially. "They copy everything I say – even when I snore, it's put on record!" There was another rumble. The audience was over.

CHAPTER 23

Shock

It was by sheer good fortune that the Captain of the Venetian guard spotted figures on the hillside, for in the fading light they could easily have been missed. But then Count Crito had selected the officer with care, a tall unsmiling man who kept communication to the minimum. Andrea found him difficult, yet he respected his professionalism.

"We need to get the ladies off the road as quickly as we can," he said forcefully to del Monte.

"There's a small church nearby, as I recall."

"I hope it's close, Sir, for when the sun dips we'll still be visible, while they'll become invisible against the darkness of the hillside."

"It's close," del Monte asserted calmly, hoping his memory was correct.

Del Monte was right, and by hurrying they reached it just as the sun began to set. The church was far too small but cool, thank heavens, though the smell was stale. Now what to do? he asked himself. They were some way from their intended stop, and the ladies had neither privacy nor anywhere to sleep. The short fat priest, resenting this invasion of his church, was hostile. He feared the soldiers would disturb his flock and refused completely to believe that there were any bandits in the area.

The Captain of the guard ignored him and tersely muttered, "We'll go outside to do a sweep. Bar the door behind us."

The priest, his bald head glistening with perspiration, was indulging in a tantrum, throwing his arms about and wailing like a grieving woman at a funeral.

"Be quiet," del Monte bellowed.

The priest froze, and a shocked silence suddenly descended on those in the church, a look of horror on their faces. No one spoke to priests like that, except for drunks and madmen.

"Father, we are sorry to invade your church like this, but the Countess and her daughter need sanctuary," del Monte explained evenly. "Have you facilities where the ladies can refresh themselves?"

At once the priest became co-operative, bowing repeatedly before the Countess. "My house is just a step or two away," he fawned.

Del Monte found the sycophancy tasteless. Stepping across to Portia, he whispered softly, "he obviously likes titles! Do you think that I should *play* the Duke?"

"If it affords your Grace's leisure some amusement!" Her eyes twinkled.

Good, he thought, she's coping well. By heavens! – he had just realised – her heaviness had gone and her sparkle had returned!

"Father, we'll accept your gracious offer when the Captain of the guard returns."

"My humble house is yours to use." The cleric bowed once more.

A knowing glance from Portia almost made del Monte laugh. Still, they needed to be cautious, very cautious. Maybe it *was* a band of children who had shadowed them. But, no – he almost shook his head – children would never keep their distance so consistently.

There was a loud knock, followed by a muffled shout, at which the bar was pulled aside. The Captain of the guard was back more quickly than del Monte had expected.

"It's very serious, Sir," the Captain reported briskly. "The waxing moon exposed two men – scouts most probably. Assuming they might be villagers, we approached without aggression, but the fools rushed at us, so now they're with their Maker. The trouble is, Sir, they each had golden florins in their pouches."

"How many?"

"Three."

"My God, is life as cheap as that!"

"The war's over, Sir, and the mercenaries are out of work and looking for employment."

"The question is, who paid them?"

"That's a question, Sir, I hope we have the leisure to pursue."

A grim smile played on del Monte's face, but the Venetian Captain showed no emotion whatsoever.

"What do you suggest we do?" del Monte prompted.

"Well, Sir, with mercenaries hired for such scant reward we can't proceed. We need to send for help and we also need a bigger place than this in which to wait," he added, turning to scan the tiny church.

The priest, who had overheard the Captain's final words, was quick to recommend a nearby monastery, less than a mile away. Was it safe to risk the journey? That was a question for del Monte and the Captain to decide. Playing down the danger, the priest was enthusiastic, eager to free his church from trouble and the soldiers. The Captain, very much a Venetian, was thorough and, after his men had scouted the terrain next morning, the party made the short journey to the monastery – a low stone-built clutch of buildings.

At last del Monte could relax. Though constantly alert, he had done little. The Venetian Captain was the hero of the hour. Again, del Monte was surprised that his second bodyguard had volunteered so readily to ride to Florence and to risk the hazards of the road. Previously he had been thinking of replacing him, so grudging was his service.

It was Portia's transformation which really heartened him. The shock, the straitened circumstances, whatever it was, had released her from the final bonds of her depression. Her old quick-witted brilliance had returned, yet Andrea knew that less than generous thoughts had nagged him in these last three months. Was he marrying someone who was flawed?

The question was, who had hired the mercenaries and for what reason? Del Monte assumed the ladies were the target, but the Captain, objective as ever, made no assumptions, only suggesting how easily del Monte could have made an enemy.

"You were at Lodi, Sir?"

"Yes, I was."

"You probably didn't notice, but I was also there – on guard duty. I witnessed the blazing row you had with two rather self-important Churchmen."

"Yes, of course, I do remember; they got very heated when I suggested that a saintly cleric they were praising was a fraud."

"I think 'very heated' is an understatement, Sir. One got so red about the face I thought he would explode. Then Piccolomini's secretary joined them and they started ridiculing Francesca Sforza."

"That's when I left, for it was my turn to explode. You may not know, but the Duke did not include Piccolomini's secretary in his delegation. That didn't please, of course, but using some excuse he attended anyway."

"Well, Sir, after you left you were described in entertaining detail as a godless heretic, an anti-Christ. They said that burning was too good for you and, worst of all, you were a Platonist!"

Del Monte laughed heartily.

"I didn't know that I warranted so much attention!"

"Sir, they meant every word of it. They were not joking."

"How do you know all this, Captain?"

"When you're standing guard people often look at you as if you are not there."

"Yes, I can well understand that, Sebastiano!"

★

The Alpe di San Benedetto was not far from Florence; indeed from where they were, it was three days on a mule at most. So when ten days had passed, del Monte grew restless. "We'll wait another day," held for two days more. Then he reluctantly concluded that his younger bodyguard had come to grief.

Sensing the need, del Monte's older and most trusted guard offered to make a second attempt to summon help, but del Monte insisted that a Venetian guard go with him, who, with the Brothers' amused connivance, was dressed in a monk's habit. So the party settled down to wait again.

The monastery was Spartan, but no one could complain that they were underfed or did not have a bed. The strain on the foundation, though, was telling, and del Monte assured the Abbot of generous compensation.

"We always have enough," the good man said. "The Lord provides, though sometimes He tests our faith and keeps us waiting." Del Monte was impressed. The Abbot was a good man, and such men kept the Church alive.

The monastic life was much more difficult for the ladies, and access to the gardens was restricted, yet, even though they were accustomed to the greatest luxury, they made no complaint. Even so, the hours of inactivity became a strain, and del Monte feared that Portia might once more succumb to melancholia. Thankfully, this did not happen. Her good spirits seemed to be established and it was difficult to believe that she had ever been disturbed.

★

Four days after del Monte's chief bodyguard and his Venetian companion left the monastery for Florence, a troop of twenty horse arrived with both men riding out in front. At last the waiting was over and the Countess and her party's journey could proceed, but disturbing questions still remained: who was the unseen hand behind the trouble? What had been the motive and would this unseen hand stretch out again? For del Monte such unanswered questions were disquieting. Was there a connection with the earlier incident on the walkway? If so, the author of the trouble was almost certainly Venetian.

CHAPTER 24

The Masterstroke

After the Doge's intervention Valeria's fate became a public obsession. No longer confined to her rooms, she was free to walk outside, but that soon became intolerable, for knowing looks and whispers followed her no matter where she went. "Poor girl," some said, while others called her 'headstrong,' 'disobedient,' and 'a witch'.

The gossips did not know it all, of course. Indeed, the atmosphere within the Tiepolo Villa was, if anything, worse than their inventions. Her brother was vitriolic. "You've disgraced your father and you've made me into a laughing stock. Know this, *sweet sister,*" his jabbing finger came close, "you'll never marry him! Never! I mean it!"

Her father simply ignored her, from time to time pronouncing in her hearing that he had no daughter, yet he did not cast her out or rage as did his son.

A letter from Portia, delivered in early August by the usual connivance of the Dandolo and Tiepolo servants, lifted her spirits.

"Mother and I have settled in at Fiesole," Portia began, "and we're enjoying ourselves immensely. Unfortunately, we had a little trouble on the way." This she described in detail. "Andrea in his easy way was full of jocular asides, to keep us happy, I assume, but the upshot of it all, my dear Valeria, is that I simply can't remember why I was so terribly depressed. Probably the shock and drama of it all released me.

"Now," Portia had started her third page, "this is something you will want to hear. I met Carlo's unique friend Marsilio, the same Marsilio who recommended music for my troubles. He's quite remarkable. Carlo and he go walking together and apparently they're quite close. Marsilio knew all about you and guess who told him. So there you are, my dear. There's no call for doubt."

This was exactly what Valeria needed to hear, as she was beginning to wish she had never met Carlo Pucci, such was the torture of her daily life, but why had he not written? Valeria read on, though distracted by her question.

"Mother and I miss Father very much, but he's hoping to be with us in the autumn. Apparently Carlo thought Father would accompany us. So he felt it prudent not to write, not knowing how to address the letter – sending it to your villa he saw as asking for trouble. He had gone to Rome, of course, before we arrived."

"O ye of little faith," Valeria whispered to herself.

"What else can I tell you? Oh yes, Febo Loredan arrived two days ago with Ginevra Bembo and her aunt as chaperone. He's a regular visitor to Marsilio's as well. He's full of fun and quick to burst out laughing. Who would ever have guessed at such a change? Father says his ego 'was pruned to its very roots' by his skirmish with the Turks.

"How I wish that you were here as well, Valeria. Father, I know, would like to help, but custom forbids it. He hints that the Doge is sympathetic, being less than happy with his peers, due to the vindictive way they've treated Jacopo, his son. Well, I'd better say no more – certainly not on paper!"

Chatty details followed about her visits into Florence with Andrea's mother.

"Now, before I end this rambling narrative, I must say something more about Marsilio, for I've never met anyone quite like him. He's a small man, hunched by too much study I suspect. But that's only the physical, for his mind is godlike. We converse in Greek, and that's the spring of so much humour, for his Greek is basic. As you know, Father taught me as a little girl, but my classical Greek is rusty. Even so, conversation brings it back. One thing, though, any word or point of grammar that he learns is held in memory. He doesn't forget, and I'm positive he would quickly be a master of the language if he had the proper teacher. Marsilio's certainly not a pious bore; anything but, and because his humour is so quick and subtle, you have to keep alert. I enjoy our occasional conversations greatly. And Valeria, I met the great Dante expert, Cristoforo Landino. Florence is an amazing place. It's so alive but, of course, it has its questionable side. In Venice we keep our indiscretions out of sight; here every vice is public!"

Valeria began to laugh, an unfamiliar therapy, as Portia described the fashionable excesses and how some ladies caked their face so much with paste and powder that they dared not laugh or smile. "But this is Florence; the tasteful and the tasteless are pursued with equal dedication!"

"Thank you, Portia," Valeria said quietly as she put the letter down. "You've saved the day," she added in a whisper.

★

Doge Foscari had always been larger than life, but the dominant figure in Venetian politics for thirty years was failing. Yet no one but the arrogant and foolish took him for granted, for, when least expected, his mind would flash with rapier precision. This his wary councillors had learned to their cost.

Since his brief meeting with Valeria he had insisted on being kept informed about her circumstances and what he heard displeased him to the point of fury. Ignoring his wishes, Tiepolo was treating his attractive daughter with as much affection as a galley slave. The law was on Tiepolo's side, but to disobey the Doge's wishes was to slight the Ducal Office and Foscari was determined not to let the matter rest. For days he pondered, often mumbling to himself, a sign his councillors knew too well meant that something was afoot. Then he acted, and four days after Valeria received Portia's letter a liveried messenger arrived from the Doge's Palace requesting her presence with her lyre that very afternoon.

In ample time, before she would have made the journey, the Doge's litter was placed at the walkway entrance to the Tiepolo villa. The symbolism was obvious to all. The Doge was honouring Valeria Tiepolo and for three days running she was summoned.

Messer Tiepolo felt powerless, and his son, Vitale, threw vengeful tantrums, so much so that Tiepolo threatened him with all the rigours of state law should he harm his sister. Tiepolo knew Foscari had humiliated him and he knew that few, if any, would raise their voices in his favour, knowing the mood of sympathy running for Valeria in the city. He was defeated. There was no alternative but to give his grudging consent to Valeria's choice, the upstart Pucci. Yet he hesitated before this final humiliation.

It was at this point that Francesco Foscari played his masterstroke. Sending word of his impending visit, the Doge had himself carried to Tiepolo's villa. This was a signal honour, and Tiepolo met his Doge with due formality. For what seemed an eternity they stood staring at each other until the Doge stepped forward, his arms open in a sign of obvious reconciliation. They embraced and when they parted tears welled unashamedly in Tiepolo's eyes.

"You have acted with great wisdom, Serenity."

"Let's say no more, Lorenzo. Children hurt us more than we pretend, and the Doge knows this as much as any man."

★

Tiepolo's son appeared immediately the Doge departed in his litter.

"Where were you when his Serenity was here?" his father asked angrily.

"That old goat! He's humiliated us! Anyway, he's got one foot in the grave."

"We all have, even you! The Lord can take us off at any time!"

"Father, Foscari's a fossil and Carlo Pucci is a jumped-up peasant."

"Peasants don't speak Latin fluently . . ."

"Pucci has no family, father. He has no wealth, no land – he's nothing! I feel degraded. My friends make jokes about it and ask me if this Pucci has a sister. It's intolerable, father. My God, del Monte found him in the gutter, but then, as del Monte's father was a peasant, what can we expect!"

Lorenzo Tiepolo sighed.

"My son, you have a lot to learn."

"You're right, I have, for only yesterday you were raging at the Doge's meddling. What did the old fool say to you?"

"We talked about the pain our children give us and how we sometimes fail as parents."

"Sentimental rubbish."

"Vitale, have some respect!" Tiepolo snapped.

"How can I? My sister's marrying a peasant, and my father doesn't seem to mind!"

"I do mind!" Tiepolo barked. "Now get out. I've had enough of you this morning."

CHAPTER 25

The Rising Star

For Riddo everything was going well. Piccolomini, the so-called genius of diplomacy, was eating from his hand, and most were quite astounded at his easy mastery of scholastic logic. He was a rising star, and many told him so, including influential Cardinals.

Now, at last, he was a Bishop, but as far as Riddo was concerned bishops were a common currency. A red hat was his aim; anything else was useless, except, of course, the Papacy itself. In the meantime he would have to make his mark. Take a safe established line, he told himself, and hold to it. He would oppose the new and fashionable learning propagated by the heretics of Florence, financed by the Medici and supported by the incumbent Pope, who luckily would not be wielding power much longer.

Who was going to be the next Pope? That was the question. Anybody but Bessarion. That droopy-eyed Greek wizard saw through the Latin ways of Rome too well, and all and sundry bowed before him as if he were the very Oracle itself. Not he at any cost. He was much too wise. Cardinal Capranica was a favourite, but he was friendly with the Colonna which meant that the Orsini party would be daggers drawn – idiots all, but ones to use when necessary. Old Alfonso Borgia was much too ancient, thank the Lord. What they needed was a common-sense Italian who would not rock too many boats.

Things were going well, too, for his other self – the one that revelled in his frequent perfumed nights as well as in the sweetness of vengeance, though this he had suspended, being ever careful of his Bishop's image. But no one knew about this secret world and no one would, for he had devised the perfect cover. There was a price to pay for such indulgence, though, for agitation and impatience ruled in place of peace of mind. He hated silence, and ambition, towering in his mind, demanded its fulfilment. Despite all this, Riddo had abundant energy and the glitter of his personality drew men to him.

His confidence in his own pre-eminence, though dominant, was covered by pretended modesty. In fact, he played his roles with skill and with an actor's instinct for convincing detail.

Where was that weasel Pucci, for he would dearly like to wring his neck. There was a rumour that he was in Rome, something that the Medici Bank denied, but then they would, of course. Only yesterday he thought that he had glimpsed him; a side profile had alerted him. He had heard that Niccolo, the malcontented brother of the pro-Medici Tommaso Solderini, was certain that 'Messer Pucci' had set out for Rome. He had also heard less than complimentary comments voiced by the solid Medici supporter,

Diotisalvi Neroni, that he did not understand 'why Cosimo had picked this Pucci out', as he was inexperienced, not too clever and not even a Florentine. "He's an innocent, for heaven's sake!" Such remarks made Riddo smile with satisfaction. Clearly the favouring of the weasel was resented in some quarters and in the highest reaches, too! Riddo's smile narrowed to a sneer. 'Pucci the paragon!' Even when Pucci was in his employ he loathed him! His quiet manner, his respectful behaviour, his modest way of living, all too good to be true. 'Watch your back Messer Pucci. I meant it in Milan and, by God, I mean it now.' Riddo hissed the words with relish. 'And your great friend del Monte and his Plato-loving clan – heretics every one of them, and if Rome won't light the faggots Ubaldo Riddo will!' What Riddo had decided as a calculated move to gain support, he began to follow with the certainty of conviction.

Being an able orator, he soon attracted followers and in the process he acquired a certain grandeur. This he nurtured. The cynically clever Riddo was receding and the pillar of established dogma was ascending. This process was occurring with amazing speed. "He is inspired", his friends began to say. What had been a calculated self-promoting move was now a righteous cause sealed by unquestioning belief.

★

Most of Carlo Pucci's time was spent sitting in taverns or on benches where the old and toothless sat and where a few questions were enough to prompt an endless stream of gossip. Disguised as old and crippled, he lingered near the mansions of the great, watching who arrived and who departed but, without a nearby tavern or a bench where he could pretend to doze, this was not easy. Was it worthwhile? This was a question never far from Carlo's mind. He was ever careful to avoid what seemed an unproductive loitering, yet even then a sudden gem of information would emerge, such as the head of the Colonna family calling on Cardinal Capranica, who many thought would be the future Pope. Carlo simply could not understand such ineptitude, for even if the Cardinal were friendly with Colonna such a public demonstration would inflame Orsini opposition to the Cardinal's election. He could only conclude that the strutting arrogance of the Roman families was totally insensitive.

In Carlo's view the great man was Bessarion. He was head and shoulders above them all. A Platonist and a scholar who would continue the humanist policies of the ageing Pope, but he was a Greek. How could a Greek preside over Latin Christendom? Carlo had heard the same question repeated many times.

Although Pope Nicholas was declining and although thoughts of the succession were on the people's minds, the Pope himself was still in charge and, never having learned the art of delegation, tried to do everything himself. Yet withal, most people thought that he had only months to live.

When Carlo asked about Bishop Riddo, the answer was generally the same – hard working, always at the Papal secretariat and a staunch supporter of church charity. "A Red Hat will be his for sure." Carlo was sceptical, of course. The only work that Riddo laboured at was self-promotion, and judging by the comments he had been successful.

Carlo had lingered near his residence on the Aventine, though only briefly, but with the incentive of a few coins he enticed an enterprising urchin to watch the entrance and report on those who came and went. The boy's reports were of marginal import, for the names he knew were few. One thing he said with certainty, no nuns or young women servants had entered.

Carlo, weary of his prickly disguise, employed the urchin for as long as he remained in Rome but the routine at Riddo's residence remained the same. Then, towards the end of Carlo's stay, the boy added a casual aside: "There's an old boy just like you, Sir, who sometimes leaves after dusk, all by himself. That happens two or three times a week, but it isn't regular."

"Probably some old part-time servant," Carlo responded casually. Riddo used to give the halt and lame employment. It helped his image, Carlo thought cynically, for he never could credit Riddo with genuine compassion.

★

Still heavily disguised, Carlo and Bernardo were approaching Siena on the hot and dusty Via Cassia when Carlo suddenly reined his mule to a halt.

"I've been a complete fool, Bernardo," he exclaimed, wiping the beads of perspiration from his forehead.

"What are you talking about, Messer Carlo?" Bernardo grumbled. The big man was suffering from the heat. "I think we should find some shade."

"Soon. The mules need rest."

"And so do we! This monk's habit is killing me, and how you can stand that beard . . ."

"Yes, it's prickly, but Bernardo, listen – we were handed the answer on a plate!"

"What answer?"

"You remember the boy telling us that an old man with a stick left Riddo's place some time after dusk on more than one occasion."

"Well, what of it?"

"That was Riddo! I'm certain of it. He's using a disguise – just like us!"

"But what for?"

"To see his ladies and to swill wine, of course!"

"So he goes to a brothel or some such place and comes back in the morning? Did the boy see him return?"

"No, not the old man, but he saw Riddo in his Bishop's garb walking as the sun came up."

"But, Messer Carlo, this is all speculation!"

"There is no proof, that I agree, but I still think I'm right. Riddo leaves at dusk disguised as an old man but he doesn't go to a brothel . . ."

"He might see too many of his friends!" Bernardo chuckled.

"As I said, he doesn't go to a brothel. He goes to another house, his own house, registered in the name of his fictional persona. In the morning when the ladies have gone, he dresses in his Bishop's garb and walks back to his residence as dawn begins to light the sky."

"You tell a good story, Sir!"

"It is a story. You're right, but I do believe it's true!"

"He could have more than one persona," Bernardo suggested pensively.

"He could. You're coming round to my way of thinking I see."

"Maybe, but more so, Messer Carlo, if you find some shade!"

"You're doing it, too – Messer Carlo this, Messer Carlo that – why?"

"I'm your bodyguard, Sir. It seems right. Carlo on its own – no, Sir!" Bernardo shook his head.

"So be it."

CHAPTER 26

Confession

Things had gone from bad to worse in the Tiepolo household, with father and son at loggerheads over Valeria's future. Row followed row, while Vitale ranted that his sister had stained the family name for generations. Driven to extreme by their last volcanic exchange, Messer Tiepolo barred his son from the villa.

Tiepolo was despondent. He had driven out his only son, and his daughter was marrying a common scribe. He felt completely broken, blaming himself, if not Venice, for the trap in which his family had been caught. A few days later he learned that Vitale had left for Rome, but that brought little comfort. Rome was a vice-ridden lawless den, ten times worse than Florence. Why had he gone there? Meanwhile, Valeria comforted him in his loneliness. He dreaded her departure. Even so, he had promised Doge Foscari that she could attend her best friend's wedding. Tiepolo was under no illusion, knowing that once in Florence she would meet her Messer Pucci, but he had given his word to Francesco, and Francesco was his Doge.

*

Andrea del Monte and Marsilio had just visited an artist's workshop near the Porto Romana. It was late afternoon and the heat of the day had lost its intensity.

"Let's go and see how Luca Pitti's folly is progressing," del Monte suggested. "Actually, Marsilio, I have a motive, for I told Febo Loredan he might see us there."

Marsilio assented readily, with the usual twinkle in his eye. "All we need is Carlo to turn up and we'd have our happy band."

"It might well happen, for he's due back very soon."

Marsilio glanced up at his friend walking casually beside him. Andrea always looked well dressed, he thought, no matter what he wore. Marsilio saw him as a natural aristocrat whose wealth and privilege were carried as easily as his clothes, yet his languid manner belied a sharp incisive mind and that was no doubt why Cosimo was employing him on what seemed endless diplomatic missions.

"Where are you off to next, Andrea?"

"Naples, but no one is supposed to know that yet. Cosimo would like to calm Alfonso down. He's acting like a spoiled boy at a party whose present was forgotten."

"So it's not an easy mission?"

"No, and the timing's awkward, especially with the Count due here in not too many weeks."

"Cosimo knows, of course."

"Oh yes, but this embassy cannot wait, he says, for he fears that King Alfonso may make stupid moves. I'm to smooth the way for consultations at a higher level."

"Has the great man said much about your coming marriage?"

"No, he seems supremely indifferent, but nonetheless I'm certain that he's pleased, for both my father and the Count he views as personal friends. But there's no indifference in the villa at Fiesole! My mother and the Countess and my lovely wife-to-be are locked in endless plans. Father and I contrive to escape. In truth, I'm not unhappy to be disappearing for a while."

"You seem to be of Cosimo's persuasion."

"No, I'm not in his class!"

Both men laughed and the conversation lapsed into an easy silence.

As often was the case when walking with Marsilio, del Monte noticed how those they met invariably seemed to smile. There were exceptions, of course, hard dark-edged faces, but most appeared to light up when they saw him. It was clearly Marsilio's sweet nature which brought relief to strained and troubled faces. Could this young man, just twenty-one, have found the secret of the one great universal love, Plato's One? It was a question that del Monte often asked himself and one he never quite dismissed.

"By heavens, Marsilio, you've become prophetic! Look! There's that mountain of a man, Bernardo, and there's our Carlo as large as life with Febo Loredan. Marsilio, your happy band is gathered!"

The greetings seemed to last for ever, until eventually, when the energies died down, Carlo gave focus to the conversation.

"What news from Venice, Febo?"

"Good news for you, my friend. Doge Foscari strongly sided with Valeria, and she's received permission to attend the wedding of her friend, Portia."

Carlo was stunned.

"How is she coming?" he stammered.

"With Count Crito."

"Is the road safe, Febo, for Andrea and the ladies just escaped being ambushed?"

"The Count will have a proper guard. But even at his age, who would dare attack him!" Febo, of course, was well aware that all the party knew of Crito's warrior reputation.

Carlo was too shocked to follow up his questions, so del Monte took the lead.

"I still keep wondering if the Romagna and last year's walkway incidents are linked. I don't think that they are, but I wish I could be sure."

"Seize the hour, Febo," Marsilio said quietly.

Febo grew bright red, spluttered incoherently and then, jutting his chin even further than its natural prominence, he burst out defiantly: "There is no connection, for I was Portia's attacker on the walkway!"

"Well, that's that, then," del Monte replied easily.

"Why are you so casual?" Loredan reacted.

"Febo, I suspected that you were behind the walkway incident, for every time the subject was discussed you went completely quiet – you practically disappeared! In fact, Febo, you did me a favour, for the incident brought Portia and me together."

Febo grinned, glancing at his friends in turn.

"Well, Sirs, I recommend confession! But, Andrea, what about Count Crito?"

"You can tell him after we have tied him down!"

Febo exploded into laughter with relief and all the party joined in.

"But what about the Count?" Febo pressed when the laughter had subsided.

"Leave Portia and the Count to me," del Monte responded quietly.

"Thanks, Andrea, and thanks, Marsilio, for your advice," he added turning to Ficino.

Febo felt free, the same open freedom he had felt after the sea-fight south of Modon. His eyes scanned the partially completed structure of Luca Pitti's palace. Yesterday he was enraged at its pretension and its massive slabs of stone. Today all that had passed. Let Luca build his palace; who knew what future function it might serve when he had left the world of flesh. He turned, conscious that Carlo was beside him.

"How did the Doge achieve the impossible, Febo?" Carlo asked. "I find it difficult to credit, for Messer Tiepolo was so completely fixed. What made him change his mind?"

"The age-old way. He used the mob."

"The mob!"

"He fed the story to the walkways and let the people know exactly where he stood. Old Francesco's not been Doge for thirty years for nothing." Febo's words were heavily ironic. Carlo knew, of course, that Foscari and the house of Loredan were not exactly on the best of terms.

"So the Doge exploited public sentiment," he said mildly.

"Exactly, yet amazingly he and Lorenzo Tiepolo have been seen walking arm in arm. But there *is* a problem Carlo – Valeria's violent brother."

"It's hard to think of Valeria's brother being violent."

"Well, he is – a dark, unreasoning man. Even I, in the full flush of my arrogant stupidity, had enough natural sense to avoid him. Now is not appropriate, but I think we'd better have a word sometime, and soon!"

"What are you two in secret session about?" del Monte called from where he and Marsilio were viewing the work in progress at the Pitti palace.

"Luca Pitti's modesty!" Febo quipped.

"We know of no such word in Florence!"

"In Venice it's not a word we overuse as either, except when hiding ducats from the tax assessors! Marsilio says we ought to head for San Miniato."

"The air's much fresher there," Marsilio explained.

"Bernardo, what about the mules?"

"There's a watering trough on the way, Messer Carlo."

"I thought you'd want to go home to your long-suffering wife."

"I can't, Messer Carlo. The great one said I was to guard you."

"I'm sure Messer Cosimo didn't want your duty to be slavish."

"That wouldn't be much of an excuse, sir, if anything happened."

"I've no enemies here, Bernardo. Anyway, I'm much too unimportant."

"What about the mad Bishop in Rome and the crazy brother you were talking about?"

"They're both in Rome."

"We've just travelled from there, and they can ride here, too!"

"Bernardo, I'm grateful for your care."

"Thank you, Sir. Not many say that, and not many stop to think I've got a wife at home!"

"What do they say?"

"They want me there, and when I'm there they don't want me!"

"Sounds familiar, Bernardo. Let's get going or we'll be left behind."

Carlo and Bernardo walked together, each leading one of the mules. Carlo's thoughts were busy for the unexpected news about Valeria had set his mind on fire. He felt elated, the tiredness of the journey totally forgotten, but riding with elation were his doubts and fears – doubts about his income and ability to provide and fears that when they met the magic might be missing. Anticipation and reality did not always coincide. There was something deeper, though, that knew, and that was the rock to which he held. What an amazing afternoon, meeting all his new-made friends together. And Febo's confession was matched, if not surpassed, by Andrea's casual acceptance, but then around Marsilio events unfolded in the most unusual way.

"Why are you all the same?" Bernardo asked suddenly.

"What are you talking about, Bernardo?"

"All the friends of young Marsilio – you're all the same. You look different. There's Messer Febo's chin and you and Messer Andrea have the features of the great Julius. You have different habits, different ways of laughing, different everything, yet you're the same. I don't know what it is. I haven't got the words."

"Why don't you ask Marsilio?"

"I couldn't do that. It's not my . . ."

". . . place. Don't be stupid, Bernardo, ask him!"

"All right, Sir, I will!"

CHAPTER 27

Doubts

Although a warrior of unquestioned reputation, Count Crito was a compassionate man. He always treated women with respect and none more so than his beloved wife and daughter. In her youth his wife, Caterina Dandolo, had been 'the flower of Venice' and her daughter had inherited her grace and beauty. But Portia also had an intellectual brilliance far beyond the average.

These qualities provoked a sharp-edged jealousy amongst her peers, however, and repeated slander gave to her a cold and haughty reputation, which was confirmed when suitor after suitor was rejected. Amidst all this, Valeria Tiepolo had been a blessed exception. She adored Portia, admired her regal beauty and enjoyed her wit and humour. The two were inseparable, but through her loyalty to Portia Valeria also suffered from unreasoning slander. So when she was barred from visiting her sick friend, both were understandably distressed. In fact, the Count was certain that it added to his daughter's depression.

Lorenzo Tiepolo had not been unaware of her heartache, but he was a Venetian nobleman intent on securing an acceptable marriage for his daughter and, if possible, one that would enhance the standing of the family. So, as Valeria's opposition grew stronger, a father's love began to turn to anger, especially when the full import of her love for Carlo Pucci dawned.

It was the vicious, vengeful ranting of his son, Vitale, which drove him into shocked admission of his own excess. So a parent's natural love returned and, even though exasperated by her headstrong opposition, he secretly admired her steadfastness.

Whilst at first incensed by Foscari's intervention, he was overwhelmed by the old man's sympathy and understanding and by the very fact that Francesco was his Doge. Tiepolo softened, and when his daughter left for Florence with Count Crito he only just managed to maintain his dignity.

Valeria should have been ecstatic, but she was tearful on parting with her father and was distressed at his distress. As well as her departure, he was acutely worried for Vitale, now in Rome and subject to the doubtful company that his violent nature would attract.

Valeria was moved by her father's efforts to reconcile himself to the impossible – her attachment to one of no known family. He kept repeating, as if to convince himself, that Messer Pucci was a friend of the nobility and was greatly favoured by Cosimo de Medici. That, at least, was something. Even so, the whole unfortunate business was a bitter disappointment, but in the last few days before she left, he kept that to himself.

On the journey the Count was kindness itself and was solicitous about her every comfort, so she made a show of being happy and contented. The truth was very different, though, for her doubts were ranging free. She had met Carlo so briefly and, at times, he seemed to be more a dream than a reality. Had he forgotten? Would he treat her as a little sister, for his letters had been so remote. Yet the news which she received from Portia told another story. He spoke only of Valeria, she reported, and 'only' had been vigorously underlined.

Valeria was unsure of her attractiveness. She was smaller than Portia and did not have her regal air. People called her 'sweet', which annoyed her greatly, for it made her feel like some retiring creature whose only thought was sewing. She was naturally warm and friendly, Portia had often emphasised, and her father more than once had told her that she had the finely fashioned features of her much-missed mother. Valeria, though, could only see herself as plain.

During their progress Count Crito was always gracious, dropping little gems of praise when he sensed that she felt down. For someone from the watery city, the hills of the Romagna were a wonder. There were many distractions but, with every turn the cartwheels made, she knew that she was drawing closer to that moment when she and Carlo would eventually meet. She desperately wanted it to happen, yet she dreaded it as well, for then she would have to face her doubts and trembling nervousness.

★

When he called in the afternoon, hoping to join Marsilio on his walk, Carlo often met young Giovanni Cavalcanti. He was only ten, yet even so, he seemed to enjoy an instinctive affinity with Marsilio's way of thinking. This was doubtless the fruit of his many visits.

Being from a noble family, young Giovanni also received instruction in the martial arts, and when Carlo arrived at the Ficino home, intent on sharing his concerns about Valeria's imminent arrival, he found Giovanni busy describing the various attacking and defensive moves in sword-play. Subduing his impatience, Carlo listened, for he had no doubt that Giovanni was knowledgeable and diligent in his practice. The strange thing was that Carlo seemed to recognise the moves, but he thought little of it, for such things were known in a general way.

Giovanni left shortly afterwards, accompanied by a family servant, and at once Carlo bared his soul.

"What can I offer her, Marsilio – a house in Florence? Not in the narrow smelly streets where I could afford accommodation! I feel it would have to be Fiesole. The air is much fresher there and she would be close to Portia – that is, if Andrea intends to settle there. Valeria Tiepolo has been used to gracious living. I fear the shock of poverty may be too much. It's such a lot to ask of her, Marsilio."

Marsilio smiled.

"I've never seen you so agitated, Carlo and you must know that nothing is resolved in agitation, so resume your natural tranquillity, my friend. That is your strength. You have shared your problems with me, now share them with the Lord and wait upon his Will."

"It's not easy, Marsilio, for the problems are real."

"I know."

Marsilio fell still, and Carlo sensed the potency. At such times he had learned not to disturb him.

"How old were you, Carlo, when you were brought to the priest's house?"

"About five or six, I think."

"Do you remember anything about that time?"

"No, Marsilio. I only know what I was told – that an old woman, somewhat odd in her behaviour, deposited me there and told them that my name was Carlo Pucci. Then she fled, close to panic, seemingly."

"Why so, I wonder?"

"It was assumed she was deranged."

"I see. I wonder what *really* happened."

For a time Marsilio was contemplative. Then he inhaled vigorously. "Time for our walk, Carlo. Shall we explore the hill of Bellosguardo?"

"Is it accessible?"

"That we can discover."

As was often the case, they walked in silence, soon leaving the city behind them. The vista opened up, with vineyards stretching out on either side. Marsilio walked freely, his senses active and his mind alert, but Carlo found Marsilio's questions playing on his mind. It was the old puzzle he had thought about so often. Why, if he were local to the priest's house, had no one ever heard of him? Surely they would have remembered something. But if not local, where had he come from? How far had the troubled lady journeyed? The good Father had enquired at Assisi without success, and even now the whole thing remained a puzzle.

Carlo looked about him. The vines still extended on both sides, and up ahead the road swung to the left, rising steadily to the top. Then a row of cypresses betrayed the presence of a villa.

Suddenly Carlo stopped. Was Pucci his real name? The thought shot through him like an arrow. Was it a cover to protect him from vendetta? Why had he never thought of this before?

"Is anything wrong, Carlo?" Marsilio called back.

Catching up, Carlo explained his sudden inspiration.

"A very valid question, Carlo. You should pay a visit to Assisi."

"It happened twenty years ago, Marsilio!"

"There could be records detailing events of that time and you know, from your experience in Rome, how old men like to reminisce. By the way, where's Bernardo got to?"

"He's down the road a bit. Look." Carlo pointed.

"What's he doing?"

"He's found a new flower, I suspect. He loves flowers and the tender way he touches them would make you weep – such a big man and such gentleness!"

"Love does not choose between a duke and peasant. It simply enters through the heart that's open."

Once more they continued up the gentle slope.

"I'm serious, Carlo," Marsilio said firmly. "You really should go to Assisi."

"Valeria's on her way to Florence, Marsilio!"

"I know, but I'm told the Count is being hosted by a number of local lords, and that will mean diversions and considerable delay."

"The Count's well-known, then?"

"He's a legend!"

"All right, Marsilio, I'll go."

"Good. It's only three days to Assisi. You'll have time in plenty. Even if Valeria does arrive before you're back, she'll need a while to settle in."

CHAPTER 28

Orvieto

It was now November. Andrea del Monte had enjoyed his stay in Naples, and the hospitality of his hosts had been unstinting. He had also seen the dominating Vesuvio, ever menacing those who farmed its fertile slopes. He had been made to feel at home, but the lack of positive progress was embarrassing – so much so that he decided to fix a definite date for his departure. If Alfonso still prevaricated, then that was how it was! His mission would have failed, but that was better than being dubbed an idiot, which would reflect upon the dignity of Florence.

The move proved fruitful, for in having to choose between his own ambitions and the censure of the northern cities Alfonso compromised, fixing a date for further negotiations in the early spring. Del Monte had won, but he did not give the slightest hint of victory, showering praise instead on the prudence of his hosts.

He was rewarded with gracious words and a practical invitation to join a well-guarded delegation on its way to Rome, so his security was assured at least for the initial part of his journey.

The delegation reached Rome on the first Monday in December. Thanking its leaders, he took his leave and, after accommodating his guard in the Florentine quarter, he set out to find his friend Paolino at the Vatican library. Paolino was on duty and in a doleful mood. Pope Nicholas, his master, founder of the library, was failing fast.

"Bessarion should be his successor. His scholarship demands it, but Latin sentiments run deep."

"You're right. They'll elect some compliant Italian, no doubt. But, Paolino, how is our new Bishop Riddo?"

Wordlessly, Paolino edged del Monte into a less public corner of the library.

"He's grown stridently anti-Plato and appears to have the passion of belief. He's certainly not a Bessarion supporter. Look, Andrea – over to the left – there he is!"

"An impressive figure!"

"Yes, but I wouldn't trust him with a toothpick!"

Del Monte suppressed a chuckle. He had no wish to attract attention.

The whispered conversation continued for some time, but as del Monte was leaving by first light and as Paolino's obligations forbade it, they could not meet again on neutral ground, so they resolved to continue their correspondence.

Being occupied with Paolino's observations, del Monte failed to notice that Bishop Riddo was also heading for the exit and as chance would have it they accidentally collided. Del Monte apologised automatically, but Riddo glared with obvious annoyance, his smiling graciousness forgotten. The moment passed, but once outside del Monte quickly stepped behind a pillar, hoping to preserve his anonymity. Whether he did or not, he could not fail to recognise Vitale Tiepolo greeting Riddo as a long-lost friend.

Had Riddo recognised him, del Monte wondered. They had seen each other frequently at Lodi, yet had never been in conversation. But had Vitale seen him, for if he had, he would have recognised him instantly, since they had passed each other often on the Grand Piazza when not a friendly word had been exchanged. Such enmity was always full of trouble. It was just as well, del Monte thought, that he was leaving in the morning.

★

After two days on the Via Cassia they reached Lake Bolsena, which they skirted on its eastern side. The air was cold but more invigorating than bitter, and although they were delayed on the first day, a brisk pace soon made up the time.

Since midday del Monte had noticed that the Captain of the guard was acting strangely. He felt the need to question him, though normally he never interfered. As it happened, the Captain broached the subject first.

"I've been uneasy for some time, Sir, but now I'm almost sure. I think we're being followed!"

"How many are there?"

"Four, as far as I can see, but they may possibly be a vanguard. Perhaps they're as innocent as babes, but I don't think we can take that risk."

"They can't be thieves, for six armed guards are hardly easy pickings. So who are they?"

"A rogue element from Naples perhaps, Sir."

"Maybe. They certainly wouldn't have attacked us on the way to Rome! But, Captain, why bother with us? Anyway, what do you suggest?"

"Give them the slip, Sir. We're approaching the town of Bolsena, and it'll soon be dark. They'll assume we're staying overnight, but we'll head east. The sky's clear and there's a moon."

"And I had hoped for a blazing fire and some wine!"

"Well, Sir, if we hurry we could be in Orvieto before midnight."

"All right. Let's hope our friends don't have the same idea!"

"They'd never dream we'd be so mad!"

"They could be right!"

The climb into the hills above Bolsena and its lake was slow, but they did not have the time to dwell upon the panoramic scene behind them. The going was easier on the higher ground and their progress quicker than Andrea had anticipated. Even so, it was dark when they started to descend towards the valley and the table prominence of Orvieto. Without the moon, travel would have been impossible. It was not easy, though, especially with the horses shying at imagined danger. In the valley the dark prominence of Orvieto loomed above them. It was a perfect defensive site, the Captain enthused, with cliffs wrapped round it like a skirt. But all Andrea could think of was a blazing fire, a jug of wine and bed. In the event, these hopes were fulfilled with surprising ease, as the Captain knew an influential official at Orvieto's cathedral. So, even though it was late, the doors of hospitality opened wide.

★

"This is a fine building," del Monte remarked to the wizened old doorkeeper in the morning.

"Used to belong to the Carrucci family – a fine family. I worked for them for years, until it happened."

"What happened?" del Monte prompted.

"An awful tragedy, an awful tragedy. All killed, every one of them, even the dogs!"

"Good God! A vendetta, I suppose."

"Nobody knows, master. They were here one day and gone the next." The old man lifted his hands to heaven.

"Did no one survive?"

"No," the old man answered bluntly.

Del Monte looked through the open doorway. A pale morning sun had penetrated the narrow street, but the air was damp and chilly.

"There's usually someone who survives," he remarked, taking a seat beside the doorman.

"Here," the old man called to a woman hobbling through the doorway. "Did anyone survive the killing?"

"One," she admitted grudgingly, glowering at him.

"But you've always said that there were none!"

"I did, but it doesn't matter now."

"Why, mother?" del Monte questioned.

Abruptly, the old woman turned away.

"What did they call the boy?" he shouted after her.

"Coluccio!"

"After the great Florentine Chancellor?"

She turned, apparently furious.

"Yes," she snapped. "And a lot of good it did him." Then, tossing her head, she hobbled off towards the main hall.

"When did all this happen?" he asked the doorman.

"About twenty years ago. The sun got up the next day just the same." The old man's head dropped lower. Then he straightened up. "And it still gets up!"

CHAPTER 29

'I Thought You Called'

On returning to Florence Carlo went immediately to see Marsilio.

"I believe I've been to every church and every tavern in Assisi, Perugia and Cortona, but not a clue, not the faintest whisper. It happened twenty years ago, Marsilio. Most people looked at me quite blankly."

"It's a start," Marsilio answered mildly.

"A start! More like a stop, Marsilio!"

There it was again, that enigmatic smile.

"Where's Bernardo?"

"Downstairs, talking to your mother."

"Well, you can tell him he has one more duty, after which he can take a well-earned rest. The duty is escorting you to Fiesole, where you're to present yourself – Andrea's orders! He's back before you."

"And Valeria? Is she here?"

"She and the Count arrived about a week ago. Oh, don't worry. Your absence has been fully explained – but what kept you so long?"

"When I asked leave from Messer Cosimo, he found other things for me to do!"

"I can imagine!"

"Will we be seeing you at Fiesole, Marsilio?"

"Andrea has invited me and Cristoforo, and young Giovanni too. He's very keen to meet the Count!"

"And what about your studies?"

"They're still a voyage of discovery, but it's quite a labour."

"Knowing you, that's the understatement of the year!"

★

Agitation was in waiting. He could feed it so easily. Despite his constant efforts, it kept happening. "Rest in your natural tranquillity, Carlo," Marsilio had exhorted. It wasn't easy, not easy at all, but he did try.

The mules, daunted by the slope rising before them, had almost stopped. It was time to dismount. It would not be long now. "Stop it, Carlo! Attention out," he told himself as he alighted.

"Not a word of thanks!" he accused his uncomprehending mule.

Bernardo laughed. "They're wiser than we think. They know when to play at being under strain! Look, the real slope hasn't even started!"

"In your case they have my sympathy. Bernardo, we're almost there; why don't you go. I can manage the last stretch."

"Right to the door, Messer Carlo."

"I don't know why I bother," Carlo grunted in mock exasperation.

"I know what it is — it's the del Monte wine. This show of duty is a fraud!"

"I hardly ever drink the stuff," Bernardo exclaimed carelessly.

"I know, just the odd cask now and then!"

The banter continued, despite their heavy breathing from the exertion of the climb.

"I hope all goes well, Sir," Bernardo ventured as they approached the villa.

"I'm sure it will. Thank you."

The big man had read the situation perfectly.

★

"Carlo has arrived, Valeria. I can hear him joking with old Jacopo and Bernardo. Just stay here beside the fire and I'll step outside and bring him through." Portia could see her friend was very nervous. "Don't worry, Valeria dear, all will be well. I'll just be a moment."

Suddenly the room was silent and the crackle from the fire seemed to emphasise her isolation. She watched the door in frozen fascination. At any moment it would open, the moment she had dreamed of yet dreaded. A sudden desire to flee rose like a compelling force, but she stayed rooted to the spot, immobile like a statue. The fire sparked loudly and captured her attention.

"Valeria, dear." The sound was so gentle yet so potent, a thousand words would not have justified its meaning. She turned.

"Carlo!" Her whisper filled the room. Her doubts and reservations simply melted, but the tremor in her body still remained. She grasped his out-stretched hands.

"You're just the same, dear Carlo; we're just the same. All my stupid doubts are nothing, simply nothing! Oh, Carlo, I'm so very happy."

"Stay calm, my dear, stay calm, or else we'll have to call a stern matron to your side!"

She laughed. How open, he thought, how lacking in anything that might offend the ear.

A gentle knock at the door was repeated more firmly before it gained their attention.

"We're all waiting," Portia said gently.

"What for?" Carlo asked absently.

"You, Carlo! Giovanni de' Medici has called unexpectedly."

"The boss's son," he whispered to Valeria. "We'll come at once. Valeria, keep beside me."

"Yes, Carlo," she agreed happily.

Carlo, of course, had met Giovanni a number of times at the Villa Medici on the Via Larga. An efficient, kindly man, with an open friendly face, Giovanni liked good food and wine. Judging by the goblet he was holding when Carlo and Valeria entered the main reception room, he was keeping up his reputation. It was said that he was Cosimo's favourite son, and this was Carlo's first opportunity to meet him informally.

"Ah, Messer Pucci!" Giovanni's hand rose in recognition. "And who is this lovely lady?"

"Valeria Tiepolo, Sir."

"The brave and beautiful lady I've been hearing about! I'm very pleased to meet you."

"I fear you flatter, Sir," Valeria said lightly.

"Not so! Not so! Everywhere I turn I look in wonder! Our lovely hostess, the Countess, and her graceful daughter, and now you, my dear."

"And what about us, Giovanni?" Andrea's father joked, leaning heavily on his stick.

"Handsome all!" Giovanni boomed grandly, the generosity of his nature shining through.

"Father was greatly impressed by your report from Rome, Messer Carlo. Who do you think will be the next Holy Father?"

For a moment the straitened nature of Carlo's past flashed before him. What was he doing here? How did he get here? It was a brief indulgence, for Giovanni de' Medici had asked him a question.

"Bessarion should be elevated, but they'll see him as a Greek. The other powerful candidates have powerful enemies. I feel that someone old and safe may well be chosen."

"Will the 'old and safe' remain so when he tastes the heady juice of power?"

"A good question, Sir."

As the conversation widened to include Messer del Monte and the Count, it became animated. Andrea could see that his father was enjoying himself. Such conversations were life and blood to him, but he needed to sit down, otherwise his leg would give him trouble.

Andrea and Portia were standing apart from the group, a pace or so behind Carlo and Valeria. This was the perfect time to try the experiment, Andrea thought, but he needed to pitch his voice just right, not too loud and not too soft.

"I sense there's something on your mind, Andrea," Portia prompted.

"There is, and I haven't burdened you with it, but please watch Carlo closely." He paused. "Coluccio!" The sound was just above the level of the conversation.

Carlo turned at once, but the others, busy with their conversation, showed no reaction. Carlo looked puzzled.

"Yes, Carlo?" Andrea said, with pretended expectancy.

"I thought you called."

Del Monte shook his head.

"You two are up to something!" Carlo grinned. "Excuse me while I return to my friends!"

"Carlo's confidence is growing," Portia whispered.

"He has Valeria at his side."

"Do *you* feel confident?" she asked playfully.

"Brimming with it!"

She chuckled.

"Andrea, what's all this about Coluccio? Why the mystery?"

Briefly, he described his visit to Orvieto and his chance meeting with the old woman.

"This changes everything – and you kept it a secret; you didn't tell me!" she added coyly.

"I'm sorry, but you're very close to Valeria and secrets can generate awkwardness."

"Yes, I would have found it very difficult. But Andrea, it worked. He turned when you called Coluccio."

"He could have been reacting to the sound, of course."

"No one else turned and it wasn't loud, and he did say 'I thought you called'. I'm convinced, Andrea! This will work wonders with Valeria's father."

"But little else, my dear, for our new-found Coluccio can't walk into a Medici bank and claim his own. Indeed, if he declares himself he could put himself in danger, real danger."

"You mean that the usurper of Coluccio's rightful inheritance, whoever he might be, would be less than pleased at his appearance!"

"Exactly, and I doubt if they'd accept Coluccio's flimsy proof of identity – the word of just one very old and demented woman, for families usually have branches and connections and there could well be someone else who knows."

"This could hatch a nest of scorpions."

CHAPTER 30

'No wonder he's the foremost man in Florence'

Giovanni de' Medici had just left the del Monte villa; Andrea's father and mother and the Count and Countess had retired to rest, and Andrea was about to confront Carlo concerning Coluccio, when the sound of laughter filtered through from the main entrance.

"That can't be anyone but Febo," del Monte exclaimed.

"Yes, only he can laugh like that," Carlo agreed.

"I met him here two days ago. He's changed so much," Valeria remarked.

"He has, indeed," del Monte said, "and Marsilio's made it permanent!"

"I hadn't thought of it like that, but you're right."

"It's good to see you all," Loredan said cheerfully as he entered.

"Febo, where's Ginevra?" Portia asked.

"My lady Bembo is with her guardians. Apparently, I'm too relaxed about the formalities of courtship!"

"You must agree, you are a bit unorthodox, Febo!"

"Should I reform?"

"No!"

"Then perhaps I will! Life is such a game; it has to be a comedy!" At once Febo launched into an enthusiastic description of an artists' workshop he had visited.

Del Monte took the opportunity of this diversion to draw Carlo aside. It was time to tell his friend all he had discovered at Orvieto. Carlo listened passively, but he showed no excitement whatsoever.

"Well!" del Monte prompted. "All you need is the enigmatic smile and you'd be another Marsilio!"

"I'm sorry, Andrea; it's a lot to take in, that's all. I'm grateful to you. Does Marsilio know?"

"Yes, he's certain that we've found your real identity."

"Did he say why?"

"No."

"There's so little evidence. All we have is the word of one bad-tempered old woman!"

"But the facts fit. It happened twenty years ago. The demented woman who brought you to Assisi would have been deranged by the slaughter of the family and she spirited you as far from Orvieto as her meagre savings would allow. That's my reading of it."

"Apparently, she gave me to the priest's housekeeper, refused to wait to see the priest, and fled!"

"She would have had to answer the priest's questions, that is, if she was at all devout. She may have been demented, but she wasn't foolish. In fact, she was a brave soul who did the best she could for your survival. Is she the bad-tempered old woman I met, I wonder? You, Coluccio, really need to visit Orvieto, for, as far as I'm concerned, you *are* Coluccio. Remember when I called, you answered to the name!"

"That could be easily explained away! You're right, though, there is a compelling case, but so far it's just assumption and deduction. We need simple proof."

"We do, but we'll be proving fact, not fiction."

"It would seem Coluccio has an ally!"

"But, Carlo, you seem singularly unenthusiastic!"

"I sense trouble, Andrea, for a rival claimant's life is often brief! Yet this is a road that I may have to travel; if not, I'd cast myself a coward."

"This will greatly help with Messer Tiepolo!"

"Yes, when we can tell him. It's only our informed opinion, though, and not yet courtroom proved. Where will it end, I wonder?"

"You're determined to be pessimistic!"

"Realistic, Andrea, for usurpers don't give up their gains without a fight."

"When have you been asked to Careggi?"

"Tomorrow, mid-morning."

"I would like to be a fly on the wall!"

"The great man usually says little – 'Thank you Messer Pucci . . . well perceived' etc. and that's the sum of it. You know his ways!"

"Well, tomorrow he may be more talkative."

"Perhaps."

"Meanwhile, you'd better tell Valeria the news."

"Yes." Carlo paused. "This is a long way from the streets of Rome, Andrea."

"It certainly is!"

"I've just remembered – I forgot to tell Bernardo about Careggi. That spells trouble!" Carlo chuckled.

"You're staying at the Count's hired villa?"

"Yes."

"I wager that tomorrow Bernardo will be on the doorstep, waiting."

★

The contrast between the warmth of Count Crito's villa and the dull, damp, cold December morning did not fill Carlo with enthusiasm for the journey to Careggi, but when he saw Bernardo waiting his spirits rose.

"How did you know?" he asked him in surprise.

"Well, it struck me that you hadn't seen the Great One and it also struck me that you might have forgotten to tell me because your lady was distracting you, so I called in at the Via Larga to check."

113

"That *is* devotion to duty! I'm sorry, Bernardo, for I'm sure we could have found you a bed."

"Don't worry, Messer Carlo."

"How do you propose we get to Careggi from here?"

"Down the hill to San Dominico, then cut across country. It's not too far."

They rode mostly in silence, two distinct entities hunched against the cold and flinching at each sudden blast of icy wind. Only when they were approaching the Careggi villa did Carlo speak about the soon and certain visit to Orvieto.

"Orvieto," Bernardo remarked, "I've got a brother there I haven't seen for years."

Carlo smiled but made no comment. Someone local like Bernardo's brother might well be a vital contact.

★

As Carlo had predicted, Cosimo was taciturn as usual, only speaking when Carlo had finished his report.

"You've confirmed my thinking in some detail. I agree with all you say, and I certainly won't be dealing with that smooth-talking merchant from Cortona. Now to your personal matter. What have you discovered?"

Carlo reflected for a time, his eyes scanning the impressive Medici library, and as his thoughts focused he began to speak. It was not long before Cosimo became visibly animated.

"That was a crime, a dark crime," he exclaimed. "They never found the perpetrators. My feeling is they never tried! A cover-up; some Cardinal was in charge, but he is no longer with us. Giovanni Carrucci was an honest man whom I was pleased to deal with. You're very like him, Carlo, or should I call you Coluccio?" Cosimo shook his head. "I should have thought of this; but then it's twenty years ago, and memory fades. There's a portrait somewhere. I've seen it here in Florence." Cosimo lifted his hand as if in benediction. "I'll ask my good friend Donatello to enquire. We'll find it. It was a commission, but your father died – well, you know the devilish story."

For a time Cosimo was silent. Carlo watched, though somewhat stunned, for only now was he absorbing the full import of his change of circumstance. Certainly Cosimo appeared to entertain no doubt at all, so why should he?

Cosimo emerged from his reflective mood, his thinking marshalled. "Go to Orvieto, but don't reveal yourself. Don't even say you're Messer Pucci. You must know the peril you'll be in should your real identity be known. You may well need to go to Rome, for, as I've said, a Cardinal took charge of the enquiry and the records will be there. Andrea has a friend at the Vatican library, I believe."

"Yes, Sir, Paolino, but I've never met him."

"That's just as well. Don't tell him your name. You can say you're making enquiries on behalf of a Medici client. This will not be easy, Coluccio, and the dangers that you face are very real, certainly more so than from your vengeful Bishop 'friend'. You're happy with Bernardo?"

"More than happy, Sir," Carlo replied, promptly elaborating on Bernardo's morning appearance. "I warned him that we might be going to Orvieto and he told me that he has a brother there . . ."

"Coluccio, be careful. Don't get over-friendly with Bernardo's brother, for he'll have friends and rumour travels like the wind."

Cosimo got slowly to his feet, indicating that the meeting was coming to a close. "First steps, Coluccio; you're returning to Fiesole, I assume?"

"No, Sir, Florence first."

"To see the young Marsilio perhaps?" Cosimo's eyebrows lifted in their now familiar way. Carlo nodded. "Ah yes, like is drawn to like, but Coluccio, on the darker side of things a similar law applies, so be very careful when you're asking questions in your father's town. Now, could you ask Bernardo to see me before you go." Cosimo nodded gently, his lips lightly pressed together. It was a friendly gesture.

"Yes, Sir; thank you."

★

They were on the road for at least ten minutes before a word was spoken.

"Messer Cosimo has made me a permanent member of his staff," Bernardo blurted out. He was clearly moved.

"Congratulations, Bernardo! You deserve it!"

"You spoke for me, Messer Carlo."

"I spoke the truth, Bernardo."

"I'm grateful, Sir."

"I hope you'll still be grateful when we're on the road to Orvieto in January!"

"The Great One said it could be dangerous and asked if I needed an assistant!"

"And how did you answer?"

"I said yes – someone who could be a scout."

"And?"

"He asked me if I knew of anyone."

"And did you?"

"I suggested my nephew, Pietro."

"And what did Messer Cosimo say to that?"

"He wants to see him; to 'get the measure of him' was how he put it."

"Amazing – with such care for detail no wonder he's the foremost man in Florence."

CHAPTER 31

A Useful Agent

Riddo had believed his lies too long to have them culled by reason. Certain that his view was right, he preached his cause with passion, and hard-line elements in the Church in growing numbers saw him as their champion. This power was much more heady stuff than women, and with surprising speed Riddo was transforming from a clever opportunist to a pillar of unbending orthodox belief. All was justified as a creature of his holy cause. His vengeance was a righteous fury fixed against the wicked, and the punishment of his enemies was the retribution of the Lord.

His delusion ran unchecked, and the women he enjoyed were seen as valid comfort for a tireless advocate of the Church's orthodoxy, facing the rapid rise of pagan heresy! Riddo's metamorphosis, though apparently sudden, had been going on for years, fuelled by the firm belief that what he said was true. This habit, married to a passion for the letter of the Church's dogma, had found its home. So the change from opportunist to fanatic evolved, and with it he had found a certain calm – something that convinced him he was right. Ubaldo Riddo was dangerous, but his adherents saw him as inspired, if not divinely so.

One of Riddo's new and passionate followers was Vitale Tiepolo. Riddo, of course, knew all about the young Venetian. The Church had always been an efficient carrier of news, and Vitale's towering rage against his sister's infatuation with the upstart Pucci was common knowledge. Cunning as ever, though he would never have admitted it, Riddo saw Vitale as the perfect instrument for his own righteous rage. So he invited the impressionable Venetian to a dinner of sumptuous proportions, in the company of other young aristocrats of like opinion. Vitale Tiepolo was enthralled and would have charged a row of cannon at the Bishop's nod. Now Riddo had a useful agent to exploit, but he did not rush to act, being too astute for that. There would be a time to move, a time divinely chosen. Such was his newfound dignity; self-delusion was complete.

All this was witnessed in his unobtrusive way by Paolino, yet there was little he could do. His high-placed contacts were few, and they were not impressed by either Riddo or his orthodox pretensions, though Paolino sensed their real concern was to stay on neutral ground, especially as the Pope was in uncertain health. Riddo's star might rise, but equally it might fall.

Riddo, however, entertained no thought of failure. He could see only a glittering future when he would lead the triumphant army of the Church.

★

Andrea del Monte, Carlo Pucci and Febo Loredan, the 'happy team' as they had dubbed themselves, met with Marsilio when they could. If the weather was fine they often headed for the ground below San Miniato; when it was cold they found a friendly tavern. On the last gathering of the year it was a tavern, its blazing fire a welcome comfort from the biting wind.

"What is the subject today?" Febo questioned, challenging the mood of contented silence, his chin jutting forward provocatively.

"Reality! The question that's engaged philosophers for countless generations!" Carlo suggested firmly. Although accepted, the name Coluccio was not yet spoken openly.

"That question's been forever dancing on a pinhead!" Febo exclaimed, "for as far as I'm concerned there are as many realities as there are people!"

"Yes, opinions, Febo, but surely not reality."

"Are we, sitting here, not four realities!"

"Bodies, yes . . ."

"And minds full of beliefs and certainties that we hold as real."

"Are they true, though? That's the question."

"True enough to those who hold them."

"It seems we're dealing with opinion and belief again, but are we dealing with reality?"

"Suddenly, I don't know what we're talking about."

"Febo, you're ducking the question!" Carlo quipped.

"Yes, that's the reality!" Febo countered mischievously.

"No, a fact!"

Febo chuckled. "How would *you* answer?"

"With difficulty. However, let's take the high ground. Say there is only one reality, then a person would be real according to his measure of that same reality."

"Carlo, that's too obscure for me!"

"Let's put it another way. If we agree that the most beautiful thing is beauty itself, then a thing is beautiful according to the fullness of that single beauty it reflects."

Febo grinned. "I capitulate. God is the one reality, and men are real according to the presence of that one."

"Excellent, Febo!" Marsilio exclaimed, clapping his hands.

"He's a fraud, Marsilio! He knew the answer all along," del Monte joked.

"I know, but it was fun!" Marsilio returned.

Febo's sense of fun was infectious, and they were laughing when the wine was poured by the landlord's boy.

Apologising for lowering the tone, del Monte confessed his continuing concern about the suspicious behaviour of the horsemen trailing them on the road near Lake Bolsena.

"When was this, Andrea?" Febo asked.

"Just over a week ago."

Febo grinned. "How many horsemen were there?"

"Four, we guessed."

"That was me!"

"You!"

"Yes, I was escorting Ginevra and her ladies back from Rome and we were having trouble with the carts."

"Thank God for that! Well, it made us head for Orvieto, and we know what happened there. What was the guiding hand, I wonder?"

"I've heard it said that what we call a miracle is a law we haven't understood," Carlo ventured quietly.

"That appeals to me," del Monte responded, but Marsilio remained silent. He was simply happy to be with his friends.

"Andrea, did you ever discover the author of the trouble in the Alpe di San Benedetto?" Carlo asked.

Del Monte shook his head.

"It was probably bandits, but why the golden florins in their pouches?"

"Perhaps I've got a vested interest, but I don't think it can be Valeria's brother."

"I agree. It happened well before he fell out with his father. Anyway, he's too angry to be so calculating!"

"And it's not me! Febo said brightly.

"Yes, how convenient to have pinned the charge on you and how inconvenient of you to have reformed so thoroughly!'

There was a ripple of good-natured laughter.

"Andrea, the Venetian guard, Captain Sebastiano, was witness to very bitter words at Lodi," Febo prompted.

"They were just crusty old clerics venting their spleen. In any case, they're much too fond of florins to give them away! But we don't want to trouble Marsilio with all this. What's the next question? – A question for the new year."

Even though del Monte had diverted attention away from the question, it still remained an unsolved problem in his mind.

"I have a question," Febo said at once, putting his hand up like a schoolboy. "Am I to be invited to your wedding?"

"You are all invited; that goes without saying. Now another question, a real question this time!"

CHAPTER 32

Narrow Escape

Since its restoration to the family in the late 1430s, the Alberti del Monte fortress and its township had become a haven of tranquillity. Previously, while under the thrall of the opportunist warlord Riario, ruthlessly enforced taxation had reduced all but his cronies to stark penury. That ended abruptly when Sforza forces led by Count Crito stormed the fortress twenty years previously.

The present rule of Andrea's brother Giovanni, the keeper of the family lordship, was in total contrast to Riario's. Giovanni was popular, if not loved, especially by the older tenants who in straitened circumstances were merely asked for token rents. He had no need for bodyguards, yet prudently, at the prompting of his wife, he always had a well-built servant by his side.

This idyll was shattered suddenly in the early days of January 1455, when Giovanni narrowly escaped an assassin's bolt. He was saved only by a spontaneous reaction to his young son's playful antics. This was his sturdy servant's view, but Giovanni felt the arrow had been wide. He immediately placed the blame well beyond the borders of the lordship, hoping to avoid finger-pointing in the town, for their mood was unforgiving. Abandoning his crossbow, the assassin had disappeared and no one could recall the presence of a stranger.

Andrea was horrified when he received his younger brother's letter. This was family! It was *his* brother who had escaped assassination. Though shaken, he could not bring himself to tell his father, certainly not his mother, and neither did he tell his bride-to-be. With the impending wedding, it seemed unfair to trouble her. Instead, he sought Count Crito on his morning walk.

The Count listened gravely to all that Andrea had to say. Then, as they neared the ruins of the Roman baths, he stopped, gazing pensively across the valley to the villas on the hills beyond. "Riario and his aides were just about as brutal as they come," he observed. "One was positively demonic; his name was Gonzaga. Such men father children from their many drunken trysts, and they're most probably in their twenties now. It's just conjecture, of course, but some deluded son might feel impelled to seek revenge – though I'm the one they should be seeking!"

"I feel strongly, Sir, that I should journey to the Marche and show Giovanni some support. I'll tell father that I'm making sure he's coming to the wedding, for Giovanni's reluctance to travel is a family joke!"

"Take a substantial guard, Andrea."

Nothing more was said, but both men were well aware of the uncertainties. As they walked on, Andrea's mind was busy. Was there a link between the Alpe di San Benedetto incident and the failed attempt on Giovanni's life? Was the del Monte family as a whole the target? He breathed deeply, as if to clear his head. Facts, Andrea, facts, he murmured to himself, but much too softly for the Count to hear.

★

Portia was tired of waiting. First her illness had delayed her marriage and now the unexpected news that her beloved aunt and uncle were journeying all the way from Corfu had delayed things further. In any case, no one favoured a winter wedding.

On coming to Florence Portia learned much more about the nature of Andrea's life. It was surprisingly busy. His languid easy-going manner, of course, gave a wholly different impression and was one he seemed to cultivate. The truth was that his advice was always in demand. There was only one better man in the world of commerce, his proud father claimed, and that was Cosimo himself – a father's exaggeration, Portia guessed. Although Andrea was a partner in two merchanting ventures, he never took the reins of power but jealously guarded his independence. True, he was solidly Medicean, but he did not join the party apparatus.

Why was Giovanni, the younger brother, lord of the Alberti fortress? It was a question which had always puzzled Portia and one she felt she could not ask lest a contentious note might be construed. Without her bidding, however, Andrea's father explained it all.

"Right from the beginning I had no desire to live in the Marche and neither did Andrea, but Giovanni loved the place. So that was how it happened. It's a partnership, of course, but Andrea only takes a nominal amount. Money isn't his first concern, but men like him always have enough and plenty."

"I can't understand why he's going to the fortress," Portia said outright. "Is Giovanni so reluctant to travel?"

"He finds Florence too busy." The old man patted her arm affectionately. "Portia dear, I suspect Andrea's escaping from all the pre-wedding fuss!"

Though far from convinced, Portia smiled, but when she learned that Andrea would be travelling with a twelve-man guard she felt certain that something was afoot and, true to her nature, she confronted him. Del Monte looked at his future wife for quite some time without speaking. She was so incredibly beautiful, he thought.

"I'm sorry, Portia, my dear," he said somewhat stiffly. "It seemed unfair to trouble you, with the wedding day approaching." Reluctant to explain, he paused, breathing deeply. "Giovanni just escaped assassination!" The words burst out suddenly. "The arrow missed!"

"Dear God!"

"I'm afraid if mother knows, her nightmares might return. She had some terrible experiences when she was young."

"Does your father know about Giovanni?"

Del Monte shook his head. "I fear if father knew, mother would quickly sense that something was amiss. They're very close. Your father knows, though."

This unexpected threat of danger had caught Portia by the throat. For a moment she could not speak another word. Andrea, too, could be the bowman's target. Oh God in heaven, what if he should be attacked. Suddenly her safe world had fallen into chaos.

★

In the early days of January Carlo set out for Orvieto, and all Valeria could do was wait. Indeed, after hearing what the Countess had endured when the Count was on campaign, it seemed that waiting was the lot of women. There was so much uncertainty, the most persistent being Carlo's safety. She was also worried for his health, as the open road in wintertime was harsh. In fact, there was no end to all her doubts and fears.

While everyone, including Cosimo, assumed he was Coluccio, Carlo still insisted that he needed further proof. Valeria, though, had little faith that he would find such evidence and was anxious that, in pursuit of this, he might reveal himself, with all the dangers that could bring. She confided in Portia, who listened but seemed to be preoccupied, and she also spoke to the Countess, whose own painful experiences made her sympathetic.

"Valeria, dear," she advised, "I tried everything when I was young but in the end I had to surrender to the Lord and trust. That brought rest when I was desperate."

The Countess was a good listener, and Valeria opened her heart to her about her father and her violent brother. "Father's very lonely and I feel conscience-stricken to have left him," she confessed.

"Well, my dear, let's invite him here!" the Countess exclaimed.

This suggestion took Valeria completely by surprise. She sat bolt upright in astonishment and as the room grew still, the only sound was the crackling of the fire.

At last she ventured hesitantly, "He would never come, my lady. The climb down would be too humiliating!"

"I wonder."

"And any hope of reconciliation with Vitale would be lost, for if father came, Vitale would condemn him for joining the 'enemy'."

"But Vitale will change his tune when he hears about Coluccio Carrucci."

"My brother loves contention. He'll attack Coluccio's lack of fortune."

"Let's not concern ourselves too much with that. Have you heard about the portrait?"

"No. What portrait"

"Donatello's found the portrait of Giovanni Carrucci and Carlo is his very double!"

"Oh, how wonderful, how wonderful." Valeria exclaimed delightedly. Then her face fell. "But Carlo will only say that look-alikes are common!"

"Yes, but even he will notice that the evidence is building up! Now, my dear, returning to my suggestion – invite your father but make no mention of Coluccio. Why do I say that?"

"It could put Carlo into danger, my lady."

"Yes, but that's not the only reason. I'm still enraged, Valeria, when I think of how your father stopped you visiting Portia when she had that terrible depression. I feel he ought to make his choice without the help of 'Coluccio Carrucci', for that would make it easy. Here is an opportunity to put his love for you before his hard Tiepolo pride, and if he does he'll be the better for it!"

CHAPTER 33

Nurse

It was cold though dry on the road from Florence, but as Carlo, Bernardo and young Pietro approached the table outcrop that was Orvieto the heavens opened in a sudden downpour. The surrounding cliff-sides of the volcanic prominence were impressive, though they saw little in the driving rain. Pitying their plight, the guards waved them through the gates; a useful anonymity, Carlo thought.

As Andrea had suggested, they headed for the Cathedral hostel, where they had no trouble in finding rooms. In fact, the place was almost empty. Clearly early January was not a popular time for travelling.

That evening the refectory was deserted, and the staff, bored by inactivity, were quick to talk. With Carlo's prompting, one toothless old man pressed on him the dismal history of Orvieto's recent past. The town, he said, was now firmly in the grip of the Papal authorities. This was both welcome and unwelcome – welcome because the factions had been driven out and unwelcome because the Church stuck its nose into everything and the taxes were just as bad! Whether the old man was speaking truth or simply grumbling was another question, Carlo thought. "What about the factions?" he remarked.

"Ah, master, the Viper were the worst, but Papa Niccolo drove them out three years ago, when two members of the Monaldeschi family were expelled. The Viper were devils, master, devils!"

"Has the Church owned this property for long?" Carlo asked casually.

"For as long as I can remember, but then I only came here fifteen years ago."

"The Carrucci were the owners," a woman's harsh voice interjected. Carlo turned, to see a portly matron waddling towards him and his two companions. "This lot couldn't hold a candle to them!" she continued, swinging her arm around dramatically. "My sainted mother worked for them."

Carlo's show of polite interest was seized upon immediately.

"They didn't leave a living thing!"

"Who didn't?" Carlo prompted.

"The factions!"

"But why?"

"Old Carrucci wouldn't pay. He'd always defied them, but the young bloods, the Viper or whoever, were furious and made Carrucci an example; dogs, cats, everything was slaughtered!"

"Who took over the estate?" Carlo asked.

"The Church."

"The Church!" Carlo reacted.

"Yes, they stepped in, for the massacre was so sickening even they noticed." Suddenly she stopped, at once aware of Bernardo's monkish disguise. "Sorry, Brother . . ."

"That's all right, sister. Speak your mind," Bernardo encouraged.

For a moment she hesitated, then the thrill of holding centre stage took over. "They sent papal mercenaries to subdue the factions and this was how the Church took over – the list of clerics that we now support!" She threw her hand up in a gesture of disbelief. "The sons of Cardinals. Sorry, Brother, I mean nephews!" Her hard-edged laughter echoed round the room. Dramatically she stared at the ceiling. "If you're listening up there, Messer Carrucci, I mean no disrespect." At that she waddled off without another word.

Carlo could have continued plying her with questions, for it was clear she loved to talk, yet he let her go. She was obviously not the soul of discretion and he did not want his curiosity to be the subject of tomorrow's gossip. The toothless man had shuffled off as well, so they were now alone, except for one man sitting by the door – the night watchman perhaps. It was time for bed.

*

The sky was clear next morning, but there was a biting wind. Carlo was tempted to break the rules and slip out to the cathedral on his own. Instead, he waited for Bernardo and Pietro in the refectory. All the staff seemed elderly, crippled or deformed. No doubt employment at the hostel was the Church's way of dispensing charity.

All last evening and again this morning Carlo was alert, watching for the ill-tempered old woman that Andrea had described. How could he effect a quiet meeting, he wondered, for according to Andrea she was explosive and not given to discretion.

There were more people in the refectory this time, probably escaping from the cutting wind outside. Bernardo and his nephew were late, but then the morning was never the big man's favourite time. Suddenly Carlo saw her, an old, unkempt, bent figure, dragging herself across the refectory floor. Movement was obviously painful, and she quickly found respite on the nearest bench. This was the moment, Carlo thought, and he slipped across and sat beside her. Luckily, there was no one else close by.

"Coluccio Carrucci," he said quietly.

Her head jerked up; her red-rimmed eyes were full of suffering. She peered at him intently, her lips pressed tightly as if all speech were locked inside. Impulsively she caught his left wrist, pushing his sleeve back with violent urgency. The scar! Carlo suddenly remembered. She's looking for the scar, an old injury, but he had no idea how he had come by it. In an instant tears were softening her hard features, but she made no sound. He simply held her hands.

"My boy, you have survived!" she whispered. "Thanks be to God! The son of Giovanni Carrucci lives!" The suffering written in her face had gone. "You are so like your father!" But all at once her features darkened. "Don't tell them who you are! None of them!" she muttered anxiously.

"Nurse," he said gently. She smiled, and he knew his guess was right. "Nurse," he repeated, "let's find a quiet place where we can talk."

"I'll lose my job here if I don't turn up!" she said fearfully.

"This drudgery's not for you. I'll see that you are cared for," Carlo reassured her, but she insisted on fulfilling her morning's work. With little option, Carlo acquiesced, for she could not be gainsaid.

Bernardo and Pietro had just arrived. They were late, but that perhaps was just as well. Saying he would explain later, Carlo sent them off to locate the Medici agent and to ask about caring accommodation for an old lady. "If you must, grab a hunk of bread before you leave, but hurry, for my instinct tells me that we haven't time to waste."

After they had left, Carlo settled down to wait in an ill-lit corner of the refectory. The whole place was so dreary – tired, broken people looking after people in not much better health. The scene reeked of poverty.

Suddenly the full import of his new identity struck him. "My God," he mouthed in shock, "I *am* Coluccio Carrucci!" There was no doubt. His scar had been the final proof. "I played here as a boy," he whispered. This fact seemed both real and yet unreal, and he watched amazed as the sense of ownership began to surface.

Here is something different he thought, as a dignitary and his minions entered – a bishop by the look of things. He was greeting everyone and blessing all that he approached. The refectory was at once transformed. The bishop turned and Carlo saw his face. It was Riddo! Carlo felt trapped, his heart thumping as if it wanted to escape his body. If he left now it would be seen as disrespectful, whilst if he stayed he would be recognised!

He sat immobile, frozen by indecision. Then he remembered the square of cloth stuffed up his sleeve. Working feverishly, he tore it into two and pressed each strip into his mouth, puffing up his cheeks and generally distorting his appearance. With all attention focused on the bishop he hoped that no one noticed.

All too soon Riddo was before him. Riddo smiled and asked him where he came from. Carlo answered, "Assisi", but the cloth so restricted his speech that he was rendered almost inarticulate. Tactfully, Riddo avoided further questions and moved on.

"That was close," Carlo breathed, but who was the young nobleman amongst Riddo's followers, he wondered.

Contrary to his nature, Carlo was very much on edge. In the immediate situation he had escaped detection, but a brief look of recognition had crossed Riddo's face and the memory of that moment haunted him. Suddenly, Orvieto was a dangerous place. Even his nurse could be in danger should it be known that he had spoken to her.

He knew too much, and Riddo knew he knew too much. That was how it had been right from the beginning and nothing had changed. Was he, Carlo, being obsessive? No! Riddo would never rest until the 'weasel Pucci' was destroyed. What was more, he would convince himself beyond all doubt that he was doing God a favour. How often he regretted that he did not quit Ubaldo Riddo's service when he first began to sense the truth. But then he had been timid, new to Rome, an innocent wont to think that his opinion went for little and was mostly wrong. That was until sheer chance discoveries proved his suspicions to be right.

When Bernardo reappeared, Carlo knew decisions were imperative and, after describing Riddo's visit, he quickly listed his priorities.

"You're instinct's right, Messer Carlo," Bernardo affirmed. "There isn't time to waste!"

"Not a minute. I'll grow a sudden beard and walk bent double, but you must keep well clear of me, Bernardo, just as we did in Rome. Pietro, though, can hover close. I need to speak to the crippled woman and I need a quick word with the Medici agent and then we'll disappear. But now, Bernardo, your brother lives nearby?"

"Yes, Messer Carlo."

"He may well be our salvation."

"You haven't told us everything, have you, Sir?"

"Later; now we must *move*! This isn't Sforza's Milan or Medici Florence. This is a Papal fief. Here Bishop Riddo's word holds power!"

★

Riddo paced up and down, his bishop's robes swishing as he turned, his right fist hammering his left hand's open palm in sheer frustration.

"We've missed him, Vitale! We've missed the weasel, that social climbing peasant – the anti-Christ who wallows in the heresies of Florence – the man who would defile your sister. How did I fall for such a stupid trick!"

"What trick, Sir?"

"He'd stuffed his mouth with paper or whatever to distort his features, and I fell for it! The trick's as old as time!"

"But if you'd caught him what could you have done? No law's been broken."

"*Law!*" Riddo bellowed. "He's a *heretic*, Vitale, and stop being such a set Venetian. Your city is obsessed by law. He's a heretic, and heresy poisons the people. It *must* be rooted out!"

★

Upstairs in the Bishop's Palace another conversation was proceeding.

"This Riddo is a useful tool, your Eminence." The Cardinal's secretary smiled, while pouring a generous beaker of the local vintage, a pleasing white.

The well-fed, round-faced Cardinal chuckled. "Yes, Matteo, he's a timely check upon the Platonists. My friend, the Church is like a stately ship. It needs to keep an even keel and not lurch too much from one side to another. Hmm – a delightful wine. I sense our brief stay here in Orvieto will be a very pleasant one. Just one thing, Matteo, no more pigeon pie. I know the town is famous for the dish, but I've had it twice already and that is quite enough!"

CHAPTER 34

The Crossbow

Del Monte checked the Church records in every village as he neared the family fortress, but he found no clues. In fact, this only made his journey more protracted, for none of the names Count Crito talked about were listed.

When he eventually reached the fortress, his brother and his family greeted him with much affection and gratitude for his support. Andrea and Giovanni, though very different in their way of life, had always been firm friends, and when the brothers toured the town together there was no doubt at all as to their popularity. So who had fired that arrow? Who had soiled the atmosphere of trust? It was a total mystery.

Giovanni, more stocky than his brother though similar in looks, had scoured the countryside, sending agents to detect pockets of dissatisfaction and resentment. There were grumbles, of course, but nothing serious, for the horrific past was still remembered, and compared with that Giovanni's rule was saintly.

Giovanni was convinced and kept repeating that the enemy was well beyond the Lordship, but the question still remained – how could a stranger fire an arrow, abandon his crossbow and then escape without being challenged or remembered? Within the town a lingering fear remained that the assassin was one of them and living in their midst. No one, not least the brothers, could ignore this festering disquiet.

Andrea still had ten days, he calculated, before he needed to return, hopefully with his brother, but at present Giovanni was worrying about the trouble which might surface in his absence. His public face was brave and trusting as before, but his faith was weakening and he entertained a growing fear that there was someone wreathed in smiles and friendliness waiting with his allies for the chance to grab the fortress.

Giovanni had been building up his guard with part-time auxiliaries. He had also encouraged a local town militia under his command. He knew the high taxation needed to support a full defensive guard could cause distress and widespread discontent.

If attacked by an outside force, he could, of course, appeal to Rome as his overall protector. At least that was the theory. So there was always uncertainty, and the shock of the attempted assassination was a sharp unwelcome reminder of his vulnerability. So to disappear to Florence for a month or so with such misgivings seemed at the very least unwise. On the other hand, if he missed Andrea's wedding it would be noticed and they would sense that something was amiss. This was not at all the message that he wanted to convey. Of course, he wanted to attend Andrea's wedding; he wanted to see

Portia and to meet the Count and Countess, and he longed to see his parents. Plagued by indecision, Giovanni became restless and irritable, and sensing this, Andrea kept his 'helpful' comments to a minimum. He had been thinking of his friend Marsilio and the quiet practical way that he approached a problem. So he asked himself once more what were the facts and what was the evidence, if any.

The facts were simple. His brother had escaped assassination, and the assassin had apparently melted into thin air. And what of the evidence? There was none, other than a crossbow and an arrow.

"What happened to the crossbow?" he asked his brother, who was busy reading a report submitted by the town elders.

"It's in the armoury — I'll show you," he added, glad of an excuse to put the lengthy document aside.

The crossbow looked like any other crossbow. No inspiration here, Andrea thought. Then, not quite knowing why, he took the weapon from its bracket and held it up against the other crossbows on the opposite wall.

"It's smaller, a good deal smaller than the others!"

"What does that prove?" Giovanni snapped, his irritation surfacing.

"It's easy to conceal and easier to use!" Andrea looked hard at his brother. "Your assailant may have been a woman!"

"A woman! That never even crossed my mind. — Andrea, don't look at me like that. There hasn't been a mistress!"

"I know, Giovanni; you're much too dull!"

Giovanni laughed, his first laugh for some time. "You know, I think you're right! No one thought it was a woman, for a woman with a crossbow is incongruous, but she could have slipped away without the least suspicion. It all fits. Thank you, Andrea. I'll send someone immediately to investigate. No! Better still, I'll go myself."

"Get someone to check the stables."

"I will."

Two hours later Giovanni returned bright and cheerful as if a load had fallen from his shoulders.

"Rosanna's the name," he called out on entering the hall. "A real fireball, they tell me — all the young bloods were after her. She's not from any of the local villages, and two days after the attempt she simply disappeared.

"Where was she staying?"

"The Old Inn. She was visiting an aunt, she said, but she didn't venture her name."

"Surprise, surprise! What about the stables?"

"My secretary was lucky. At the first stable he visited the old proprietor said a young girl fitting Rosanna's description bought a donkey."

"Bought!"

"Yes, she seemed to have some money."

"Did the donkey have a name?"

"Why in heaven do you want to know *that*?"

"A donkey's name is what it answers to, but I'll vouch Rosanna's not the girl's real name!"

"Oh, the ways of Florence are all too much for me! – Antonio!" Giovanni called out as his secretary came through the doorway. "What was that donkey's name?"

"Apollo, Sir."

"You're devious Andrea, but you're right. Children love donkeys, and with a name like Apollo they're bound to remember. So it's follow the donkey!"

"Yes. I couldn't phrase it better!"

The brothers laughed.

★

Portia was very much relieved by the news that Andrea, his brother and his family were already on the road to Florence. But with her wedding just weeks away and with her much-loved aunt and uncle due at any time, she found it difficult to stop excitement taking over.

Marsilio's example had been an inspiration. He called, the day after she received Andrea's letter, to make his routine check on Messer del Monte's leg. The medical duty was brief, as usual, but the subsequent conversation with her father and Andrea's father lasted well over an hour. Portia did not intrude, but she found herself experiencing Marsilio's tranquillity. He seemed so utterly *present* for someone of only twenty-one. His powerful example calmed her completely, and, what was more, the calmness lasted.

Portia was glad that Marsilio also talked at some length with Valeria. Dear Valeria, she was so fine in all respects, yet totally without pretension. It was clear, though, that her conversation with Marsilio had brought relief, for she was very anxious for Carlo and understandably so.

"What did Marsilio say?" Portia asked when he had left.

"He told me plainly that Coluccio would be tested, but advised me not to worry since men like Coluccio – he kept calling him Coluccio – were protected. I don't quite know what he meant. I believed him, though, for he was very convincing."

Portia made no comment. Marsilio was a mystery, and she was loath to dismiss anything he said.

CHAPTER 35

The Road to Bolsena

Heavily disguised as an ageing peasant, Carlo headed for the road to Bolsena. Bernardo was some way ahead, in the clothes of a labourer and, being the most unlikely to be recognised, Pietro followed with the mules, as it was decided not to use them until well clear of the town.

It was cold, though the winter sun eased the bitter intensity. In fact, it was perfect for stepping out. The quick way to the valley floor was steep but, once on the level ground, Carlo pressed on rapidly. Then he zigzagged up the other side on the road towards Bolsena. As he looked back, the scene was dramatic. Orvieto was an incredible defensive site and it was hard to imagine how any enemy could prevail against it. But, of course, it was also the enemy within that proved to be the weakness. He trudged on, yet was drawn to stop from time to time and wonder at the town called Orvieto, the town where he was born. He heard a noise behind him and, expecting Pietro, he turned to see instead a lone priest riding on a donkey and busy talking to himself.

"Ah, brother," the priest called out, dismounting as he did. "May I walk with you?"

"You bring the blessing, Father," Carlo responded respectfully.

"I wish I did, my friend, for at present I'm consumed by anger and frustration!"

"Is there something wrong?" Carlo questioned mildly.

"Oh, I shouldn't trouble you with this, but they're turning Orvieto upside down to find a heretic – one heretic!"

We've got out just in time, Carlo thought with some alarm, and knowing Riddo he'll be scouring the countryside as well, and soon.

"Did they say who the heretic was?"

"Pucci is the name. Riddo is incensed!"

"Who's Riddo?"

"A bishop, and because he comes from here he thinks he owns the place."

"Is he Orvieto's bishop?"

"No, he's based in Rome."

"So he doesn't like this Pucci."

"Doesn't like! He *hates* him, and to burn him is too lenient! My friend, I'm just a simple parish priest but I know this: when someone hates as he does, Christ cannot be their guide!"

"Father, you're the priest for me. May I know your name?"

"Francesco. My little church is in Bolsena." He patted his donkey's neck.

131

"Virgil and I have quite a journey before us, and what is your name, my friend?"

"You can call me Marco, Father."

"Have you far to journey?"

"No, not far – a village close by," Carlo said, with studied casualness. He sensed the priest was watching him, which was disconcerting, for his disguise did not bear close scrutiny.

"Sugano, perhaps," the priest prompted. Carlo nodded, as he could not think of what to say.

"It's much further than you think, but I wouldn't go there, Messer Pucci!"

"So much for disguise!" Carlo reacted, and the priest laughed.

"What gave me away?"

"What didn't give you away is more like it! I'm sorry, but you don't talk like a peasant, you don't walk like one and you've put your beard on in a hurry!"

It was Carlo's turn to laugh, then he suddenly became cautious. "Are you in disguise as well?"

."No, I'm a priest all right, but there's a little more to it than that." Looking straight at Carlo, he continued, "I was in Florence in the autumn and heard all about Messer Pucci and his friendship with that young prodigy Ficino. I was present when Marsilio gave a talk. It was inspiring. So, on hearing Bishop Riddo's hymn of hate and the shouts of his supporters, I knew I had to act."

"You contrived this meeting?"

"Yes, but with no small difficulty; we nearly missed you."

"You say 'we'."

"I had trusted friends watching the gates."

"I see. It looks as though I'm being protected."

"That's what I hope . . ." The priest stopped short. "Horses! Dear God, it's too late. We'll have to brave it out. Now, if they ask you questions, mumble, stammer and don't look up. Keep your head bent forward. This could be difficult." The priest was clearly agitated.

The galloping horses slithered to a halt. There were four riders.

"Have you seen three men? One is large," their officer barked.

"No, Sir," the priest replied respectfully.

"And him?" The officer pointed.

Carlo stammered. "Tr . . . tr . . . try . . . Ph . . . Por . . . a."

"Get on with it, idiot!" the officer barked. "Look at me!"

Carlo pretended great effort.

"I think he's trying to say Porano, Sir. There's a turn-off quite soon to the south," one of his companions suggested.

Without another word or even an acknowledgement of the priest, the officer spurred his horse and the troop galloped on.

"My God, if they meet Bernardo they might guess the truth and gallop back!"

"Let's get off the road," Father Francesco urged. "We can hide behind those cypresses," pointing to a row of five close by.

The horses did not return, but they continued listening until another sound began to dominate from the direction of Orvieto.

"It's my young bodyguard, Pietro, with the mules."

"I passed him earlier. He was having a lot of trouble. They're contrary beasts but, Messer Pucci, a mule's exactly what you need."

Pietro was told all that had happened and was instructed to pass it on to Bernardo, who was hopefully unscathed and further up the road. Bernardo's instructions were to proceed with Pietro to Sugano, meet up with his brother then, after ten days, head for Bolsena, letting Pietro seek out Father Francesco. The plain truth was that Bernardo, being easily recognised, had become something of a liability.

Now, with Carlo on a mule, and with Father Francesco on his donkey, they hurried on towards Bolsena. They soon passed the turning to Porano, where the troop of horse had headed. All seemed well, yet they stopped regularly to listen intently for the tell tale sound of approaching horses. They knew the officer would realise his error at some stage and that he had been tricked.

It was difficult to talk on the road, for the wind snatched at their voices and they had to shout, so in the main they rode in silence. When they reached the last stage of their journey in Father Francesco's reckoning, they stopped at a small vineyard to take refreshment. At last Carlo could ask the questions which had been brewing in his mind.

"You said Riddo came from Orvieto. Is there a family estate?"

"Not that I know of. Riddo is a mystery, for even before he became a bishop he would strut about as though he owned the place. I have a feeing that he receives an income from these parts, but it's all hidden somehow. The truth is I don't know, but one thing I do know: the break-up of the Carrucci estate was a murky affair."

"How murky?"

"The slaughter of the Carrucci was so appalling that the city was in shock. The factions denied involvement, but some, including my good father, believed they had combined to punish one who would not acquiesce in their corruption. The Church became involved; it had no option. No one, of course, would admit to having benefited from the carnage, but many did – have no doubt of that and have no doubt there was corruption amongst the clergy."

"That's pretty strong, Father!"

"And so it should be. I've been waiting to say this for years and I'm glad to get it off my chest and I'll tell you more – this so-called Bishop Riddo is a bishop of Barabbas *not* of Christ."

"Father, shouldn't we be on the move? It's getting late!"

"Don't worry. I could navigate this road blind-fold! One of them survived, you know."

"Who, the Carrucci?"

"Yes, the youngest son. Coluccio was his name, after the great Chancellor of Florence."

"This wine is pretty potent, Father!"

"It's good. I always stop here. Anyway, we deserve it. Just think how we foxed that stupid Venetian!"

"Venetian?"

"Yes, young Tiepolo. He doesn't know it, but Riddo sees him as a useful fool!"

My God, Carlo thought, this whole affair is getting out of hand.

"Are you all right, Father?"

"My legs are displaying a certain independence, but not to worry – the faithful Virgil knows the way."

★

Bernardo had just joined his brother in Sugano when Vitale Tiepolo and his troop clattered into the tiny village centre. At once they demanded the heretic Pucci.

"We know no heretic here," was the chorus from the sullen crowd.

"Then where's that ape, Bernardo?"

No one answered. Their anger was explosive, but Vitale did not seem to notice. He drew his sword.

"Maybe this will help your memory," he snapped.

"For God sake, Vitale, put that sword away!" his deputy pleaded. "There're only four of us and one's a boy!"

"There he is." Vitale pointed triumphantly. "That's the heretic's man, Bernardo!"

"I'm not Bernardo, but I have a brother of that name."

"Do you expect me to believe that?"

"No, but you can ask my brother."

Bernardo's brother now suddenly appeared. "If you're looking for Bernardo, he never comes here. He's much too high and mighty up there in Florence."

"You mean there're three of you?"

"Four, Sir. We'd challenge anyone in Italy."

"All right, all right," Tiepolo spat in exasperation. No doubt one of the two was Pucci's man, but with just four men facing such a hostile crowd what could he do? Nothing!

CHAPTER 36

Late Arrival

Cardinal Latino Orsini had enjoyed his visit to Orvieto and he was pleased to have obliged his friend the Bishop, who had been called away. A brief visit and a fatherly eye, he had suggested, and Orsini had been glad to help as it allowed him to escape from Rome.

Handling Riddo was an amusing diversion. He chuckled. Telling men that they were fools in words both flattering and gracious was a skill he had perfected, and with Riddo he had enjoyed the further opportunity to exercise this art. He smacked his lips. That Orvieto wine was delicious, and thankfully the irreplaceable Matteo had ordered a supply. Yes, all in all it was a most enjoyable visit.

A gentle knock disturbed his reverie.

"Cardinal Borgia to see you, Eminence."

"Show him in, Matteo," Orsini responded easily.

Almost at once Borgia's ageing figure filled the doorway.

"Alfonso, this is a pleasant surprise!"

"Latino, my call is overdue. A month in Rome without paying my respects is much too long."

You old fraud, you're snooping, Orsini thought, while smiling widely.

As the conversation unfolded, Borgia ventured: "The Pope is very frail."

"Indeed, my friend, and speculation has outstripped all decency."

"Well, Latino, I'm too old to be a threat to anyone, but you, my friend, are an Orsini." Borgia's Italian was thickly covered by his Spanish accent.

"Which means I'll never wear the tiara."

"Your reason, Latino?"

"The Colonna would oppose, and we in turn would do the same to them."

"Martin V was a Colonna."

"Odo Colonna was elected in Constance – even so, he was a disaster!"

"How so?"

"He practically made the Papal lands Colonna!"

"So Cardinal Capranica has a difficulty," Borgia said mildly.

"Yes, he's a friend of the Colonna, and I doubt if my brother Napoleone would be pleased!"

"So it looks as if we'll have the Greek!"

"Bessarion – perhaps, Alfonso, perhaps. We might even have the Spaniard."

"I'm much too old, Latino. Even the prospect of the labour wearies me."

"Ah, here's Matteo with the wine. He always anticipates my wishes. You'll like this, Alfonso; it's from Orvieto."

"Orvieto white – this makes Church affairs quite refined," the Spanish Cardinal crackled with a laugh.

★

Everyone had arrived; even the acutely embarrassed Lorenzo Tiepolo was becoming more comfortable amidst the pre-wedding routine, but Carlo Pucci had yet to climb the hill to Fiesole. With three days to go, the air of concern was impossible to ignore. There had been a verbal message by way of the Church saying that he was on the road to Florence, but that was all. Valeria was very worried, and her restless mind invented endless dangers. She was all too aware that his absence would blight the celebrations. Andrea remained confident. "He'll be here," he said, "even if he has to travel through the night."

That was exactly what Carlo did. He should have left at least two weeks earlier, but just as he, Bernardo and Pietro felt it safe to travel, Vitale Tiepolo appeared with young and passionate supporters to hunt down the 'heretic', Pucci. Tiepolo boasted that he was not subject to any pagan-loving Cardinal, but his arrogant bullying behaviour soon alienated the townsfolk of Bolsena, so much so that, fearing for his life, he had to flee.

Once more they were about to leave when both Bernardo and his nephew succumbed to fever. So, leaving them in Father Francesco's care, against all the rules Carlo took to the Via Cassia alone but disguised in the clothing of a priest. For the last two nights his sleep was minimal, though he had to give the mule some rest and in this manner he arrived at Fiesole the day before the wedding. He was exhausted.

★

To Messer Lorenzo Tiepolo the arrival of Carlo Pucci was the moment of truth, as sharp and potent as a sword thrust. So much seemed to hinge on first impressions. Could he trust him? Would he even like him or would he see him as a fraud?

Tiepolo was a trim, sharp-featured man, fastidious in his habits, whose word was very much his bond. He was a Venetian nobleman, sensitive to offence and intense in his reactions. Strangely, he knew it; indeed, this was his saving grace. The loss of his wife had been a blow from which he never quite recovered. With her he'd known real devotion, and in her gentle way she had firmly made him face his weaknesses. Valeria was so like her, and when his daughter fell for what he saw to be a common peasant's son, he was appalled. It was a double blow. Yet here he was, eating humble pie and now about to meet this Carlo Pucci.

Still in his priestly garb, Carlo took Tiepolo completely by surprise. Somehow he had expected Pucci to be quiet and apologetic, but his quick exchange with young del Monte summarily disposed of with that illusion. There *was* a sense of quietness about him, but he was certainly not apologetic, and now he was coming towards him with his hand outstretched. If anything, it was he, Tiepolo, who felt apologetic.

136

"It is an honour to meet you, Messer Tiepolo."

"My pleasure, Messer Pucci. You've had a trying journey, it would seem." Though feeling awkward, Tiepolo responded with a measured dignity.

"It wasn't easy, Sir, but luckily it didn't rain."

"Rain would have spoiled his finery, Sir," del Monte interjected, conscious that Tiepolo was ill at ease.

"Where are the ladies, Andrea?" Carlo asked.

"At the Count's villa. Jacopo's already gone to tell Valeria that you're here. Now, Carlo, meet Portia's uncle, Giovanni."

Carlo immediately turned to face the broad-shouldered Venetian.

"You seem to be living a rather full life, Messer Pucci."

"Sir, having heard of your exploits, I feel my life is rather tame. Ah, here's Valeria! Valeria, dear," he called in greeting as she joined them. He seized her hand.

"What happened, Carlo?" she exclaimed. "We were so worried!"

"My 'friend' Riddo was in Orvieto and he proved somewhat troublesome. I just escaped his clutches, but apparently a visiting Cardinal reined him in. Unfortunately, Riddo had a young nobleman who was his enthusiastic follower and he pursued me to Bolsena. This delayed me considerably. However, here I am, my dear; the 'heretic' is free to do his worst!"

"Carlo, you're making light . . ."

"Later, Valeria, later."

"Who was the young nobleman?" Tiepolo interjected, fearful that it was Vitale.

"Sir, I hoped you wouldn't ask."

"My son!" Tiepolo prompted, his sound aggressive. Carlo felt Valeria stiffen.

"I'm afraid so, Sir."

"I'd heard he was consorting with some charismatic Churchman, but there's nothing I can do. He won't listen!"

"Perhaps he will if . . ."

"Carlo, be careful!" del Monte interrupted forcefully, fearing his friend might say too much.

Tiepolo looked hard at Carlo and then at del Monte. The Count and his brother-in-law were deep in conversation with del Monte's father and out of earshot.

"There's something I don't know," he said pointedly.

"There is, Messer Tiepolo. Do you mind if we sit down. For the last three nights I've hardly closed an eye."

They gathered chairs together. Carlo sighed; he felt completely drained. "Riddo comes from Orvieto or thereabouts. It seems certain that his family was a beneficiary when the Carrucci estate was broken up." He scanned the gathering wearily. "There's no doubt now – I am Coluccio Carrucci."

Valeria gasped.

"My God!" Tiepolo whispered, the colour draining from his face. "I met your father when I was young. Our families traded and father always said your father's word was like a rock. What a dreadful crime that was! Dreadful!" Tiepolo shook his head. "Coluccio, you are in danger, for Riddo's family was surely not the only one to share the spoils! I dare not tell Vitale. For a father it's an awful thing to have to say this, but I cannot trust him."

"Our records here in Florence maintain that the Church had care of the Carrucci estate," del Monte interjected.

"I wish I could believe it!" Tiepolo reacted with an edge of bitterness. "Coluccio, you need to rest."

"Thank you, Sir," he said gratefully, while getting to his feet.

Valeria followed him as he left the room, and once outside he held her closely. "My love, it's so wonderful to be back," he murmured.

"Oh Carlo, it's such a mess. What are we going to do?"

"I don't know, Valeria my dear, I simply do not know." Sleepily, he added, "Is Marsilio coming tomorrow?"

"Yes, both he and his father."

"That is good. Very good."

CHAPTER 37

The Red-Faced Priest

The Ring Ceremony, which followed a solemn betrothal in church, united couples in marriage and, being a contract between families, it was also witnessed by a notary. It was performed in the bride's house, though in Portia's case this custom was suspended. Marriage was often a hard practical alliance designed to advance the standing of both families. In this respect Messer Tiepolo's anger at his daughter had been understandable.

With Andrea and Portia, however, such details were adhered to in a nominal sense. Hard bargaining was out of the question, for the families already felt at one. Nonetheless, the details were completed with due care.

The Mass of Union, traditionally the only religious rite, was said some time after the Ring Ceremony when the marriage had been consummated. A church blessing made a private matter public and was growing in popularity. The celebrations attending on Piero de' Medici and Lucrezia Tornabuoni had been lavish and in keeping with the city's leading family – indeed, a necessary political statement. With Andrea and Portia, the occasion was subdued, as neither of the families wished to be pretentious, yet it was seen as a requirement and certainly expected by the Medici, since they had suggested their family church of San Lorenzo as the venue.

The guest list was extensive. It had to be. It was a question of 'invite one, invite all', for offence was easily taken.

★

When Carlo entered the church on the morning of the celebration, Giovanni de' Medici bowed and boomed out loudly, "Welcome, Messer Carrucci." No doubt he had heard his father's proclamations of certainty. Luckily few understood, but the incident was a potent confirmation of his new identity. He *was* Coluccio Carrucci, and trying to keep it quiet after what had happened was a fantasy.

Giovanni was representing his father. Gout was the official reason for Cosimo's absence. Unofficially, though, he was careful about showing favour publicly, as the sensitive pride of certain families was excited by the merest smile.

Coluccio Carrucci sat with Dr Ficino, Marsilio and Febo Loredan, sent by the Doge to be his special representative. Valeria, of course, was attending on her best friend, and their entrance together with the two families would be the final act before the ceremony. Coluccio scanned the congregation. There were many that he knew. Cristoforo Landino, with young Giovanni Cavalcanti and Donatello in the company of artists that Coluccio knew, though not by name. Messer del Monte had always been friendly with the artist community.

There was a perceptible rustle in the congregation. Heads turned, somewhat indiscreetly but, like Marsilio, Coluccio waited until the reason for the flutter was apparent – Piero de' Medici with his much-loved wife, Lucrezia, on his arm. Coluccio had expected Giovanni but not his elder brother. This was indeed an honour.

Suddenly Coluccio jerked upright. Was it him or was he mistaken? The red-faced priest! Yes, it was him all right – Riddo's drinking friend from the early days – the endless insults he had suffered from this man. Riddo and he had quarrelled violently and after that he seemed to vanish. Coluccio shuddered, the past at once alive. My God! Had he and Riddo joined up again? Was he here on Riddo's orders to cause disruption?

"Marsilio, that priest over there, to the left, beetroot-red from drinking, do you know him?"

"No, he's not someone I have met."

Unusually for Coluccio, he felt the rise of panic. What could he do? Who could he approach? The del Monte and Dandolo families had yet to take their seats. Giovanni de' Medici! He suddenly remembered. He was the man, and luckily he was close.

Coluccio felt hopelessly exposed as he approached Giovanni and whispered in his ear. Immediately the young Medici led him to the back of the church, the buzz of speculation all too evident.

Giovanni, usually amiable, was tight-lipped and angry, not with Coluccio, he was at pains to stress, but with the twisted mind that would even contemplate disrupting such a glittering occasion.

"Leave it to me, Messer Coluccio. You can resume your seat."

Coluccio was much relieved that he had acted. He could so easily have watched and waited. His fears were soon confirmed for when approached by two Medici guards, the priest refused to leave the church.

"I don't answer to you," he shouted, so that all could hear. "Heretics all!" he screamed, before being gagged and marched outside, while fighting all the way.

The excitement amongst the congregation had risen to a babble, and unable to resist a barb, Febo leaned across. "Be careful, Marsilio! One word from him," he quipped, nodding to Coluccio, "and out you go!"

They chuckled, but all knew a hateful incident had been avoided.

There was a sudden hush as the Dandolo and del Monte families took their seats. They had entered from the side. Then, as though from nowhere, Andrea and Portia stood before the altar. Coluccio, intent on the movements of the Medici guards, had missed their entrance, though he saw Valeria and Andrea's brother with his children going to their seats. The blessing had begun.

In the Roman era marriage happened by mere consent of families. The Ring Ceremony appeared to come of this, but Coluccio sensed the custom was about to change. Fashionable church ceremonies would bring a measure of prestige, something that ambitious families craved. Again, the church would emphasise the spiritual dimension.

The proceedings were lengthy and, to Coluccio, tedious, and of course in the echoing church it was difficult to hear. Then all at once it was over.

Andrea and Portia, her veil drawn back, turned towards the congregation. The splendour of Portia's patrician beauty drew an audible gasp. It was little wonder that, like her mother, she had been named 'the flower of Venice'.

CHAPTER 38

The Bishop of Siena

Febo Loredan had been ordered back to Venice to command a convoy bound for Crete. It was an honour to have been chosen, as the competition for such posts was stiff, yet he could not bring himself to be enthusiastic. His last remaining hours in Florence were spent with Marsilio. On this he had been quite determined, but when he grumbled at his posting with its consuming labour Marsilio showed him little sympathy. "Philosophy can be practised at the tiller of a ship. No excuse, Febo!" The gentle admonition was delivered with the usual smile. "You're not much help, Marsilio, but at least in Venice I'll have Ginevra's shoulder to dampen with my 'anguished' tears." With Febo, laughter was always close.

Florence being a city enamoured of its art and beauty, praise for Portia's bridal splendour was on every lip. The del Monte and Dandolo families were naturally proud, but the Count and Messer del Monte urged restraint. Envy needed little fuel, especially with the wild exaggerations growing by the minute. Then late in the afternoon news came, like a chilling wind across the city. The Pope was dead.

*

Cosimo had been monitoring the Roman scene for months. Of course, the news from Rome had been expected and it spelt uncertainty. The Medici bank had handled Pope Nicholas's affairs, but would the new Pope continue the arrangement? This was no small matter, for the papal account was substantial business. Certainly vigilance was vital. Thankfully the branch in Rome was very well informed, but finally the decisions would be Cosimo's.

His relationship with Pope Nicholas had been established long before the Pontiff reached the papal chair. In fact, it was Cosimo's backing that had made his progress possible. It had been a risk for Cosimo, but it had proved most beneficial. These were the hard commercial facts, but Cosimo respected Nicholas as a man and was saddened by his passing.

*

Aeneas Sylvius Piccolomini, Bishop of Siena, knew at once that the place to be was Rome. As a bishop he was not a candidate, of course, but with his contacts and negotiating skills he could be of help to one who was and one, indeed, who might succeed and thus be grateful. Perhaps a Cardinal's red hat could be his prize at last. Yet too swift a rush to Rome might well be judged unseemly. Yes, he would linger for a day or so and then proceed. Rome was not far distant from Siena.

The evening before Aeneas was about to leave for Rome his ageing secretary burst in on him, very much upset.

142

"By saying he's a servant of the Medici he's got past the guards and servants and now he's trying to get past me! He demands, yes, demands to see you!"

"Tommaso, you're uncommonly agitated. Calm down and tell me what this is all about."

"A common youth in peasant garb. I've never been so insulted, and this the bishop's palace!"

"Yes, yes, but what does he want to see me for?"

"He has no respect for the cloth at all!"

"A servant of the Medici, you say. He's a Florentine! What do you expect?" Aeneas teased. "Now, Tommaso, please tell me *what is going on.*"

"Well, Sir, this youth named Pietro has an uncle called Bernardo who's been wounded. A big man, according to the servants. The youth insists he knows you. No respect at all; no respect at all," the old secretary muttered resentfully.

"Tommaso, stop worrying about the Church's dignity. Get a physician and show this young man in. Bernardo, if he's the same man, saved me from a drunken mob five years ago!"

Pietro entered the bishop's chamber, gripping his cap tightly, bowing and looking, as indeed he was, very much distressed.

"Is your uncle badly injured, my son?" the Bishop asked gently.

"Yes, my Lord. He told me to tell you it was the friends of Bishop Riddo who attacked us."

"Riddo!" Aeneas snorted. "He'll disown them!"

"You were the only one I was to tell."

"You did well, my son. Now take me to your uncle."

The bishop, whose gout was troubling him, followed slowly. Riddo was an ass, Aeneas thought angrily and to think at one time he had considered him as clever and intelligent.

Bernardo was lying on a bench to which he had been carried from the peasant cart. Their attackers had simply ridden off, their laughter harsh and callous, leaving Pietro helpless until the cart arrived, as if from nowhere, to rescue them.

Alarmed at the wounded man's condition, a servant had already summoned the surgeon, and the torches surrounding the courtyard were now concentrated where he was at work, frantically attempting to halt the loss of blood.

Bernardo's eyes filled with tears when he saw the bishop, but Aeneas put his finger to his lips.

"My Lord Bishop," the surgeon reacted with surprise.

"Carry on, my friend, and care for this good man as if he were the Bishop of Siena. Let me know when he's well enough to speak."

"I can speak now, my Lord," Bernardo murmured weakly.

"May he, doctor?"

"Briefly."

"Who was it?" Aeneas asked quietly.

"The mad-eyed followers of Bishop Riddo. Young Tiepolo was their leader. The worst one was called Gonzaga. He kept screaming 'vengeance'. There was a ferocious row when Tiepolo called him off. He would have killed us both."

"Why did they attack you in the first place?"

"We're the bodyguards of Carlo Pucci, who Riddo has denounced."

"As a heretic?"

"Yes, Sir. The young bloods are his unofficial army."

"That's enough. Conserve your strength, Bernardo. God's blessing, my son."

For a moment the bishop stood quietly, his head bowed, before turning away. He climbed the stairs slowly and painfully, his secretary by his side.

"I hope they're not going to keep the big man in the courtyard longer than is necessary."

"No, Sir. He'll be moved as soon as the doctor thinks it safe. The wound is not too deep, but he's worried about the bleeding."

"Of course. Tommaso, I think I'll delay my journey to Rome for another day. Make sure the household knows."

"Anything else, my Lord?"

"No. I'm going to do a little writing tonight. Just keep me informed about the patient's progress. That's all. Good night, my friend."

"Good night, Sir."

Once the door closed behind him, Aeneas smiled. "Tommaso," he mumbled to himself, "you're not too bright. You're set in your ways, but you're a good man." What a contrast to the clever Riddo. Aeneas felt a sudden rush of anger. "You may be clever, Riddo, but there's someone just as devious as you and that man is Aeneas Sylvius Piccolomini."

CHAPTER 39

'We have a Pope'

The del Monte family villa had an empty and deserted air. Andrea and Portia were still in the country, now the guests of the Medici at Cafaggiolo, and Giovanni and his family had returned to the fortress in the Marche. Valeria was with her father, who was deeply concerned for his son and determined to confront him. For security they had joined an official Florentine delegation on its way to Rome, a Rome buzzing with the drama of a Papal election. Coluccio Carrucci, protected by a strong Medici troop, willed on him by Cosimo, had gone to Siena to visit Bernardo. The Count and his brother-in-law were in Milan, being feted by their old friend Sforza. Only the Countess and her sister, Portia, were resident, though even they were often absent, visiting friends in Florence. So when Messer del Monte learned that Marsilio was due his spirits lifted.

With the aid of a stick he finished a circuit of the garden, then thankfully settled down on his favourite couch underneath the awning. Maddalena had called, so his wife was busy listening. Dear Anna, she was so patient and, knowing that Maddalena's endless chatter wearied him, she managed, thankfully, to keep her well away.

He always knew when Marsilio had arrived, for old Jacopo never failed to make a fuss.

"Marsilio and Cristoforo, too, what a pleasant surprise!" del Monte exclaimed as Jacopo led them through to the garden. "Are you the new Pope's emissaries!?"

"No, we're much too ill kempt. Who's it to be, Sir?" Landino asked lightly.

"The wrong man!" del Monte returned with obvious cynicism.

"We'll have to wait for God's decision," Landino prompted, guessing how del Monte would react.

"I wouldn't trouble God with that circus, my friend! Bessarion should be Pope, but he's a Greek and Latin bigotry will block him! What's your view, Marsilio?"

"As you know, Sir, I much admire Bessarion, though I share your doubts."

The conversation continued, relaxed and humorous, as they recalled highlights of the wedding celebrations. Though uplifted by the occasion, del Monte had felt exhausted in the days following, so Marsilio judged it necessary to conduct a thorough examination, during which Landino discreetly took himself around the garden. When he returned, Jacopo was arriving with refreshments.

"How are your studies progressing, Marsilio?" del Monte asked.

"Cristoforo and I were discussing this on the way here . . ."

"You should continue your project, Marsilio," Landino interjected. "From what I've read so far it's a wonderful distillation of Graeco-Roman thought."

"Yes, but it's taking so much time and sometimes I feel I'm clearing out an old and dusty cupboard."

"You must complete your study, Marsilio. Half-finished works are a burden on the mind."

"It's the time, Cristoforo. Father is anxious that I spend more hours on medicine. And now one of my brothers wants to leave and make his own way, so he's calling for his family share, which of course puts pressure on Father."

"You must continue, Marsilio," Cristoforo stressed.

"Even clearing out a dusty cupboard is evidence of work," del Monte added. "And when you go to see Messer Cosimo you will need something to offer him."

"I know, and I appreciate your encouragement, but family pressures are all too real. Father has been most indulgent and has taken advice from our good Archbishop Antonino, who would have me focus much more on the Christian Fathers, but despite his known severity, there has been no coercion, none at all. Father knows, of course, that I'm not just gathering and accumulating knowledge. He knows I seek a living knowledge that can liberate the soul, but it's his duty to be practical. The family must be fed and housed and his eldest son must share this burden."

"Is a crisis imminent?" del Monte asked.

"No, there's still some space. Father has been very patient, but now I feel that time is finally running out."

★

A report awaited Giovanni del Monte when he returned from Florence. The would-be girl assassin had been traced as far as Assisi. Andrea's idea of the donkey's name had been of little use. It was the 'girl with the donkey' that reawakened memory, especially as she was both pretty and vivacious. In Assisi, though, Apollo, the donkey's name, proved the only lead; a conversation overheard by chance in which Apollo was the subject of some bargaining. Enquiries revealed that the girl had sold the donkey two days previously and had bought a horse. The stable owner was effusive. She was a real bundle of fire named Maria and the rumour was that she was heading north. So the search continued.

★

Lorenzo Tiepolo and his daughter were guests of the Orsini family, not the premier house in Rome but still Orsini. Though they were polite and generous to a fault, Valeria could not help contrasting their rather stiff formality with the freer attitudes of Florence. Rome was Rome, however, and the

146

sheer scale of the ancient ruins outstripped all her pre-conceived opinions. Her hosts indulged her interest and were pleased to show her all the major sights. It saddened her, however, to learn that stone was still being plundered from the numerous crumbling structures. What bliss it would have been to have Coluccio by her side to share these sights.

When, oh when, would she be married? Coluccio's noble birth had solved one problem only to produce another – his inheritance – and there was little hope of realising that. She asserted often that a modest house would be more than good enough, but as she was a Tiepolo her father would not even contemplate that option.

★

As soon as he was able, Tiepolo called at Bishop Riddo's villa and, with Venetian formality, politely asked to see him. The elderly doorman hurried off, soon returning to convey Riddo's 'great pleasure' and 'sincere welcome', and to show him to an ornate reception room. After a lengthy wait Tiepolo grew restless and increasingly annoyed. This rudeness was crude posturing, in his opinion, for a truly busy man would send someone to apologise and to offer some refreshments.

Tiepolo's sharp features grew sharper as his anger rose to boiling point. Then Riddo entered quietly, tall, urbane, gracious and so full of apologies that Tiepolo was won over, though not completely, for he was a shrewd Venetian merchant not given to premature enthusiasm.

"Thank you for seeing me without a prior appointment, my Lord Bishop," he began formally. "You have probably guessed already the reason for this call – my son. I'm told he is your close adherent and I would dearly like to contact him."

"A high-spirited young man, Sir; a credit to you, but as far as I know he's not in Rome at present."

"Is he due back soon?"

"Messer Tiepolo, I'm sorry to disappoint you. I really have no idea. Young men, like your son, hear me speak but I have little knowledge of their movements." Riddo was determined to keep his distance. Young Tiepolo's excesses were his own affair.

"He was in Orvieto recently and in your company," Tiepolo pressed forcefully. In his opinion, Riddo was a liar.

"Yes, that was some weeks ago. As I've just said, young men hear me speak and indeed follow me around." Riddo's urbanity did not falter. "Sometimes," he continued, "these same young men become, shall we say, 'enthusiastic'. I, Sir, am not their keeper."

"They become 'enthusiastic' when they hear you speak!" Tiepolo's anger was not disguised.

"Young men sometimes interpret my words with a certain youthful immaturity!"

147

"And that youthful immaturity was pursuing a so-called heretic whom you had denounced!"

Riddo smiled. Tiepolo was a predictable fossil. "Ah, young men, Sir – their energy can so often be misplaced."

"So misplaced that the so-called heretic's bodyguard was almost killed!"

"Good Sir, from what I hear they were provoked. Heresy is a canker eating at the roots of Christendom, and I make no apologies when I say it must be rooted out!"

"In Florence, and not only Florence, what you call a heresy is applauded. The late lamented Holy Father was also sympathetic!"

"Far be it for me to question the wisdom of Papa Niccolo, but I do believe he was mistaken and many now agree with me. That I know!"

"This conversation is going nowhere," Tiepolo spat, no longer able to contain his rage. "I'll be blunt with you, my Lord Bishop. I don't believe a word you say. Good day to you."

"And to you, Messer Tiepolo," Riddo responded quietly as Tiepolo headed for the door. "Well, well," he murmured mildly to himself, "you played that well, my son."

Tiepolo strode from the building in a fury, Riddo's self-satisfied smile mocking him as he left. The Orsini guard, generously provided by his host, followed his angry stride. God help Vitale, seduced by that man's serpent tongue, he thought. Vitale's nature, prone to anger like his own, could so easily get him into trouble, in which case Riddo wouldn't lift a finger to defend him. Indeed, for some brief advantage, he would as likely cast him to the wolves. Tiepolo was certain that he knew his man. He *had* to find his son.

In his headlong haste he almost collided with a group of revelling Spaniards in the street. They were very drunk and one leered at him with unashamed abandon. "We have a Pope, Sir!" His accent was rough and thick. "We have a Pope! Our Pope! And his name is Borgia."

CHAPTER 40

Façade

Not long after Lorenzo Tiepolo left, Bishop Riddo received notice that the Bishop of Siena wished to pay respects. This was a wholly different situation, for Piccolomini was a wily fish. Riddo had not been his secretary for nothing. Keeping Piccolomini waiting, as he had Tiepolo, was out of the question. So when the time approached Riddo himself was waiting at the door to greet him.

"My Lord Bishop, this is an honour," he enthused warmly. "Welcome to my humble villa."

"Ubaldo, we are both Bishops now. To you I am Aeneas."

"Generous as ever, my friend. You've heard the news?"

"Yes. Alfonso Borgia is now the Holy Father. A worthy choice, Ubaldo."

"Indeed. He may be old in body, but he's old in wisdom, too," Riddo assented graciously. The old goat is senile, he grated to himself.

"Well spoken, Ubaldo. I will relay your comments to him," Aeneas responded, with a knowing look. He smiled. That was the last thing he would do.

"Come, Aeneas, let me give you some refreshment."

"My dear friend, dilute it well. My gout is more than troublesome these days."

"How tedious for you, Aeneas." Riddo's tone was sympathetic.

They took their seats, and an attendant nervously offered wine.

"You have been busy, Ubaldo," Piccolomini continued. "I hear praise from every quarter. Stemming the tide of heresy is a worthy cause for any lover of our holy Church." Aeneas bowed graciously towards his former secretary.

"One does one's best, Aeneas, yet the trouble is I'm labelled a fanatic for the gentlest of reproofs."

"It was ever thus, my friend. A burden we must bear."

"One's tolerance is tested, Aeneas. However, it's a question of balance. We have no love for witch hunts."

"Of course, my friend," Piccolomini said reassuringly. Riddo's dissembling was so total that it was amusing. "We had a nasty incident near Siena recently," he added casually.

"Not too serious, I trust, Aeneas."

"As it happened, no, but it could too easily have gone the other way. A group of young horsemen attacked and wounded an old friend of mine and I'm afraid it's said that these same youths are your close followers. Now, Ubaldo, I wouldn't for a moment hold you responsible, for as we know the energy of youth runs to wild excess. Some in their excitement turned quite savage, and how can you be held accountable for that!"

"How well you understand, Aeneas. A mild aside is seized upon and blown up out of all proportion."

"A familiar hazard, Ubaldo, and, of course, we get the blame."

"How can we combat such slanderous insinuations?"

"With difficulty, Ubaldo, with difficulty. Now there is a slight problem, my friend, which may cause you some minor embarrassment or rather, tedium. The unfortunate incident I've just mentioned took place within the jurisdiction of Siena. There'll be an enquiry of sorts and you may be asked some questions. You will, of course, have nothing to worry about." Aeneas shook his head. "How did we get entrapped in such a weary subject? No matter. Let's talk about our new and much applauded Pope. You know he's somewhat set against the Turks."

"He may be, Aeneas, though when it comes to soldiers, who will send the numbers needed and who would sacrifice the gold? A battle with the Turks would be no skirmish, and who would queue with eagerness to fight the Janissaries?"

"Well analysed, my friend. Yet, with your ability to fire a crowd, who knows what we could do! A word from me . . ."

"Aeneas, I'm a man of peace, not war."

"I have much sympathy with that Christian view, but give my words some thought when you have the leisure to reflect."

Aeneas stood up and sighed wearily. "More meetings call, Ubaldo. Alas, none so congenial as this. Did I tell you the Pope has chosen the name Calixtus?"

"That will be the third."

"Indeed it is. Few know that so readily!"

"My head is full of trivial information," Riddo laughed dismissively.

Aeneas bowed. "My Lord Bishop, God's blessing."

"And to you, my Lord Bishop," Riddo returned, bowing with equal solemnity.

"How very civilised," Riddo murmured to himself as he watched the Bishop of Siena leave. What was he really saying, though, for with Piccolomini you could read at least three meanings into every sentence. And the proposition of preaching a crusade – a failed crusade before it started – would be death to his career. Yet it would help him with Calixtus.

As his next appointment was close by, the Bishop of Siena preferred to walk. His gout had eased, and he felt the need of exercise. He walked slowly, surrounded by attendants, all the while smiling to himself, for the meeting with Riddo had amused him. The air of cosy friendliness, the man-to-man approach had been exactly right, at least for the present. One day it would be different.

*

Coluccio had secured accommodation overlooking the Campo. Siena was a beautiful city, and all he wished for was Valeria to be with him. It was his second week of virtual inactivity, but the physician was hopeful that Bernardo would soon be fit enough to travel. Coluccio, of course, was not completely idle for, being fluent in Latin, he spent most mornings in the large cathedral library. He had also contacted the authorities, who were most co-operative, not always the case in their dealings with Florentines, but Bernardo was the friend of their much respected Bishop and that was more than good enough for them. In fact, they were adamant that a full enquiry should proceed. Certainly, Tiepolo and Gonzago would be traced and summoned, an order they would probably ignore. Riddo, too, would not escape attention, but he could not ignore a summons quite so easily, for his dignity as a bishop would necessitate his presence.

CHAPTER 41

Good Friends

Cosimo's ageing face lit up with pleasure. It was an image few were privileged to see for he was mostly reticent and certainly not given to public demonstration.

"Carlo, my dear friend, when I heard that you were coming I cancelled all appointments."

"Not so, Cosimo. I saw a waiting delegation as I arrived!" Carlo del Monte returned in obvious jest.

"As sharp as ever. You're right; I told my son to walk them round the garden and let them see the vines across the valley. The delegation is from England. They'll be quite happy, for in that dull and dreary country they rarely see the sun!"

Cosimo pulled the bell cord. "Let's have a decent glass of wine. Dear, oh dear, the dramas that we've lived through! Crito called just before he left to see Francesco. He called earlier, of course, but this time he brought young Giovanni. Young, did I say? He's fifty-five at least! Anyway, it was good to see them after all these years." Cosimo was being unusually expansive.

"Francesco's feeling his years," he continued, "but then, aren't we all? Ah, here's the wine. I think you'll like it." He watched as Carlo took a sip.

"Excellent, Cosimo!"

"Our very own from the Careggi vines! Let's toast your son, Andrea, and the lovely Portia."

They raised their goblets.

"You must be very pleased," Cosimo said quietly.

"Anna and I are more than pleased."

"Where are they going to settle?" Cosimo ventured, for he knew the question to be sensitive.

Carlo sighed, his animation ended. "The Dandolo estates need looking after," he responded flatly.

"Andrea's much too fond of Florence!"

"He certainly loves Fiesole, and so does Portia."

"Carlo, my friend, there'll be a compromise, I'm sure. Let's not get too gloomy. But I have a feeling that you've come to tell me something, and certainly not to ask a favour, for you never have!"

"Am I that independent?"

"Yes," Cosimo answered bluntly. "So what is it you've come to say?"

"It's Marsilio. I'm certain that his family situation is quite strained, and soon there'll have to be a choice between his studies and following in his father's footsteps as a doctor."

"Your visit is most timely, for only yesterday I chided myself for my inaction. Ever since I met Gemistos Plethon here in Florence, the nagging need to found a school upon Athenian lines has never left me, but before the Peace of Lodi it was quite impossible. The pressures were enormous and it was in the balance as to whether we survived or not. Only the few, including you, knew how desperate it was!"

"It was a sobering time."

"Now there's both space and stability, but I move slowly. It's my nature. I must be absolutely sure. There's no decision that I've ever made that's so important. Clever people, well, they're commonplace – you can sweep them off the streets, and, as for scholars, well, we're inundated. Take Argyropoulis, for one. I can't ignore him."

"He's in love with Aristotle and anyhow, he and his friends are too, too comfortable!"

Cosimo laughed heartily.

"You haven't lost your touch my friend."

"I'm convinced, Cosimo. Marsilio is wise. I know he's only twenty-one, but that seems quite irrelevant. He *lives* philosophy. That's what impresses me. He's made a study of the soul's relationship to God."

"Is that in book form?"

"I don't know, but when I asked what he had discovered, he answered 'little', that is, apart from a casual aside, that 'he would only know by the grace of experience'; – the relationship between God and the soul, no less! Cosimo, give Argyropoulis Aristotle, but keep Plato for Marsilio."

Again Cosimo burst out laughing.

"Well, old friend, your word means much to me and I'm very grateful that you've come. It has helped to clarify my mind. Now, just for a little while let's indulge ourselves. Let's talk about old times."

Carlo del Monte laughed, took up his goblet and drank deeply, and for a full half hour the good friends reminisced.

Suddenly Cosimo got to his feet, held out his arms and the two men embraced. "If you don't pay another visit within a decent interval, I'll send a troop of horse to fetch you!"

"That might get me moving!"

"It's been a well-spent afternoon, but now I'd better see this English delegation. Gregory called them angels, I believe, but I doubt if that's a true description!"

★

Banter, with all its poignancy, kept the realities of age from growing sentimental, and certainly there was banter when Carlo del Monte took his leave. Cosimo was clearly reluctant to bid his friend farewell, but he had to meet the delegation. However, he did suggest his friend should linger and enjoy the garden for a while and, finding an arbour in the shade, Carlo took the offer up.

Insects! They were swarming everywhere, myriad in shape and number. So much movement – such apparent urgency and to what purpose? A greater being watching humans might well ask the self-same question. It was a lovely afternoon, hot, yet with a breeze. He would stay for half an hour and then depart.

He heard footsteps approaching from behind. They were on the other side of the tall hedge providing him with shade.

"Cosimo is a giant," a voice said. "Who and what comes after him? That's the question."

"Piero and Giovanni and their sons. We have a dukedom. All that's lacking is the name!"

"That's a bit excessive, Luca, and don't forget we're enjoying Cosimo's garden. This is not exactly the time and place!"

"Right as ever, Diotisalvi."

The footsteps on the gravel path began gradually to recede.

Interesting, Carlo mused. Diotisalvi Neroni, the trusted friend of Cosimo and the up-and-coming Luca Pitti. Pitti he had never met; Neroni, though, he knew quite well. An ambitious self-important man, yet Cosimo relied on him. What indeed would happen after Cosimo? That was a fair question. Florentines were wont to speak their minds, yet discretion was a wise precaution, and by the sound of Pitti's voice this quality was sadly lacking.

Just like the old days, Carlo murmured, when as the so-called master of disguise he had stumbled on so many 'indiscreet' discussions. His eyes felt heavy, and for a span he dozed, waking suddenly to find his three attendants waiting. It was time to head back to Fiesole.

CHAPTER 42

Todi

Giovanni Alberti del Monte's agents were enterprising, persistent, but above all fortunate. Their quarry, being vivacious, if not wild, was completely unconventional. She left a trail behind her, though finding it was far from easy. Tricked by a rumour that she was travelling north, they headed for Perugia, then, realising their mistake, they retraced their steps and set off in the opposite direction. Luckily they caught up with her, but at Spello she vanished amidst the twisting alleys of the ancient Roman hill town. In fact, they had resigned themselves to having lost her. Then, as if conjured out of thin air, she appeared astride a mule, swearing loudly at its tardiness and answering to the name Maria. Immediately they followed and soon found out that she was heading for Bevanga. This was it, they thought, but they were mistaken. Maria only halted over night. However, the next morning, when she took the road to Montefalco, they were certain they had reached their journey's end, but this they could not prove for, just as at Spello, she disappeared. The town, it seemed, had swallowed her and all enquiries were dismissed by blank uncomprehending looks.

They liked Montefalco, especially the Piazza at its crest, though they guessed it could be cold in winter. Now, it was idyllic, and the tavern that they patronised was ideal as a place to watch the general bustle. When three days passed without a hint of Maria's whereabouts, they grew despondent; then, only by sheer chance, they overheard a conversation that described a wild-eyed girl chasing an aggressive suitor with a sword. It had to be Maria.

The man that they had overheard was garrulous and was pleased to tell them all he knew. The girl hailed from Todi, he maintained, and had been urged to leave at once, lest her 'admirer' sought revenge for his humiliation.

This time Maria's pace was relentless. Indeed, she was behaving like a creature on the homeward path. Her stops were brief, so the agents, too, had little time to rest or wonder at the fortress town now dominating the horizon. They passed through the gates just as the sun was sinking, and the agents, a father-and-son team, were exhausted. In fact, the father took to his bed at once. A good night's sleep restored the son and, leaving his father still recovering, he strode off to the Piazza del Popolo to make enquiries. Being approached from the end opposite the Cathedral, with its many steps, the long expanse of the Piazza was impressive, as were the official buildings. Indeed, they spoke of wealth and pride. Subduing his natural curiosity, the young man quickly sought a tavern, copying his father's casual way of questioning, but no one named Maria fitted his description. Then the landlady burst out laughing, her ample proportions shaking with mirth. She slapped the bar.

"That's not Maria!" she bellowed. "You've got the wrong name. It's Lucrezia! Everybody knows Lucrezia Riario. She can use a sword as well as any man but, mind you, she plays the pious daughter when she's in her mother's company. One thing's for sure, they're not short of a ducat!"

Concerned that he might have drawn too much attention to himself, the youth from the Alberti del Monte fortress retired to a table just inside the entrance. He could barely contain himself and, when he had finished his wine, he set out at a lazy pace, while all the time restraining the urge to rush back to his father, but once clear of the Piazza he started running.

"We've found her!" he called out, bursting into his father's room. "She's Lucrezia Riario and she lives nearby."

"My God – the daughter of our one-time lord – that murderous madman Riario. I never knew he had a daughter. I suppose her mother told her all about her 'noble' father and she, being pretty mad herself, set out to take revenge.

★

Rome was already having second thoughts about the elevation of Alfonso Borgia. Once a mild old man approaching eighty, he was now inflexible, overbearing, brooking no contradiction. Lorenzo Tiepolo was witness to this change of personality, and being a guest in an Orsini household, he was soon acquainted with the details.

"A tide of Catalans is about to drown this city and, mark my words, Lorenzo, his dissolute nephews will be cardinals within the year. Rome will soon become a Spanish fief!"

Tiepolo smiled at the poetic exaggeration, but he knew that much of it was true.

Although the Orsini would not hear of it, Tiepolo felt he had imposed too long upon their hospitality. His embarrassment was eased however with the arrival of a friendly note from Piccolomini whom he had met briefly, to say that Vitale was presently at Todi.

At last he and his long-suffering daughter could take their leave but he needed an escort for the journey. Once more the Orsini assisted him, and in return he offered his Venetian villa as a home should his host or any of his family ever wish to visit.

★

Carlo del Monte and his wife Anna had accepted that Andrea would now be spending much more time in Venice, for, being heir to the Dandolo fortune, he was duty-bound to help manage the estates. It would be lonely without him but, of course, he was not gone for ever and, having bought a villa in Fiesole, he had given substance to his promise to be a frequent visitor.

For months the centre of activity, the del Monte villa now felt quite empty. Anna was concerned, for her husband needed stimulating company. Coluccio would call, of course, and Marsilio – by heaven, she had almost forgotten about Marsilio! She knew that he was very busy, but what would stop him writing in Fiesole? There were rooms in plenty and, at least, he could stay a night or two. Carlo would be more than pleased. "When Marsilio's next here," she murmured, "I'll have a quiet word."

Jacopo's sudden laughter alerted her. It could only mean one of two things: either Febo or Coluccio had arrived, and as Febo was in Venice it had to be Coluccio. She hurried to the portico.

"Coluccio, my dear, how good to see you. Come through." She almost danced before him as she led him to her husband. "You are the very tonic I've been praying for!" she whispered.

"Coluccio," del Monte beamed. "Back from Siena, and how's that rogue Bernardo?"

"Almost his old self."

"Good. Now you'll have news to tell me."

"I have, Sir. One of the attackers was Vitale Tiepolo."

"Vitale! Oh, that's awkward for you, Coluccio," del Monte exclaimed.

"Yes, Sir, I know, and another member of the party, the one who almost killed Bernardo, was named Gonzaga."

"Gonzaga! – Like father, like son. So Gonzaga had a son! We never knew."

"I'm sorry, Sir, I don't understand."

"Gonzaga was the name of Riario's mad-eyed henchman."

"The Riario who terrorised the Alberti lordship?"

"Exactly."

"This Gonzaga could be from another family, Sir. It's not an uncommon name."

"I doubt it. Sit down, Coluccio, sit down. I, too, have news." Del Monte paused almost theatrically. "I received a letter from Giovanni yesterday. You remember the would-be assassin?"

"Yes, Sir."

"Well, it seems she was a woman!"

"A woman!" Coluccio interjected.

"Yes, a vivacious creature, I am told, and they've traced her back to Todi."

"That's quite close to Orvieto."

"I know, but guess what her name is."

"You'll have to tell me, Sir."

"Riario! No one even dreamed he had a daughter. Hers clearly was an act of vengeance."

"That's exactly what Bernardo said. Gonzaga kept repeating 'Vengeance'!"

"Misguided fools. Ah, here's the good Jacopo with refreshments."

As they sipped the light Trebbian wine that del Monte favoured in the afternoon, Coluccio began describing his journey to Siena. Del Monte was fascinated, as every corner, hill and stream traversed so often was etched upon his memory. Then suddenly he returned to speak of Gonzaga and Riario.

"Gonzaga is the one to watch. Even if he only has a little of his father's blood, he'll be raving mad."

"What about the girl? Do you think she'll try again?"

"She'd be very foolish if she did, for she's lost her anonymity."

"She could send someone else . . ."

"I doubt it. I don't know why, but I feel there's now no longer any danger from that quarter. I know, I should be howling for her blood, but I'm not. I just have a feeling, irrational no doubt, yet quite persistent, that conclusions here may be premature. I've often had premonitions in the past, and often they were right. So I've learned to treat them with respect. I've read the reports a number of times, and have formed a liking for her wild, spontaneous ways. The urge is past; it's over. In fact, she may be quite relieved she missed."

"With respect, Sir, that seems sentimental!"

"You may be right. All I can say is, that on reading the reports that's the sense I got. She's unpredictable, yet, in a way her unpredictability *is* predictable."

"What about Vitale? He could be my brother-in-law!" Coluccio spoke with unusual passion.

"Brothers-in-law come with the marriage contract and Vitale is Valeria's brother. That's the truism. I know Messer Tiepolo is most concerned and is attempting to contact him. His son's volcanic, he maintains, and this quickly turns to violence if he's not restrained. He's both proud and impressionable – not the best of combinations. He needs good company."

"In that case Riddo's a disaster! What if he hears that Pucci is Carrucci?"

"He'll scoff and call you an impostor. His strutting pride would *not* admit an error. But Coluccio, are you not concerned about Carrucci becoming public knowledge?"

"Messer Cosimo was insisting on a guard long before Carrucci was dreamed of. I'm used to being careful. In any case, when Giovanni Medici boomed 'Messer Carrucci' at the celebration, the world was bound to know."

"I used to wear a breastplate underneath my tunic."

"I doubt if I could stand the heat!"

"Better hot than terminally cold! But now, Coluccio, let's address the major question. Who stole the Carrucci estate?"

"Everybody seems to think the Church benefited."

"A convenient cover, and 'benefited' is such a useful word. I prefer an honest one like *stolen*, though I don't mean stolen by the Church as such, for by definition the Church of Christ in its purity is incorrupt. I mean stolen by the pious frauds who pose as Bishops and their like. For them the Lord takes second place to ducats!"

Coluccio smiled. Andrea's father was still true to his anti-clerical opinions.

"The whole thing will be mired in complication, Sir, and Churchmen always cover for each other."

"Because they're all at it, that's why!"

Coluccio laughed at what was clearly a colourful exaggeration. "But, Sir, what would you suggest I do?"

Del Monte paused reflectively. "I can't believe I'm saying it, but you need to find a senior Churchman – a very senior Churchman . . ."

"Who lives in Rome!"

"Precisely!"

"The current very senior head?"

Del Monte shook his head. "He's too busy feathering his Spanish family nest!"

"So for the moment I should curb my urge to buy a villa on the hoped-for Orvieto fortune."

"I'm afraid so, but you never know, some unexpected ally may appear. Coluccio, it's just struck me: I hope you've got the nurse's statement recorded by a notary."

"Yes, the Medici agent saw to that."

"Good. Now, my boy, you must stay the night. After being empty so long, those rooms of yours will be bleak and uninviting."

"I'd love to, Sir, especially if you tell me all about your journeys to Constantinople and to Mistra."

"The Greek Constantinople. It will be a pleasure, Coluccio. Old men love to talk about the past!"

CHAPTER 43

Lucrezia

It was morning and the May sun was already hot. Gonzaga, his round face glistening with perspiration, stood by the old shack amongst the olive groves where they usually met. Lucrezia was late, he grated, his small sharp eyes stabbing with anger everywhere he looked. It was deliberate. There was no excuse, for her mother's villa was less than half a mile away. Of course it was deliberate. She did it to excite his fury. Damn her for the way she had entrapped him. Damn her unbridled passions.

Suddenly she appeared, striding with a man's aggression up the hill towards him.

"You're late!"

"Who says I'm late!"

"I do!"

"Should I get excited?"

He grabbed her hungrily.

"Stop it! You're such an idiot."

Enraged, his hand went automatically for his sword.

"I'll kill you!"

"Again," she mocked.

"Mocking me is dangerous," he snarled, approaching cat-like, his sword in readiness. "I don't miss – not like you!"

"If you're so clever, *you* go to the fortress. That is, if you're man enough." Her sneer faded as she saw someone approaching through the olive grove. "Who's that?" she snapped. "Another that you've fooled with words and little action?"

"I called him here to help assuage your passions."

"I'm not an animal!" she shouted fiercely, "But you are!"

"Never call me that – never!" Gonzaga bellowed. It was what they called his father. Using all his strength he slashed at the wooden shed, his sword digging deep into the timber.

He's mad, she thought, absolutely mad, and she was tired of it. She had been tired of him for ages, but now she'd simply had enough.

"Vitale," Gonzaga called out.

"Zaga. Is that the way you show affection to a lady?"

Both men laughed too loudly.

Lucrezia's dark eyes shone defiantly. "Is no one going to introduce me?"

Tiepolo bowed. "Vitale Tiepolo at your service, ma'am."

"Lucrezia Riario," she returned, with all the courtesy expected of nobility.

Instantly Gonzaga felt jealous. She had never behaved like that to him. So what was so special about Tiepolo? The Venetian peacock was spineless but he had ducats. Perhaps she smelled them. She loved wealth.

"Go back to your mother, Lucrezia. We have things to talk about," Gonzaga barked.

"How dare you. This is our grove. Get off our land!"

"Make me!" The hatred in his eyes was plain and menacing. "Go to your mother," he screamed, the veins on his neck standing proud like cords.

"Get off our land," she spat fearlessly, her long dark curls swinging as she jerked her head.

"Calm down, you two," Tiepolo intervened, his sharp features showing alarm.

Gonzaga and Lucrezia, facing each other like cats about to spring, began to ease their confrontation.

Tiepolo bowed again towards Lucrezia with Venetian formality. "Zaga and I will move aside to exchange some business and then we shall return."

"Thank you, Sir," she answered brightly.

Gonzaga ground his teeth together, his volcanic temper close to an explosion. The way she played up to the smooth Venetian was absolutely maddening, but he moved away as Vitale had suggested. Reason had not totally disappeared.

Lucrezia waited. With her flashing energy and her wild appearance most said she was of gipsy origin. But now she fell quietly reflective. Tiepolo had treated her like a proper lady and it seemed that something hidden for a long, long time had suddenly been uncovered. She liked the feeling and she liked Tiepolo.

★

Bishop Riddo, accompanied by a burly servant, was progressing with due dignity between Castel Sant' Angelo and the Vatican when he saw Piccolomini walking slowly in the same direction. Obviously his gout was still troubling him. Riddo soon caught up.

"My Lord Bishop," he called out. "I see, like me, you enjoy the morning air. And Aeneas, you're the very man I hoped to see."

"My friend, what a pleasant surprise." Piccolomini's smile was disarming. "Well, Ubaldo, what can I do for you?"

Riddo's pace had slowed to Piccolomini's gingerly progress.

"You may recall mentioning that I might be contacted by the Siena authorities. You were right. I've been summoned, though in most deferential terms."

"What tedium, Ubaldo. I assume you will ignore this presumption," Piccolomini responded casually.

"The trouble is, Aeneas, your name is used as a supporting authority."

"Ubaldo, my name is used for many things. Of course, there are advantages in obeying the magistrates, for you'll be seen as humble and compliant and there'll be an opportunity, no doubt, to advance your worthy efforts in protecting holy doctrine."

"Indeed," Riddo answered easily. "I hadn't thought of that."

"And there are other towns to visit on the way. Your work has no frontiers, Ubaldo."

"How well you understand, Aeneas." Riddo's self-importance mushroomed, for Piccolomini seemed sincere. He could sense no hidden currents.

"My friend, I'm rather slow this morning," Piccolomini said confidentially. "The gout is tiresome, so why don't you carry on?"

"How considerate of you, Aeneas. I *will* rush on as I've a rather busy morning. I do hope your gout eases."

Smiling with satisfaction, Piccolomini watched Bishop Riddo stride ahead. Aeneas chuckled, "My friend, I'm fearful that Siena will not be to your liking."

CHAPTER 44

'Take the Battle to the Enemy'

When Messer Tiepolo thought he had at last secured a meeting with his son, he was once more frustrated. It had happened in Rome and again at Todi and then at Orvieto. Each time his son had moved a day or so before. Was this deliberate? He feared it was, though he had no way of knowing this for sure.

No longer angry, for that fire had long since died, Tiepolo resigned himself to failure and set out for Ancona and then to Venice. He had left countless messages and had humbled himself in ways he never thought he would, but he could wait no longer; Venice and his merchant interests demanded his return.

Valeria had no option but to accompany her father, for since Portia was married and, the Count and Countess were back in Venice, there was no one suitable to act as chaperone. That was Tiepolo's genuine opinion, for he had no wish to cause his daughter further pain. His love for her had deepened. Her stoicism amazed him, and he felt humbled by her uncomplaining nature. Indeed, father and daughter had grown close, their mutual affection forged on the anvil of suffering. Tiepolo did not know it and, if he had, perhaps would not have understood how his daughter had been much influenced by Coluccio's friend, Marsilio. His friendly conversation and advice had given her the strength to face up to frustration and the all too frequent temptation to indulge her moods.

★

Coluccio, fully employed by the Medici secretariat, attended daily at the villa on the Via Larga. He had hoped to observe the magistrate's inquiry into the wounding of Bernardo, but that had been inexplicably delayed without the declaration of a forward date, and Coluccio feared 'delay' was just a diplomatic word for 'closed'. Cosimo was surprisingly upset, yet, with a new Pope recently installed, he did not want to stir too many pots. Bernardo was a Medici servant, and while Cosimo might presently ignore the attack he would not forget. His agents in Siena were certain that Piccolomini was sympathetic. So who had got to Aeneas? Perhaps he was also treading cautiously. Aeneas, of course, wanted a Cardinal's hat, and for a man of his ability it was understandable. In fact, he might well see Calixtus as his last chance, so he would have to move with care.

★

The news that Bishop Riddo was preaching a crusade, the passion of Pope Calixtus, came in a letter from Valeria to Coluccio. Her father's Orsini host had written suggesting that the all-pervading Riddo could become a

Cardinal, such was his prestige. Orsini also mentioned a rumour that Piccolomini had initially recommended Riddo. So what was going on? – for the rumour was contrary to the best opinion in Siena, where it was felt their Bishop was disdainful of his former secretary.

Could it be that Piccolomini had been out-manoeuvred? If so, it was certainly an exception, for general opinion held that Aeneas was a master of diplomacy. So what was happening? Coluccio felt very much in the dark, and the more so when thinking of his family properties in Orvieto. The del Montes had regained their fortress with the aid of a Sforza army but he had nothing. There was always Messer del Monte's suggestion to seek a senior Churchman's help – even the Pope's! He had never taken the suggestion seriously; perhaps he should have done. The question was, whom should he approach? Certainly someone who had real and present influence. Calixtus III? He was almost eighty and obsessed by his crusade against the Turks. Not hopeful was, with little doubt, an understatement.

Coluccio yawned and stretched himself. His work was finished for the day, so he put his desk in order, left the secretariat and strode out into the Via Larga. Marsilio was at some gathering with Landino, so instead of his customary walk he headed for the stables housing his reluctant mule and then for the del Monte villa at Fiesole.

It was during conversation over supper, when Andrea's father made the flippant aside: 'It's not the present Pope, it's the next one that you need,' that Coluccio replied with equal flippancy that 'prophecy has never been my dominant gift'. But somehow he knew that he had found the key; why, he could not say.

★

The next morning Coluccio set out early for Florence. He had no body-guard. In fact, he had been lax, for there was an arrangement for a Medici guard to be available. The previous evening, though, it had seemed totally unnecessary and an imposition on Medici generosity. In any case, Bernardo would soon be back with him.

What he had thought last evening as being the key now seemed both vague and fanciful, yet a spark remained. His future was not unlike Marsilio's – high potential, shadowed by uncertainty and with a sense of imminent crisis.

As Valeria's suitor, he was without the means to visit Venice. The chances of recovering his inheritance were tenuous at best. Hopelessness, like a substance, was waiting to engulf him, but he kept his interest outward on the passing scene of scattered dwellings while riding as quickly as his stubborn mule would tolerate.

Someone dropped a plank of wood nearby and the mule bucked in reaction. There was a thump and looking down he was amazed to see an arrow sticking in his saddlebag. The mule began to trot. The arrow tip, he guessed,

164

was acting as a spur. No one was following and soon he was well out of range, so he stopped, extracted the arrow from the saddlebag and rode on. Then he began to shake as if he had a violent fever. 'Shock', he gritted through clenched teeth. He had experienced it only once before. Slowly his body settled, but his mind was racing. Who was it? Who had shot the arrow? Was it Riddo, Vitale or a present owner of Carrucci property? At one stroke his freedom was now drastically restricted, and what was more, his walks with Marsilio would be hopelessly circumscribed. In fact, his very presence would endanger him. Unusually for Coluccio, he felt angry. Could it be that even in Fiesole he would have to wear disguise? No! He would take the battle to the enemy.

CHAPTER 45

The Scribe

Coluccio had lost his inner tranquillity, and an unusual buzz of agitation seemed to have possessed him, yet, strangely, it was not fear. True, the arrow cutting into his saddlebag had been a shock, but now he was being faced with a decision. It was as though some power was forcing him to action. 'Don't wait for the next arrow' his inner voice commanded. 'Act!'

He was tired of being guarded and tired of the restrictions it imposed. Passivity no longer ruled. Was he being stupidly naive? Perhaps he was, yet he held to this command with unrelenting stubbornness.

Once the decision had been made, his inner tranquillity returned as rocklike as before. This gave him confidence to make his plans and order his affairs.

Since his last attempt at a disguise, his knowledge of the art had been transformed under Messer del Monte's astute direction. He was cautioned not take a mule or donkey on any journey, for when gathering information in the enemy's camp they could be distracting and might mark him out as having some small wealth.

Taking everything Andrea's father said to heart, he stayed out of sight for long enough to grow a beard, tingeing it with grey, a technique del Monte had taught him.

He wrote an explanatory letter to Cosimo at his country villa and called on Marsilio, who made no comment one way or the other. Then he warned Valeria not to expect letters for a little while as he was journeying incognito to the south. She had no need to be concerned, he wrote. He would be in touch again as soon as possible.

With everything in place, using the common name Tommaso, and confident in his disguise, he set out on foot through the Porto Romano, heading for Siena.

It was now early September, still hot but not scorching, an ideal time to travel. He had decided to play a scribe-cum-secretary down on his luck, who had heard that there was work in the next town up ahead. It was a much more realistic role than the peasant he had tried before.

To discover why the inquiry had been postponed or, more likely, abandoned he journeyed to Siena first. After that he planned to head for Orvieto by way of Bolsena, then to Todi and finally to Rome. That was the ideal, but what would happen as the days unfolded was another matter.

Travelling without a mule or donkey was quite a discipline, and on the first day his patient nature was sorely tested, for it was not until the late afternoon that he got a lift from a creeping farm cart. The driver was talkative and suggested a deserted barn where he could spend the night, which, as it happened, was surprisingly comfortable. The next day an early lift in a fast two-wheeled cart sped him on to a village close to Monteriggioni, where he found cheap accommodation. The omens were good, for with luck he could reach Siena in the morning, which in fact he did. What was more, he found employment at the cathedral, where he registered as Tommaso da Roma.

When he felt he had the trust of his fellow scribes he asked his first casual questions. "What is the Bishop like?" – "Is he popular?" The answers were not ambiguous. He was a scholar who looked after his staff and yes, the people liked him. Not that they saw much of him of course, for he was often in Rome.

"I know someone", Coluccio responded, "who maintained that the Bishop was more than kind to a friend of his who was wounded hereabouts. A big man, I believe."

"You must mean Bernardo," one of the scribes responded without hesitation. "The Bishop visited him every day. There was going to be an inquiry, but it was stopped."

"Why was that?" Coluccio asked innocently.

"Pressure from the Pope, so the story goes, for the Bishop was determined to proceed."

Coluccio let the matter drop. He had heard all he wanted to know. Calixtus was protecting the crusading Riddo from embarrassment. A few days later Coluccio took his leave.

The journey to Bolsena was not so easy, as farm carts were his only help and they, of course, were slow. It took five days before he entered the familiar town, and he studiously avoided his old friend, Father Francesco. The security of his disguise was vital, especially at this point.

Coluccio did not expect the final stage of his journey to Orvieto to be easy, but by good fortune another farm cart took him all the way. The driver, an old garrulous individual who maintained that he was fit for nothing except sitting, talked freely, and whether Coluccio liked it or not he was subjected to a running commentary on who was husband to the land on either side of the narrow roadway. Coluccio listened intently as the heavy cart slowly crunched its way along the stone-strengthened road, but no familiar names were mentioned.

"Where were the old Carrucci properties?" he asked.

"They're nearer to Orvieto."

"Who owns them now?"

"They call them the Church lands," the old man answered. "They've done so ever since..."

The cart slewed violently.

"Ever since what?" Coluccio pressed.

"The massacre – the Carrucci – they were..." The old man drew his hand across his throat.

"What happened to the killers?"

"The Church came and threw a blanket over everything."

The cart lurched again.

"This road's getting worse and they're far too mean to fix it. You're interested in the Carrucci, are you?"

"I was here before and heard about them."

"Well, you can take it from me, Giovanni Carrucci was a good master. I should know; I worked for him. I was a young man then," he added wistfully, nodding his grey head in silent benediction.

A surge of emotion caught Coluccio unawares, but he recovered quickly.

"What's your name, my friend?"

"Benedetto."

Benedetto stopped a mile or so short of Orvieto, so Coluccio walked the rest of the way, a climb, until he reached the plateau table on which the town was built. Being confident in his disguise, he headed for the hostel where he had stayed before, while remembering all the mannerisms Messer del Monte had suggested as giving subtlety to his acquired persona.

He stammered slightly as he booked accommodation and after settling in sought employment as at Siena. There was little on offer other than a filthy job in the town's archive room, where the dust of generations covered everything. They were paying a pittance and it was easy to disguise enthusiasm, but the truth was it was the very place that he was seeking. His overseer, an elderly man named Stefano, looked as dusty as the archives he was handling.

"You take that lot over there,' he said, pointing to a muddled heap of papers, his voice muffled by the cloth that covered both his nose and mouth, a wise precaution which Coluccio immediately copied.

With astonishment Coluccio realised he was scanning property transactions of the past fifty years or so, though not the recent ones. Some names such as Filippeschi and Monaldeschi were dominant, but there was nothing at all concerning the Carrucci. This was puzzling, for how could anyone have extracted the Carrucci files from such a mess, yet it seemed that someone had. Coluccio bided his time, and when it was appropriate he brought the matter up with his overseer Stefano during a welcome draught of well-diluted wine.

"An obliging driver called Benedetto gave me a lift from Bolsena..." Coluccio began.

"Benedetto! Did you get a word in? He never stops!"

"You're right. He wasn't short of conversation. He said among other things that the Carrucci family owned extensive property hereabout, but it's surprising that the name doesn't show in these records at all."

"I know," Stefano replied flatly. "All the Carrucci papers were taken to Rome..."

"All of them! Why would that be, for heaven's sake?" Coluccio tried to maintain a casual tone.

"Rome sticks its nose into everything!"

"But however did they find the Carrucci papers? The records are in such a jumble!"

"That's the way they left them, my friend, and after twenty years we're still trying to tidy up. You're interested in the Carrucci?"

"It's just that Benedetto went on about it so that I was curious. How do you stand this dust day after day?" Coluccio thought it best to change the subject.

"A few more months may finish it," Stefano said somewhat doubtfully.

"I'm sorry, but I fear my chest won't stand much more of this."

"Well, Tommaso, if you're troubled with your chest, this is the wrong place to be."

"I'm sorry."

"More so me, my friend, but there it is."

Coluccio had contrived his exit. He worked another day then, taking a fond look at the Cathedral, he set out for Todi, the haunt of Gonzaga and the girl Riario, and possibly Tiepolo. He had no idea what to do or what he should expect, but he sensed danger.

CHAPTER 46

Birds of a Feather

Coluccio did not know, of course, but the day after he set out for Siena a letter arrived at the del Monte villa from Valeria, saying that she and her father would be due in Florence by mid-October.

Messer Tiepolo's official reason was to strengthen trading ties which he had established during his last lengthy stay. His unofficial and real reason was concern for his daughter. She had become withdrawn, and the happiness of Portia and Andrea only emphasised her loneliness. She was also losing weight, something she could ill afford.

All the hoped-for marriage alliances that would have helped the family climb the oligarchic ladder had lost their meaning as love for his daughter transformed Tiepolo in a way that he or any of his friends would never have imagined. Throughout those weeks in Rome and the desperate search for his fiery son, Vitale, Valeria had been a loving and supportive companion, never once complaining. Now he was reciprocating. They were bound for Florence, for that was where her heart resided.

When they reached Fiesole and learned from the del Montes that Coluccio had journeyed south, Tiepolo reacted more overtly than Valeria. She was very disappointed, of course, but in missing Coluccio her father was subjected to the vivid memories of Todi and Orvieto, where Vitale had deliberately avoided him – a sharply hurtful experience to which he had not wanted to admit.

While Valeria received a gentler report from Messer del Monte, Tiepolo was informed of all the detail. This did not help his mood, except that he much admired Coluccio's spirit, in taking the fight to the enemy. Yet he was very much concerned, even fearful, that Vitale would be there amongst that very enemy.

On the Tiepolos' second day at Fiesole, Marsilio called to carry out del Monte's routine check. It had grown to be a custom that he stayed over-night, so in the evening he joined the del Montes and their guests for supper.

The conversation was a revelation to Tiepolo. He knew that Marsilio was a friend of Coluccio and that Valeria much respected the young scholar. Tiepolo had a passing knowledge of Platonic reasoning. When young, it was something that he had been made to learn, but since then he had never given the subject much thought. He was a busy merchant and church devotion seemed quite adequate. Now he was amazed, for no one had ever explained Platonic principles in such direct and simple terms and, what was more, the young man was so patient.

Valeria could see her father was enthralled and could hardly wait to ask him his opinion when Marsilio retired.

"I was captivated, my dear. What he said was so straightforward. Even I could understand it!"

"Father!" she exclaimed in mock reproof.

"You understand, my dear, for you put the principles into practice."

"I try to."

"More than try, Valeria."

"Father, I asked Marsilio if Coluccio was in danger."

"And what did he say?"

"He didn't give an answer, but he said that Coluccio had been greatly tested and now he is much favoured."

"I read hope in that." He kissed her on the forehead. "Sleep well, Valeria."

★

Anticipating the approach of winter, Coluccio bought a heavy coat and cape, funded by his earnings at Siena and Orvieto. They were not new, of course; that was beyond the limited means he had secreted on his person. The coat, though, proved a prudent buy, as the very day that he set out for Todi the weather grew much colder.

The hilly terrain between Orvieto and Todi made the going tortuous and doubled the direct distance. Indeed, leaving Orvieto at dawn, it was two days before he saw the hill of Todi filling the horizon.

Lifts from passing farm carts had been few and brief, and his feet were sore and swollen. He felt exhausted, and all that he could think of was the comfort of a fire and wine. He was descending now towards the narrow valley where the Tiber flowed and where there was a bridge spanning its far from insignificant width. On the other side there was a village where he hoped to find some generous household.

The Tiber was full and flowing at a pace. He stopped and watched the water slipping by. How much of what he saw would find its way to Rome? Most of it, perhaps. It was a question he had never thought to ponder. Once over the bridge, he began to knock on doors, but few, if any, that were willing, had the space to house a traveller. So, despondent, he trudged on. Then to his right he saw a wisp of smoke curling up behind a screen of bushes. He left the road to find a small low-roofed cottage. Being at the edge of the village, it was his last hope, or so he thought, before the climb to Todi. He knocked, expecting rejection. Instead he was greeted warmly by a middle-aged couple who were just about to eat and who invited him to share their simple fare. Being able to sit down and with warm food before him, Coluccio felt that heaven had come down to earth.

Where had he come from? Where was he going? What did he do? Coluccio responded with ease to the natural questions of his hosts. Simone and Maria told him that they tended the vineyard close by. It was Church property and the Church were kindly masters. Yet it was obvious that the couple were very poor, for though their table was sturdy, their chairs, except for one, were little more than boxes. Nonetheless, their home was spotless. One unusual feature was the stone slab floor. Someone at some time had been enterprising. It was, however, slippery

Coluccio was complimenting them on their wine and homemade goats' cheese when suddenly there was a loud knocking at the door and before Simone could get up the caller was already in the room.

"I've lost my dog! Have you been feeding him again?" a man demanded accusingly.

"No, Messer Gonzaga," Simone answered anxiously.

"You're always feeding him!"

"The children used to give him scraps, but I've told them not to."

"Where are they?"

"They're in bed, Sir."

"Get them up!" Gonzaga's eyes were blazing, agitation driving him to pull his sword half way from its scabbard in rapid repetitive movements.

Simone hesitated and Gonzaga exploded.

"Do I have to repeat myself? The dog's probably with them!"

Simone still hesitated, a father's protective instinct making him resist.

"Sir," Coluccio interrupted quietly. At such times of crisis he was often calm. "Is that your dog waiting at the doorway?"

Gonzaga spun round, almost falling over on the slippery floor.

"Where have you been?" he snarled, lunging to kick the hound. The dog growled, and Gonzaga stormed out without another word.

"Phew," Simone exhaled. "I should be laughing but I don't feel like it!"

"Who was that madman?" Coluccio asked, hoping for more information.

"He's our neighbour. Thank God the road divides our properties, for he has a habit of disputing boundaries. Are you all right, Maria?" he added softly, "You're very white."

"I was so worried for the children, but I'm fine now. Thank you, Sir, for pointing out the dog."

"I suspect he beats the poor creature," Coluccio ventured.

"I know he does," Maria confirmed.

"He's a vicious bully," Simone added bluntly.

"He never had a father to keep him in his place," his wife explained.

"My dear, they say his father was just as bad."

"What happened to him?" Coluccio prompted.

"He was killed in a sword fight by one of Sforza's friends."

Count Crito – Coluccio had often heard the story from Messer del Monte.

"A soldier's life might tame this son of his," Coluccio suggested quietly.

"Maybe, for he often practises with his cross-bow," Simone said easily.

Coluccio was immediately alerted, but he said nothing and the conversation casually turned to Church affairs at Todi. Simone was clearly devout and respected his Bishop, but Coluccio was puzzled and after a little while he brought the subject of Gonzaga up again.

"Simone, have you complained about Gonzaga to your priest?"

"Yes, and I know that both Gonzaga and his mother were cautioned but it's made no difference."

"But why do they tolerate his arrogance?"

"He's got high-placed friends in Rome who find him useful and Rome looks after him!"

Coluccio said no more. Riddo had the favour of the Pope and a network which was influential.

★

Physical tiredness and the strong local wine brought instant sleep, despite the hard floor, softened marginally by rugs. Coluccio rose early, refreshed yet somewhat stiff. For a while he forgot the happenings of the night before and when they did return, they seemed so totally unreal. Had Gonzaga been drinking? Was that the cause of his bizarre behaviour? If not, he was quite mad and dangerous, for rage possessed him. It was frightening. And the way he juggled with his sword was like an omen that one day he would use it, if only for the mere frustration of a whim.

After warm goats' milk straight from the milking, and some bread softened with oil, Coluccio set out for Todi. Maria and Simone would take nothing for his fare, which was generous yet most embarrassing. So he resolved that one day, without fail, he would repay their kindness.

Simone suggested that he contact Father Vanne, and this he did, finding his employment almost automatic. The recommendation of the devout Simone must have carried weight, but the earnings proved as meagre as at Orvieto, though they were quite enough for lodgings and for food.

For the first week he did little other than acquaint himself with the secretariat's routine. The second week was similar, but his expertise in Latin had been noted and the nature of his work was changed.

All the drama he had envisaged concerning Tiepolo, Gonzaga and Lucrezia simply had not happened. He disciplined himself not to mention them at the secretariat lest some suspicion might arise, but at the tavern in the evening he was not so circumspect.

"Lucrezia!" one old wizened greybeard picked up his question. "She's a bright one. You'll always see her at the festivals. Gonzaga used to be her man but they say she has a new man now."

"Gonzaga won't like that!"

"Well, he'll have to lump it, won't he! The story goes she fought a duel with him and she won!"

"Maybe he let her," Coluccio suggested.

"Not Gonzaga – he's a bastard!"

"That's plain enough. So who's the new man?"

"Some young dandy from Venice."

"Venice! Plenty of ducats there!" Coluccio prompted.

"They weigh themselves in ducats, my friend!"

"So what does this Gonzaga think? He can't be pleased."

"Zaga gets his slave girls by the cart-load!"

This was the first break-through, and from then the old man fed Coluccio nightly with the gossip. All he needed was a jug of wine. The picture was becoming clear. Lucrezia's new lover was Vitale, and Gonzaga had been cast aside. But would the madly proud Gonzaga take this insult lying down?

Two weeks later, in mid-January, the answer was made tragically evident. Habitually Coluccio enjoyed a brief early morning walk before going to the secretariat. He had his favourite routes, some up and down the winding steps leading to the piazza. This particular morning the ground was white from an overnight fall of snow and when Coluccio saw a trail of blood he swiftly followed it, coming in horror upon the gasping Lucrezia.

"Zaga," she wheezed, but Coluccio did not wait for further words. Instantly he lifted her – to his surprise she was quite light – and rushed as quickly as the icy ground allowed to the sanctuary of a church, where he shouted to the nearest priest to bring a surgeon. There he waited until a frantic and distraught Vitale, alerted by a friend, rushed in to hold her hand, and when the surgeon came Coluccio quietly slipped away.

For days Lucrezia's life hung in the balance, and all of Todi seemed to hold its breath. Then slowly she began to gain in strength. Vainly Vitale sought the man they called Tommaso who had found and saved his love.

Coluccio had left and was already on the busy road to Rome. Love had tamed Vitale and Lucrezia in a way that no one would have guessed.

"It's as if I've just remembered who I am," he told Lucrezia.

"Then, who are you?" she quipped.

"Ah! That's too difficult!"

Their laughter erupted.

Gonzaga had fled, no doubt unrepentant, and was travelling with the main bulk of the family gold. He was still a threat and even more so than before, for who could find him if he changed his name and habit? Coluccio felt defeated until he thought of Riddo, for where the Bishop Riddo was there would be Gonzaga. They were birds of a feather, crows both black and cruel.

CHAPTER 47

Rome

Brief coded notes to Messer del Monte at Fiesole were the only communications from Coluccio. Over Natale there was no news and it was not until the end of January that a short note arrived via the Medici Bank in Rome. The relief to Valeria was enormous, for she was sick with worry, even though every message repeated the refrain 'Tell Valeria not to be concerned.' Coluccio, of course, did not know that she was now in Florence.

Messer del Monte acted, in a sense, as Coluccio's agent, for he kept Cosimo up to date and informed Coluccio's special friend Marsilio of the latest news. Although acknowledging Ficino's vastly superior mind, del Monte felt paternal towards the young scholar and was concerned that his future still remained uncertain. Marsilio was under considerable pressure. His prodigious capacity for study seemed labour enough, but he was also helping to support his family by tutoring the reluctant offspring of the rich, something not greatly to his liking. He also helped his father with his patients, so his study time was much curtailed, delaying the completion of his four-book project on the nature of Platonic philosophy.

Landino had told Cosimo about Marsilio's writing, and the subject had also come up in conversation at Careggi during Marsilio's occasional visits, but nonetheless he had been slow to publicise his work. Even so, Cosimo knew about it, and Marsilio's continued delay in completing it would give unflattering impressions. But why was Cosimo still delaying his support, which would give Marsilio his much-needed freedom for his studies? Del Monte knew the great man's thinking well. Seemingly, Cosimo was still unsure, still waiting. From his viewpoint, Italy was awash with brilliant scholars, like Platina, seeking patronage, scholars well-versed in Greek. Marsilio's Greek was not as yet of a standard needed for translation, though, even with that, few could meet Marsilio's penetration. Cosimo was aware of this but he was waiting for the moment. It was not yet time.

Messer Tiepolo and Valeria had by now become part of the del Monte household. Anna welcomed this, for she knew her husband relished both company and intelligent conversation. In any case, the villa was large enough for all to have their privacy. Tiepolo, though, often rode to Florence, where he hoped to establish a branch of his merchant house – one perhaps that Coluccio could manage, but he did not tell his daughter this.

It was his worry about Vitale which kept Tiepolo awake at night. His son was rash and foolish, but then he, Tiepolo, had been just as bad when he was young, and had he found an evil genius such as Riddo, he too would have followed and believed his lies. Damn Riddo's arrogant and dissembling soul! It was so easy to corrupt the young with hate-filled aims on which to vent their excess energy. Please God his son would see the sham for what it was. Unfortunately, though, Riddo was a favourite with Calixtus and could well wear a red hat all too soon which, of course, would add to his attraction.

There was nothing Tiepolo could do, absolutely nothing, but he prayed that his son might still recall the strong Venetian training of his youth for, when not being totally stupid, Vitale still knew right from wrong.

★

Coluccio was fortunate on the road to Rome. Two fast carts took him practically all the way but, though dry, the wind was icy, and when he reached the city it was no less bitter. Rome, of course, was a familiar place. Cheap lodging was known to him, and he quickly settled in.

It was now the Rome of Calixtus, and the great projects of the previous Pope, the Holy Father Nicholas, had been abandoned. New Papal wealth was focused on the grand Crusade against the Turkish menace and the brazen enrichment of the Pontiff's nephews. The 'Catalans', as they were called, straddled Rome, and resentment was fermenting.

Coluccio's self-appointed tasks were daunting. The first, to locate and then to study the Carrucci papers transferred from Orvieto. This would not be easy, for it required the penetration of the Vatican archives – sensitive archives which, if disturbed, could prompt a harsh reaction from the vested interests. Of this Coluccio had no doubt; there *were* vested interests. He had one well-placed contact, Andrea's friend Paolino, but he would have to re-veal himself. Though reluctant, he could see no alternative, yet he hesitated, for the currents of conflicting interest coursing round the Vatican were treacherous.

Watching Riddo was his second task. Had he still the same nocturnal habits, or had the Pope's crusade become his mistress? The heady rhetoric was potent, as were the fame and adulation. Riddo was like a weather vane which followed the changing wind of fashionable opinion, but his vindictive streak prevailed, and forgiveness was not a word he understood. While masquerading as Tommaso da Roma, Coluccio knew he dared not overdo his prying lest he be discovered. He would have to move with care.

His third task, no less pressing, was to trace Gonzaga's whereabouts. He had disappeared after Lucrezia's near fatal stabbing. Had he fled to Rome and was he now under the protection of his so-called mentor, Riddo? This was a strong possibility and hopefully easy to confirm, for anonymity was not Gonzaga's strong point. But, of course, he could be anywhere, holding dear his hatreds and his jealousy.

★

Santa Sabina on the Aventine was full. Coluccio was lucky to get in and to find a seat quite near the front where the senior clergy were arrayed. He

176

recognised Latino Orsini amongst a group of fellow Cardinals, a bright red array. There were Bishops, too, and representatives of the major families in seats especially reserved. He could just see Napoleone Orsini and also the Colonna dignitaries and noted they were seated well apart. Piccolomini was standing talking to – great heavens – Andrea's friend Paolino, and it was *Paolino* who escorted Bishop Riddo in! Dear God, what was going on? Was Paolino one of Riddo's converts? Or was he simply an official of the Church? Coluccio had no way of checking and no one to turn to for advice. Certainly, after what he'd seen, he dared not trust Paolino. His one hopeful lead was now unsafe.

Reluctant as he was, Coluccio had to admit that Riddo was impressive. The moment of prayer before his sermon was self-effacing and not at all pretentious. Sincerity seemed to sanctify his movements. Who would believe that this man was a fraud? 'Even I find it difficult', he thought. And Piccolomini – what did he think, sitting passively at the side? Indeed, the Bishop of Siena was totally inscrutable, while Paolino sitting close to him looked bored.

Just as at Todi, Coluccio was on his own. 'Trust, my friend,' he told himself, 'and be alert.'

Riddo's sermon had begun, and the passion of his rhetoric was powerful and compelling. The congregation was enthralled. Coluccio glanced side-ways. Piccolomini remained impassive and Paolino still looked bored; not everyone was trance-like in their listening. In fact, Coluccio found Riddo's sermon narrow and predictable, a polished and sophisticated tirade focused on the Turks, while Christian division and ineptitude were cleverly glossed over. True, many would applaud the Pope, but few would sacrifice their gold.

After the sermon came prayers and then the final benediction. Slowly the church began to empty. The dignitaries filed out together, no doubt to a reception of some kind. Coluccio watched intently, hoping by a stroke of fortune that he might see Gonzaga.

Piccolomini and Paolino were standing now but had not yet moved away. Piccolomini, of course, was busy chatting to his many friends, but Paolino was simply watching. For a moment Coluccio turned to scan the slowly receding congregation, hoping he might spot Gonzaga. He had been alert throughout the whole proceedings. Perhaps it was too much a chance – too unreal an expectation. His gaze casually returned to Piccolomini and Paolino, but they had gone. Then, with a jolt, he saw a figure going through to the reception clothed in the habit of a cleric. It was Gonzaga. Coluccio had no doubt.

CHAPTER 48

Father Sebastiano

To many in Rome the Turkish threat seemed distant, an obsession of the Pope, and even academic. In Venice, though, the mood was wholly different for, with their fortress ports feeling a new and unfamiliar sense of insecurity, the Turkish threat was all too real. Again, constant vigilance was required at sea – the experience of Febo Loredan was not unique. Indeed, Count Crito predicted that a major clash would be inevitable. Andrea, apprised of news from Buda, was certain that a confrontation was now imminent, for the Sultan was building up his strength, his aim to spread the rule of Islam to the very heart of Europe. Andrea could only think of one man who could stop him, Janos Hunyadi. He had the will, the strength and courage and the ability to inspire. The situation was dire, but a rare mood of common purpose uniting central Europe was coming to his aid. The outcome of the next few months would be crucial.

Born in Venice, Andrea never felt a stranger in the city, but the Venetian authorities offered no role to Count Crito's heir. Seemingly, they were unable to deal with what was termed 'a dual identity'. Busy with the Dandolo affairs, Andrea was not at all concerned. He had quite enough to do and was enjoying his new challenge. It was not surprising that the Venetian bureaucracy was unable to employ Count Crito's son-in-law, as the ducal administration was in virtual suspension. The ageing Doge Foscari was declining and was much affected by the exile of his wayward son. For a man who had dominated Venice for three decades it was a tragedy.

It was mid-February, six weeks or so away from the anniversary of Andrea's marriage. A blissful year had passed with his loving, gifted wife. They were a popular couple, never short of invitations, and frequent visitors to Febo and Ginevra Loredan, now also man and wife.

Portia was disappointed to be still childless, but her father dismissed her worries. "The Dandolo women," he said flippantly, "were always tardy!" Yet privately he felt concerned, for the continuity of the house was a vital issue for every family.

Portia and Andrea planned to visit Florence some time after Easter, and the Count and Countess guessed that that might be the pattern for the years ahead. Children, though, would change all that.

★

As usual, Lucrezia's hair cascaded about her and now that her energy was flooding back, getting her to rest was difficult. Impossible, Vitale protested.

"I want to go to Florence," she said suddenly.

"Why Florence?"

"All the people your friend the Bishop rails about are there . . ."

"Lucrezia, you're not planning something silly!"

"Of course not! I want to hear what they've got to say. The Bishop could be wrong. Are you still with him?"

"I've lost interest, Lucrezia and I can't remember why I got so damned excited. Well, I suppose it was something to do. I was so worked up about Valeria and the social-climbing Pucci, but now I learn that Pucci is Carrucci!"

"A Carrucci of Orvieto! No social climbing's needed there!"

"I don't like it! Pucci has the last laugh. It makes me look a fool!"

Lucrezia stamped her foot.

"You're being selfish, Vitale. Think of your sister!"

"You know, if anyone else spoke to me like that I'd blow up, but with you I only smile."

"So I'm a good influence."

"It seems so."

"That's the first time I've been told that! So *are* we going to Florence?"

"Have I a choice?"

"Of course." She smiled demurely.

"You'll need a chaperone."

"Chaperone! I've never had one, ever!"

"It might be wise to play the game."

"I could bring my old nurse."

"Would your mother mind?"

"She ignores her!"

"And you as well, as far as I can see!"

"Mother had a difficult time when I was little and I remind her of it."

★

Vitale was happy and certain that Lucrezia was a gift from heaven, but there was a shadow, the shadow of Gonzaga. He would neither forgive nor forget, and it made Vitale shudder.

★

As he moved out of the church after Bishop Riddo's sermon, Coluccio struck up a casual conversation with an elderly priest.

"A magnificent performance," he ventured.

"A speech for warriors, my friend, but we're too old for that."

"Dare I say, thank heavens!" Coluccio answered lightly, sensing that his acquaintance was far from ardent.

"To dare to speak the truth is always wise, old friend."

'Old friend' Coluccio noted with amusement – the disguise was working well!

"Tell me, who was beside the Bishop of Siena?" he asked casually.

"His new secretary."

Of course, that explained it all. But was Paolino still reliable?

"Paolino is his name, I think," the priest said easily.

Coluccio was loath to let the conversation lapse. "Do Bishop Riddo and the Bishop of Siena share the same passion for crusade?" Immediately he felt he might have pushed too far.

"Aeneas is a diplomat, a poet, a man of letters. He will obey the Pope's instructions." Clearly this priest admired Piccolomini, but he made no mention of Ubaldo Riddo, which to Coluccio was equally revealing.

"Thank you, Father," Coluccio said respectfully.

As they emerged from the church various knots of people were busy talking, while others stood waiting no doubt for friends still amongst the press of people.

"The evening has a pleasant freshness," the tall priest said, turning leisurely towards Coluccio. "A pleasure to meet you. You're new to Rome, I sense."

"Yes, I just arrived a few days ago and am hoping for work as a scribe or secretary."

The priest's head drooped further as he pondered. "Call tomorrow morning at San Pietro in Vincoli, say at ten. Ask for Father Sebastiano. Your name?'

"Tommaso, Father. I am most grateful."

The priest smiled and hobbled off, stiff with pains, Coluccio thought, and once away from the blazing torches by the entrance he, too, was soon swallowed in the darkness of the evening.

CHAPTER 49

Gonzaga

Pope Calixtus was deeply grateful to his good man Bishop Riddo, and the Bishop's small request that a friend of his be given a commission in the Vicar General's soldiery was seen as trivial and granted without question.

Riddo was gloatingly pleased at the Pope's easy compliance, for in one move he had gained Gonzaga's gratitude (that is, if Gonzaga was capable of such an emotion) and had also distanced himself from his embarrassing disciple. In future any incidents – and knowing Gonzaga, there would be incidents – would be the Vicar General's problem. Eventually, of course, the Turks would tame his reckless ways with final permanence.

Riddo's expectations had soared, and rightly so, he felt. A Cardinalate was his due, and many said it openly. He, of course, publicly dismissed such views as fanciful. He had already abandoned his 'youthful excesses', his way of describing or, indeed, justifying his womanising. He would still have a slave girl, but that would be discreet, an understandable indiscretion to most.

The only annoyance was the pretender, Carrucci, his one-time clueless secretary. Gonzaga's hired assassin had missed him in Florence. Since then the weasel had disappeared, probably shivering in a Medici fortress, fearful of the next attack. Anyway he had vowed to rid the world of the so-called Carrucci.

Riddo's mind, forever presenting pictures of his glittering role and forever taking it as real, was slow to sense his underlying fear, manifesting as unease. 'Pucci' – the very name filled him with aversion, hinting at a subterranean world in which Riddo's whole persona was a fraud. Though weak and hardly seen at all, this alien presence was disturbing, and Riddo was determined to be rid of it, believing that if Pucci went it, too, would go.

But he wanted to be rid of Pucci for another reason, too, one that struck at the very foundation of his income, the Carrucci estates. The pretender might be genuine after all and investigations would, to say the least, be undesirable. Though not personally involved in the Carrucci massacre, he suspected that his family was. It was a subject no one talked about and questions were forbidden. Some years earlier he had tried to penetrate the mystery, but the papers buried in the Vatican archives were under strict security, so he let the matter rest. Anyway, he had the income, but few, if any, knew that it was linked to the Orvieto estates.

★

Eyeing his new uniform, Gonzaga threw his clerical black into the corner with disgust. There was no need for such disguise, for at last he was a soldier like his father, whom no one dared oppose. He'd been the only one the Lord Riario feared. But he had been murdered. The 'beanpole Count' had killed him in a duel, so the story went, though his late mother never thought the story to be true. No one could have killed him in a straight fight, she said. Her strong and passionate husband had been *murdered,* and revenge had burned in her, a fire that scorched her son.

Oh! There were many scores to settle, not least the Jezebel Lucrezia and her lackey, that rich man's son, Tiepolo. But the Bishop had advised him to move slowly, to play the model soldier and thus build up a reputation as a solid and respected servant of the Papal power. After that some private soldiering would be much more acceptable. The Bishop had been careful of his words, of course, but that was his insinuation. Restraint, though, would be difficult, if not impossible, for he had so indulged his violent moods that his frustrated appetites resulted in a towering rage. Resignation was not a word he understood, and he despised the fearful yet compliant smile of the oppressed. However, for all his self-opinionated arrogance, Gonzaga had not stood his ground in Todi. On the contrary, he had fled with unceremonious haste. Was this the prudence of the cunning or was it simply fear? Gonzaga shunned such self-examination. He had fled to escape the whining questions of the tottering elders, and that was that.

CHAPTER 50

'You stay put and let him come to you!'

Messer del Monte was enjoying the afternoon breeze as he sat under the awning in the garden. Reading was difficult, and he could only manage a few lines at a time. He was dozing when approaching footsteps jerked him into wakefulness, to see Lorenzo Tiepolo standing close.

"Lorenzo! You look like a man alive with purpose!"

"Carlo, you'll not believe this, but I saw my son this morning. It *was* him. I stood like a rabbit in a trance and before I'd regained my wits and rushed towards him, he'd vanished. I looked everywhere, asked all and sundry but . . ." Tiepolo shrugged his shoulders in exasperation, "not a trace!"

"Sit down Lorenzo, you need a drink to calm you." Del Monte rang a bell beside his chair. "Where did you see him?"

"Near Santa Croce."

"Ah, you could lose an army in those alleys. Did you see who he was with?"

"A girl. From the distance she looked quite wild, her hair spilling about her, and there was another woman dressed in black. They were all laughing about something and didn't hear when I called out."

"Oh good, here's Jacopo with the wine."

"I brought the Trebbian, Sir."

"Perfect, Jacopo. Messer Tiepolo needs a generous draught. He's just spotted his son in Florence."

"But I missed him, Jacopo. He simply vanished before I reached him."

"Don't you worry, Sir. You stay put and let him come to you!"

Del Monte burst out laughing.

"But, Jacopo," Tiepolo protested, "he doesn't know I'm here!"

"Well, Sir, my guess is, he's only just arrived, for in Florence we know each other's business within the hour! And by noon tomorrow he'll learn exactly where you are!"

Del Monte, who was trying to subdue his mirth, started to laugh again.

★

After a fortnight working at San Pietro in Vincoli, Coluccio was transferred to the Vatican secretariat. "Your Latin and your basic grasp of Greek has impressed us all, Tommaso," Father Sebastiano beamed, clearly pleased that his protégé had been successful.

Tommaso da Roma was now earning even more than had Coluccio. His situation was bizarre, if not laughable, but it was frustrating, too, as he had as yet found little which was useful to his purpose; though being at the very hub of Vatican activity, he was bound to encounter discoveries and surprises.

His disguise still held. In fact, his stammer had become automatic and his stoop was second nature, both habits which would have to be undone, he thought ruefully.

On his fifth day he chanced upon Paolino and at once set out to cultivate his friendship, not a difficult task, as Piccolomini's secretary had a genial disposition. Nothing much was said during those easy meetings in the corridors and often it was little other than a nod or smile, but a week after their first encounter Paolino beckoned him.

"Tommaso, I often walk to the Palatine to clear my head of diplomatic documents. Would you like to join me? But you may think it much too hot, it being near to midday."

"Heat doesn't worry me, Paolino. It's the cold that I find difficult. Yes, of course, I'd be delighted."

They strode out, Coluccio, though, pretending to be less than nimble. Once over the bridge at the Castel Sant' Angelo, Paolino led the way in the shade where possible. Passing the Pantheon, they carried on until the Capitoline appeared in front of them, and continuing round on the Tiber side, they entered the ancient Forum with the Palatine on their right. Why such a long walk? Coluccio wondered, but he let the question pass.

"Let's climb up here." Paolino pointed to a path that zigzagged to the table summit of the Palatine. He was certainly very definite in his aim, stopping only on a platform near the top from where they viewed the ruined Forum stretching out below.

"Rome was Rome when this was full of glittering marble," he said with certainty.

"It must have been magnificent," Coluccio echoed. "Today, though, it's a powerful testimony to impermanence."

"Indeed it is."

Coluccio, still reluctant to lead the conversation, stood quietly, as did Paolino, and for what seemed ages they remained immobile, watching the sun-baked scene below. Coluccio connected naturally with the peace, such was his nature, and the sense of stillness deepened.

Paolino was certain. This *was* Andrea's friend. In fact, del Monte had described him perfectly. He had also said that 'C', meaning Coluccio, had disappeared on one of his missions. And how could an old man walk at such a pace without complaint? The final proof, though, was the stillness. This resonated exactly with Andrea's account.

"Here I renew myself," Paolino remarked eventually. Turning deliberately, he looked directly at Coluccio. "Three years ago I met a friend of yours at this very spot. Andrea Alberti del Monte is his name. We corresponded. I'm pleased to meet you, Messer Carrucci!"

"And I thought that my disguise was perfect!"

"Good, not perfect, but without Andrea's letters I doubt if I'd have looked so closely."

"Does anyone else know?"

"No; Aeneas is curious, though."

"The Bishop of Siena!"

Paolino nodded.

"He's impressed by your abilities, and I'm certain he will question you. In fact, it may be better that he knows exactly who you are."

"But, Paolino, can we take the risk?" Coluccio's face reflected his alarm.

"Don't worry. Aeneas is a diplomat. He never tells his left hand what his right is doing. You'll be completely safe. I mean it. So why are you here, Messer Carrucci? What are you looking for?"

"Paolino, it's Coluccio!"

Coluccio then explained his hope of finally perusing the Carrucci papers and also spoke of his concern about the dangerously violent nature of Riddo's man, Gonzaga.

Paolino did not respond immediately. Instead, he pondered, his eyes scanning the expanse of the ruined Forum and focusing on the arch of Septimius Severus. The position of the sun had moved and they were now in shade cast by a bush growing amongst the general dereliction.

"The Carrucci papers will doubtless be amongst the sensitive archives," Paolino began. "You know, those diplomatic exchanges which if made public would be damaging. They're very difficult to access unless you have a valid reason, but Aeneas has, so my advice is speak to him. I can arrange that."

Coluccio nodded his assent.

"As for Gonzaga," Paolino shook his head, "he causes trouble everywhere he goes!"

"He certainly does."

"You'll not like this – Gonzaga's just been given a commission with the Vicar General. Riddo spoke for him, and Riddo is the apple of the Holy Father's eye."

"My God, they've legitimised an assassin! I'll have to warn the fortress – I mean Andrea's brother! Gonzaga's bound to go there. He'll manufacture some excuse!"

"They say that Riddo's told him forcefully to restrain himself."

"And he's obeying?"

"Apparently. Riddo seems to exercise some power over him."

"Even so, I fear restraint will be a temporary curb," Coluccio said bitterly.

"And you, my friend, are you in danger?"

"Let's put it this way. If I charged a troop of Turkish Janissaries single-handed it would please Ubaldo Riddo well. I was his secretary; I know too much. Also, I'm a Carrucci. Riddo came from Orvieto, and if his family gained from the break-up of the estates it could be most embarrassing, but that's not yet proven, of course."

"Coluccio, you must see the Bishop of Siena. Tell him all!"

CHAPTER 51

Meeting

The small villa was delightful, the servants helpful, and the view from the portico was magnificent, and what was more, Brunelleschi's dome was visible. Nothing more it seemed could add to its enchantment. But Lucrezia was raging against fate and determined that she would not meet Vitale's sister.

Never of a patient nature, Vitale's tolerance was at breaking point.

"Lucrezia," he burst out, "We've been waiting for your mood to change for two weeks now. Show a little common sense, for goodness' sake. There *is* no problem, other than cold feet. You only panicked when you heard that father and Valeria were in Florence. Before that you were your old self."

"Enough of the 'old'!" Lucrezia protested.

"Good. Where humour sparks there's hope!" he teased.

"You don't know what it's like, Vitale. I ran wild. I've no idea of how to be a lady."

"For heavens sake, Lucrezia, you *are* a lady. I tell you what we'll do. Let's get the cart out, leave it at the Porta Romana and have a morning walk. Then we can eat somewhere that's fashionable and return before it gets too hot. What do you say?"

Still agitated, she stood up and began to pace the floor. "All right." Her nervousness was palpable.

"That's settled then. We'd better move quickly."

"You haven't made some arrangement..."

"Lucrezia, don't be so suspicious. We're simply going to Florence for the morning."

"It's not easy, Vitale. There's your sister, your father, and the del Montes – what am I going to tell them?"

"What you told me."

"They won't believe me, and I wouldn't blame them, for what I did was stupid!"

"Tell them you purposely missed so that you could tell your vengeful mother that you tried. You could have told a lie, of course."

"I don't like telling lies!" she answered forcefully. "Anyway, a lot of good it did me, for after telling her that I missed she barely spoke to me. 'You're not his daughter' she spat at me. 'His daughter never would have missed!'"

"And what did you say?"

"What could I say? I just walked away."

"Well, enough of this, Lucrezia. We're off to Florence!" he said as brightly as he could.

"What place is that?" Vitale asked a passing tradesman.

"Luca Pitti's doghouse!" the Florentine answered flippantly.

"Big dogs!" Vitale countered.

The man laughed, saluting as he continued on his way. Vitale had heard of Pitti but only vaguely. Turning to Lucrezia's nurse he added, "Why don't you make an offer, Maria?"

"Maybe, if they add another wing!"

Lucrezia clapped her hands with glee. "Nurse always has an answer."

They strolled on over the Ponte Vecchio, and turning right they headed for Santa Croce. Vitale was being deliberately unambitious on this first occasion. The Duomo and Piazza della Signoria could wait. Walking arm in arm with her nurse, Lucrezia looked quite at ease. 'Deo volente', Vitale repeated to himself, 'all is going well.'

"Who's that?" she asked suddenly.

"Who, Lucrezia?"

"That small man with the stoop – looks like a scribe. It's remarkable!"

"What's remarkable?"

"He seems to be surrounded by . . . I don't know what."

"I can't blame the wine, Lucrezia, for we haven't eaten yet. Let's have a word with him."

With the excuse of asking direction, Vitale contrived a conversation.

"Do I detect a Venetian accent?"

"Vitale Tiepolo, at your service, and you, Sir?"

"Marsilio." He paused quietly for a moment. "I believe I know your sister, Sir. She *is* a blessing to all who meet her."

"She's well, I hope."

"She is, but she would welcome a visit, Sir, as would your noble father."

This Marsilio was direct, Vitale noted, yet there was not the slightest hint of accusation, nothing to prompt reaction.

"Please tell them, if you see them, that we hope to visit soon. There may be some delay, though." Vitale shot a glance at Lucrezia, who was standing there transfixed. What was going on?

"May I introduce Lucrezia, Marsilio, and her nurse, Maria?"

"Ladies," Marsilio acknowledged with a bow. Then unhurriedly he moved away.

At once Vitale rounded on Lucrezia. To his astonishment she was weeping, something that she scorned to do.

"Are you all right?" he asked anxiously.

"Yes, of course," she muttered roughly, trying to hide her face. "Let me be."

"But why the tears?" he persisted.

"Oh, don't you see, Vitale?" She gulped, trying to command herself and, turning to him full face, she said, "I've never met such gentleness before, never, ever!"

★

The Count was almost sixty and, though still in reasonable health, he tired more easily and his war wounds often troubled him. The needs of state, however, were indifferent to such infirmities, and those needs frequently required his presence at the Ducal Palace more and more; as all could see, the Doge seemed quite content when he was there; otherwise the old man fretted and grew uncooperative.

Because of the pressures on his father-in-law, Andrea kept putting off his plan to visit Florence, which he knew would disappoint his parents. His conflicting loyalties were also fuelled by a letter from his brother. Giovanni had received a terse note from Coluccio, who was enraged that Gonzaga had been given a commission with the Vicar General. Giovanni wrote that he was increasing both his bodyguard and the town's defences, but that meant raising taxes and inevitably some discontent. All this because of one madman! Could something not be done? 'Very little', Andrea thought, though he did not say this in his letter.

The danger was that most would trust a Vicar General's man before Giovanni. Venice and Florence might ask questions and complain, certainly Sforza would, but it was Rome which held authority. However law, though fostered, was frequently irrelevant and in the Marche, where might was largely right, local alliances were more of a deterrent. Andrea could only hope that Giovanni had been prudent. The Marche was volatile. Indeed, in many ways it was amazing that Giovanni's peaceful tenure had lasted quite so long. Hopefully, his pessimism was unfounded.

Andrea strongly desired to join his brother, yet his concern for Portia was even more demanding. It was also plain his place was at Count Crito's side.

When Andrea raised the matter, his father-in-law's response was swift. "I'll write to Sforza. They were his soldiers who restored the fortress to your family. He'll not be pleased that this demonic offspring of the man I fought is left to roam unchecked!"

"Milan is very distant, Sir!"

"Yes, but when Sforza speaks men listen."

"Will Calixtus?"

The Count made no answer.

CHAPTER 52

Aeneas Sylvius Piccolomini

Aeneas Sylvius Piccolomini had the appearance of a man who approached his dining table with discrimination. His naturally disarming nature was one suited to diplomacy, and he was slow to take offence. Even when his face looked stern there was a feeling of underlying amusement. A man of some refinement, he was generally respected as a diplomat and had rubbed shoulders with the great for years. Some said he was ambitious, while others felt that he had merely risen to the level of his known ability. When Coluccio was conducted by Paolino to the Bishop's rooms, he knew that he was fortunate and he was grateful.

After the initial greetings, the three men sat round in an informal circle. Urbane and courteous, Piccolomini took time to put his visitor at ease by talking generally of happenings in the city – indeed, the gossip of the day – joking about the idiosyncrasies of those his guest might know. Then he addressed the question which was uppermost.

"I must congratulate you, Messer Tommaso da Roma, for penetrating the Vatican's defences! It was an astonishing achievement, Messer Carrucci!"

"Sir, praise is due to the good priest who taught me Latin and some basic Greek."

"Without a pupil, what's a teacher?" The Bishop's smile revealed his sense of humour. "Well now, down to business. Paolino has apprised me of your situation and your search for the Carrucci papers. What a dastardly business. The Carrucci were an honest and respected family but the ruling factions demanded their collusion and compliance, not honesty. That's not in the papers, of course, but it was the opinion of the time."

"But why the savagery, Sir? No one has explained that . . ."

"Fear! Fear breeds cruelty. They feared your father would lead a popular party, as did the Medici in Florence. I'm fairly certain that my theory's right."

"I see," was all Coluccio could say.

"This brutal crime happened twenty years ago," the Bishop continued, "and at that time the power struggle between the Albizzi and the Medici was uppermost in people's memory. Your father's enemies did not want a second Florence in Orvieto. That's what I suspect. Of course, it's only speculation, not fact."

"It has the ring of truth, though." Coluccio responded quietly.

"It does." The Bishop paused briefly, his head bowed. "May I call you Coluccio? Messer Carrucci seems a little formal."

"Of course, Sir," Coluccio answered, somewhat bemused by the Bishop's sympathetic stance.

"Well, Coluccio, I have perused the Carrucci papers and what I read was not unexpected. The Carrucci estate was made a partnership. The Church *was* a beneficiary, but only one of four; the other three were families. I'll not burden you with names, for the beneficiaries are now second generation. However, there is one name that you should know – not Riddo but Riddileschi – and Riddo still receives an income."

"I had a sense that that was so," Coluccio acknowledged. Strangely, he felt no emotion, just the flat, dull sense of anti climax.

"You'll have to exercise some patience, Coluccio, but I promise I will do what I can, when I can. I'm afraid the Church is to blame, not for fraud as such, but for sheer incompetence. The busy Pope of the day delegated the matter to the Curia, the Curia to a Bishop who in turn passed the matter to the lawyers and they were bought. That's it plain and simple. All those involved have now passed on, but the Church still has responsibility. Getting the Curia to accept this, of course, will not be easy. Have you anything you would like to say, Paolino?"

"There's the question of Gonzaga, Sir."

Piccolomini sighed. "Oh yes, that commission should never have gone through. I must say, though, Riddo has him on a very short rein at present. It's a pity we didn't send him off with Cardinal Scarampo, on his 'Aegean tour'!"

"I'm sorry, Sir, I don't follow." Coluccio interjected.

"Sixteen crusading galleys have left Ostia for the Aegean. Their Admiral, Cardinal Scarampo, said he needed thirty at the very least, but the Pope insisted that he sail, since he had promised they would leave in March. Don't broadcast my opinion, but I have doubts of their efficiency. I'm surprised you hadn't heard."

"I may have, Sir, but certainly not in such detail. Perhaps I dismissed it as a fiction, as such news often is."

"Indeed."

"Gonzaga troubles me. How long will Riddo keep him tethered?" Paolino pressed.

The Bishop suddenly looked tired.

"Coluccio, I think you should travel north with me. I'm leaving for Siena in a week's time."

"That will be an honour, Sir."

"A pleasure for me too, my son."

That was the signal. The meeting was over.

★

It was June and it was hot. Tiepolo and his daughter were resting in the cool centre of the del Monte villa. No sound disturbed the stillness of the early afternoon. Tiepolo was near to sleep.

"Father."

"Tiepolo shook himself. "Yes, my daughter."

"You're spending a fortune on messengers to and from Venice, and I feel that I'm the cause."

"Valeria, I've discovered that the world gets on quite well without me. In fact, my nephew and our senior clerks only need a few words now and then, and the branch in Florence is booming. They know that I'm a friend of the del Montes, and for del Monte read Medici. I can do no wrong. Business flows in and the Florentine manager is competent. The more I keep away and stop my meddling, the more it grows!"

"And you used to worry so much!"

"I know, my dear. Who's that?"

"It's Marsilio! Jacopo speaks much more softly when he comes."

After a brief wait the door opened.

"Messer Tiepolo, Valeria, I fear I've disturbed your midday rest."

"Never, Marsilio," Tiepolo said forcefully, rising to greet him.

"I've good news for you both. I met Vitale yesterday near Santa Croce. He said he hoped to see you soon."

"At last," Tiepolo exhaled. "At last," he repeated, sitting down heavily as if the news were hard to bear.

"Was he alone?" Valeria asked.

"He was accompanying a lady named Lucrezia and what I took to be her chaperone."

"Was . . ." Valeria hesitated. "Was this Lucrezia nice?"

"Striking. Her honesty shone forth." He smiled. "I have other good news too – Coluccio is on his way from Rome . . ."

"Oh, Marsilio." Spontaneously, she kissed him on the cheek.

"Heralds can be blessed, it seems." Humour danced about his eyes. "Now I'd better slip through to the garden. I assume Messer del Monte is in his usual seat."

"He is," they both returned in unison.

CHAPTER 53

'This is new Territory, Lucrezia'

Lucrezia was still hesitating, still afraid she would receive a cool reception, if not plain rejection. Vitale knew he could not force her, no one could, but he'd noticed how impressed she'd been by the young scribe, Marsilio, who clearly knew his father and his sister. So, early in the morning, he left in haste for Florence. He had conceived a plan.

★

"Where have you been?" Lucrezia raged. "I know you go out riding in the morning, but it's after midday. You shouldn't do that, Vitale. I was very worried, for Zaga's out there, no doubt stoking up his vengeance!"

"Stay calm, Lucrezia. I went to Florence."

"Florence!"

"Be patient. Just hear me out."

"Oh, very well." Her agitation was beginning to subside.

"I went to find the scribe, Marsilio, who you were greatly taken by."

"Why did you do that?"

"Just listen for a moment, *please.*"

"Did you find him?"

"Yes, easily. My description was recognised immediately. He's a son of a Dr Ficino, who attends on the Medici no less. Marsilio himself is somewhat of a prodigy, it seems. A Platonist, I was told – the kind of person that Bishop Riddo would consign to hell. Anyway, a youth named Calvacanti escorted me right to the Ficino door. He enthused endlessly about Marsilio."

"So you met Marsilio?"

"I was received most graciously."

"And what did you talk about, for you're no Platonist, Vitale!"

"Agreed. Now, Lucrezia, listen. I explained our reservations about meeting not only father and Valeria, but also the del Montes and I asked if he would come with us to smooth the way."

"That was a liberty!"

"I know, but he agreed – in fact, he seemed enthusiastic! We're to meet him in the morning."

"Tomorrow!"

Vitale nodded.

"But what am I going to wear?"

"Clothes, I hope!"

"Vitale, don't be stupid."

"Now, please Lucrezia, don't spoil it all."

"So you expect me to go!"

"I do."

Impulsively, she embraced him. "You're a clever old thing, Vitale!"

★

Lucrezia was uncharacteristically silent as they were driven into Florence, and Vitale could see that she was holding tightly to her nurse's hand. In fact, Vitale had long concluded that her nurse had been the only one to lavish love on her.

They left the cart at the Porta Romana, it being foolish to negotiate the busy streets at this time of day. Marsilio was ready when they called and, with the briefest of formalities, they set out towards Fiesole. At the city wall Vitale hired a cart for the ladies and mules for Marsilio and himself.

Lucrezia was tight-lipped, and Vitale only partially heard what Marsilio was saying as he pointed out the various sights and villas on the way to San Domenico. Once there, they headed for the hill leading to Fiesole, and when the climb reached its steepest they abandoned both cart and mules to be cared for by the driver and continued on foot, pausing frequently so that the nurse could catch her breath.

Lucrezia's usually vivacious features were drawn and tense. Marsilio approached her casually.

"You'll find the del Montes delightful company and I'm certain that Messer Tiepolo will be gracious and that Valeria will welcome you with open arms. Don't worry."

Her face relaxed.

"Thank you, Marsilio. Do they know we're coming?"

"Oh yes, we sent a message yesterday."

"Vitale didn't tell me." For a moment she almost rounded on him, yet she held herself in check. 'This is new territory, Lucrezia' she told herself, feeling much more content, until the del Monte villa came in sight. Then panic suddenly took over. Vitale gripped her hand tightly. This was what she needed. She no longer felt alone.

★

Valeria was concerned as to how her father would react, for Lucrezia had been described as striking and fiery, and her father was so reactive. Of late, though, he had mellowed, but his nature was still volatile. Valeria's own view was simple. If Vitale was happy and the family was reconciled, she would be content, providing, of course, that Lucrezia kept within the bounds of decency.

Marsilio was coming, too, thank goodness. He would bring calmness, and it augured well that her brother had seen fit to ask him. Poor Marsilio – he was so busy. How had he spared the time? She knew the answer. He would have responded without the slightest hesitation. In this respect need was his master.

194

Though his wife, Anna, had powerful reservations, Messer del Monte was not on edge. If anything, he was simply curious. At the time when he had read his son's report, he had been strangely drawn to the vivacious firebrand. He could not quite believe she was a murderous assassin, speculating that she could have missed deliberately. He had dismissed the sentimental feeling then, but now he wondered if he had been right.

He would soon know, for she was due at any time, to meet the father of the man she had hoped to kill. To any mode of thinking the situation was quite bizarre.

★

Hearing Jacopo's voice outside, they knew the visitors had arrived. Everyone was ill at ease except del Monte. He remained unnaturally calm, watching in fascination as Jacopo announced the guests. What *was* going on?

Bowing politely and exchanging formal greetings, the company was frozen in embarrassment. For her part, Valeria felt entrapped. Her instinct was to embrace her brother and Lucrezia, but in showing easy friendship to Lucrezia she feared upsetting the del Montes. After all, Lucrezia was the failed assassin of their son! Valeria was certain that her father's thoughts were similar.

The stilted atmosphere was awkward, if not explosive, and, being host, del Monte knew he must do something, otherwise young Tiepolo might well stomp out. But it was Marsilio who spoke.

"Vitale," he began quietly, "I think you should explain to us the truth about events at the del Monte fortress. What actually happened? We need to clear the air." His smile was completely disarming.

Taking Marsilio's lead, Vitale cleared his throat to ease the tension in his voice. First he described how Lucrezia had been instilled with stories of her noble father and the monsters who usurped him. Her mother had made it plain that she desired a boy. How could a useless girl avenge her father? So, in short, Lucrezia had decided to show her mother that she wasn't useless.

"It was so stupid," Lucrezia burst out, "but nurse here was my saving grace. She taught me that there are often two sides to any story and that I should behave and speak with honesty. Mother never told me anything. So, when I arrived at the little town underneath the fortress, I learned a different tale. It was father who had been the monster! The del Montes were admired. Mind you, I didn't like this, but as nurse had taught me to be honest . . . well, I couldn't do it!"

Lucrezia looked defiantly at everyone in turn. Vitale smiled. Lucrezia was herself again.

"Then I did something really stupid. Wanting my mother's approval and to be close to her, I decided to shoot the arrow but to miss deliberately. This didn't help with mother, of course. Anyway, the rest you know."

"I was right after all," del Monte chuckled. "I guessed you hadn't really tried. That was the sense somehow conveyed in my son's report."

Suddenly a dam of feeling was released. Valeria hugged Lucrezia, and Tiepolo embraced his son.

"I have no reservations, Vitale. It is enough that you are back with me." Tiepolo's voice was clearly audible above the hubbub, and Marsilio beamed.

No one noticed the bearded figure at the door, but suddenly Lucrezia saw him and stood stock-still. It was Tommaso! The picture of the snow-dusted alleyway flashed before her. This was the man who'd saved her life, but what was he doing here?

"Coluccio!" Valeria's high-pitched whoop arrested everyone's attention and in that instant Lucrezia realized the truth. Tommaso was Coluccio Carrucci! Excitedly, she whispered in Vitale's ear. He was dumb-struck.

Initially Coluccio's eyes only sought Valeria but now, with her beside him, his attention widened. My heavens, Lucrezia! He had registered the shock of hair but had not made the connection.

"Lucrezia, I'm glad to see that you've recovered," he called out, moving towards her.

"Thanks to you, Tommaso. Without you I'd be very still and cold in Todi. But, I'm sorry, I should be calling you Coluccio."

"When I shave my beard, you'll find it easier!"

"Sir, we are both grateful, eternally grateful." Vitale stretched out his hand with vigour and Coluccio grasped it. "We looked everywhere for you in Todi."

"I'm afraid I disappeared to Rome."

"Did you hear anything of Zaga there?"

"Yes. Riddo got him a commission with the Vicar General . . ."

"What!" Vitale exclaimed. "Zaga in command of soldiers! That's madness. I know him all too well."

"Has he a weakness?" Coluccio asked

"Well, he's afraid of pain," Vitale volunteered.

"That doesn't seem credible."

"It's true, but he also loves inflicting it! – Ah, here's Marsilio – You, Marsilio, are the unsung hero of the hour, and we owe you thanks for smoothing the way for us."

"Unsung heroes have no reputation to live up to," Marsilio quipped.

"I'm lost," Coluccio interjected. "What have you been up to, Marsilio?"

Briefly Vitale described the meeting, its initial awkwardness, Marsilio's intervention, and Lucrezia's explanation.

"I was so occupied by the memories of Todi I completely forgot about the incident at the fortress, but I'm very pleased that it's resolved. I sent a letter to Andrea's brother, alerting him to Zaga's new legitimacy, but I'll not trouble Messer del Monte with this just yet."

"Do I hear my name being called?" del Monte asked loudly.

"You do, Sir, and I must say your advice about disguise worked perfectly. Only one man, Andrea's friend Paolino, saw through it. Incidentally, he's now the Bishop of Siena's secretary."

"Piccolomini! Excellent, an excellent contact." Del Monte rose stiffly to his feet. "Now, my friends, it's well past noon and you've no need to return to Florence today. My son's villa stands empty, so there's plenty of accommodation. My wife's friend, Maddalena, has a host of maids and cooks that we can borrow. No polite dithering! Yes or no?" Del Monte only waited briefly. "Good, that's settled. Valeria will show you to your rooms. But first enjoy the garden."

★

That evening was a defining occasion in the lives of the Tiepolo family. Father and son were reconciled, as were brother and sister, and Lucrezia was a favourite with them all.

She rose at dawn next day and had already explored the town before Vitale emerged.

"You were unescorted!" he protested.

"Vitale, I've always roamed alone. Anyway, in the early morning all the nasties are lying in their beds!"

What could Vitale do but laugh? He then told her that he planned to stay a week or so in Fiesole, assuming that Andrea del Monte's villa was still vacant.

"Father and I have much business to discuss, in particular about the new branch he's set up in Florence. Meanwhile you, my dear, can get to know Valeria."

"She's lovely and so open, yet wonderfully efficient. It was very obvious last night that she was in control, and Madonna Anna seemed quite content."

"I think she's been 'helping' for some time. You had a long talk with Marsilio, too."

"Yes. I told him about Riddo and his conviction that all Platonists deserve hell's fire. I asked him if he was ready for the heat!"

"Lucrezia, that's a bit . . ."

"He laughed heartily, Vitale. He's so natural, so unassuming."

"Do I have a rival?"

"Vitale! Don't be silly! Marsilio's not like that. He's a friend, a confidant, and a teacher. My dear Vitale, Marsilio loves God and God reciprocates! I feel we have little understanding of the world he knows. But, he's such good company and, when I questioned him, he explained the nature of 'the One' and how we need to distinguish between the permanent and impermanent. It was all quite clear last night, but this morning it's pretty hazy, I must confess."

"Well I'm hazier, but, Lucrezia, you've only just met the man! How can you be sure of what you say?"

"Vitale dear, you don't need time to know such things."

"I do! There's one thing, though, I'm sure of, and that is my good fortune to have met a lady named Lucrezia."

"You're a sweet old thing, Vitale," she quipped lightly, kissing him on the cheek, but she was close to tears.

"I'm hungry! When are we going to eat?"

"Now – Coluccio didn't shave his beard off,' she added casually.

"He said that he was going to show it off to Cosimo, but that was for Valeria's ears. Coluccio's still in danger, Lucrezia, but don't alarm Valeria. Last night was wonderful, but there are still many uncertainties."

CHAPTER 54

'A Terrible Thing has happened'

The Doge's wayward son, Jacopo, had been foolish yet again and rashly so for, by corresponding with the Turkish Sultan in the hope of escaping his Cretan exile, he had intrigued with a foreign power and a belligerent one at that. This news, received in June, outraged the Council, who ordered his return. Now all Venice awaited his appearance and his trial. Naturally this distressed the ageing Doge, especially as he knew that vengeful elements in the Council would press for execution. Andrea's hoped-for stay in Florence could not be contemplated. The heir to a powerful branch of the Dandolo family needed to be circumspect.

Other news arrived – chilling news – that the Sultan's forces were massing and moving inexorably towards Belgrade. Frightening rumours circulated, while the Muslim forces grew in number by the day – one hundred and fifty thousand men, some said – but Andrea knew that only they who faced the storm could estimate the total with any accuracy. Europe had to waken up, but Andrea doubted if it would. Too often the enemy was hammering at the gates before men strapped their armour on. He thought of Janos Hunyadi, the Hungarian Captain General. So much depended on that resourceful and impressive warrior.

★

Andrea had written to his brother, exhorting him to cement local alliances and ensure his bodyguard was loyal and, above all, vigilant of strangers in the town. Perhaps it was pretentious to write in such a manner, but the family bonds were strong and, after all, he was the elder brother. The dangers were real, for with Riddo and Gonzaga armed by legitimacy anything could happen. It was doubtful if any major crime could be pinned on either. True, Gonzaga had wounded Lucrezia and Bernardo, but that was hardly news in Italy, which was suffering, in many places, from a culture of impunity.

Paolino's letters told all this in code. As the Bishop of Siena's secretary, he had to show some caution, yet he wrote regularly.

So far Gonzaga was quiescent and Paolino was quite certain that Riddo had him in his power. What was his secret, Andrea wondered, for Gonzaga was behaving like a model officer, busily training his recruits for the crusade? All this paled, of course, before the drum of destiny now sounding near Belgrade. What would be the outcome? No one knew, though there was little doubt that many prayed with fierce intensity.

★

As a proud father, Dr Ficino knew that Marsilio was very special. His capacity for study, his amazingly retentive memory, his level of understanding, were all impressive. True, he grew melancholic from time to time and like most he had his off-days, yet somehow these moods seemed mere ripples on the surface of his deeper self.

Ficino had always done his best to free Marsilio from time-consuming daily needs, but his eldest son was one of six. All his children would expect the family patronage. Indeed, one son had already received his share. Being a doctor, Ficino was all too aware of life's uncertainties, and if he were taken the family would be in Marsilio's charge, and for that he would need an income. Once his book was finished, Marsilio must needs journey to Bologna to qualify in medicine at its prestigious university. There was no option.

Although he never showed it openly, Ficino was frustrated by his noble patient, Cosimo. Why was he holding back, for he could so easily support Marsilio? Of course, the great Medici's mind was stretched by myriad concerns of state and business, while his firm intentions, though not yet spoken, were left for quiet contemplation at some convenient time. This, though, never seemed to come. Perhaps if Marsilio went to Bologna, Cosimo might focus on the problem, or was this all illusion, for men like Cosimo made decisions not by sudden whim but by well-considered thought.

★

At Cosimo's command, Bernardo was back at Coluccio's side, careful as ever and using street urchins as scouts – an idea he adopted after listening to Coluccio's adventures in the south. Cosimo's indulgence in providing this protection for one so junior in his secretariat puzzled Coluccio. There were numerous explanations but none satisfied, that is, until Piccolomini revealed the presence of a popular party of which his father at that time had been the focus. The Medici, also at the centre of a popular party, had won their struggle, whereas the Carrucci party failed.

Having known his father well, it seemed reasonable to conclude that Cosimo was moved to protect the son of an old and trusted friend who had shared similar ideals.

★

The hoped-for marriage had been unresolved too long and needed to be settled, yet Valeria had said nothing. Tiepolo had not even hinted, and Vitale was too busy enjoying the delights of Florence with Lucrezia, but all were very well aware that it needed resolution. There was also the unconfirmed assumption that he and Valeria would live at the del Monte villa, for, as it was, Valeria was practically running the household. Madonna Anna saw Valeria as the daughter that she never had and gladly let her take control. All that was missing was an income, for Coluccio knew his employment at the secretariat did not pay enough.

Having been absent since the previous autumn, Coluccio did not know that Lorenzo Tiepolo had established a branch of his merchant house in Florence. In the flurry of events nothing had been said and, although most guessed, they all refrained from speaking until Tiepolo stated his intentions openly.

As a woman, Valeria was reluctant to push herself. And knowing male independence to be sensitive, especially in their role as the provider, she kept silent. Coluccio had to act, but Coluccio's income didn't match his station. Something had to happen, for awkwardness was hours away.

At the time that Valeria was trying to subdue her restlessness, Coluccio was walking with Marsilio and describing his adventures in the south. Suddenly he stopped and abruptly changed the subject.

"Something has to happen!"

"What, Coluccio?"

"Marriage! Valeria and I can't live for ever in this limbo. We're flesh and blood. The pressures are too much!"

Marsilio quietly resumed his walk.

"Well?" Coluccio prompted.

"Have you spoken?"

"To Valeria?"

"No, to Messer Tiepolo."

"But I have nothing . . ."

"No matter. You should speak. He admires you greatly."

"What can I say, Marsilio? – 'Sir, I want to marry your daughter, but I cannot keep her. Will you?'"

Marsilio made no response and both men continued until they reached the riverbank downstream from the Ponte Vecchio. For a moment they watched the lazy flow of the Arno, shallow from the summer heat.

"Just ask him, Coluccio," Marsilio said quietly. "Don't try to work it out."

This time it was Coluccio who made no answer. So there was another moment of silence, but as always with Marsilio and Coluccio there was no awkwardness.

"The river's not exactly smelling sweet, Marsilio," Coluccio said laconically.

"No. Let's walk across the bridge to Santo Spirito, and then we can return."

★

Coluccio, shadowed by Bernardo, climbed the hill to Fiesole with mixed feelings. Valeria would be waiting, but so would Messer Tiepolo. Marsilio was, as usual, right. He had to speak. There was no alternative.

The last stretch was always the worst, he mused, as he trudged up the incline from the town's piazza, but as he approached the familiar villa he sensed that something was amiss. There was no visible reason for this except that the wall gate was wide open, which was most unusual, for Jacopo was always fussy about such details. But when they passed through into the

201

garden and saw Jacopo half running, half hobbling towards them, Coluccio was certain of his premonition.

"Master Coluccio, Bernardo – a terrible thing has happened. Master Giovanni and his wife were attacked a week ago not far from the fortress. Master Giovanni was badly injured and his wife died instantly. Master Andrea is already on the way to the Marche."

"My God!" was all Coluccio could say.

All thoughts of speaking to Messer Tiepolo were suddenly forgotten.

CHAPTER 55

'Ah, the Good Bishop'

"Now I know what you experienced, mother," Portia said wearily. They were sitting sewing by the first-floor windows overlooking the Molo and the entrance to the Grand Canal. "The worry, like the waiting, is oppressive. The Marche's such an awful place!"

"Yes, my dear. I know it all too well," the Countess nodded. "But in Andrea's case I can't imagine too much trouble. He has safe passage from the Vatican, and Father picked his guard – the best soldiers in Venice, he told me."

"But he's not a warrior. He's not like father!"

"Thank heavens!" the Countess replied, "For he'll not go charging into danger, the way your father did."

"Father looks so strained."

"Indeed. He's always at the Palace, trying to keep Francesco co-operative and battling with that flint-faced Council. It's not easy, for Francesco's son is due at any time. And, of course, they're all on edge about Belgrade. The Muslims are besieging the fortress there and the news is most alarming." She shook her head and sighed. "We live in troubled times, my dear. Life's very short and full of trials."

★

Yesterday had been difficult, Piccolomini thought wearily, as he made his way towards the Papal chambers, and his gout was nagging. Yes, Calixtus had been particularly irritable, insisting on his will, regardless of the obstacles – the same obstinacy that had sent sixteen galleys off to fight the Turks. The plain fact was that Cardinal Scarampo's expedition was a farce, for sixteen galleys could do little other than avoid trouble. The Pope and his arrogant nephews could blame no one but themselves.

He had some sympathy for the Pope, though, for the wealthy were so niggardly, while the Dukes and Princes wasted revenue in petty squabbles with their neighbours. 'Vanity of vanities, all is vanity,' he muttered to himself.

The guard came stiffly to attention as he passed through to the Papal presence. What would be the Pontiff's mood today, he wondered.

"Ah, the Bishop of Siena, my strong right arm," the Pope called out.

Promising, Aeneas thought and, even better, he was on his own – not a nephew in sight.

"Sforza is blustering about this latest outrage in the Marche. Not only that, but both Venice and Florence have asked questions. Our Holy Office condemns all crime, and this latest brutal incident, in a territory under our protection, offends us greatly. But, Aeneas, who are the del Montes and why such widespread interest?"

"The del Montes have powerful friends, Holiness," Piccolomini answered respectfully.

"And who is this Gonzaga that Sforza rails against?"

"He's a member of the Vicar General's staff."

"The way Sforza writes you might believe he was the special agent of the dark Satanic Lord himself! Who put him on the staff?"

"With respect, you, Your Holiness. It was the Bishop Riddo's wish."

"Ah, the good Bishop. Aeneas, deal with all this if you will. We really must preserve our strength to focus on our plans to thwart the Turkish threat. How are our appeals progressing?"

"Little is happening at the moment, Holiness, for all intent is frozen, waiting on the outcome from Belgrade."

★

After his audience with the Pope, Piccolomini made his way to the main corridor and at once saw the Bishop Riddo striding purposefully towards him. He held up his hand in greeting and both men stopped, each bowing graciously to the other.

"Ubaldo, all I hear from the Holy Father is 'the good Bishop' and all know, of course, he means the Bishop Riddo!"

Riddo beamed. "You're being much too kind, for I'm sure His holiness calls other bishops good, including you, Aeneas. Your labour is quite awesome!"

"No more than yours, my friend. Why only this morning, when we were discussing that awful incident in the Marche, your name came up and immediately His Holiness reacted with real feeling: 'Ah, the good Bishop'. I tell you noble Sir, you can do no wrong!"

"How was my name connected with that appalling tragedy?" Riddo asked with innocent surprise, but Aeneas caught the caution in his eyes.

"Only indirectly, Ubaldo, only indirectly. That young man Gonzaga, whom I believe you know, was mentioned as harbouring a possible grudge. Apparently his father was killed when the fortress was restored to the del Montes."

"This is all news to me, Aeneas," Riddo lied convincingly.

"I'm sure. In any case, Gonzaga has been behaving like a model officer by all accounts, though he's certainly being watched. He's quite playful in the evenings, I believe." Piccolomini shot Riddo a knowing look.

"Young men are full of spirit, Aeneas!" Riddo answered evenly. Gonzaga was becoming an embarrassment, he thought with irritation.

"Yes, indeed, we must make allowances. I know *my* youth was not exactly pious!" Aeneas chuckled, and Riddo was quick to join the intimate tone. "Gonzaga, of course, is the Vicar General's man," Piccolomini continued,

"But we're told the young blood listens to you — so a fatherly word from time to time would help to keep him out of trouble, I'm sure. It is a pity that he missed Scarampo's expedition." Aeneas shrugged his shoulders. "Then perhaps he doesn't like the sea!"

Riddo's laugh masked his unease. What did the wily Piccolomini know? Damn, he thought bitterly. He didn't need this sort of problem. Gonzaga was a definite liability, but he knew he dared not slight him. Those eyes of his burned too intensely. What kind of demon had he nurtured?

"Ubaldo, I've kept you back quite long enough. My friend, your persuasive oratory is much appreciated, but we need more galleys to appear at Ostia!"

"I feel that no one's listening at the moment. All eyes are focused on Belgrade."

"Sir, I fear for Europe and all those German towns I know for, if Belgrade goes . . . Ah, but let's not think of it."

★

The warm July evening was perfect for a stroll, so Coluccio and Valeria set out, with Bernardo keeping a discreet distance. Walking up the hill from the villa, then down the other side towards the old Gothic wall, Valeria felt supremely happy. Coluccio had spoken to her father, who in turn had offered him a partnership in his merchant house in Florence. Everything was falling into place. Her uncertainties were over, and but for the tragedy in the Marche she would already have been married.

This evening, though, she sensed that Coluccio was preoccupied and strangely uneasy in himself.

"Is there something on your mind, my dear?" she asked gently.

"I'm sorry, Valeria. You won't like this, but I feel I should be with Andrea."

She stiffened. She had not even dreamt of such a prospect.

"What could you do, Coluccio?" she reacted. "Andrea will have all the help he needs. The Countess wrote to Madonna Anna saying that his body-guard had been especially selected."

"I know, but I owe him some support, even if it's only the presence of a friend. Remember, Valeria, without Andrea's generosity there'd be no Coluccio Carrucci today!"

"Have you spoken to Messer del Monte?"

"No. If I speak to him, I go! Tomorrow, though, I'm due to meet Marsilio, when doubtless he will quickly tell me in the plainest terms if my plans are ill advised or simply sentimental. Your father, of course, may not be pleased, since I've only just started at his office."

"He'll understand. He'll see it as a noble gesture."

"And you, my dear?"

"You must do what you think best, Coluccio, though my heart is most reluctant. It's the waiting. There's been so much of it!"

He turned and gently touched her cheek. "I know," he said. The sound was no more than a whisper.

As they walked back to the higher ground, to mask the worry racing through her mind, Valeria said easily, "It'll soon be August." Then stopping in her tracks, she said, "Listen. Are those bells I'm hearing?"

"I do believe they are, and all the way from Florence. It's very still. Ah, there's San Dominico's."

Then suddenly the church bells in Fiesole joined in sounding, loud and clear.

"What is this celebration?" Valeria was puzzled.

They stood quite still as the pulsing notes washed round them.

"My sweet Valeria, I dare to hope that Belgrade has been saved!"

CHAPTER 56

'O Pietà Grande'

They ate supper in almost total silence. The Countess did not try to lead the conversation, for her husband looked so tired. Indeed, she was concerned, and seeing him collapse onto a couch afterwards confirmed that there was something wrong.

"You look exhausted, Crito," she ventured quietly.

"And I feel it, Caterina. Since the Doge's son returned to exile it's not been easy at the Palace. Francesco seems to have lost his fight. He signs papers and does all that is required in a dull mechanical way. In the past I've always managed to elicit a response, but no longer. He's lost his spark."

"He may recover, Crito."

"I doubt it." He shook his head. "That last meeting with Jacopo – well, I think I felt the pain myself. There he was, sitting in his chair, trying to be Doge, while all the time suffering as a father. And when Jacopo was led away he collapsed completely, sobbing. *O pietà grande!* he called out, for he knew full well that he would never see his son again. To watch the once indomitable Francesco Foscari in such a state was heart-rending. So things have been very difficult, Caterina."

"You should share these troubles with me, Crito."

"I'm sorry. It's my old habit. I didn't want to burden you."

"Crito dear, it's not a burden, and do you know you look better already, having got that off your chest."

"You're right. – Caterina, you know what I would love to do?"

"What my dear?"

"Spend the winter in Fiesole."

"Fiesole! That wine you drank this evening must be strong!"

"I'm serious. Business will be near to dormant in the winter, and the clerks can cope with all the routine work. What do you think?"

"I'd love to go, but what about the Doge?"

"For the last two weeks he hasn't seemed to notice I was there. Anyway, we don't need to make our minds up yet."

"It's a wonderful idea, but winter travel could be cold."

"Caterina, if you can survive the Venetian walkways in the winter, you can survive anything!"

★

Marsilio asked Coluccio only one question: what practical need he hoped to serve by going to the Fortress.

Coluccio's reply was equally direct. "To try and discover who is guilty of the crime, for no one seems to know and the assassins are still at large."

"It will be a shot in the dark, Coluccio."

"I agree, but at least I will have tried."

"Does Messer del Monte know?"

"Not yet."

"He'll be grateful," Marsilio concluded. There was no advice to go or not to go and Coluccio did not press him. This was not untypical of Marsilio. Coluccio looked to him as a kind of mirror in which thoughts were seen in high relief. At least he always found his thinking to be clearer after meeting with his friend.

★

Parading the pretence that he'd been given a lift, Carlo used a farm cart, driven by Bernardo's nephew, for his journey to Assisi. The idea was Messer del Monte's, to speed Coluccio's travel. Being much too easy to recognise and thus a danger to 'Tommaso's' anonymity, Bernardo was barred from journeying with him.

Once at Assisi, Coluccio was on his own. His abilities were soon recognised, and he quickly gained employment. It was familiar territory, and his Tommaso persona fitted like a well-used garment.

The strangers' refectory at the monastery was full of pilgrims. They came and went, but after four evenings he soon picked out the regulars and as usual it was the old and often toothless men who liked to talk. And how they could talk! It was endless, yet with a guiding question here and there they were fruitful channels of information.

"Do you get much trouble here with all these visiting pilgrims?" he asked a bent and greying lay monk.

"No, brother. St Francis guards us."

"Marco!" another man cut in irritably. "Have you forgotten already?"

"What, Masseo?" Marco looked up blankly.

"The four men who smashed the tables and the chairs when they were told to leave . . ."

"Did they?" Coluccio prompted.

"Oh yes. When the guards came they left quickly. They were mad with wine."

"And they weren't held?"

"We don't like bloodshed here – not near the blessed shrine."

"So they left and that was that?"

Both men nodded, but another who had been listening soon spoke up.

"They went down the hill and wrecked the first tavern that they came to!"

"So you *do* have a little trouble now and then," Coluccio responded casually. "Let's have some more wine." His suggestion found unanimous approval. And there Coluccio let the matter drop, for he had no wish to sound too curious.

The following evening he walked down the hill to the tavern that had been mentioned. He could see that most of the furniture was new so he guessed he had chosen rightly. For three nights he took wine there and the landlord grew gracious towards this new and valuable customer. Yet Coluccio held back. It was not until his sixth visit that he complimented the landlord on his furniture. This was the key, for then the floodgates opened.

"They wrecked everything." The man's face flushed with anger. "And the guards all kept well clear! I went into debt to replace all this," he barked, pointing to the furniture. "And they were soldiers with the Papal livery, what's more! Acting like animals, and just a stone's throw from the holy shrine! And, of course, nothing's been done about it!"

"Papal livery, you say," Coluccio prompted.

"Yes. They were bound for Rome. At least, that's what I heard them shouting. One had a big heavy face. They called him Bull."

"And the others?" Coluccio questioned casually.

"There was one with a narrow beak-like face. They called him Hawk."

"Do you get much of this?"

"No, my friend, most are respectful of the shrine. Here, let me fill that beaker up. This one's on me!"

For an hour Coluccio chatted amiably with the landlord, but there was a limit to his intake, so as graciously as he could he took his leave. He returned the following evening and the next. To have disappeared too soon after learning about the Papal soldiers might have seemed suspicious. Messer del Monte had been emphatic that such detailed care was vital.

When Coluccio eventually told the landlord he was heading for Fabriano, the wine-induced directions became a jumble of confusion. Nonetheless, Coluccio thanked him profusely. The general direction was clear enough, of course: head east, join the Via Flaminia going north, then turn east again.

Coluccio was very well aware that the four undisciplined soldiers were not necessarily the assassins he was after. The only way he could find some semblance of proof was to discover evidence of them passing through the area between the Fortress and Assisi. 'Not an easy task, Coluccio,' he muttered to himself, for the road through the mountains was tortuous. Occasional rides on farm carts helped to ease his weariness but did not speed the journey, as they moved at little more than walking pace. The drivers, though, were quick to tell him places he could rest at night and places that he should shun completely. Such local information was vital. At last, he arrived at Fabriano, a thriving town noted for its paper making. But no one had seen or heard of the four soldiers, and once more he was reminded that his search was based on an assumption. Yet, it was a fair projection and, in any case, it was his only lead. So he continued on towards Ancona, but veering south towards the fortress.

One by one he checked the townships until at last he found the evidence in the lowly tavern of a village that was perched precariously on an outcrop.

"Yes, they were here all right," the stout landlady confirmed in response to Coluccio's question. "And the big one, the bully, was called Bull. But they weren't soldiers."

"Are you sure?" Coluccio pressed.

"Well, they were dressed like peasants."

"What was their footwear like?"

The landlady nodded pensively before answering. "You're a shrewd one, old man. You're right, the peasant stopped at the knee!"

He smiled. The good lady had a colourful way of putting things. He was gratified that his disguise was still working. Indeed it continually surprised him just how natural 'Tommaso' had become.

"So, where are you heading?"

"The Alberti del Monte Fortress." Coluccio saw little point in being evasive. "Is it far from here?"

"With a mule, you'd do it in a day."

"And walking?"

"A day and a morning. So why are you interested in those four bundles of joy?"

Oh dear, Coluccio thought, he had asked his questions too directly. No matter, the days of pretence were almost over.

"They caused a lot of trouble in Assisi."

"And you know about the murder of del Monte's wife and you also know that four men were involved?"

Coluccio nodded.

"Where the killing happened is only half a day from here," the woman continued. "I'll get one of my idle sons to take you in the morning. He'll introduce you to Maria, who runs a little place like this."

Coluccio thanked her warmly.

"It's nothing," she protested. "The del Montes are well liked round here. The old widow next door hasn't paid any rent for years and she's not the only one. *You* don't work with your hands," she added unexpectedly.

"I work as a scribe and secretary," he answered, but had she spotted his disguise?

CHAPTER 57

'The Moment will come'

Piccolomini's secretary was privy to much of his master's thinking, and in turn Paolino shared his secrets with the Bishop. So, when a letter arrived from Coluccio giving details of his findings in the Marche, Paolino immediately showed it to his master.

"Your friend has been busy," Piccolomini commented pensively, "but *we* will have to be as sly as serpents. We cannot trust the Vicar General, for he'll be much too anxious to avoid a scandal and 'Bull and partners' could well be spirited away. Then we'll never know who paid them. There's little doubt in my mind that they're hired assassins. Who handed them the ducats, that's the question."

"One word from you, Sir, and half of Rome would know."

"So it's up to you, my friend, to probe."

"But how, Sir?"

"Paolino, violent men have violent pastimes – bear-baiting, dogfights and the like. There are also the taverns."

Paolino shuddered visibly.

"Take two trusted bodyguards but don't divulge a thing. Let's hope our quarry has returned to Rome and still remains here. But it won't be easy. As the ancients would have said, we need the gods to smile."

★

It was now September, yet the heat and smells of Florence were still oppressive. Marsilio decided to escape to Fiesole, seeing some of his father's patients on the way and ending with the elder del Monte. He was close to San Marco when he heard his name being called.

"Cristoforo," he responded warmly to the familiar voice.

"Where are you heading, Marsilio?"

"Fiesole, eventually."

"May I join you? I'm going in the same direction."

"A pleasure."

"How's the book – or should I say books?"

"Almost completed, Cristoforo. It's being copied and bound. There'll be one for you, of course."

"Marsilio, Cosimo's the priority. Give him the first copy."

"Could you do that for me, Cristoforo?"

"I could, but you should present your own work."

"It feels so . . . well . . . self-serving."

"Come Marsilio, *you* give it to him. Grasp the opportunity, my friend. – Have you heard from Coluccio?" Landino asked.

"Yes. He's at the Fortress with Andrea and his brother."

"How is Giovanni?"

"Almost recovered. Andrea is planning to return to Florence in a month or so and doubtless Coluccio will be joining him and his Venetian guard."

"Is Giovanni coming too?"

"No. He won't leave the Marche. He often remarked that 'a fortress without its lord is an invitation to the greedy.' His wife's death and the attempt on his own life will have steeled him to protect his Lordship."

"Of course, that's understandable."

They were almost at the wall and Landino stopped. "This is where I leave you. Now, don't forget, Marsilio. Give your book to Cosimo yourself!"

★

Riddo was brimming with confidence, as praise was heaped on him from all directions. A Red Hat was surely his. Even so, he felt a measure of unease as influential men such as Piccolomini and Orsini, while showing due courtesy, kept their distance. There was a hint of condescension in their manner which made him furious, an anger that he dared not show, though it burned inside beneath the polished gloss of the crusading Bishop.

His hatred of the 'weasel Pucci' had grown obsessive, for he was certain that his former secretary had destroyed his reputation in many influential quarters. Now, he could not use Gonzaga as his arm of punishment, since the vicious fool was being watched. His frustration fuelled agitation. In truth, Riddo's tortuous thoughts coursed continuously beneath his hard-set self-belief, and every now and then his fraudulence broke through, especially in dreams; dreams which held a mocking presence that had always haunted him, even as a boy – and they were growing frequent. Yet these were soon forgotten in the busy schedule of the day. In his mind he was the popular Bishop, always in demand and soon to be a Cardinal, after which, perhaps, the Papal Chair!

★

Paolino was a mild-mannered churchman, not given to missions or burning causes, and although he avoided the excesses of the worldly clergy he did not sit in judgement. But after visiting two bear-baiting 'entertainments' he was sickened.

Sandwiched between two burly bodyguards, he was secure, but his third attendance was too much and he left abruptly, protesting loudly: "I can't stand any more of this. Someone else will have to find Gonzaga and as for dog-fights – no!" He had said too much, of course – his aversion had overruled all prudence.

"If you're looking for Gonzaga, Father, why didn't you tell us?" one of his bodyguards exclaimed. "He's always at the tavern where the soldiers go, though I'd keep well clear of him!"

"So would I!" the other bodyguard agreed. "He flares up without the slightest reason. He's full of spite."

"Does he have cronies?"

"One or two."

"Do you know their names?"

"We could find out. But that tavern's not for you, Father. In fact, we were puzzled by our visits to the bear pit."

"Well, now you know – but keep your questions casual."

"You mean don't make Gonzaga and his drinking friends suspicious?" the self-appointed leader of the two returned.

"Yes. It's important; in fact, it's vital."

"Don't worry, Father."

"When people tell me not to worry, that's exactly what I do! So don't be over-confident."

"What happens to men like Gonzaga? Do they go to hell?"

"It could be warm."

The two men laughed. "But what does happen?" the leading bodyguard pressed.

"Men who hate so much also hate themselves. You can't hate everyone and love yourself."

"I'm sorry Father, but it doesn't seem like that – they love themselves – they're like peacocks!"

"They seem to love themselves, but that self is a surface fraud, for all the while they're being devoured inside."

"Deep down, they think they're real bastards! Is that it?"

"You could put it that way."

Paolino had drawn directly on a conversation he had had with Coluccio: the Platonic concept that the tyrant is a tyrant to himself as well.

"We'll be very careful, Father."

★

When Paolino confessed his outburst at the bear pit, Piccolomini waved the matter aside. "Bear baiting is not a spectacle for a man of your refinement. I should have known better than to have suggested it. Yet, it's worked out well – that is, assuming we can trust your bodyguards."

"They seem reliable, but, Sir, supposing we discover Gonzaga and 'Bull' are drinking friends, what can we do?"

"Leave that to me, my friend. I will choose my moment well. For it's not only Gonzaga I want to trap, it's the pompous fraud as well!"

"Riddo! Oh, be careful, Sir. Riddo is growing very friendly with young Cardinal Roderigo Borgia, the Pope's nephew."

"Roderigo would throw Riddo to the lions tomorrow if it proved expedient! My good friend, it may be months, indeed it could be years, but the moment *will* come."

CHAPTER 58

Giovanni

Giovanni Alberti del Monte did not share his brother's philosophic leanings. His regular and sincere devotions at the altar were quite enough for him and served as an example to his people. He had been overwhelmed by their outpourings of sympathy, and when fit enough he mingled in the town and toured the local villages, strengthening further the bond between the people and their lord. So Andrea was not surprised when Giovanni declined to leave the Marche. It was a pity, Andrea thought, for here was the perfect opportunity to journey safely, but Giovanni simply loved to be at home and never favoured travel. There was doubtless another reason for his reluctance to visit Fiesole. Andrea well understood that happy couples such as Portia and himself and Coluccio and Valeria could be too painful and too poignant a reminder of his loss.

Giovanni's agent was devoted to him, his staff were loyal and his absence would be understood, yet he refused to contemplate the journey.

★

Andrea and Coluccio left in the first week of October. Coluccio had remained 'Tommaso' throughout, playing the scribe and secretary and avoiding the public eye, but on nearing Florence he would become Coluccio once more.

Both brothers were grateful for his efforts. The conclusive evidence that the assassins were not from the town was especially welcome to Giovanni. His initial and understandable reaction was to despatch an angry accusation to the Vicar General, but both Andrea and Coluccio vigorously counselled patience. Without real evidence in the hands of someone influential the Vicar General could well condemn the accusation as malicious slander, aimed to undermine the credibility of his men.

Giovanni found it difficult to believe that such a devious world existed. Even so, and even though outraged, he did obey. Coluccio was concerned, for Giovanni's guileless nature could easily fall prey to the unscrupulous. Yet, strangely, this had not happened. He was surrounded by wholly loyal men whose common sense and honesty were beyond debate. Was it that the good Lord was careful of the good, whereas the devious, thinking they knew all, were left to their devices?

Coluccio himself felt joyful. He had done what he had felt to be his duty and had succeeded to a large degree. Now he was returning to Fiesole, where Valeria would be waiting. There was nothing to stop their marriage. All that needed to be settled was the date.

It was already agreed that they would make their home at the del Monte villa. "Coluccio, you are a son to both of us," del Monte had said emphatically. "And Valeria is our daughter." Certainly the rambling villa was large enough for them to have their own apartments. The future also seemed secure, for Messer del Monte hinted strongly that the villa would eventually be theirs, saying that both Andrea and Giovanni had more than ample. Idyllic though it seemed, Coluccio knew that life was ever changing and uncertain, but it was just as foolish to dwell on this as it was a foolishness to take God's grace for granted.

★

Andrea, too, was joyful, knowing that Portia and the Count and Countess would soon be on their way to Florence. It was the first separation they had experienced since their marriage, and he greatly missed his wife – her wit, her charm and the natural intimacy that marriage brought. Why he had felt indifferent in the early days was now a mystery, for he adored her. Like her mother, she was the 'Flower of Venice' – to whom all heads were forced to turn.

They were nearing Florence when suddenly they came upon a scene of total devastation. Across a wide swathe of land, stretching from east to west, buildings were flattened, vines, olive groves and trees uprooted and cast about, as if by some giant hand. What had happened? In shock, they asked the first man that they met.

"A whirlwind," he replied, gesticulating wildly.

"When?" Andrea pressed.

"Late August. It was God's warning to us to mend our ways, for we are sinful folk."

"Have you lost your home, my friend?" Andrea asked evenly.

"Everything, just everything. I was in the fields and when I came home there was nothing. I searched for my wife for weeks, but nothing! Nothing!" The man seemed close to madness.

"Where do you sleep?" Andrea asked as he dismounted.

"That barn," replied the man, pointing to a near-roofless shack some way away. "The monastery's full."

Del Monte looked at the man passively for what seemed ages, then handed him a pouch. "Here, take this and find somewhere to stay, for the winter's on its way – and mind you eat hot food."

"Thank you, Sir, thank you. God bless you."

"Remember – hot food!"

"Yes, Sir. What is your name, Sir?"

"Del Monte."

This question was the first glimmer of normality. Andrea watched closely. Beneath this unkempt mess a young man's heart was beating.

"Remember, find somewhere warm to stay and keep those ducats out of sight!"

"Yes, Sir." By now the man's voice was much more steady.

Nodding briskly, Andrea mounted, and they resumed their journey.

The man had received much more perhaps than a year's earnings, Coluccio reflected as they rode, and he could not help recalling similar generosity which had transformed his life in Rome all those years ago. He looked across at Andrea riding stony-faced beside him.

"Our educated minds would say a whirlwind is but a whirlwind, yet are there other factors? Was that unfortunate man correct? Was all this death and devastation some form of punishment? The thought repels me, but I cannot rule it out. The truth is, Andrea, I don't know."

"Neither do I, Coluccio, but it sets the mind enquiring."

CHAPTER 59

'The Die is Cast'

Marsilio felt empty, and his mule's lazy walk seemed an eloquent reflection. Gone was the briskness of his outward journey to Carreggi, but the rows of vines, dormant for the winter months, were just the same.

Cosimo had been gracious and complimentary but made it very clear he wanted more. A work on Plato, based on the commentaries of others, even Boethius and Cicero, was not enough. The great man had been direct. Only a straight translation from the Greek would be acceptable; platonic knowledge had to come direct from Plato.

The challenge, if he took it up, was daunting, for Greek of a standard to translate could not be mastered overnight. However, there was no hint of a commission, and in these circumstances Bologna and a medical career was his only option. Though Marsilio entertained no criticism of Cosimo, he felt deeply disappointed. Reflecting on this outcome of their meeting, Marsilio braced himself. Wise men like Socrates were untroubled by the wheel of fortune, and when misfortune struck they used it as a tutor for the good, allowing reason to find blessings in the darkest hour. "So, Marsilio," he muttered to himself, "you have a little way to go."

The morning's message was simply 'study medicine and master Greek'. That was the way ahead and with that clean decision – no creature of a mood – the dullness vanished on the instant and the seeming weight about his shoulders dropped away. In Caesar's famous words 'the die was cast'.

What would his friend Landino think, he wondered. Probably the same as Cosimo, for it was so obvious. Cristoforo's prompting was simply to make sure the work was hurried forward and completed. He could almost hear him speak: 'Well, Marsilio, you've got that off your chest. Now you can get down to work.'

Marsilio chuckled. Sensing his master's change of mood, his mule flicked its tail and quickened pace. On a sudden impulse Marsilio headed for San Dominico and Fiesole. Andrea and Coluccio had been back for weeks and Messer del Monte's routine check was overdue, but the last month had been so busy with the final stages of his presentation. Thankfully that was over and new horizons had opened up.

*

An icy wind began to stir as Marsilio approached San Dominico, and it gusted strongly as he started up the hill to Fiesole. The del Monte villa's comfortable warmth was a welcome goal and indeed predictable, for Messer del Monte liked the heat and always had a generous fire in winter.

Only Andrea, his father and Coluccio were there when Marsilio entered, the ladies being at Andrea's villa directing preparations for the imminent arrival of Portia and her parents. The weather had been particularly bad, and they were much delayed.

"Where have you been hiding Marsilio?" Andrea asked with mock accusation. "Coluccio and I called a number of times, to no avail."

Marsilio smiled as if concealing a secret. "I was overwhelmed by a sea of paper," he confessed and then described the busyness of the past weeks and his visit to Careggi.

"You're amazingly sanguine, Marsilio," Coluccio observed.

"Well, I think Messer Cosimo *is* right. I've always had an uneasy feeling, but Cristoforo and you, Sir," nodding to Andrea's father, "both encouraged me."

"It was necessary labour which you needed to complete. Now your real work can begin and, Marsilio, the Count is due, even today perhaps. His master was Gemisthos Plethon, so you must take the opportunity to learn from him while he is here!"

"The trouble is, Sir, I'll be going to Bologna."

"Oh Cosimo, why are you so tardy!" the elder del Monte muttered. "You're being too careful." His last words were inaudible.

"You're being tested Marsilio," he said directly. "But as far as I'm concerned you've already passed. Just do as my good friend says and learn Greek."

Andrea smiled with amusement. His father's relationship with the first man of the state had always been 'domestic'!

Jacopo entered with hot drinks and the conversation turned to the happenings on the Marche. An hour slipped by as though it were merely minutes. Then, seizing his opportunity, Coluccio told them about the whirlwind's devastation.

"Are such happenings the whim of chance or are they the design of fate? How would you answer, Marsilio?"

Marsilio appealed to Andrea's father, who vigorously shook his head. "Your question, my friend."

Marsilio breathed deeply. "Well, if all things happen by chance we labour in vain who hope to control completely and if all things come by fate those who strive to avoid the unavoidable surely must be more entrapped."

"Yes, Marsilio, that's the analysis, but what's the answer?"

Marsilio's face shone with energy. He loved such questions. "Those who willingly unite with the divine will find stern fate and unreasonable chance are tempered by the good."

"And if we don't unite, we're tempting fate? Is that it? Marsilio, this isn't easy." Coluccio shook his head.

"It's easy when we accept the divine will!" Marsilio's smile was mischievous.

"But don't we have the perfect example in Marsilio's visit to Careggi?" Andrea interrupted. "In similar circumstances most would have railed against the fates, but you, Marsilio, have accepted the situation and so the self-same situation is your friend."

"My conversion wasn't instant, Andrea; I needed to apply a little reason!"

"Yes, Marsilio, but that's the lesson for us all!"

"I still balk at the storm and its devastation," Coluccio protested.

The elder del Monte cleared his throat, and in deference all turned towards him.

"The storm is the work of nature, but nature is under the divine witness, and what that witness knows is only known when we are at one with it."

Marsilio clapped his hands. "Sir, you were not idle when you studied at the feet of Plethon!"

There was a draught of icy air as the door opened and Messer Tiepolo entered.

"Welcome, Lorenzo," the elder del Monte greeted. "You've just missed a most excellent conversation. But you look absolutely frozen, my good friend!"

"I am! But listen, I have good news. As I started up the hill I saw a troop of horse approaching San Dominico. I'm certain it's Count Crito and his party. No one rides as tall as he does!"

CHAPTER 60

A Cardinal at Last

Calixtus's zeal for a crusade was only rivalled by the shameless enrichment of his nephews. Don Pedro Luis de Borgia had been made Gonfalonier of the Church and Prefect of Rome. All the castles in the neighbourhood of the city were committed to his hand, and he was greedy still.

Friends of the Borgia, hearing of the easy wealth, flocked to Rome and all the while Cardinal Roderigo Borgia was busy gathering preferments. But opposition was growing.

Paolino wondered at the behaviour of his master, for Piccolomini was openly conniving with Roderigo. The Bishop was playing a long game, he guessed, with a Cardinal's hat as the principal objective. Paolino did not blame him for, as he saw it, Aeneas was only striving for a post that would exercise his talents. He needed a large role. Yet the jealousies of Rome were unforgiving. Nothing was certain, but as December progressed Paolino noticed an unusual agitation in his master's habits. Aeneas didn't breathe a word, but Paolino sensed that something was afoot.

On December 18th, the Pope elevated five Cardinals, with Piccolomini amongst their number.

"At last!" Aeneas said with feeling to his secretary. "No Cardinals ever entered the college with greater difficulty than we," he confided.

Paolino knew exactly what he meant, for the College, solid in their opposition to Calixtus and his nephews, resisted as long as they could. To Paolino's great surprise Riddo was not amongst the five. Why had the Pope's great ally and the bosom friend of Roderigo been forgotten? He was mystified and, when at last he had a private moment with his master, he posed the question.

"Eminence, why was Riddo overlooked?"

"A good question, Paolino, for I'm just as mystified as you are. I've noticed one strange thing, though. He's forever showered with public plaudits, but rarely do I hear a word of private praise. I have the feeling no one quite believes him."

"The Pope does."

"He finds him useful, Paolino!"

"Then what about Roderigo? Riddo and he have been inseparable."

"Perhaps the College simply would not entertain another Borgia creature."

"With respect, Eminence, you had Borgia backing."

"Yes, but I also had the German Emperor's support. As you know, I've written to convey my thanks."

"Riddo won't like it."

"That *is* the understatement of the year! He'll be seething, yet unable to display it!"

"The Pope's 'good Bishop' and for ever being lauded from the Papal chair – it's still a puzzle."

★

Riddo was indeed seething and the well of hatred in his being, sealed briefly by his rising fame, was once more explosive. Calixtus had been spineless. He had forced the College to accept the five, but when it came to Bishop Riddo, his faithful, tireless advocate of crusade, he'd failed to press the case. It was plain betrayal and Roderigo's smooth assurance that a Cardinalate would be his next year might well mean never. Yet there was just a possibility that the Borgia Cardinal was sincere. It was maddening, for once more he would have to bow and scrape to those he viewed as his inferiors. Damn the Cardinals Capranica and Orsini. Their gracious smiles meant nothing, and pomposity was their sole achievement. They had blocked his elevation; he was sure of it. Damn them, damn them all. He wanted to strike out, to wound, to maim, to punish.

No! He would once more wrap himself in pious dignity. He would be a man of God, indifferent to the lure of worldly office. This was the role that he would play and, true to his determined nature, he lent to it a measure of belief. Even so, the pressured subterranean pool of hatred was moving with a slow deliberation to the surface.

★

Gonzaga knew he was being watched, and he also knew his drinking friends were under scrutiny, but 'Bull' and 'Hawk" were too thick-headed to be cautious. So he threatened them with imprisonment in the darkest dungeons if their drunken blabbering grew explicit.

He himself was not, of course, the model of discretion, but he had a sharp-edged cunning and he listened to the Bishop. In fact, Riddo deftly used Gonzaga's superstitious nature to control him. There was another factor, subtle in its nature, for Gonzaga found himself attracted to the Bishop as if by some magnetic power.

★

Two days after the elevation of Piccolomini, Riddo was proceeding towards the Vatican when the influential cleric Estouteville beckoned him.

"My friend," the Frenchman bowed. "I greatly admire your sermons and your tireless work in promoting a meaningful crusade."

Riddo was a mirror of humility as he relished the unexpected praise.

"We were disappointed, Ubaldo, indeed aggrieved, that you were not amongst those elevated. But then," he added, putting his arm round Riddo's shoulders, "no prophet is accepted in his own country." Estouteville smiled warmly, and Riddo responded in fluent French, which greatly pleased him.

As they went their separate ways Riddo wondered what the wily Frenchman wanted. Why the sudden warmth? Yet he was flattered, despite his doubts. He had dealt with the French before, of course, but the question still remained. What was Estouteville up to? It was not in Riddo's nature to trust a simple compliment.

CHAPTER 61

'May I honour you'

Lucrezia's enthusiasm never seemed to wane. She was fascinated by Venice. "She's dragged me to every island and pushed me through the door of every church. Her curiosity is insatiable," Vitale told his friends. "But she's such good company. What's more, her nurse, at first so self-effacing, has shed her village black and become a most attractive lady!"

Whether gondolier or banker, Lucrezia talked to all. Some thought her completely wild, but even so they liked her. Her honesty, with its lack of airs and graces, made her popular with both servants and nobility. Indeed, her sense of freedom was infectious. Those who labelled her uncouth held their tongue in public, since it was a common sight to see her walking arm in arm with Ginevra Loredan and, more surprisingly, with the Countess Dandolo and Portia. Her friends were clearly from the highest level of society.

The Countess was particularly fond of Lucrezia. "You remind me of my much loved sister. Like you, she talked to all without distinction. She drove poor father mad, but he adored her!"

When Lucrezia learned that the Dandolos were bound for Florence, she immediately wished to join them. Persuading Vitale was easy as he had a similar desire, though at first he played at being reluctant for the fun of it.

"You should be with your father and your sister for Natale. Christ's birthday festival is for the family," she stated forcefully.

"Our merchant house needs full attention, Lucrezia," he countered.

"Vitale, your grey-haired manager knows just as much as you. He's been running things for months!"

Vitale laughed, while reflecting that at one time such blunt honesty would have put him in a towering rage.

"Well, are we going?" she pressed.

"Of course, my dear."

Impulsively she embraced him.

★

Messer Tiepolo was right. He had seen Count Crito on his horse, but the party was much bigger than he'd imagined, and when they arrived outside the villa he was overjoyed to see Vitale and Lucrezia amongst their number.

The ladies had returned from Andrea's villa and the del Montes' large reception room was full, though far from crowded. All were busily talking, and tears of joy were not infrequent as the party slowly settled. Andrea and Portia shone with the happiness of being united and were in conversation with Coluccio and Valeria. The Count and Countess were sitting with their old friends, Carlo and Anna del Monte, and laughing heartily as Crito described the 'comforts' of their storm-plagued journey. Messer Tiepolo was in animated conversation with his son, and Lucrezia, with her nurse beside her, soon sought out Marsilio.

As often happens in such gatherings, there was a sudden unexpected silence, and Messer del Monte seized the moment to invite everyone to stay for supper. "And, Lucrezia," he called out, "there are two letters for you."

"For me!"

"Yes. They've been here some time. Here they are."

Coluccio handed her the letters and Lucrezia broke the seals. As she read, the buzz of conversation started up again, but it slowly faded as the shock on Lucrezia's face was seen. She had everyone's attention, and when she spoke her words were simple and direct.

"The first letter is unsigned and promises my certain death. The second is from my mother and is full of bitterness. 'You're not a Riario,' she writes. 'Your real father was the traitor nicknamed 'Brain'. I deeply regret the affair and I regret your birth!'"

"What an awful thing to say," Valeria whispered.

The Count was instantly on his feet. He caught Lucrezia's hand impulsively and kissed it. "May I honour you, my dear, for your father saved my life and was murdered for his pains. Riario never tolerated a defector."

"That's true," Andrea's father confirmed.

Suddenly Lucrezia crumpled, sobbing, but she recovered quickly when Vitale put his arm about her.

"Nurse is *my* mother," she said defiantly. "But who would want to kill me?"

"Gonzaga," Vitale spat. "Who else? Damn him, for now we'll have to be perpetually on our guard – just like you, Coluccio!"

"Take the battle to the enemy," Coluccio exclaimed. "Send *him* a letter – unsigned, of course – and tell him that the secret arm of Venice has him on their list!"

"That can be arranged," the Count said casually.

"But will that stop him?" the elder Tiepolo questioned.

"He's a blusterer," Vitale countered, full of scorn. "We rode together when I was fooled by that fanatic Riddo. I know Gonzaga well."

"From what I hear he has the temper of a madman."

"Yes, Father, but he's in Rome and we're in Fiesole. Anyway, what idiot would loiter with intent on such an evening? He'd be an icicle within the hour!"

"Well spoken, Vitale," Andrea's father spoke with a note of finality. "Gonzaga's trying to scare you and, in my opinion, that's his only option. According to Piccolomini's secretary, Gonzaga and his cronies can't even sneeze without it being noted. Now, after such a journey I'm sure you'll all want to wash and change before we eat."

★

To his own surprise, Lucrezia's uncertain parentage did not trouble Lorenzo Tiepolo. "Just two years ago I would have raved and ranted through the Grand Piazza", he confided to del Monte. "But now, Carlo, I accept God's will with equanimity, for Lucrezia has transformed Vitale, and Coluccio, of course, is special."

"Yes, Coluccio is impressive," del Monte agreed. "He's very close to Marsilio, you know, and so is Lucrezia. She tells me his presence is so stilling. I had a long talk with her last night at supper. Vitale's been very lucky, Lorenzo."

"Indeed, the gods have smiled upon the Tiepolo, but this death threat makes me most uneasy."

"Yes." Carlo del Monte drew the word out pensively. "It's Riddo who worries me. He's full of rage, Coluccio says, and he should know! Riddo's dangerous, Lorenzo, and if he fails to land a Red Hat, will he keep the lid on his frustration?"

Tiepolo made no response, and for some time both men sat silently gazing at the flickering fire. Except for themselves, the large reception room, so full of life the night before, was empty.

"Where's everyone?" Tiepolo enquired.

"The ladies are at the Count's hired villa and the men have gone to Florence. Crito thought he'd take advantage of the sudden mildness in the weather and pay Cosimo a visit."

"With no appointment!"

"He doesn't need one. Lorenzo," he suddenly changed the subject, "Valeria should be married!"

"Carlo, you're almost as direct as Lucrezia!"

Del Monte chuckled. "I haven't reached that summit!"

"Easter, my friend. It will be Easter for a double ceremony. I've given my consent to both Coluccio and Vitale."

225

CHAPTER 62

Crisis

In late February news arrived from Venice that Doge Foscari's son had died in Crete. The news devastated his father in his declining years, and he was now refusing to co-operate or even attend meetings. As a result the government was drifting in a state of semi-paralysis. Count Crito's presence was required and, although disappointed, duty bade him leave Fiesole. Caterina joined her husband, even though she knew that she would miss the April weddings. She hated prolonged separation from the Count; a lifetime of waiting for her warrior husband to return had left its mark.

Count Crito's private view, shared with his wife, did not flatter the Venetian elders, especially the leading branch of the Loredan family. They had been unbending and vindictive, for young Foscari had not admitted, even under torture, to the crime of which he was accused. No one had actually proved that he had killed Ermolao Dona, a member of the powerful *Ten* The only evidence was a denunciation placed in the *Lion's Mouth*; the rest was circumstantial.

Crito had expressed his feelings strongly at the time, but no one listened to the 'Greek', a convenient name they gave him when they wanted to ignore him.

The Elders had created their own problem. Crito felt like washing his hands of the whole affair, but need demanded action, for Venice dared not drift too long.

Venice was divided, and the division was largely personal. Even so-called rational discussion seemed overlaid with volatile emotion. The Doge had reigned for thirty years and had been a Doge indeed! What were they to do?

Many hoped Foscari would recover sufficiently to resume some of his more important duties, but the situation continued unresolved. Twice in the past he had asked permission to resign and twice he was refused. Now *he* refused to contemplate his abdication unless the full constitutional requirements were met.

Francesco was being stubborn, but Crito was not surprised. He was even sympathetic, for to his mind the *Ten* had behaved abominably and there was little doubt Foscari blamed them for his son's untimely death. The Doge was eighty-four. Such wrongs bit deep.

The Count was once more a regular visitor to the Ducal Palace and once more back in favour. For him, at least, the Doge emerged from isolation.

"Where have you been, Count? I thought you had abandoned me." Foscari managed a weary smile.

Crito told the old man all about his visit to Fiesole, and for a time

Foscari brightened. But Crito knew he dared not raise the subject of the all-consuming crisis lest the Doge dismiss him as a creature of the *Ten*. Franceso would have to bring the subject up himself, though Crito doubted that he would. He was at war with the *Ten* and all those who had hounded his son. It was his last battle, and while he had the strength he would not contemplate surrender. All Crito could do was wait and hope that in some way he could help to bring about an honourable solution.

★

The ring ceremony uniting Coluccio and Valeria and also Vitale and Lucrezia took place in the first week of April at Fiesole. It was a modest and subdued event as, in a sense, only one family, the Tiepolo, was represented, for Coluccio was an orphan without inheritance and Lucrezia had uncertain parentage. She, too, had been denied her due.

In the hope of reconciling her mother a message had been sent to Todi inviting her to attend the wedding, but the messenger was brusquely turned away. "I have no daughter," she said bluntly. Lucrezia had done all she could.

The del Monte family, of course, stood for both Coluccio and Lucrezia. Indeed the ceremony, conducted in the presence of a notary, was a quiet, intimate affair. In keeping with the general trend, however, a blessing was conducted in the church.

After a few days Vitale and Lucrezia set out for Venice by way of Bologna, at Lucrezia's prompting. "We can call on Marsilio and receive his blessing," she announced.

"But he's not a priest!" Vitale protested.

"Yes, I know, dear, but he's a priest inside."

Vitale chuckled. With Lucrezia life would be full of surprises.

Mindful of the death-threat to Lucrezia, and using Bernardo as a recruiting officer, Vitale hired a bodyguard, but the nurse did not travel with them. Her role as chaperone had ended, and it was decided she would travel later with Valeria's father. He was staying longer, until he felt his son-in-law was well established at the Tiepolo branch in Florence.

At the insistence of Messer Tiepolo and with his funds, Coluccio hired two further bodyguards. So with Bernardo as their leader, he and Valeria were well protected. As Messer Tiepolo pointed out, none of the threats had gone away. He was particularly worried by Coluccio's plan to bring his old nurse north from Orvieto so that he could care for her in person. In fact, Tiepolo made Coluccio swear that he would hire a troop of horse for such a mission.

Valeria was blissful. Coluccio was so gentle and considerate. Yet he was also firm, and when he had decided on a course of action he kept to it. She dreaded his planned journey to Orvieto, but she kept that to herself. Anyway, it was two months off.

Right from the beginning she sensed that Coluccio wasn't much enamoured of the merchant business, but she did not sense aversion. He did his duty and was conscientious, yet despite his clear detachment he was surprisingly successful, securing business where other more dynamic merchants failed. To Valeria the answer was quite simple. People liked him and he liked meeting people.

★

It was now July. Crito's hopes of a reasonable solution were fading. The *Ten* were being insensitive in their dealings with the Doge – so much so that they sent a Loredan to treat with him. Francesco dug his heels in, and Crito felt, with some anger, that the *Ten* were being tyrannical. A tragic close to a thirty-year reign seemed unavoidable.

CHAPTER 63

Guilt in Venice

Andrea and Portia were now back in Venice, and the Dandolo household was buzzing with the news that Portia was with child. But such news was always tinged with anxiety, and shafts of worry struck Andrea just like any other man who loved his wife.

Because of his father's friendship with Foscari, Andrea's sympathy was naturally with the Doge. "Francesco was always larger than life," his father often told him. So Andrea had a feeling for the current drama, even though he was brought up a Florentine. The *Ten* were hard-faced men whose humourless rigidity appalled him. The Doge, of course, was being awkward, very awkward, but after all the man *was* eighty-four! To force an abdication after such a reign would leave a lasting blemish on the page of history.

Andrea was also exercised by the disquieting news from Buda. Following the victory at Belgrade, the sudden death of Janos Hunyadi left the country virtually leaderless and subject to Ladislas V, the young unstable king. Two opposing parties, one being the Hunyadi, vied for power. Janos Hunyadi's son, Laszlo, executed the leader of the enemy faction but was captured by them one year later, together with his brother, Matthias. Laszlo was executed by the king and his brother held. The Hunyadi were popular and a rebellion erupted, led by Janos Hunyadi's widow, but news had just arrived that Ladislas had died. Now young Matthias was the favourite for St Stephen's crown. Still, little was certain in such a volatile situation. Matthias was only seventeen, maybe eighteen, but Andrea had heard that he was both intelligent and cultivated. If chosen, how would he rule? Only time would tell, and all Andrea or anyone could do was wait and see, and that was what he said to those who asked him his opinion. He, of course, had been to Buda and many saw him as an expert, an illusion he vigorously denied.

Venice, of course, could not be indifferent should a new and powerful sovereign grow ambitious in the north, for Hungary and Venice had clashed before.

★

Foscari refused to resign without the Grand Council's order and the proud *Ten* refused to compromise. October had arrived and, exasperated, the *Ten* decided to force the issue by giving the Doge an ultimatum. Either he resign within the week or be forcibly removed and his property confiscated. Still Francesco did not bend, and a week later, with Venetian precision, his ring was removed and ceremoniously broken. The old man simply did not have the strength to resist. But the next morning, when given the opportunity to leave by the side door, he barked defiantly, 'No!' He would descend by the stairs by which he had entered.

One week later the new Doge, Pasquale Malipiero, was attending All Saints Day Mass when the news broke that Francesco Foscari was dead. At once guilt descended like an all-pervading cloud enveloping those assembled. Seven days later the new Doge walked behind Foscari's bier, dressed as a simple senator, while the full ducal splendour bedecked the coffin. The symbolism was obvious, but the old Doge's widow was bitter. "It was a little late," she said, "to make amends."

That evening the mood at the Dandolo palace was sombre. Something large and grand had gone. Crito had been with the Doge on his last day at the Ducal Palace, and the old man had expressed the hope that they could tour the monasteries together, but that never happened. The Count was also angry and, indeed, concerned. "The *Ten* are much too powerful," he growled to Andrea. "The seeds of future trouble have been planted!"

★

Andrea's father, although adopted by the Venetian state, eventually settled in Fiesole, where he found the mode of life less formal. That was years ago, of course, but he was fond of Venice and regretted that his leg and general health would not allow him to return and wander on the so familiar walkways. His son had in some ways inherited a not dissimilar dual allegiance. He, too, loved Florence and was also heir to a Venetian fortune. The problem was that cities were possessive, and divided loyalties were not encouraged. Even so, the del Monte family had always managed to escape state censure. The reason was quite simple – Carlo del Monte's friendship with both Cosimo and Doge Foscari. In a practical sense, of course, both leaders had a back door contact which they both completely trusted. What the future held, though, was uncertain.

Andrea and Portia had many friends and acquaintances but their closest friends, where no one stood too much on ceremony, were Febo and Ginevra Loredan and Vitale and Lucrezia Tiepolo. They met once a week for supper and had dubbed themselves 'The Friends of Marsilio', for that was their common bond.

The Tiepolos had called on Marsilio in Bologna, and since then Lucrezia had corresponded regularly, while reporting in her witty way on 'The Friends' and their conversations. Marsilio replied to all her letters with matching humour, but there were also his deeper comments and the sheer lack of any criticism. Indeed, this was something which 'The Friends' had adopted as a rule. They would be honest and straight but at the same time avoid all criticism. It was not an easy rule at first, but it prevailed and its surprising bonus was a sense of freedom.

★

The year was drawing to a close. Coluccio and Valeria were now well settled in their wing of the rambling del Monte villa. Valeria still assisted Madonna Anna, so in that respect there was little change. Coluccio journeyed to Orvieto as he had intended, returning with his old nurse without incident. For Valeria, the relief was considerable.

The nurse had rooms close by with help constantly at hand. Indeed, the warmth and comfort of her new abode, so lacking in the past, had subdued her prickly temper and her guarded sense of isolation. Coluccio called in frequently, and once a week she was the guest of the del Montes.

Messer Tiepolo was still resident at the villa. "I've not been so contented for years," he confided to his friend, del Monte. "But I must return to Venice, otherwise the city fathers will begin to fret."

Del Monte smiled but made no comment. It was obvious to all that Messer Tiepolo and Lucrezia's nurse were fond of one another.

CHAPTER 64

Birth

Fourteen fifty-seven was not a good year for Bishop Riddo, as all the sugar-coated promises had come to nothing. He was still a mere Bishop and it was his firm belief that his 'friend' Roderigo Borgia had made no effort to promote his cause. Calixtus, of course, was too busy feathering the family Borgia's nest. Yet Roderigo still maintained the mock sincerity, dangling the carrot of hope as if he, Ubaldo Riddo, were a donkey!

Riddo's scepticism made him reckless, and finally he asked directly: 'When?'

"The Feast of the Ascension, my good friend," Roderigo purred, but Riddo wasn't fooled. Borgia had fobbed him off as usual. His uncle's 'good Bishop' and all such papal praise was only meant to keep him on a string.

Riddo's remaining hope was Cardinal Estouteville, for the Frenchman continued to be friendly. Why, he could not fathom, for the Cardinal's wealth was more than considerable and he certainly did not need Ubaldo Riddo. The more Riddo pondered the more convinced he grew that he was right. Estouteville was his man, and when preaching he made frequent mention of the Cardinal and was lavish in his praise. This was not lost on Estouteville, and when the Cardinal was in Rome Riddo was regularly included on his guest list. The coming year might well hold promise after all.

Even with this new hope Riddo's frustration was at boiling point and his drinking bouts with Gonzaga were becoming frequent. More alarming were his nightmares which were now a regular occurrence, their pattern often ending, when he woke, with harsh and mocking laughter echoing in his head. This experience worried Riddo more than he was willing to admit.

★

Calixtus was eighty, and speculation and manoeuvring regarding his successor were barely kept within the limits of decorum. Paolino was not surprised that his master, Cardinal Piccolomini, was being mentioned as a favourite. He was head and shoulders above most members of the College. Aeneas, of course, remained completely silent, though Paolino had no doubt that he was busy fostering alliances, the essential foundation for election. His drawback was his lack of wealth. The Piccolomini were a noble family, but their fortunes had diminished.

On the other hand, his chief rival, Estouteville, was immensely rich and had innumerable benefices with which he could reward his backers if elected. The battle, when engaged, promised to be keen and bitter, and on the face of it Paolino feared that much too much was stacked against his master. But

Aeneas was a brilliant diplomat and kept at least two moves ahead of most, and he was, of course, Italian. A French pope conjured memories of the schism.

Meantime Calixtus was still vigorous, even reckless, in the advancement of his family. He could be sitting on St Peter's chair for years.

Paolino kept his friends, Andrea and Coluccio, well informed. He was amused, he wrote, to watch Ubaldo Riddo ease himself towards the French. A clever move, no doubt, but only if it proved to be the winning side.

★

It was February 1458 and Messer Tiepolo was still at Fiesole, but was planning to return to Venice when the weather was more settled. Maria, Lucrezia's nurse, was his certain companion and he had asked Bernardo to arrange a bodyguard. Even so, Lorenzo Tiepolo felt a strange reluctance to leave for his native city and his home, as he had enjoyed more peace and real contentment in Fiesole than he had ever known.

"You can always come back!" del Monte said laconically, "And don't forget to bring Maria," he added with a knowing look. "You should marry her!"

"I'd never get away with it."

"Not in Venice, but in Fiesole not a soul would mind."

"Vitale might not like it overmuch."

"Get Lucrezia on your side! You're sixty. You need a hearth companion!"

Tiepolo laughed. "You're right, you're absolutely right. We walk abroad together daily in the town, and most appear to treat us as if we were already man and wife, but my flouting of convention might reflect upon Valeria."

"Valeria!" del Monte exclaimed. "You're talking nonsense, Lorenzo!"

"You *must* have given lessons to Lucrezia!"

There was another peal of laughter. "Lorenzo, Valeria is like Piero Medici's wife, Lucrezia Tornabuoni. Everyone adores Valeria, and nothing you might do will make a jot of difference!"

"Well, that's plain enough," Tiepolo returned, still close to laughter. "Carlo, to change the subject, there seems to be a lot of activity just down the hill towards San Dominico."

"Yes, that's to be Giovanni de' Medici's villa."

"Piero's younger brother?"

"Yes. He's a likeable man, but he eats too much."

With characteristic suddenness they fell silent. He would return to Florence, Tiepolo decided, and the Tiepolo branch could afford some occupation. Coluccio was doing well. People liked him, but he was no merchant. Still, he was generating a reasonable income. The attempt upon his life, which had happened some time ago, had not been repeated. Also, no threat to Lucrezia had manifested, but there was always the lingering doubt.

Gonzaga and his friends were being closely watched. Not only that, Count Crito had alerted the secret arm of Venice. They also had a brief to watch the movements of Ubaldo Riddo. Yet, in such a world, nothing could be certain, and any slackening of vigilance would be unwise, to say the least.

★

As Easter approached, the mood in Rome was far from happy. The Pope's indulgence of his nephews and their Catalan friends was storing up a deep resentment. Cardinal Orsini had been virtually driven from the city, and Cardinal Capranica had fared little better, their fault being the voicing of their opposition. Paolino's letters were circumspect. They had to be, though reading between the lines the message was quite plain. Rome was weary of the Borgia.

The news from Naples was also depressing. The reigning King Alfonso was ambitious and vainglorious. By attacking Genoa he had hoped for easy gain, but as the French had hurried to his victims' rescue he found that he had bitten off much more than he could chew.

Coluccio and Messer del Monte discussed such topics regularly, but the news from Buda was confused, though it seemed certain that young Matthias Hunyadi was still being held in Prague by the party of King Ladislas.

With his mother leading an uprising in Hungary, Matthias, who was a similar age to Ladislas, was in a precarious position. Anything could happen.

The news, of course, was not all dire. Sforza's Milan, Medici Florence and Venice were all stable. Peace had brought renewed prosperity. The Serene Republic, as Venice called herself, was indeed serene. She had made a treaty with the Turkish Sultan, Mehmet II, and trade now seemed secure, but Messer del Monte was sceptical.

"Venice has always played with compromise to protect her trade," he grumbled to Coluccio. "But compromise is not a word Mehmet knows. He's only resting for a while before he surges on. His Muslim heart will never be content!"

Coluccio listened respectfully, for Messer del Monte knew about the East, but Coluccio did not think the Turks would march for ever. Their obsessive drive would turn upon itself in time.

★

In late May joyous news arrived from Venice. Portia had given birth to a baby boy. Both parents and grandparents were overjoyed and mother and son were in the best of health. That evening the del Montes celebrated.

"What will they call him, I wonder," Anna asked her husband.

"Crito!"

"They might even call him Carlo!"

"My dear, he'll be loaded with names!"

234

CHAPTER 65

Speculation

It was July, and a sudden embassy to Milan had absented Coluccio from the Tiepolo office. Cosimo wanted someone who was outside the circle of his close advisers and someone who had already met Francesco Sforza.

"It's Calixtus," Cosimo confided. "He's being particularly irresponsible, but the Duke will explain the situation. I've told him he can tell you all."

Coluccio was flattered. It was quite a mission and an honour to be asked, but why, he wondered.

After a hot but uneventful journey, Coluccio was welcomed at the impressive Sforza fortress by the Duke himself. "I am honoured to receive the son of Giovanni Carrucci," he announced, warmly welcoming his young visitor, and with no lengthy preliminaries he was quick to get down to business.

"As you probably know," he began easily, "King Alfonso of Naples died on the 27th June, and the Neapolitan nobles have declared his illegitimate son Ferrante as their new sovereign. The Pope has other ideas. He wants the Kingdom of Naples, or at least a part of it, as a fief for his nephew Pedro."

"But, your Grace, this would plunge Italy into conflict, and France and Spain would not stand idle. As it is, they're only waiting for an excuse."

"Yes, that's the nightmare. Well, Messer Coluccio, you can tell my good friend Cosimo that I've refused to help the Pope in his designs. That will put the great Medici's mind at rest!

"The Pope's ambitions seem so childish!" Coluccio's voice mirrored his puzzlement.

"My friend, when it comes to his nephews, our Holy Father is quite blind. Now, Coluccio, the first time we met you were in the company of Andrea del Monte, your destination Buda." Clearly the first formality was over.

"Yes, Sir, I was Andrea's secretary."

"It may interest you to hear that I've received good news from Buda. Matthias, the second son of Hunyadi, the hero of Belgrade, is soon to wear St Stephen's crown."

"That *is* good news. I met Janos Hunyadi when I was there. He was most impressive, and if his son reflects his qualities in any way Hungary can look forward to a stable reign. What happened to Ladislas?"

"He died some weeks ago, from natural causes, it seems." The Duke paused briefly. "Tell no one of our conversation about the Pope, except perhaps my old friend Carlo del Monte. He can keep a secret."

That evening the Duke was engaged in official business, but he saw to it that Coluccio was hosted by two of his trusted aides. In the morning he left early, his brief mission completed, but he was still puzzled by the secrecy

★

After reporting to Cosimo, Coluccio returned to Fiesole, but Valeria was out with Madonna Anna when he arrived. So he sought out Messer del Monte, who was, as usual, in the garden, and told him all Francesco Sforza said.

"The Borgia are a menace," del Monte growled. "Imagine the old fool thinking he could get away with it!"

"But why were Messer Cosimo and the Duke so secretive?"

"The Church – allegiances can be confused, and when the Holy Father speaks even reasonable men can lose their common sense. In any case, the Medici don't want to prejudice their privileges in Rome. Open knowledge of collusion between Florence and Milan might ignite the irascible Calixtus."

"It's all so convoluted!"

"Yes, Coluccio, but it's also very simple! Have you seen Valeria yet?"

"No, she's out visiting with Madonna Anna."

"Oh yes, I'd forgotten. Did you bring her anything from Milan?"

"Yes, I remembered!"

"Good. Such things mean much to the ladies."

What was all that about? Coluccio wondered. It was most unlike Andrea's father to mention such domestic matters.

"Have you heard anything about Marsilio?" Coluccio asked.

"Yes. Dr Ficino called yesterday. He said his son had found a tutor to help him with his Greek."

"So he's taking Messer Cosimo's words to heart!"

"Very much so, according to the Doctor. Ah, I can hear the ladies. Off you go, Coluccio."

Coluccio obeyed without question. Clearly something was going on.

Something was indeed afoot, for immediately Madonna Anna saw him she waved and disappeared. Coluccio embraced his wife affectionately.

"It's good to be back," he murmured.

"Was it a successful mission?"

"Yes, dear, but I'm pledged to secrecy, at least at present. I brought you a little gift from Milan," he added, handing her the parcel. She opened it eagerly.

"Oh Coluccio, what a lovely shawl. Now *I* have a present for you!"

"Do I close my eyes?"

"If you like. I'll whisper in your ear."

"A little Valeria," he exclaimed, embracing her again.

"Or maybe a little Coluccio!"

"You kept this very secret, dear."

"I didn't know for sure until Dr Ficino called yesterday."

"What a wonderful homecoming!" Coluccio exclaimed.

★

Coluccio had only been back two weeks when momentous news arrived from Rome. Pope Calixtus had succumbed to fever on August 6th, and already the Orsini were plundering the houses of the hated Catalans. Don Pedro just managed to escape by way of the Tiber.

The old Pope was buried with scant respect, a mere four priests following his remains to their resting place.

"The world has changed," Messer del Monte breathed after he finished reading Paolino's note.

"Yes, Sir," Coluccio echoed. It was evening and they were still outside. The air was balmy. "My journey to Milan might as well never have happened!" he added, turning to the man he had grown to view as a father.

"No need for secrecy now! In truth, God's will is the only secret!"

For some time they sat in companionable silence.

"Who will it be, I wonder?" Coluccio eventually mused.

"The new Pope?"

"Yes."

"Landino was here yesterday and he feels that Estouteville has the patronage and wealth to sweep all before him."

"Do you agree, Sir?"

"I agree about his wealth, but he's French, Coluccio."

"That shouldn't matter."

"It shouldn't, but it does. Can we trust the French to keep the papacy in Rome? An irrational fear perhaps, but it's there, even if it's only faint. The schism left a scar and its mark remains. *I* can remember when we had *three* Popes!"

"Well, if it's not Estouteville, there are many more contenders – Latino, Orsini, Piero Barbo, the nephew of Eugenius IV, Capranica, Calandrini, Prospero Colonna."

"You haven't mentioned Piccolomini."

"He's only just been made a Cardinal."

"Yes, but he has great skills. Cardinals may be self-seeking, but generally they admire ability."

"Well, I hope you're right, Sir, for I rather like Aeneas, as Paolino calls him."

"You should pray that he's elected, for he's your best chance, judging by all you've told me . . ."

"You mean in restoring the Carrucci estates?" Coluccio shook his head vigorously. "I doubt if that will ever happen. It would upset too many people."

"Maybe, maybe. Come, I can hear the ladies. It must be close to supper time."

237

CHAPTER 66

Election

Bishop Riddo felt like a merchant who had seen his long awaited ship heave into sight, for Estouteville was almost certain to be Pope. His wealth and magnificence had gathered a considerable following, including men of substance like Bessarion. Nothing could stop the Frenchman, and nothing could stop his faithful advocate, Ubaldo Riddo, from being a Cardinal. It was simply a matter of time. His former employer, Piccolomini, was casting about in desperation for support, but he was wasting his time. Even Calandrini could do better, Riddo thought disdainfully. In any case, Piccolomini was a pauper.

Unlike Riddo, Paolino was uncertain. It was either Estouteville or an Italian, and that Italian could be Calandrini or some other unexpected name. His master was by no means the only candidate, but all knew of his unusual ability and few could match his diplomatic skills. The conclave in the Vatican Palace was due to begin on the 10th and his master had predicted that all eighteen Cardinals, who were in Rome, would attend. Once they were assembled, the world would have to wait.

★

The confidence of Estouteville's supporters was palpable and was attracting waverers to their camp. On the first scrutiny Aeneas and Calandrini had each received five votes but Estouteville could count on six. However, Aeneas knew the first scrutiny was of little consequence, other than as a means of opening private discussions. Each Cardinal was allowed one servant and had his own cubicle containing a bed hung with silk curtains and marked with his coat of arms. The windows of the hall had been blocked up and three rows of guards ringed the hall. To say the least, security was strict.

Piccolomini had heard from one of his backers that Estouteville was dismissing him as poor and gouty and had scornfully condemned his heathenish poetry. Estouteville was even saying that 'Piccolomini will take the Papacy to his beloved Germany'. What rubbish! The man was a fool, yet Aeneas learned with disquieting certainty that the Frenchman was amassing votes.

At midnight Calandrini visited Piccolomini's cell, maintaining that Estouteville was unstoppable and would be elected on the following day. Calandrini counselled Aeneas to cast his vote accordingly, for it was most unwise to be caught on the losing side.

Aeneas dissented, saying it was against his conscience to vote for one he thought unworthy, but he was nonetheless disturbed, and in the morning he visited the Cardinals Borgia and Castiglione, who both expressed similar sentiments to those of Calandrini.

Borgia produced a document in which Estouteville promised to confirm him in the post of Vice-Chancellor, an office he had held under his uncle. Aeneas countered that the Chancery was also promised to the Cardinal of Avignon and asked which promise the new Pope was most likely to honour.

Unlike Calandrini, Castiglione, and Borgia, Cardinal Barbo felt the Frenchman should be stopped and, setting his own hopes aside, he decided to select the best Italian candidate and to do so he summoned all his fellow countrymen. Six answered the call, and Aeneas was selected. Now the battle was in earnest!

Shortly after this there was another scrutiny. Aeneas noted that Estouteville's face was white with excitement. He was keeper of the chalice in which the votes were cast and with deliberation he emptied its contents on the table. As the votes were counted the silence grew profound.

"The Cardinal of Siena, eight votes," he called out.

"Count again," Aeneas said quietly.

Embarrassed, Estouteville admitted his mistake. "Nine votes to the Cardinal of Siena."

Estouteville had six, which meant that three Cardinals had still to indicate their preference. Aeneas watched. There was no bodily movement. It was as if the members of the conclave were frozen in their seats. Only their eyes moved. Who would speak first?

At last Borgia got to his feet. "I accede to the Cardinal of Siena." No doubt he had remembered his conversation with Aeneas.

Aeneas had now ten votes and, in a desperate attempt to stop the election, two Cardinals left the conclave, but no one followed, and they soon returned.

Again they sat immobile until Cardinal Tebaldo rose. "I also accede to the Cardinal of Siena."

Only Prospero Colonna remained, and as he rose Estouteville and Bessarion upbraided him for desertion and tried to lead him from the conclave. But Colonna shouted loudly, "I also accede to the Cardinal of Siena and make him Pope."

It was over, the intrigues were at an end, and in a moment the Cardinals were prostrate at the new Pope's feet. Then, resuming their seats, they formally confirmed his election.

Bessarion rose to speak in the name of those who had opposed him. "We are pleased with your election, which we doubt not comes from God; we think you worthy of the office, and always held you so." Bessarion went on to ascribe his lack of support to Aeneas's bodily infirmity and his gouty feet. "It was this that led us to prefer the Cardinal of Rouen. Had you been strong in body there is no one we would have chosen before you. But the will of God is now our will."

Aeneas answered graciously. "You have a better opinion of us, than we have of ourselves; for you only find us defective in the feet. We feel our imperfections to be more widely spread. We are conscious of innumerable failings which might have excluded us from this office; we are conscious of no merits to justify our election. We would judge ourselves entirely unworthy, did we not know that the voice of two-thirds of the Sacred College is the voice of God, which we may not disobey. We approve your conduct in following your conscience and judging us insufficient. You will all be equally acceptable to us; for we ascribe our election, not to one or another, but to the whole College, and so to God Himself, from whom comes every good and perfect gift."

Aeneas took off his Cardinal's robes and assumed the white tunic of the Pope. He was asked what name he would bear. He smiled and, with a Virgilian memory of *Pius Æneas*, he answered *'Pius'*.

★

Paolino was waiting when Aeneas retired to the peace of the Papal apartments.

"The mob have pillaged your house, Holiness."

"That's not unexpected. There was little to take, anyway. And they know I have no use for it."

"Bishop Riddo handed me a note of congratulations."

"What! That barefaced fraud. I have unfinished business there."

"Your election has been popular, Holiness."

"Paolino, my good friend, ambitions have been fulfilled and success has come. But the greater part of me is cautious, if not fearful. Even for a man in perfect health the task ahead is daunting."

CHAPTER 67

'Gonzaga – disappear!'

Riddo ranged about his palace like a madman, while Gonzaga watched, his wine-soaked leer uncomprehending. That French idiot, that over-privileged pampered idiot," Riddo ranted. "He has thrown it away. And here I am a Bishop, a mere Bishop, and likely to remain that way while Piccolomini lords it over us!"

Riddo picked his beaker up and drained it dry. Gonzaga obligingly filled it up again.

"Piccolomini Pope!! That sly gout-ridden fox. It's unbelievable. What were those fat-headed Cardinals thinking of?" Riddo drained his beaker once again. "You're free, Gonzaga. I have no reputation to protect!"

Gonzaga's eyes gleamed. Riddo looked at him. A ferret's eyes, he thought. Why did he bother with him?

There was a knock, and an attendant entered cautiously. "Cardinal Bessarion is waiting downstairs, Sir," he said nervously.

"I'll be down directly. Gonzaga – disappear!"

Without hesitation Gonzaga headed for the back stairs with unquestioning obedience. As far as he was concerned, the Bishop knew what he was doing and it was not the first time he had had to 'disappear'.

Bishop Riddo composed himself, then descended the stairs to meet the much-respected Cardinal. What did the old droopy-eyed Greek want? he wondered. He swept grandly into the reception room, where the Cardinal was waiting.

"Eminence, this is indeed an honour."

"My good Bishop, after all your tireless work on behalf of Cardinal Estouteville it's the very least that we can do – to thank you for your unstinting efforts on our behalf." Bessarion spoke with easy dignity. "God has spoken, and Aeneas is our Pope. That is now unquestioned, but the Cardinal of Rouen feels a man of your ability needs a larger sphere in which to operate."

"What does his Eminence mean?" Riddo questioned mildly. "My abilities are surpassed by many men."

"The Cardinal of Rouen will speak for himself, I'm sure. I know he was most impressed by your fluency in French. Now that may give an indication of his thoughts."

"I am most grateful that the Cardinal should think of me in such a way and indeed, Eminence, for your consideration. Now, may I invite you to my humble table, for it is time to eat."

"That is most kind," Bessarion returned, "But a previous appointment means I must decline. Otherwise, it would have been an honour."

"Another time, perhaps; another time," Riddo responded easily.

Riddo smiled to himself as he escorted the old 'Plato lover' to the door. Had Bessarion forgotten his attacks on 'heathen Platonists'? It seemed so. Anyway, it was in the past.

"Where's Gonzaga?" he demanded brusquely as he went inside.

"He's gone."

"Get him. It's important!"

Gonzaga had to be restrained. Riddo *had* a reputation to protect.

★

Paolino's letter arrived at Fiesole just as the church bells signalled Piccolomini's election. Both Andrea's father and Coluccio were elated, but it was the new Pope's choice of name that particularly caught del Monte's attention.

"It's *Pius Æneas* – Virgil's *'Aeneid'*. It has to be. It's what a literary man would choose!"

"Pius is Pius; we can't be sure."

"That's the point, Coluccio. *'Pius Æneas'* is Pagan and not a title for a Christian Pope, but as you say Pius is simply Pius, so no one can accuse him. It's his little joke, and for me it shows a healthy detachment."

"According to Paolino, Riddo backed Estouteville, no doubt hoping for a Cardinalate. He won't be happy!"

"An understatement Coluccio! And he can't be the new Pope's favourite Bishop, for Piccolomini was instrumental in linking him with the drive for a crusade. You were in Rome; tell me, why did Piccolomini help someone whom you said he really didn't trust?"

"I think Piccolomini miscalculated. He thought Riddo would fall flat on his face, whereas exactly the opposite happened."

"Calixtus didn't reward him, though, so he turned to Estouteville and that has failed. No, he won't be happy. Is he dangerous? That's the question, or is all his blustering hot air? I don't really understand Riddo. He keeps changing somehow, like those creatures that can alter the colour of their skin."

"You're right. He changes with the wind. First he was the staunch defender of the Church, the anti-Platonist, then the great crusading Bishop, and recently the champion of Estouteville. But it's all for Riddo. Ambition drives him This he covers with the passion of belief. To put it simply, he believes his lies."

"Yes, you said that before, but there's something else."

"He's obsessive in his hatred. It's a fire within him and it never cools and never lets him rest. He loves to hate, and in private his tongue tears everyone to ribbons. I was his secretary, and I can't remember him saying a good word about anyone."

"That's it!" del Monte asserted. "That's why a Red Hat has eluded him, and I would wager that he has few friends."

"You would win your wager, Sir."

"The inner language of a man, though hidden, can attract and can repel. Riddo lives in hell, God help him."

Coluccio was startled. He had never heard anyone speak of Ubaldo Riddo with compassion.

★

In Venice Lorenzo Tiepolo's perspective was wholly different, and what had seemed possible in Fiesole was now considered quite impossible. He neither approached Lucrezia nor spoke to his son, as Carlo del Monte had suggested. Instead, he sought the company of Count Crito. As he expected, the Count was sympathetic and understood the difficulties, for the written and unwritten rules of Venice were fixed in stone.

Lucrezia's mother was the wealthy widow of Riario, lord of a township in the Marche. That was good enough for Venice. The fact that Riario was a criminal was beside the point. But Lucrezia's nurse was judged to be a servant who had only lately shed her village black.

"My dear wife's sister, Portia, married the son of a gondolier," the Count said in encouragement.

"I remember it well. But Portia was Portia and a great favourite of the people. She was young, and Giovanni proved himself with distinction as a senior officer on Sforza's staff; and Count, our Doge was Francesco Foscari! Crito, Maria and I are both elderly. The gossip would be cruel. It would be unfair to Vitale and Lucrezia and, indeed, Maria."

"Why don't you go back to Fiesole? Over there they'd view you as the mad Venetian friends of Carlo del Monte. You would have the Tiepolo merchant house in Florence to give you some employment; you'd be close to Valeria and you wouldn't be an interfering nuisance to Vitale. Lorenzo, Florence would accept your marriage, and in due time Venice would as well."

"I'd miss Vitale and Lucrezia."

"Lorenzo, your daughter-in-law will make sure Vitale visits Florence!"

"Why?"

"Marsilio's there, and she's an ardent follower!"

Tiepolo's sharp features softened. He laughed. "You're right. You're absolutely right!"

Later that evening Crito recounted the conversation to his wife Caterina. "I still find it difficult to believe. Lorenzo's transformation is so total."

"Crito, love won. Love for his daughter and, my dear, he almost lost his son!"

"I know." He put his arm around his wife for, like himself, she was thinking of their late son, Giorgio. "We have our grandson, dear and that is indeed a blessing."

"We've given the poor infant so many names! Carlo Andrea Gemistos del Monte Dandolo."

"Andrea calls him Crito, and I suspect that that will stick."

CHAPTER 68

The Carrucci Estates

Gonzaga and his ally, Bull, had disappeared, and Riddo feared the worst. What was more, he knew that he could only blame himself for, by telling Gonzaga that he was free, he had unleashed a madman.

Gonzaga's beady shining eyes haunted him, linking with the nightmares he had suffered twice within the last five days. The mocking laughter and the gloating eyes were very similar. What could he do? If Gonzaga were on his way to wreak revenge on the del Montes and something happened in the Marche or Fiesole, he would be blamed and not the Vicar General. In fact, the Vicar General had named Gonzaga 'Riddo's hound'. He could not stand apart so easily as before and, if there were a scandal, the anticipated favours of Estouteville would be stillborn.

Riddo paced his study anxiously, the image of the urbane poised Bishop forgotten and, being used to his master's bursts of anger, his secretary watched anxiously. Then, caught by sudden inspiration, Riddo stopped.

"Send a note to Piccolomini's secretary," he barked. "Tell him I need to see him. It's about the del Montes, and it's urgent. Put it in suitable language, but don't spend all day. I want it sent immediately."

"Brilliant, Ubaldo', Riddo praised himself. The name del Monte would get instant access to Paolino, and Riddo knew the part that he would play. He, of course, had little interest in the del Montes, the 'Weasel's friends' as he was wont to call them. He simply wanted to cover himself and so stand apart as blameless, and hopefully rid himself of Gonzaga. He was sick and tired of his brainless devotion, his crudeness and the fear that one day he might bare his fangs.

★

As Riddo had anticipated, he gained instant access to the new Pope's secretary.

"How considerate of you to see me so quickly," he said smoothly. "For the Pope's secretary, especially that of a new Pope, cannot have much leisure."

Paolino nodded, letting the platitudes wash over him.

"I'll be straight, my good Sir. Gonzaga has disappeared with his associate 'Bull'. You may not know it, but for some time I have restrained him. How, I do not know. This time, however, he has broken free, and I fear revenge is burning in his mind. Bluntly, Sir, he sees the del Montes as guilty of his father's death. An absurd belief, of course, but the mind of man is often caught in such delusions."

"Quite so, Bishop, and what do you propose?"

Riddo had expected an emotional reaction and a promise of immediate redress. This Paolino was a cool fish.

"I'm told you are on friendly terms with the del Montes, and I feel that you can best alert them of the danger."

"Indeed, but you befriended and protected this Gonzaga."

Damn this jumped-up secretary. He was rubbing in the salt. "True, I have befriended him, but I feel that I no longer have an influence. He sneers at moderation."

"Well, he's the Vicar General's man," Paolino said dismissively. He paused, looking calmly and deliberately at his visitor. "Rest assured, Bishop, that all will be done that is necessary."

"I am much relieved." Riddo spoke quietly, but his mind was turbulent within. This secretary was much too big for his sandals, and he clearly had no wish for further conversation. Who did he think he was? But taking his cue, Riddo bowed deeply. "My sincere devotion to His Holiness."

"I will convey your words to him, do be assured." Paolino smiled correctly.

The short meeting was clearly over. Even Riddo could not spin it out with further platitudes.

★

Paolino knocked gently and pushed open one of the tall twin doors to the Pope's private chambers.

"Ah, Paolino. Has he gone?" the Pope asked, looking up from his papers.

"Yes, Holiness. It seems that Gonzaga has disappeared, and Riddo's worried that he may be bent on vengeance."

"Against whom?"

"The del Montes."

"Why didn't we send Gonzaga down the mines?" the Pope snorted.

"He was given a commission under Calixtus at Riddo's prompting."

"And now Riddo's trying to back away! One thing's certain, *he's* not interested in the del Montes. We'll have to warn them."

"Messengers are already on their way, Holiness."

"Excellent, and Paolino, the Vicar General must put his house in order. Convey this in more diplomatic language, my friend," he added casually, pausing, his eyes scanning the ornate ceiling of his chamber. "Young Carrucci may be in danger."

"He lives with the del Montes now, so he'll also receive the warning."

"I hope you're right. I liked Carrucci when we met – an intelligent man and, Paolino, we need to peruse those secret files regarding the Carrucci estates. Can you arrange that?"

"Of course, Holiness."

"Well, well, so Riddo's covering his tracks!"

Paolino was elated, for his master had brought the subject up himself. Indeed, he was surprised, if not amazed, that the busy Pope had recalled his brief and distant conversation with Coluccio. But then, that was why he was the Pope.

Riddo's warning had been sent by escorted messenger to both the Marche and Fiesole. Paolino had done all he could, but he was still concerned. Gonzaga was dangerous and his intention murderous. In this respect he believed Ubaldo Riddo, and as far as Paolino was concerned the Bishop's motives were beside the point.

Florence was hot and airless, and the Tiepolo merchant house was like an oven. Business was completely dead, with only brief activity in the early morning, so Coluccio left and headed for Fiesole. He liked the ride, despite the heat, but was weary of the tedious need for bodyguards. Yet that was how it had to be. Both Messer Cosimo and his father-in-law insisted.

He reached home just after midday, and a slight breeze was moderating the heat as he approached the villa. Bernardo led his horse away as he opened the iron gate into the garden. Suddenly he froze, for standing with his back to him was the familiar thick-necked figure of Gonzaga confronting an alarmed yet stubborn Jacopo.

"Either you let us in, or we *go* in. Your choice, old man," Gonzaga barked. Clearly he had not heard the gate opening. "What do you say, Bull?"

There was a rasping laugh. "You're wasting your time, 'Zaga. Just go in!"

For Coluccio the shock brought intense awareness, but he felt no fear. "So 'Bull' was present, too. A bush was hiding him from view. Strangely, there was so much time, time to think and time to notice very detail Amazingly, he also knew the menacing Gonzaga was full of fear, for his harsh and brutal self grew brittle when the testing time arrived. Yet this was covered by a savage reckless courage.

"Messer Gonzaga, you will address me," Coluccio commanded evenly.

Gonzaga spun round. "Ha, the Weasel," he sneered.

"Get on with it 'Zaga. Finish him off!"

"How can I, Bull? For the Weasel has no sword! Throw him yours."

"But you're wasting time," Bull shouted.

"Do it!" Just like a cat, Gonzaga relished playing with his victim.

A sword fell at Coluccio's feet, and as it did there was a scream from the shadow of the portico. It was Valeria with Madonna Anna restraining her.

"Go inside, ladies," Coluccio said, with an authority that amazed him. There was so much time!

"Pick it up," Gonzaga bellowed, shaking in his agitation.

Coluccio bent down and Gonzaga lunged as he grasped the handle. Effortlessly Coluccio parried. There was so much space. Enraged, Gonzaga lunged again and once more Coluccio parried. Then he tripped briefly, and with a shout of triumph Gonzaga slashed wildly, but Coluccio leapt outside the arch with ease, his sword catching Gonzaga on the side. There was a piercing scream as he retreated backwards. The wound was only superficial. Coluccio waited, but Gonzaga did not lunge again. He had seen Bernardo and the other bodyguard.

"'Zaga, let's get out of here," Bull bellowed. At once they raced towards the garden wall and with the energy of desperation scaled it in an instant.

"Don't go after them!" Coluccio ordered. "Pursuing an enemy is always fraught with danger and we cannot leave the villa unprotected."

★

"Messer Coluccio, I didn't know you were a swordsman!"

"Neither did I, Jacopo. Someone must have taught me when I was young."

"There was more to it than that!"

"You're right; something took over. I wasn't the usual Coluccio!"

"It's all that time you spend with Master Marsilio!"

"What do you mean, Jacopo?"

"You're very like him. You both have a deep well!"

"I hope I don't fall in!"

"I'm serious."

"I'm sorry, Jacopo. I know you are."

"Why did you not call me?" Bernardo burst out.

"I'm not sure, Bernardo. It was stupid, but as I've said to Jacopo something took over."

"You could have got yourself killed!"

"It didn't seem like that, and, Bernardo, my knees aren't knocking!"

"Well, mine are!"

★

Coluccio had just reassured a tearful Valeria when Jacopo knocked and entered. "A papal messenger has arrived with an armed escort. He has a message for either you or Messer del Monte and has been asked to wait for a reply."

"Send him in."

The messenger, in full papal livery, bowed respectfully and gave Coluccio the roll despatch, which he handed on to Andrea's father. Del Monte broke the seal, read the content and handed it back to Coluccio without a word. Meanwhile the messenger stood immobile in the middle of the room.

"We are deeply grateful to the Pope's secretary for his prompt action," del Monte said quietly, getting to his feet. "But the men in question beat you here by less than half an hour and were promptly scattered by Messer Carrucci and his bodyguard. Now, my friend, you've ridden hard and far and I insist you rest and take refreshments – and that includes your escort."

"Sir," the messenger bowed, "you are most gracious, and refreshments will be more than welcome! But Sir, should we not give chase?"

"I suggest not. Your quarry is cunning. They have horses and many roads to choose from. What's your view, Coluccio?"

"I would recommend you travel back to Rome by way of Todi. Gonzaga has estates nearby. There's every possibility that he'll go there."

After an hour of easy informality the messenger and his escort left for Florence and for promised hospitality, and it was only then that Coluccio and Messer del Monte were able to discuss the content of Paolino's letter.

"What do you think Riddo's game is, Sir?"

"One thing's clear, he's not interested in my welfare and certainly not in yours. In fact, the opposite. So it's what one might expect – he's protecting himself. Riddo's often entertained that viper 'Zaga in his home. His servants talk. He cannot gag them all. So any crime Gonzaga perpetrates will automatically reflect on him. He's covering himself, but he must have known Gonzaga's intentions."

"Yes, that's obvious."

"He might even have put Gonzaga up to it!"

"This gets worse, for that would mean direct betrayal of Gonzaga!"

"Exactly, and if Gonzaga got some wind of this, and even if Riddo didn't put him up to it, he would not be pleased!"

"He would be very much displeased!"

★

That evening, when they were alone, Valeria came to her husband and gently put her arms about him. "Jacopo said that you were very brave today. *He* was much impressed!"

"My dear, it was as though I was *being moved*!" Then he told her of the calmness and the sense of space and time.

"Marsilio's coming back from Bologna tomorrow," she announced suddenly.

"Oh, I didn't know!"

"I'm sorry. I forgot to tell you. Apparently Messer Cosimo wants to see both him and his father."

"That sounds promising. When?"

"Nothing has been fixed."

"Is there anything else that you've forgotten?" he joked, poking her gently in the ribs.

"Father's coming in the autumn with Maria, and Portia is bringing little Crito to Fiesole next Easter to see his grandparents."

"By that time, dear, there'll be a little Carrucci, *Deo volente*." He kissed her on the forehead. "It's been an eventful day; bed is now the order of the hour."

CHAPTER 69

'God help me, for no one else can'

It was at Todi that Gonzaga learned that Riddo had betrayed him. Four men in papal livery had gossiped drunkenly in the tavern, and Gonzaga's boyhood friend had heard their every word. "Has anyone seen Gonzaga?" they kept asking. "Rome is after him!" All shook their heads.

Gonzaga was devastated. Only Riddo knew of his intent; the only man that he had really followed and obeyed had callously abandoned him. Riddo had cast him to the dogs, and for a day Gonzaga wandered, grey and listless. Then slowly rising from the shock, he was possessed by an all-consuming rage. Caution was abandoned as a cold determination engulfed his thinking. He would confront the lying Bishop face to face and in his palace. Blind hatred had replaced devotion.

Advising Bull to 'lie low', Gonzaga set out for Rome. He had no wish for company.

★

Gonzaga entered, as usual, by the servants' quarters at the rear of Riddo's palace. Seeing a housemaid that he knew, he squeezed a chilly smile in greeting and rushed on down the long, familiar corridor, then up the back stairs to the Bishop's chambers.

Seeing him approach, Riddo's cringing secretary tried to bar his way. "He doesn't want to see you," he hissed.

Gonzaga pushed him forcefully aside, and the man fell backwards, swallowing a frightened scream. Violently wrenching the door open, Gonzaga entered Riddo's study.

"Ah, Gonzaga! Where have you been?" Riddo acknowledged him with studied calmness, but his eyes were full of fear, and Gonzaga saw it.

"As if you didn't know! You *betrayed me*! You went to Piccolomini's secretary! Don't try to deny it!"

Fear froze Riddo's wits. Gonzaga's rage was frightening.

"'Disappear' you snapped, as if I were a rat! Well, *you're* the rat and your home is in the sewers."

"But, 'Zaga . . ." Riddo appealed.

"Ah, the mighty Riddo pleads!" Gonzaga drew his sword and placed the point against the Bishop's chest, pushing him towards the open fireplace with its ornate iron fender. Losing balance, Riddo's heavy frame fell backwards, falling on the fender's iron spike, as if it were an upturned dagger. He tried to scream but failed. The shock delayed the pain, but the catastrophic loss of blood swiftly dulled his senses. Close to his heart, he knew the wound was fatal. In a desperate effort he lifted himself free. This exhausted him, and with a fierce intensity he grabbed the cross about his neck and kissed the hanging Christ with passion. "Father, have mercy upon me," he groaned.

Gonzaga slammed his sword into its scabbard.

"Damn you, Riddo. I wouldn't stain my sword. You're not worth it." Then too enraged to notice anything, Gonzaga crashed noisily from the room, his harsh mocking laughter resounding down the corridor.

"The nightmare! God, the nightmare. God help me, for no one else can," the dying Riddo mouthed.

All at once his mind grew calm. It was over – the endless struggle of his life was passed, and the frantic engine that had driven him had stopped. He kissed the cross again, clinging to it with the full force of his remaining strength.

★

The secretary had either fled in panic or had scurried off for help, for there was no one in the corridor as Gonzaga raced downstairs towards the servants' entrance. Outside, the alleyways were empty. It was early afternoon, and those with any sense were indoors resting.

Gonzaga gloated on Riddo's abject snivelling humiliation, as he headed for a tavern close to Riddo's other house – his 'love nest' – though the Bishop's 'dignity' had restrained him in the last year or so. "Too high and mighty," Gonzaga sneered, his voice rasping in the echoing alley as he neared the tavern.

He ordered wine and slumped into a chair, his feet stretched out in front of him and, as he had rested little since leaving Todi, he was soon asleep.

A little later he awoke suddenly, his neck stiff and painful. He could hear the sound of marching feet growing more audible by the minute. They stopped outside and, curious, Gonzaga peered through the open-fronted tavern. They were the Papal soldiery.

"He's in there!" someone shouted.

Instinctively Gonzaga knew that they were after him and, ignoring the landlord's protests, he brusquely pushed his way to the rear entrance. But the soldiers had anticipated his move, and three of them were waiting with their crossbows loaded.

"Bishop Riddo has been murdered," their officer said formally. "We're arresting you for the crime."

"Murdered!" Gonzaga burst out. "I didn't touch him!"

Who did this aristocratic whelp think he was? "I never touched him!" he screamed again.

"We're wasting time. There's no point in argument."

The officer's formal way of speaking maddened Gonzaga still further. "No one will take me in! No one!" He had seen the prisoners' cells; they lived like animals. He stood defiant.

"There are three of us." The officer's smooth tone poured fuel on his fury.

"No. Two of you!" Gonzaga barked, stepping forward as if to surrender.

"What do you mean?" The officer moved towards him, expecting to receive his sword, for like him Gonzaga was commissioned.

Suddenly Gonzaga drove his dagger home and with equal speed headed for the alleyways. The confusion of the inexperienced soldiers gave him time but an arrow, shot in panic, caught his leg. He swore loudly yet struggled on, determined to be free. A tell-tale trail of blood gushed from his thigh, but he cunningly used this to deceive, as he ran into a square; then, stemming the flow, he retreated to a hide he had remembered, for he knew the area well.

A slit between the houses, disguised by a wayside shrine, was his escape. Slipping through, he checked his heavy breathing as the soldiers ran by. Relying on the young soldiers' inexperience and the confusion after the officer was stabbed, he knew too well that he'd been lucky.

Few used this narrow windowless canyon with its crumbling redbrick walls, and even fewer cared about it. Finding a recess cut into one wall he kicked the rubbish out with his good leg and sat down on the still filthy ground. He looked up. The blue sky seemed very far away. He was free, yes, but that meant little, for he needed water badly – water to drink and water to wash his wound. In fact, he needed expert care. What hope was there of that? Pulling on the arrow, he swore softly, for its head remained imbedded and he had to use his knife to ease it out. The searing pain shot through him, blotting out his rage and the violent impulses of his nature. What a sunless hole in which to end his days.

He thought of praying, but that reminded him of Riddo and hypocrisy. Anyway, why should God think of him when he had never thought of God?

As if immersed in a dream, he became aware of two innocent round eyes watching him without the slightest sign of fright. He mouthed "water" and pointed to his mouth and leg. The young girl, ten perhaps, kept looking. All the while he was careful not to speak lest it should frighten her.

Suddenly she scampered off. That's the last of her, he thought. She could betray his hiding place, of course. Well, if she did, she did. One thing was certain; he would not be taken alive.

Amazingly, the girl came back, placing a bowl of water, a beaker and some rags beside him. Then, as before, she simply stood, just gazing at him. He smiled, a response drawn from deep within him. His usual self felt heavy, like a suit of armour, yet he made no sound, feeling it might break the magic.

The girl still watched and, when he had used all the water, she took the bowl away and filled it up again. Again she watched and then, as suddenly as

251

before, she left, this time returning with a bottle which she placed in front of him while pointing at his wound.

Was she deaf, he wondered? He mouthed his thanks and still felt he dared not speak aloud. Seeming to be satisfied with her efforts, the girl slipped away and he leant against the wall and dozed.

To his surprise the girl returned as the shadows lengthened, and this time she brought blankets and some food. It was meagre fare and he still felt hungry, though he did not give the slightest hint of this.

That night Gonzaga prayed, something that he had not done for years. He did not pray for himself, only for the girl. He was certain she was deaf or dumb or both, and he prayed with all the passion of his nature that the good Lord would take care of her.

In the morning she appeared again, carrying water, more rags to dress his wound and some breakfast. Clearly, she had adopted him. And so the pattern of the days repeated until the fourth day, when she brought a crutch. Where she got such things he had no notion.

She knew his leg was healing, and it was her way of saying that it was time to move. Yet the future troubled him. He was a wanted man, condemned for something that he had not done. His nature, practised in habitual rage, grew angry. Quickly, though, this fizzled out, for it could find no fuel. All his life he had been with violent people. His father, whom he worshipped, had been violent, and his mother's rasping tongue was quick to lash the unsuspecting. When he met Riddo, a similar violence in the Bishop's language linked with his boyhood memory. He was trapped, and Riddo gained his full devotion.

Suddenly, with an arrow in his leg, and on the run, all his bullying belligerence was useless, his future too appalling to consider. Then came the 'angel', the name he gave the girl. She had saved his life, but more than that, she had saved his soul. What he meant by soul was vague, to say the least. He only sensed that something deep within had been reborn. He could not put it into words, yet that was how he felt.

Each night he prayed for this silent little girl – not wordy prayers, but a concentration of intent, and totally sincere. By day he practised gingerly with the crutch, discovering why no one used the alley, for the other end was blocked.

Two days later the girl left a lay monk's habit by his side and he guessed now where she came from. His old self reacted violently, but he was too devoted to her to show it and so, half mesmerised, he followed her beckoning like a lamb. No one would recognise him now, for his beard had grown and dressed in the lay monk's habit, with the girl beside him, this was not Gonzaga, at least not the one that all were looking for.

Slowly she led him to a nearby monastery, and at once his old persona raged with sheer aversion. Even so, he checked his thoughts and meekly stepped inside. Clearly this was what his 'angel' wanted.

"What is your name, my son?" the Abbot asked.

"Angelo, but it's not my real name, Father," Gonzaga answered honestly.

The Abbot, who clearly knew about the little girl's involvement, smiled discreetly but did not ask the obvious question.

"Our garden needs a caring hand, my son, and you can help us there. But first, you need to get completely well."

Gonzaga had escaped, but in the following months there was a crippling price to pay, the wages of remorse.

CHAPTER 70

Angelo

Paolino was with the Pope when news arrived that Riddo had been murdered. The culprit was Gonzaga, it was said, and all of Rome was looking out for him.

"Tell the Prefect to ring Riddo's palace with guards. No one must enter!" Pius pronounced emphatically.

"Yes, Holiness."

"And, Paolino, I want you to investigate. You'll not relish what you see, I know, but I need someone I can trust. And take my personal physician." The Pope paused, looking intently at his secretary. "I want the facts, not the fiction of some frightened secretary. Make sure you take a personal guard!"

"Is there anything else, Holiness?"

"There is. I don't want that fraud Riddo ending up a martyr!"

"Holiness, that could happen all too easily."

"Not while I'm the Pope," Aeneas Piccolomini snapped.

Paolino bowed, backed towards the door and made to leave.

"Oh, Paolino," the Pope called after him, "thank you for those files. I'm sure we can restore a goodly portion of young Carrucci's inheritance. Certainly Riddo's share is his!"

"That's good news, Holiness!"

"It is," the Pope responded quietly.

★

Riddo was lying awkwardly face up beside the fender of his fireplace in a pool of blood – a most distasteful sight. Stiffening himself, Paolino questioned Riddo's secretary, a nervous agitated man, who insisted this was murder, though he had not seen it happen. He had heard Gonzaga rowing with the Bishop in a most aggressive way, and he had run for help. Those were the facts, and he insisted he was right.

The Pope's physician, however, was completely certain that Bishop Riddo had fallen on the pointed corner of the fender, since there were no other wounds. So Gonzaga's frenzied claims of innocence were true. There was no basis to justify the call of martyrdom now sounding in the streets, but where was 'Zaga?

A few days later Paolino wrote to Coluccio, relating the momentous news. Riddo was dead and Gonzaga missing. He had simply disappeared.

Two weeks passed, then another letter arrived at Fiesole, this time summoning Coluccio to Rome. The Holy Father had called him to his presence, but Paolino gave no hint of the Pope's intent. That was for His Holiness to reveal. There was still no trace of Gonzaga, but Bull, his accomplice, had been killed in Todi while resisting arrest. Before dying he confessed to the murder of Giovanni del Monte's wife. He had done it to fulfil a drunken boast that he would *do* what 'Zaga simply talked about.

★

Lorenzo Tiepolo and Maria arrived in Fiesole the day after Coluccio left for Rome. They were intent on marriage, for Vitale, at Lucrezia's prompting, had withdrawn all his reservations.

Tiepolo was full of admiration for his daughter-in-law. She was the organiser, the prime mover and the inspiration behind so much. She had written to Marsilio, when he was a student in Bologna, and peppered him with questions, and with her energy focused her wild impulsive nature was quite tamed. His son, instead of being jealous of his wife, was proud of her, and their marriage, against predictions to the contrary, was blossoming. She and Vitale were close friends of Andrea and Portia and, indeed, of the Count, who treated her with great respect.

The news from Rome added to Lorenzo's buoyant spirits. He laughed loudly. "Carlo, my friend," he said, turning to address del Monte, "do you know what Lucrezia said to me?"

"Tell me."

"'Remember God on the good days, Papa — she calls me Papa.' If anyone else had said it I would have grown livid, for such 'advice' annoys me intensely. So, now on these days of satisfaction and contentment, I remember that happiness belongs to God and not Lorenzo Tiepolo!"

"You've found a teacher in your daughter-in-law it seems!"

"She gets it from Marsilio."

All at once, they were silent. The late August evening was balmy, and the silence continued as they watched the dusk settle over Florence. Eventually Tiepolo broke the spell. "It makes me feel uneasy to think Gonzaga's still at large," he said reflectively.

"Yes, his disappearance is a mystery, yet somehow I don't feel ill at ease."

"But he's such an animal!"

"No one blessed with human birth is wholly animal. However dim, there's always a spark. A man can always turn. It's the story of the Prodigal Son, Lorenzo. Saints have often trodden on this path."

"What are you trying to tell me, Carlo?"

"Well," del Monte paused. "I have a feeling, just as I had with your daughter-in-law in those early days, that something may have happened." He paused again. "I've thought a lot about our friend Gonzaga. According to your son, he was all bluster. Vitale also noted how Gonzaga was devoted to his father's memory. He was devoted to Riddo. Indeed, the Bishop could do no wrong. But Riddo betrayed him. So who is it to be now? He'll be devoted to something, for that's his nature."

"Messer Carlo, he wounded Lucrezia and he almost killed Bernardo!'

"Such violence can be overcome, but it takes an uncommon effort and devotion."

"I'll say this for you, Carlo, you're an optimist!"

"I try to be!"

Again they fell silent. Dusk was now complete in the valley of the Arno and the evening air was soft.

"I have a letter for Marsilio from Lucrezia. Will he be calling soon?" Tiepolo asked.

"Yes, though he's very busy helping his father at the moment."

"And his Greek and philosophic studies . . . ?"

"They're much restricted, Lorenzo. Cosimo wants to see him, but the great Medici's at Cafaggiolo at present. Marsilio's done all he can, and as far as I'm concerned it's up to Cosimo. Marsilio's future is in his hands. It's Cosimo's responsibility and no one else can do it!"

"You mean patronage?"

"Yes, I mean patronage, and Cosimo is the most prestigious patron of them all!"

"More even than the Pope?"

Del Monte chuckled. "They're on a par, I'd say!"

★

Coluccio only spent a week in Rome before returning to Fiesole. His audience with the Pope was brief and business-like, though clearly Aeneas Piccolomini was pleased to be the instrument by which most of the Carrucci property was restored to its rightful owner.

Much of Coluccio's time was spent with the Pope's secretary, who, though busy, found the leisure to be with him. Coluccio learned all about Ubaldo Riddo's end and how the Pope had squashed the wild excited claims of martyrdom. Riddo, however, was buried with all the dignity befitting a Bishop of the Church, but that was all. Few tears were shed for Bishop Riddo.

As was his wont, Coluccio visited the ancient sites. Their crumbling splendour never failed to fill him with a sense of awe and wonder but, apart from his audience, his most significant experience came when visiting a small monastery with Paolino on the final day before leaving for the north.

It started with a casual walk in the area of the Trastevere, across the river from the Palatine. On impulse Paolino called on an elderly Abbot friend of his, and they were invited to take a tour of the garden. It was obviously well tended, and Coluccio was quick to praise.

"That's thanks to Angelo; he's dedicated," the Abbot beamed, pleased that Coluccio had noticed.

"Is that him over there?"

"Yes, though we'll not disturb him. Anyway, he's got his little friend

256

with him. She's deaf and dumb, but they're inseparable. Her being here will have to end quite soon, which Angelo understands."

Coluccio made no response, and as they circled the garden he had ample time to watch the gardener at work. He was a big man with a full beard, and Coluccio noticed that he had a slight limp, but when he saw his face at closer range he had no doubt. It was Gonzaga. Luckily, there was no hint of recognition on his part. He was much too intent on hoeing.

Only briefly did Coluccio consider speaking, though he soon resolved to hold his peace. Things were better, much much better, left the way they were. As he reached the gate, Coluccio turned and looked again. Gonzaga and the little girl were distant figures now. He kept watching, and as he did a stillness grew within him. This was the nearest to a miracle he had ever witnessed.

CHAPTER 71

'At last I feel like celebrating!'

Except for Messer del Monte, Coluccio told no one about his sighting of Gonzaga, not even Valeria, for he judged the knowledge was a burden that she did not need to carry. All Andrea's father did was smile. Coluccio was surprised, but then Messer del Monte often surprised him by his most original way of thinking.

"Somehow I half expected this, Coluccio, as the whole thing was a most intriguing puzzle. How did he escape? How did he avoid the watching eyes of Rome, when all were searching? It has to be the little girl. Being deaf and dumb she would not know the current gossip, nor could she chatter but she discovered him and, what is most important, catered for his need."

"And now he's devoted to her, so the Abbot said."

"A discreet man, the Father Abbot, for he must have guessed."

"I still find it quite amazing."

"God's grace always is, Coluccio, not least the restoration of the Carrucci estates. Will you be moving to Orvieto?"

Coluccio noticed an unusually forced sound in del Monte's question, and he knew the reason. Messer Carlo and Madonna Anna would miss their company. "I hope to visit Orvieto from time to time, but both Valeria and I see this villa as our home and, with your approval, we would like arrangements to continue as they are."

"Wonderful! At last I feel like celebrating! For a time I felt that your good fortune would be our misfortune. Now I can say it without reservation. Thank God for Aeneas Piccolomini! And to cap it, all we need is good news from Marsilio."

"So he hasn't met the great man yet?"

"No. Cosimo returned from Cafaggiolo about a week ago. It should be soon."

"A lot hangs on this meeting,"

"You could be right, Coluccio. Surely this time Cosimo will act!" Del Monte's frustration was transparent. "Coluccio," he added confidentially, "don't abandon the Tiepolo merchant house too readily. It might . . ."

"It's all right, Sir. I'm not intending to withdraw. Indeed, to do so would be gross ingratitude. Thank you for mentioning it, though."

"Where is everybody?" del Monte suddenly demanded.

"Messer Tiepolo is thinking of buying a villa on the other side of town and the ladies have gone to see it."

"Why the other side?"

"My father-in-law jokes that only the Medici and the del Montes can afford a villa overlooking Florence!"

Del Monte laughed, and for a moment the conversation stopped. Coluccio, still tired after the journey from Rome, felt his eyes grow heavy, but he jerked awake when del Monte started speaking.

"I received a letter from Andrea two days ago and he asked if we'd ever discovered the hand behind the attempted ambush when he was escorting the Countess and Portia."

"That was over three years ago!"

"I know. Still, he's concerned, for he hopes to bring little Crito to see his grandparents next Easter. It's a father's question, Coluccio!"

"So how did you reply, Sir?"

"I haven't answered, and I was wondering what you thought."

"I think that it was bandits, Sir. The gold florins in their pouches were a promise from their leader of more to come."

"And Riddo?"

"Maybe it was Riddo, but I don't believe so. At that time we were seeing him under every stone!"

"Good. That's my view as well. Andrea needs to hire a proper guard. The Romagna's never been a land of saints!"

Coluccio stood up and stretched, while savouring the scene below, and what a scene it was, with Brunelleschi's dome set like a jewel in its midst. Del Monte chuckled and Coluccio turned enquiringly.

"What is it, Sir?"

"I was thinking of the two Ficini on their way to Cosimo – the father anxious and the son annoyingly placid!"

"Did your imagination conjure the Via Larga or Careggi?"

"Careggi!"

"That's the picture I have, too."

CHAPTER 72

Careggi

The burning heat of August had given way to the softer warmth of mid-September. It was perfect weather for the traveller, and even the mules were willing, as Dr Ficino and his son progressed towards Careggi. On both sides of the road teams of men were busy amongst the vines. The winter months were approaching. It reminded the elder Ficino of his own imagined idyll, retirement to his vineyard in the country. But that was some years off. Now he was the busy doctor, with an ever-hungry family requiring this, demanding that. The list of wants was never-ending.

His gifted eldest son, though, was his greatest headache. Of course, Ficino wanted his son to follow his bent for study. Nonetheless, he had to be practical, for without some form of patronage Marsilio's studies would be considerably restricted. He would have to earn his living. Ficino was a doctor well aware of man's mortality, and when he died Marsilio would shoulder the family responsibility, and for that he needed income. Now at least he had a profession, but if he gained the mighty Cosimo's patronage a whole new world would open. No one, however, could take the great Medici for granted. He did things in his own time. So much hung on the outcome of this meeting, not only his son's future but the whole future of the Ficino family, for what affected one affected all. But Marsilio was taking it as calmly as if he were visiting his friends at Fiesole.

At one time he might have been infuriated by what he would have judged to be sheer indifference. Not now, though, for he had grown to wonder at his son's amazing capabilities and his tranquil nature. He was tolerance itself, yet he could be firm. Indeed, he had written to his younger brothers, sternly rebuking their disrespectful behaviour towards their father, and he, Diotifeci, had been grateful. Marsilio had had no wish to go, yet he had gone to Bologna without the least complaint. This behaviour did not issue from a warm and saintly dream-world. On the contrary, it was the product of an ever vigilant mind. Of course, he had an equitable disposition, but it was a gift that he had nurtured with ever-present effort.

"We're almost there. I can see the guards on the upper walkway." Diotifeci observed.

"They'll see a dangerous pair approaching!" Marsilio quipped.

"I don't doubt we're outnumbered!"

"Don't worry, we'll scale the walls with ease."

For a time humour eased Ficino's tensions. He had been to Careggi many times as a doctor, but this was different, very different.

★

Cosimo was sitting in the villa's large central *atrium* when the Ficini arrived. There was no one in attendance, and it was clear that the great man was set on informality with those that he considered to be friends.

"Welcome," he called out, with that hint of amusement so characteristic of his manner. "You are out of luck! There's no business here today. We're all quite fit – that is, in body! But can you heal the mind, Sirs? That's the question!"

"A troubled mind is a tragic thing," Ficino answered formally.

"It seems to me we're all a little tragic. What do you think, Marsilio?"

"The mind is much too often like a house without its master. The master needs to be in residence."

"Who is the master?"

"Our inner self, but not the one that flits from flower to flower."

Ficino was always amazed at Marsilio's answers. His mother and he had long conversations, of course, but he, Diotifeci, was always out on call.

"Sounds like the Delphic *Know thyself*, Marsilio."

Cosimo was playing, for he knew all this, but it made no matter. Marsilio smiled. Then Cosimo continued, "If all we have to do is know ourselves, why all these books you labour at?"

Yes, Marsilio thought, Cosimo was having fun, yet he was testing him as well.

"Books are the maps, the inspiration and the keys to recollection."

Cosimo nodded, obviously impressed.

"Let's go through to the library. This baronial pretension doesn't suit the conversation. – How are your medical studies progressing, Marsilio?" he asked, as they walked through.

"Very well, Sir."

"I know, for he has devoured my textbooks, Messer Cosimo," Diotifeci interjected. "In the past I had to search the text. Now, I simply ask my son!"

Cosimo chuckled, while ringing the bell beside him. "We need some re-freshments, I feel," he said casually. "So the Ficino practice has potential to expand. Indeed, I'm told already that you have a busy round," Cosimo added mildly.

"Yes, Sir, we are well employed."

"My friend del Monte speaks highly of you."

"They are delightful people."

"Yes, for a man who was the friend of Emperor and Doge and is the friend of a Duke, and even the Medici, he is remarkably unassuming."

It was a friendly meeting, but what was Cosimo up to? Diotifeci felt the rise of frustration.

"How's your Greek, Marsilio?"

"Better, Sir. Translation is much more comfortable. I think that's the word."

"That I'm very pleased to hear. Ah, here comes the wine. Well, my friends," he said grandly, holding up his glass, "to you, Dr Ficino, for your very excellent work, and to Marsilio for a very different work."

What 'very different work'? Cosimo could be infuriating, Diotifeci grumbled to himself. He felt tension mounting, for he sensed that a decision was close. Just then Cosimo turned to him.

"My good friend, encourage Marsilio in his studies. There will be no need to take account of domestic hardship, for I will see to that. You, Diotifeci, have been sent to us to heal bodies, but your son has been sent from heaven to heal souls!"

Suddenly the room was very still.

"Marsilio's work is important," Cosimo continued quietly, "more important, I suspect, than we might guess. Your task won't be easy, Marsilio, but it is a task indeed. All the works of Plato need to be translated into Latin. I've been waiting a long time to say this. Now there is no doubt."

"Thank you, Sir." Marsilio could find no other words.

"Don't thank me, Marsilio. Thank God. It is His work."

For Marsilio there was no excitement, no euphoria, just a deep profound contentment. All the uncertainty had gone. There were no doubts, no doubts whatever, and in their place a quiet gratitude now reigned supreme. Here, at last, was the confirmation of what, in one sense, he had always known – the true and sure direction of his life.